GONE ROGUE

A MIA MURPHY MYSTERY

STEPHANIE ROWE

COPYRIGHT

coincidental and not intended by the author or the artist. There are excerpts from other books by the author in the back of the book.

WHAT READERS ARE SAYING ABOUT MIA MURPHY

"A hilarious and twisty ride! ...I definitely need more Mia Murphy in my life." Five-Star Goodreads Review (Tammy M.)

"I was catapulted into the story and remained captivated until the end... Down right laugh out loud!" Five-Star Goodreads Review (Elizabeth)

"Stephanie Rowe has such a way with words! Her offbeat humour and madcap adventures are absolutely mesmerizing!" Five-Star Goodreads Review (Laura C.)

"A hoot! " Five-star Goodreads Review (Margie)

"I am so in love with Mia and her friends...this series just has me literally laughing out loud...Non-stop high jinks, great characters, and above all, wonderful and engaging writing." Five-star Goodreads Review (Penny)

"[Mia] had me laughing out loud constantly. Also, I think King Tut might be my favorite water-loving bodyguard/ kitty cat companion that I've ever read! I absolutely cannot wait until we get the third book!" Five-star Goodreads Review (Danielle B.)

"I love this book, this series and this author!" Five-star Goodreads Review (Riding Reviewer)

CHAPTER 1

MY PHONE RANG JUST as I hopped out of Turbojet, my well-used, antique pickup truck I'd acquired along with my new business, the Eagle's Nest Marina. I saw the call was one of my new besties, Hattie Lawless, so I answered. "What's up?"

"Mia. It's been ten days since we've had to deal with a corpse. Are you getting as bored as I am?"

Alarm shot through me, and I hung up on her.

Hattie was a seventy-something race car driver who owned and operated a café in my marina. She was sassy, irreverent, and an unstoppable force, which I greatly admired. Except when it got me almost killed. Which seemed to happen a little bit too often.

She called again, and I almost didn't answer. But what if Hattie was in trouble? I couldn't take the chance. "What?"

"No one has tried to kill you in ten days either. You have to ditch your new bodyguard. I think he's repelling fun."

I hung up on her again. Hattie was like a siren. The entire world seemed to want to bend to her will, not because she tried to control it, but because it *wanted* to be her friend. If Hattie invited murderers into our lives, they would probably come.

Not that I was superstitious, but Hattie was...Hattie.

My phone rang before I managed to get it back in my pocket. I answered it as I wandered away from Turbojet and headed toward the Bass Derby town green, which was teeming with people, music, tents, and small-town festivities. "Hattie. I love you. I don't love murderers."

"Yes you do. If you didn't, you wouldn't have gone undercover for the FBI against your drug lord ex for two years."

That had not been an entirely voluntary situation for me. "They made me."

"Hey! Don't give away your power by lying to yourself like that! No one makes you do anything. You wanted to because you crave excitement, my thieving friend."

I smiled at the affection in her voice. I'd been so scared that she and Lucy Grande, my two favorite people in the world, would reject me when they found out about my criminal childhood, but my pickpocketing past had been a great hit with both of them. "I just arrived. Where's your tent?"

"Pink and white striped tent at the near end of the first aisle. Best spot of the festival. You can't miss it."

"Of course you got the best spot."

"Always," she agreed cheerfully. "The world is my playground."

Up ahead, I saw the awning in question. "I see you. Coming over."

"Awesome. Ditch Ivan in the crowds, though. Seriously."

I glanced behind me at the six-foot-four jacked-up, federal agent-type suit-wearer who had been shadowing me for the last ten days, shooting looks of "I will take you down if you mess with Mia" to anyone who came close to me. I smiled at him, but he ignored me. Ivan didn't mess around, which was a great trait in a bodyguard. "I'm not ditching Ivan. You'd be so sad if I was assassinated."

"Would I, though? That's such a complex, loaded issue."

I laughed. "Bye. I'll see you in a sec." I hung up as I merged with the crowds streaming onto the grass. Tonight was the opening night of the three-day Bass Derby Strawberry Festival, an annual event that drew people from all over the state to celebrate, culminating in the crowning of the Strawberry Shortcake Bake-Off Champion on Sunday afternoon.

How adorably small-town was that?

I was so excited. The crowds were boisterous. The tents were so cute, local vendors selling crafts, artwork, pottery, candles, pizza, sandwiches and everything else that one could create. There was a big contest tent for the competitors. Tonight was round one, the strawberry contest, where contestants would present home-grown strawberries for judging. Saturday was the biscuit contest. And Sunday was the Strawberry Shortcake Bake-Off, which was the biggie. Plus, there was a palooza of other events planned for the weekend as well.

A band was playing on the gazebo, and the local baton-twirling team was performing routines. Pickup trucks lined the parking lot, and people were tailgating with barbeques and beer. The mid-June night was warm, the evening sun casting glorious light across the water, and the adjacent town beach was full of kids and families playing in the water.

It filled my soul with all the warmth and belonging that I'd wanted my whole life.

This was why I'd turned down witness protection and moved to Bass Derby.

This was why I'd bought the run-down Eagle's Nest Marina, so that I could be here, becoming a part of a community for the first time in my life, rehabbing the marina to make it my dream.

I'd even managed to grab a last-minute volunteer spot. I was part of the team patrolling the contest tent to make sure that all the competitors had what they needed. My shift started in ten minutes, and I was so pumped. I was proudly wearing my volunteer badge, and I was pretty much giddy with excitement.

I jogged over to Hattie's tent, breathing in the scent of the fresh bread Hattie was so magical at creating. She was behind a well-stocked table, and there was a line twenty-people long already. "Hey, girl. How's it going?"

"Swamped," Hattie said cheerfully. "Niko and Cris are away at some football camp this weekend, so I'm on my own."

Nico and Cris Stefanopoulos were Greek brothers who worked in her café. They were both headed to college on scholarships, and their grandma, Angelina Stefanopoulos was raising them. As a staff member at the police station, she'd been helpful to us on more than one occasion.

Today, Hattie was sporting fuchsia hair, to match her Hattie's Café T-shirt. I didn't know many seventy-somethings who could carry off fuchsia hair, but Hattie definitely could. "Jump in and help. I'll give you free food."

Hattie never gave away anything for free, so the offer was tempting. But… "My shift starts in ten minutes."

"How long is your shift?"

"Two hours."

She shook her head. "No, that won't work. I need help now. Ditch your shift."

I blinked. "I can't. I promised I'd do it—"

Hattie leaned on the table. "I need you. I thought we were friends."

"We are friends." I would never turn down a request from Hattie, but I'd been excited at the chance to volunteer, as if I actually belonged to the community. "Hattie, I—"

"Hey!" A low voice barked out the single word.

We both turned to see three twenty-something gang member-ish dudes striding across the grass toward us, wearing heavy motorcycle boots, leather jackets, gold chains, with possible gun bulges in their jackets, and enough swagger to trigger a tidal wave in Diamond Lake.

A path had cleared, and people's jaws were open in stunned shock, clutching their babies and dogs as if the trio was there to mass murder everyone. The approaching trio was so out of place that I could practically feel the earth shifting to expel them.

The woman at the front of the line hugged her loaf of Hattie's rosemary focaccia bread to her chest. "Are they coming here? They look like they're heading here. They're not getting my bread."

As she spoke, the trio strode right up to the table and stopped, arms folded, jaws jutted out, shoulders back. Every line of their bodies said that they expected to be thrown out.

I'd spent most of my first seventeen years with that stance.

They did not tackle anyone for their bread, babies, or dogs. Instead, they focused entirely on Hattie. The tallest one spoke first. "You owe us. We're here to collect."

A woman behind me made a noise like she was slowly dying, and I heard someone whisper to find Chief Stone. I heard someone else say something about me being a drug dealer, which hurt my innocent little heart just a bit.

Hattie set her hands on her hips. "Mia? Do I owe these guys?"

I'd been with her when we'd met them a couple weeks ago. I knew what she was doing, but at the same time, I felt for these guys, because that had been me. They wouldn't interpret her response the way she meant it. I knew that, because I'd been them. "Um, guys? Vinnie?"

The tallest one looked over at me, then his brows went up. "I remember you."

More people started whispering, which bothered me a little bit. Honestly, life was so much more complicated when you cared what people thought, when you were trying to put down roots. "Hattie, for heaven's sake, stop being difficult. Vinnie, you, too. You're like two alpha dogs who want to pee on each other."

Both Hattie and the guys looked at me. "You're calling me a dog?" Hattie said.

"I am. An alpha dog, though. Top of the heap."

"A Cane Corso? I'd like to be a Cane Corso."

Of course she would choose to be a one-hundred-and-fifty-pound guard dog. "Sure."

"You're calling *me* a dog?" Vinnie didn't look as thrilled with the news as Hattie had been.

"Yes. I am." I put my hands on my hips. "Vinnie, Hattie

promised you a free sandwich at her café in exchange for the favor you did. Instead, you chose to show up at the strawberry festival and try to scare everyone. But Hattie's the alpha dog, and she has to prove it by not feeding you here, since she's not at her café. So, she's going to say no to the sandwich, and then you're going to get all mad and think that no one is trustworthy. But that's a bunch of crap, because Hattie's completely loyal and amazing. We all know you're not a jerk, because you saved our lives and hers. So give it up. You two are both cute little puppies who need to go romp on the beach together instead of peeing on each other."

Everyone stared at me.

I smiled. "But Hattie needs help at the booth right now and she offered me free food to help her, so maybe you guys can make a trade."

Vinnie's eyes widened. "Work here?" He looked around, and we all did. I could see that he didn't believe Hattie would let him get behind her table, handle her food, work with customers, and take their money.

But he didn't know Hattie like I did.

Sure enough, Hattie's face lit up. She liked to nurture people with potential, and these guys were no exception. She knew goodness when she saw it, and she didn't give a hoot what anyone else thought. So what if Vinnie probably liked to steal cars in his spare time? He had a good heart buried under that gang activity, so that was all that mattered to Hattie. "Yes!" she exclaimed. "Great idea! Vinnie, get your team back here. Let's do this! One free sandwich for every hour you work the booth."

Vinnie stared at her. "You're serious?"

"I never joke about food."

Vinnie went silent, then looked at his friends. They both shook their heads and headed back down the aisle toward the parking lot. But Vinnie shrugged off his leather jacket, revealing massive, tattooed biceps that set the whispers going again. "I'm in."

Two minutes later, Vinnie and his muscles were wearing a

fuchsia Hattie's Café T-shirt that was a little too tight, a matching visor, and he was holding a credit card reader and taking money.

Hattie grabbed a muffin and handed it to me without a word.

Her way of thanks. Lucy and I owed Vinnie our lives, and Hattie was as happy as I was to offer more than a sandwich to him.

I winked at her and swiped a cookie, feeling all sorts of warm fuzzies in my heart. I was so happy to be in a position to offer belonging to someone who was an outsider, after a lifetime of being the one on the outside.

If I had tried to hire Vinnie, my marina would have paid the price in lost business. But Hattie had the power to do whatever she wanted in Bass Derby, and she'd just given Vinnie her stamp of approval.

It felt good to be a part of that.

"Mia! Hattie!"

We both turned as the third part of our trio of awesomeness, Lucy Grande, ran toward us, ducking around people. It took me only a split second to register her tension and to realize she was running hard. Alarm shot through me as she reached us. "What's up?"

"It's Rogue!"

I glanced at Hattie. "Rogue? What's wrong with Rogue?" Rogue, whose real name was Esther Neeley, was about Hattie's age. She was obscenely rich and not afraid of owning it. She was sassy, irreverent, and a member of the Seam Rippers, a local quilting group who loved margaritas, loyalty, and adventure. I adored Rogue, and she'd helped save my life ten years ago. Different situation than when Vinnie had stepped in, but equally as helpful.

"The strawberry judging starts in a half hour, and Rogue's not there. Her table's not set up. I've looked everywhere for her, and no one has seen her." Lucy looked worried. "I tried to call her, and her phone went right into voicemail."

"She should have been set up hours ago." Hattie swore. "We need to check her house. Something's clearly wrong."

Their worry was contagious. "What are you guys talking about? What table?"

"I'll drive," Hattie said. "Vinnie. You're in charge. The reputation of Hattie's Café is on your shoulders. If you blow it, I will hunt you down, and you won't like it one bit."

The gun-wielding gang leader's eyes widened, and he looked slightly alarmed. "Run your tent?"

"Yes, I'll be back soon." Hattie grabbed her keys from a corner of the tent. "Let's go!" She broke into a run, and Lucy ran after her.

They took off so fast that I had to sprint not to lose them in the crowd. They were both fitter than I was, but ten days of working out with Rogue had helped me enough that I still had them in sight when Hattie leapt into her massive, jacked-up pickup truck.

Lucy jumped into the back seat, and I grabbed hold of the passenger door and hauled myself in as Hattie hit the gas. "What is going on?" I panted as I dragged the door shut just in time to avoid taking out a telephone pole.

"Rogue has won the Strawberry Shortcake Bake-Off four times," Hattie said as she peeled out onto the main road. "The festival charter states that the championship trophy will be named after the first person to win it five-times."

"She's been entering for years, and she finally won her fourth time last year. There are four others who have also won four times," Lucy said. "Rogue wants that trophy named after her, and she's been planning for this year's festival for the last twelve-months."

"One of the four-time champions is probably going to win this year," Hattie said, the tires squealing as she peeled around the corner. "Rogue needs it to be her."

"Why?"

Hattie glanced at me. "She used to enter with her daughter long ago. It has personal meaning for her. There's no way she'd miss out on the Strawberry Contest."

"Doing well in the first two rounds can help break a tie in the finals," Lucy explained. "Today matters."

"Rogue was planning to get there at six this morning to set up her table," Hattie added. "Presentation makes a difference."

"But her table is empty. Nothing on it at all," Lucy said. "Judging starts at seven."

I glanced at Hattie's dashboard and saw it was six thirty-three. Much like Hattie, Rogue was an unapologetic, unstoppable force, but she had the added benefit of endless financial resources. If she wanted to win that contest, nothing would have kept her from being at that table. "You don't think she changed her mind?"

"No." Hattie swung the truck into the long, white-stone driveway that snaked almost a half mile through Rogue's lake-front property. "No chance."

I pulled out my cell and texted Bootsy Jones, the only other Seam Ripper I had in my phone. *Rogue's missing. Have you heard from her?*

What? No. I'll ask around. I'm at the Festival. I'll look around here.

Great. We're at her house. I set my phone down as Hattie screeched to a stop by the front door.

Rogue's cherry red Lamborghini SUV was parked out front, with the tailgate wide open.

I was the first one out of the truck. "Rogue!"

There was no answer, but the back of Rogue's SUV was loaded with gorgeous strawberries, along with other crates containing what appeared to be table decor. I could see champagne, a velvet table covering, but no Rogue.

Hattie came up behind me. "She told me she was packing her car at five-thirty this morning."

Fear trickled down my spine. "That was thirteen hours ago."

The strawberry crates were neatly arranged, ready for transport that had never happened. The berries were a gorgeous vibrant red, plump, flawless perfection. "The strawberries look really good. Does she grow them herself?"

"Actually yes. She doesn't even let her gardener touch them. They're the best around."

Lucy was at the front door. "No one's answering." She peered through the window beside the door, then swore. "You guys! The furniture inside is knocked over. It looks like someone tore the place apart."

We all looked at each other, and then suddenly, I realized that Ivan, my bodyguard wasn't with us. "We lost Ivan."

"Well, I think that tells you a lot about how useful he'd be in an emergency, right? Because right now, I feel like there's something going on that he might be needed for."

"I agree," Lucy said. "This scene is giving me the creeps. It's like Rogue was plucked right out of her life mid-stride."

A shiver went down my spine, so I immediately cleared my throat and stood taller. Fear was never allowed to win. "It's fine. Whatever it is, we can handle it."

"Damn straight we can." Hattie pushed me toward the house. "Go unlock the door, Mia. See what's going on."

"Unlock it? I mean, yeah, I love a chance to pick locks, but shouldn't we call the police?"

Hattie put her hands on her hips. "How well did that work for us recently? Involving the police in a dicey situation?"

"That was murder!" I stared at them, horror congealing in my stomach. "You don't think—"

"Well, open the door and find out."

With the exception of Griselda, my FBI handler, I didn't trust cops to believe in my innocence. Well, if Devlin Hunt was in town, I might have texted him. But he'd been called away right after he asked me out on a date, and I hadn't heard from him since. The only one we could call was Chief Stone. The fact he was Lucy's cousin didn't mean we could trust him to do what was right and handle the situation correctly.

Quite the opposite.

Which meant if we cared about Rogue, it had to be us.

I grimaced, but pulled out my lock picks, which I now carried with me more often, because life in Bass Derby was turning out to be like that. "Make sure no one shoots us."

"They'd shoot only you. *We* don't have assassins after us," Hattie said, but she took up position next to me, facing out.

Lucy did the same as I went down on my knee and got to work.

I was sure that Rogue had an alarm, but there was no sound as the lock clicked a minute later. I pushed the door open. "Hello? Is anyone there?"

Silence.

I stood up and took a step inside. "Rogue?" My voice faded as I took in the carnage. Her house usually was in pristine condition, gorgeous, designed to emulate cozy, Maine warmth with expensive perfection. But right now, chairs were upturned. Pictures and books strewn on the floor. The rugs askew.

"Go in and check it out," Hattie said. "I'll stand guard out here."

I looked back at her. "Why me?"

She smiled and waved me inside. "You're the FBI special agent. Do your thing."

"I'm not an FBI special agent—"

"Closer than I am. Go, go."

I looked at Lucy, and she picked up a small pot of geraniums and hefted it. "I'll come with you. I'm good at throwing things."

"All right, then. Let's do this." Wishing I had my hairdryer, which I'd recently discovered was very useful as a weapon, I led the way into the front hall. I looked around and saw that the family room was open to the kitchen. "That way." I pointed, my instincts drawing me toward the kitchen.

"Okay." Lucy stayed close to me, her pot ready.

As I walked past an upturned table, I grabbed the lamp off the floor and wrapped the cord around my hand, swinging the lamp gently. It wasn't as maneuverable as a hairdryer, but all corded projectiles were pretty much in my wheelhouse these days.

We stepped into the kitchen and looked around.

"Nothing in here looks like it was touched," Lucy said. "Let's go—"

"No." I knew from my own childhood training sessions with my mom that sometimes the best distraction was in plain sight. "The front hall is a mess, so maybe someone doesn't want us to notice something in here."

"Oh...right...I forgot about that. I gotta work on my criminal mind."

We both looked around, and this time, I saw a note on the center island, with messy handwriting scrawled across the paper. I walked over and peered at it. The message was short and to the point. "I didn't do it," I read aloud.

Lucy looked over. "Who didn't do what?"

"Rogue, I'm guessing. But what didn't she do? Trash her house?" I looked around, and I saw that the pantry door was open at the back of the kitchen. Instinct made my heart start to pound. "In there."

Gripping my lamp more tightly, I forced myself to walk across the kitchen. "If Rogue jumps out of there to scare us, I'm pretty sure I'm going to have a heart attack."

"You and me, both." Lucy edged up close behind me, which I greatly appreciated—

My gaze dropped to the threshold, and fear crept down my belly when I saw something peeking out from the pantry. Limp. Lifeless. Adorned with very high heels. "Are those *feet*?"

"What? Where?" Lucy looked down. "Oh, God. *Yes.*"

We lunged for the door and yanked it open. Sprawled on the ground facedown was a fifty-something woman with raven black hair, gorgeous shoes, and a bunch of strawberries scattered around her.

"Oh, God." I dropped to my knees beside her, but the moment I touched her, I knew.

She was dead.

CHAPTER 2

"DON'T TOUCH HER!" Hattie shouted it from behind me.

Startled by her sudden appearance, I shrieked and leapt backward, crashing into the shelves. One of them broke, and cans tumbled down to the floor, thudding onto the dead woman, which was just a little disturbing. Yes, she was dead, but... "Sorry," I told her, because what else was I going to say?

"Get up!" Hattie grabbed my arm, and hauled me to my feet, with astonishing strength for a sassy senior. "Lucy, help!"

Lucy grabbed my other arm, and between the two of them, they basically catapulted me out of the pantry and across the kitchen with so much force that I hit the ground and sprawled forward, just like the dead gal I'd just clobbered with cans.

I scrambled to my feet. "More dead people? Seriously?"

"Not people. Just one." Hattie threw me a towel. "Did you touch anything? Wipe it. Don't mess with the evidence."

"I know that." But I grabbed my lamp from where it had fallen and quickly wiped it down. "We need to call the police—"

"Do we?" Hattie put her hands on her hips. "Do you want to rethink that?"

I stared at her. "You're literally the one who talked me into *not* running from murder scenes." My con artist mom taught me the art of self-preservation on many levels, including not sticking around crimes scenes that you aren't responsible for. A couple weeks ago, I'd tried to put that lifelong wisdom into practice, and Hattie had talked me out of it. It hadn't worked out great, but none of us were in prison, so it was a good growth moment for me.

"Facing the police *is* a valuable life skill to be employed whenever appropriate." Hattie looked around the room, then hurried over to the sink and picked up a gorgeous crystal vase of red roses. "This is not one of those times. We gotta go."

"Go?" I looked at Lucy, but she shrugged. "Go where?"

"The festival." Hattie said it like we were both complete idiots.

I put my hands on my hips. "I kinda think murder takes priority over the festival—"

"Does it?" Hattie picked up another vase of roses and shoved both containers into my hands. "That dead woman there is Dee Dutch. She and Rogue, along with several others, are four-time champions of the bake-off. And suddenly Dee is dead and Rogue's on the run. Coincidence? I think not, my friends."

I blinked. "You think someone murdered over strawberry shortcake?"

"Who wouldn't?"

"Well, honestly, I think the list is pretty long—"

"Obviously not long enough, given that Dee's dead in the pantry." Hattie looked around. "I think the roses are what Rogue came back for when she found Dee. I don't see anything else for her table, do you?"

Lucy held up her hands. "Wait a sec. You want us to go back to the festival and set up Rogue's table?"

"Her strawberries need to be judged tonight, and she's not around to do it. Are we really going to let her get eliminated from contention just because someone dumped Dee in her kitchen?"

I opened my mouth, and then shut it again. If Rogue was innocent, Hattie kind of had a point. "I hate bullies," I admitted.

"Right?" Hattie pointed to the counter. "Rogue left us a note. She didn't do it. Therefore, she needs our help."

I had definitely not guessed that the "it" in the note was murder, but maybe I needed to level-up my thinking. "Where is Rogue? How do we know she's okay?"

"She's okay," Hattie said with absolute confidence. "She clearly was in the middle of packing for the contest, walked in here, found Dee, realized she was going to be the primary suspect, so she wrote the note for us so we'd know what to do, and then she went into hiding."

I frowned. "Really?"

"Absolutely. That was her way of asking us to get those berries judged tonight. We're not going to let her down, are we?"

Lucy and I looked at each other. "Can we present for her?" Lucy asked.

"Yep. Until the finals, all contestants can name a stand-in, in case of car trouble, food poisoning, that kind of stuff."

"Like murder," I said dryly.

"Exactly. I'm Rogue's officially designated stand-in. I'm the food maven in this region, so who else would she pick? No one. So, let's go. I made a promise, and I never break my promises." She checked her watch and swore. "We gotta go! Judging is in twelve minutes! Mother of pearl!" Hattie shot out of the kitchen, hurrying toward the front door.

Lucy and I looked at each other, then took off after Hattie.

Hattie raced out the front door, not waiting while I paused to clean my prints off the lock I'd just picked or the lamp I'd been carrying around with me.

Hattie hurled her keys at Lucy. "Take my truck. I'll drive the Lamborghini. It'll be faster since it's already packed. No time to move all her gear to my truck. We'll meet there. Mia! With me!"

"Got it!" Lucy said as she caught Hattie's keys.

Hattie shut the back of Rogue's SUV. "You stall the judges, Lucy. Mia and I will get the table set up. Go!" She practically threw herself into the Lamborghini. "Let's go, Mia!"

I launched myself into the Lamborghini just before Hattie hit the gas. I lodged the vases of roses between my feet, trying to ignore the sloshing of water soaking my shoes. Hattie tore out of the driveway with about twenty times the enthusiasm she'd driven in with. "Did you pick the Lamborghini just so you could drive it?" I asked as I braced myself.

"No smart woman ever turns down a chance to drive a Lamborghini," Hattie said as we peeled around the corner. "This SUV corners like a race car. It's a freaking brilliant machine. How long do we have?"

"Eight minutes." I pulled out my phone and called Bootsy, who I'd texted earlier.

Bootsy answered on the first ring. "We can't find Rogue—"

"She's gone underground," I said. "Hattie and I have her strawberries and her display. We're on our way there. Gather as many Seam Rippers as you can and meet us at the entrance to the contest tent to help us unload. We'll have about three minutes to set up. And help Lucy stall the judges."

"Got it!" Bootsy hung up immediately without asking for more info, which made me wonder exactly how often the Seam Rippers got into trouble.

Given what I knew about them, it was probably pretty frequent. Did I really want to hang out with them? Yes. Yes, I did.

"Great idea," Hattie said. "Those Seam Rippers are a force. Love it." She blew through a stop sign, but no one was coming, so we didn't add any more corpses to the town total, which was great.

"Who is Dee Dutch? Why would someone set up Rogue to kill her?" I couldn't quite buy into the fact that Dee had been murdered over the strawberry shortcake championship, but she was definitely dead and Rogue was clearly the shiniest choice for murder, so info was needed, and fast.

I waited, but no more information was forthcoming. "Hattie?"

"What?"

"Dee Dutch? Who is she?"

"Sorry. I was obsessing about how heavenly this engine is. How do they make it sound so beautiful?"

"Hattie! Dead woman? Did Rogue kill her?" I had to ask, right?

Hattie looked at me, which meant her eyes were off the road for longer than I wanted. "She definitely could," she admitted. "And honestly, it wouldn't surprise me if Rogue was actually a sleeper agent for the KGB or a former assassin for the CIA. She just has that vibe, don't you think?"

I raised my brows. "You're not really making a case for her innocence."

"Sure I am. She'd be so good at murder that if she killed Dee, that corpse would never be even close to Rogue's house, let alone abandoned in her pantry. No one would ever find the body. Plus, secret life aside, Rogue would never believe she'd need to kill Dee to win the contest. Between you and me, she *would* have needed to, but she didn't realize that, so there goes your motive for murder."

The logic of Hattie Lawless was astounding.

And I believed her.

What did that say about me? That I was smart, clever, and knew when I had reliable resources? Or so desperate for friends that I'd be willing to completely abandon all independent thought so I could bond with them? Or maybe I trusted my own flawless instincts about Rogue's propensity for murder and Hattie had simply confirmed them?

Regardless, I was thoroughly ensconced on the Rogue-is-innocent train, so it was time to get some info. "What was Dee like?"

Hattie hit a corner at top speed, and the SUV was marvelous handling it. "She was Miss Teen Maine as a kid, for one thing."

"A beauty queen?" That wasn't what I'd expected to find in Bass Derby. A fishing champion? Yes. A snowmobiling addict? Sure. Beauty queen? I hadn't given that possibility any thought.

"Yep. Dee was all kinds of trouble. Won the bake-off four times in a row, but just before the final judging for her fifth crown, it came out that she'd cheated. She was booted from the contest moments before the champion was announced, but it was later leaked that they'd been ready to crown her. Right after that, she took off from town and never came back. There's going to be a party when people find out she's dead."

"So, many possible suspects?" That meant a lot to sort through, but it was good because we could send the police after folks other than Rogue.

Was I actually developing a strategy for keeping my friends from being accused of murder? That was not the life I'd come here to lead...but I *had* come for friends, and I treasured every one of them. If I had to save a few of them from a murder rap so that bullies didn't get away with bad things, then I was happy to use my skills however I could.

"Yep, lots of suspects, but Rogue is the one whose kitchen Dee is in, so the police won't look much past that. Rogue was in good shape to win this year, but Dee made the best strawberry short-cake I've ever tasted. Not as good as mine, of course, but I stopped entering after my fourth win. No challenge, so who wants to bother? It's like winning a sprint against a turtle. It's an embarrassment to even enter."

I laughed softly. Of course winning the bake-off wasn't a challenge for Hattie.

"But other than me, Dee was the best around. With her in the contest, no one else stood a chance. If I'd known she was back, I would have had to enter just to keep her from winning, but obviously, I don't need to do that now." Hattie turned into the lot and hurtled past all the parked cars, heading straight for the contest tent. "Dee would have to be eliminated from the contest for anyone else to win."

"So, any of the four-time champs might have killed her?" Dear heavens. Had I just said that? No one killed over strawberry shortcake. It was impossible. There had to be something else at play. But it was a place to start, and I was starting right now.

"Damn straight." Hattie slammed on the brakes next to the main door of the tent, somehow not coming close to even a single person, animal, or car, then hit the button to open the back. As she parked, Seam Rippers popped out of the tent at varying speeds, shouting orders at each other as they emptied the back of the vehicle in less than a minute.

I grinned at the sight of all the senior quilters raiding the SUV in support of Rogue. This was the kind of place I wanted to live in. The kind of friends I wanted to have. And I was in the middle of becoming a part of them—

Hattie put the SUV in park but grabbed my arm as I reached for the door handle. "Wait. There's one more thing you need to know."

I sat back in my seat, my heart suddenly hammering. "What?"

"Do you know about the Dutch family?"

I frowned. "They have a lot of headstones in the town graveyard."

"Right. Because there are a lot of Dutches, going way back. Some of them are great people. Some of them...let's just say that Dee wasn't the worst by a long shot." She paused. "They're a close-knit family. They'll want revenge for Dee's death, and they'll take it as soon as they figure out who killed her."

Understanding dawned. "Rogue didn't go into hiding to avoid the police, did she?"

"Nope. The police she can handle. The Dutch family? She wouldn't survive for twenty-four hours once the Dutches find out Dee's in her pantry."

"So, they're like my ex-husband." Yay for that.

Hattie grinned. "Yep. And once they decide Rogue killed Dee, and then realize you're helping Rogue out, they're going to come after you."

That sounded like fun. "Me? Why me?"

"Because I'm untouchable, Lucy's cousin is the chief of police, and you're the new kid on the block. So, you're the weak link, the loose thread they can start pulling at to find out where Rogue is."

I narrowed my eyes. "Are they the type to target my cat or my marina?"

"They might, but honestly, too bad for them if they tried to mess with King Tut."

I grinned. "True." King Tut was the best.

Hattie opened her door. "No one knows that Dee's dead yet, so right now, you're safe. But if you go out there and align yourself with Rogue, they're going to remember that, and it's a big family. Lots of them, and most of them are built like moose. You're new here, so you don't owe Rogue anything. Just wanted you to make an informed decision."

I appreciated Hattie's candor, but I didn't need to think about it. "Rogue risked her life for me, and I hate bullies. So, I'm helping." I pushed open my door and got out.

Hattie grinned. "I figured you would, but I wanted you to know. But you should probably find Ivan again. He'll be good to keep around. This is going to be fun. Keep quiet about what's at Rogue's house. Everyone will find out soon enough—" She paused. "There's one of the sets of Dutch twins. Twins run in the family."

I turned around and saw two massive human beings lumbering toward us. Each one was about six and a half feet tall, with carrot-top hair, big muscles, and extra beef. "They could squash me with their pinkie."

"Yep."

I had time to turn back. To walk away, climb into my truck, and drive back to the Eagle's Nest Marina, pretending I knew nothing about their dead relative.

I didn't even consider it.

I hadn't been able to walk away when I found the white powder in my dining room cabinet, and I wasn't going to be able to walk away now.

Friends didn't let friends get revenge-killed for murders they didn't commit.

Basic friendship rules right there. "I'm in. Let's do it."

CHAPTER 3

WHEN I REACHED Rogue's table moments later, four Seam Rippers were unpacking the crates from Rogue's SUV. Hattie took over as executive director as I jogged up. With astonishing speed, the display came into gorgeous perfection. The luxurious velvet cloth was laid across the table. Strawberries were arranged to perfection on silver platters. Expensive champagne was poured into the most beautiful crystal flutes, chocolate bonbons were set out, and the roses were arranged.

"Judges are two tables down." Bootsy came running up. "Can't stall them anymore. Hey, looks great!"

Hattie moved the roses to the back corner of the table. "Good enough. Everyone vanish."

The Seam Rippers disappeared as if by magic, leaving only Hattie, Bootsy, and me. Standing there at Rogue's table, I could almost feel the target lining up on my forehead. I looked around but didn't see the red-headed twins. But who else was a Dutch?

I smoothed a wrinkle in the velvet as Lucy came running up. "That looks like it was designed by a professional wedding designer," she said. "I can't believe you pulled it off."

Hattie waved her hand toward the judges. "You don't need to stall them. We're ready."

Lucy nodded and put on her volunteer badge. "Okay, we'll patrol. Come on, Mia."

I hesitated. "You go. I'll watch this aisle." There was no way I could leave Hattie unattended. Whoever had killed Dee was around here somewhere, and I didn't feel right leaving Hattie. Where was Ivan?

"All right. Keep in touch." Lucy blew us a kiss and strode down the aisle, her head swiveling back and forth as she checked out everyone.

I stepped back as Hattie leaned forward and put her hands on the table, clearly staking her right as stand-in. The judges were across the aisle now, at the table one down from us. There were four of them, and I didn't recognize any of them.

Directly across from us was a four-time champion banner table, along with the years the contestant had won. Old years. Nothing recent. Was it Dee's table? The thought sent a chill down my spine. The table was being managed by a man and woman in their early twenties. They kept looking down the aisle and at their phones, texting, and making calls.

Waiting for Dee?

The thought was sobering. Dee might have been an evil beauty queen, but that didn't change the fact that the world still thought she was coming tonight. I nudged Bootsy, who was standing beside me. "Whose table is that?"

Bootsy narrowed her eyes, and I could see her thinking. "Those are Dutches at the table, but neither of them has ever won…" Her eyes widened. "Holy cow. Is Dee back?" She hit Hattie in the shoulder. "Those are Dee's years. Is she back? What the heck? Who let her enter?"

"Dee?" Hattie echoed, as she looked across the aisle. "Those are Dee's years," she agreed, "but she'd never be allowed back in the contest. I'm sure it's not what it looks like." Then she paused. "Holy crap," she whispered. "The head judge is Ronald Dutch. Do you see that? He must have let her in."

"Ronald is a good guy," Bootsy whispered. "He'd never let her in. He's not like his twin was."

Another set of Dutch twins? "Which one's Ronald?" I asked.

"Red shirt," Bootsy whispered. "He's a really nice guy. How did Dee's entrance get past him?"

"Family priority?" Ronald Dutch looked to be in his mid-to-late sixties. He was fairly tall, and he looked fit. He was wearing jeans, white dock shoes, and a short-sleeved button-down shirt.

Bootsy shook her head. "He wouldn't prioritize family over doing his job. He'd never let Dee in—"

"Both of you, shut it down," Hattie interrupted. "The judges are coming here." She gave me a meaningful look, and I nodded in agreement, understanding that she wanted me to check things out while she worked with the judges.

I eased away. As I moved, my gaze went to the booth next to Dee's, another table with a four-time champion banner. The man standing behind the table looked familiar, and it took me a moment to realize it was Diesel Knox, the owner of the Ugly Man Tavern.

He was a huge, rough woodsman, wearing a T-shirt with the Ugly Man caricature face on it: big nose, beard, and the logger hat. A banner on the front of the table said "Four-Time Champion," along with the years he had won, which were much more spread out than Dee's. He had a couple other rough-looking dudes with him, and they were all sitting in Adirondack chairs with a beer. Diesel was handing out beer to anyone who wanted it. He was being far more charming than you'd think a guy with that many tattoos could muster.

The Ugly Man was the sketchy man-cave bar in town, and Diesel was the man who could keep a place like that in line.

Which meant Diesel was also a man who would have no problem taking out Dee without breaking a sweat. But how could he care that much about a bake-off? He was rough and tough, practically oozing testosterone in a caveman kind of way. He was in his mid-fifties, a guy who didn't look like he'd baked anything in his life.

I peered casually to my right and checked out the blue and white striped décor at the next table. It was the same striping as on the patio umbrellas at Jake's Yacht Club, the upscale marina owned by Jake Nash, who wasn't a fan of me showing up in town and creating competition for him.

Jake looked over at me, his navy-blue Yacht Club shirt crisp and perfect. His blond hair was cut short, without a hair out of place, and his sculpted jaw had the plastic perfection of a photoshopped model. He narrowed his eyes at me, and I gave him a smile.

Jake and I weren't doing great at making friends, but I was hoping to fix that. I noticed the Four-Time Champion banner on the table, and quickly looked at the booth more carefully.

This time, I recognized the man beside Jake as the free-lancing dessert chef who Hattie had once dated.

I scanned the aisle, but I didn't see any more four-time champion banners. The judges were at a table with a sign that said Topsy's Vegan Delights. The fiftyish woman behind the counter was wearing all the colors of the rainbow, jeans with embroidered flowers, and a scarf braided into her hair. She was laughing with the judges, clearly having a glorious time simply being present.

That's how I wanted to be, not looking over my shoulders for another freaking *murderer*.

I wanted to finish this whole thing and fast. Hattie had said there were two other four-time champions. Including her, or not including her? I needed to know who they were.

The judges finished up at the vegan table, then headed over to Rogue's. I tensed as they walked up, all of them frowning when they saw Rogue was missing.

"Where's Esther?" asked Ronald Dutch, the head judge who Bootsy and Hattie had said was a good guy. A good guy who had apparently let his bad-vibing relative, Dee, into the contest, which raised all sorts of questions about exactly where his moral barometer stood.

"Rogue is detained this evening." Hattie blasted the judges with a confidence and swagger that only she could pull off. "I'm her designated stand-in." She then immediately launched into a description of the strawberries. She knew exactly how they'd been planted, treated, and harvested. She was efficient, professional, and knew how to represent them.

Rogue had known what she was doing when she'd chosen Hattie. Was there anything that Hattie couldn't handle?

As I stood there listening to Hattie charm the judges, I couldn't keep my gaze from wandering over to Dee's table. There was definite consternation there now, which made guilt inch down my spine.

We'd left a dead woman behind and hadn't told anyone.

Didn't she deserve to be noticed? Especially when whoever killed her could be after Rogue, or me, or any of us now…

"Mia."

I jumped as the low, deep voice drifted over my shoulder and down my spine. I knew that voice. It belonged to an inconveniently attractive local cop named Devlin Hunt. I'd been starting to get just a little bit interested in him, enough to agree to meet him for dinner, and then he'd disappeared for two weeks. The absence had been exactly what I needed to remind myself that I wasn't dating again. But dammit. I still liked his voice. "Hi."

"Sorry I missed our date. You got my text, right?"

I didn't turn around. "It wasn't a date, but if it had been, a text wouldn't have been sufficient. But since it wasn't a date, it was fine."

He was quiet for a sec, and I could almost hear his mind analyzing my response. I didn't like that. I didn't want to be analyzed. So I spun around. "Devlin—" I made the mistake of looking at him, which completely distracted me.

Clearly not on duty, he was in jeans and a black T-shirt that showed off a very fit physique. His brown skin was pretty much radiant in the early evening light, and his dark eyes were like bottomless chasms of mystery. He was just a man, but he did it for me, and I didn't appreciate that one bit.

"Where's your bodyguard?" he asked suddenly.

"Ivan lost me. I don't know where he is." Now that he mentioned it, I was a little surprised Ivan hadn't tracked me down when I'd arrived back at the festival.

Movement from Dee's table caught my eye, and I glanced back over. They were talking to the judges now, and the young woman was moving her hands urgently. I could tell Dee's absence was causing an uproar. No one knew she was buried in strawberries in Rogue's pantry.

I couldn't take it anymore. I knew Dee was dead, and I had to do something about it.

Devlin shifted restlessly, his cop persona kicking in. "Has Ivan called you to find out where you are? Texted you? Checked in?"

I ignored the barrage of questions, my guilt over Dee's abandoned corpse overriding my interest in my bodyguard's lack of quality work. "Devlin, you need to go to Esther's house."

His eyebrows shot up, and he gave me a long look. "What's at Esther's house? Ivan? Did you leave him tied up in the bathtub to get him out of your way?"

That was actually a somewhat valid line of inquiry. The man was getting to know me quite well...on some levels. "No, but I'll keep that in mind for the future." I cleared my throat. "We went there to find Esther, because she hadn't showed up for her table. Innocent trip. We wanted to check up on her."

"You're proclaiming your innocence before you even tell me the story? That's not a good sign." Devlin's gaze shot to Hattie, then back to me. "What happened?"

"Esther wasn't there. Her car was packed and open, her house trashed, and she was gone."

"A break in?" He looked a little relieved, as if he were expecting something more dramatic, because he was a smart man. "Esther's missing?"

"Yes, she is. So, we need to file a missing person's report."

He watched me, clearly understanding that there was more. Because he wasn't an idiot when it came to me. "Okay. And—?"

I let out my breath. "We found Dee."

"Dee?" he echoed.

I forgot he was relatively new to town. I gestured to her table. "Dee Dutch."

"A four-time champion? Was she trashing the place?" He looked almost amused by the idea.

I was glad for him, because his joy would fade very shortly. "No, not when we found her."

"Kidnapping Esther, then?"

"No." Playing twenty questions with Devlin was a delight, but not really getting me out from under the guilt of leaving Dee on the pantry floor. "I don't know why Dee was there, but let's just say she's not coming to her table tonight." I paused at Devlin's blank look. "Or *ever.*"

"Ever?" Devlin stared at me.

"Ever." I said it with as much drama and permanence I could muster, which was really quite a lot, because I'd been raised on drama.

Sudden understanding dawned on his distractingly chiseled face. "She's dead? You found a *body?"*

I nodded. "In Esther's pantry. We were looking for Esther, and Dee had these really nice shoes on—" Too much info. Right. "She's dead. I mean, I'm not an expert on death, but it was pretty obvious."

He swore again and pulled out his phone. "And you didn't call the cops? You left her there?"

I decided not to take offense at his sudden irritation. "It was a tricky situation, and we had to make a game-time decision. Plus, she wasn't going anywhere. And…" I paused, not quite wanting to admit that Hattie was an unstoppable force that I'd been no match for. "Yeah."

He looked at me as he punched a number on his phone. "I swear to God, Mia."

"I know, right? Your life would be so dull without me. I'm happy to shine the bright light of joy into your darkness. You're welcome, but no thanks is needed."

"I'm going to need to talk to all of you later."

I grimaced. "Of course. We tried not to touch anything, but we were kind of in a rush so—"

He shot me a look that was layered with all sorts of irritated emotion, then turned away, striding toward the parking lot as he spoke into his phone. Relief rushed through me as I watched him go. Yeah, we were all going to be in trouble for leaving her there, but Dee was no longer going to lie there alone, unnoticed, and unacknowledged.

But she was still going to be dead.

And a murderer was still walking freely around our little town, and maybe this very park.

And maybe this very aisle.

CHAPTER 4

"HATTIE." I kept my voice low, not wanting to draw the attention of any active murderers who might be strolling through the tent.

"Mia!" My favorite sassy senior beamed at me as the judges moved on to the Yacht Club table. "Wasn't that great? I forgot how much fun it is to win things like this. The judges asked me why I wasn't entering my famous shortcake. They all remembered how great it is. I think I should enter. What do you think? I don't need the strawberry portion to win." She wiped her hands on her jeans. "Seriously. It's great to be adored. I need to put myself in the position to be adored more often. Bootsy, take over! I gotta go check on my booth."

And with that, Hattie trotted past me, heading down the aisle.

Um...what? "Hattie!" I jogged after her. "Wait up."

"Can't. I have a possible gang leader managing my booth. Gotta check on that situation. Come on. Don't be lazy. Surely you can keep up with an old lady like me."

I had to jog to keep up with her walk. "You always say you're not old."

"I'm not, but when it's a chance to mock your lack of physical prowess, I'll play that card all day long." She ducked around a woman pushing a double stroller. "I saw Devlin sneaking off. I assume you told him about Dee?"

"I did. I felt guilty—"

"Perfect. Now we're all set." She waved at someone and blew an attractive silver fox a kiss. "This is such a great night. I really might enter in the morning. I have to think about it, you know? Do I want to crush all the little wannabees—" She stopped suddenly, so fast I literally ran into her. "Vegan? Really?"

We were in front of Topsy's Vegan Cupcakes booth. The strawberries looked amazing, and she had dozens of samples of cupcakes arranged, making it apparent that she was using the contest to advertise her business...which made me think maybe I missed out by not getting the marina involved. The number of people strolling through the aisles admiring the displays and sampling strawberries and other goodies was significant.

Topsy had many different varieties of cupcakes, and they all looked amazing. Gorgeous stacks of frosting, cool decorations, and they were arranged on fun-colored platters that felt like sunshine and confetti.

The woman I assumed was Topsy of Topsy's Vegan Cupcakes smiled, clearly overhearing Hattie's comment. "Vegan can be delicious when it's done well."

Hattie raised her brows. "And do you do it well?"

Topsy nodded. "I do it very well." She held out a tray of mini cupcakes. "Try your favorite flavor. You'll be impressed."

Damn. She had as much confidence as Hattie did when it came to baking. Topsy was a couple decades younger than Hattie, but they might be long lost soulmates.

Hattie raised her brows. "I might not like your cupcakes, but I like you."

See? Soulmates.

Hattie helped herself to four different flavors, and I grabbed a chocolate one. Hattie gave Topsy a wave and continued her exodus before trying any of the cupcakes. "You never give the competition the satisfaction of a job well done," she whispered to me as we walked away. "These look great, so we can't eat them until we're out of sight. Is she watching us?"

I looked over my shoulder, but Topsy was already chatting up someone else. "We're not even on her radar."

"What?" Hattie stopped and turned around. "Stunning. She completely disregarded us. Does she not realize who I am? I can literally make or break the reputation of her business. I'm like the Frugal Gourmet of Bass Derby."

I started laughing. "It's okay, Hattie. As soon as she realizes it, you'll find her at the door of your café, trying to sweet-talk you, panicking because she had her chance to win you over, and she blew it. She'll probably lose multiple nights of sleep over it."

Hattie turned to look at me. "I like the way you think, Mia. You're good for my journey into more self-adoration." She held up a cupcake. "Bottoms up, Thief Girl."

I tapped my cupcake against hers. "Bottoms up, Sex Pistol."

"Damn straight." She flashed me a wicked grin, then popped the cupcake in her mouth.

I did the same, and the most incredible explosion of chocolate decadence exploded in my mouth. "Holy cow. That's incredible."

Hattie spit hers out, tossed the rest in a nearby trash bin, and then walked off.

I ran after her, half tempted to fish her rejected cupcakes out of the garbage. "How could you not like that?"

"Oh, I liked it. It was incredible," she muttered. "If her short-cake is anything like those cupcakes, she's going to win. We can't have a vegan winner. What will that do for the reputations of butter and eggs? And for this town! Bass Derby isn't about vegan cupcakes! It's about indulgence, roaring fireplaces, and satisfied bellies. Where are the judges? I'm going to enter now—"

"Hattie." I caught her arm. "Hang on."

"What?" She put her hands on her hips. "Mia, this is between you and me, but she could wind up being better than I am. If she can do that without butter and eggs? She's a magician." She held up her hand. "Wait. I bet she's a liar. There's no way those are vegan. We need to go prove she's a fake—"

"Hattie!"

"What!"

"Rogue is *missing.* There's a *dead woman* in her pantry. I think we need to focus on that."

Hattie rolled her eyes dismissively. "Rogue is fine. She's probably at your house, hiding out. And the woman is dead, so what are we supposed to do about it? I lost my necromancer license, so I can't zombie her. We had our fun with the body, and now it's not our problem. But those vegan cupcakes can't be allowed to win, and I'm the only one who can stop her."

I blinked. "We're just going to walk away? Let the police handle it? Since when do we do that?" Not that I wanted to get involved with a murderer, but justice mattered.

Hattie sighed and gave me her full attention. "Is anyone you love going to jail for Dee's murder?"

I held out my hands in an "are you kidding me?" gesture. "Rogue might."

"Only if they find her."

"They'll find her. Bass Derby isn't that big, and they'll be motivated by the body they find in her pantry."

"So, if Rogue gets tossed in the pen, we'll get involved. She doesn't have to be at the contest until Sunday, so we have time."

"That's forty-eight hours."

"She's at my house or yours, hiding out. We'll talk to her when we get home, and then proceed from there. She might know who killed Dee, and then why waste time looking?" She smacked me on the shoulder. "Don't look so worried. Rogue is like me. Nothing keeps her down. I'm sure she has a good story about it, and we'll get to hear it tonight." She turned away and started heading back into the competitor tent.

"Where are you going?"

"To find Ronald so I can enter the contest. The pride of Bass Derby is at stake, plus my own ego. It's a two-fer, and I win both ways. Meet me at my booth when the festival's over, and we'll go find Rogue--"

"Wait!"

She didn't stop walking. "No. Got stuff to do—"

"Can I sponsor you?"

Hattie stopped, turned around, and walked back over to me. "What?"

"For the contest. As long as you're entering, can I sponsor you? Then I can set up marina stuff at your table and work the good-will of the town. We can do a Hattie's Café and Eagle's Nest joint promo. What do you think?"

"You want to sponge off my brilliance for your own benefit?"

"Absolutely."

She grinned. "That's my girl. I love that entrepreneurship. It's about time that you started getting some good ideas for that business that's trying to drown you."

A compliment from Hattie was like sunshine pouring down on me. "So, that's a yes?"

"No. Why would I do it? What do I get out of it?"

I blinked. "My appreciation and friendship?"

"Already have those, and no successful business was built on decisions made out of personal affection, so show me a business reason why it's good for me, and I'll do it. My reputation is stellar. I control the Bass Derby restaurant trade. And I'm pretty much the only reason people walk into the marina property. So, what do I gain from teaming up with you?"

I threw out the idea I'd been percolating. "I'm going to put in outdoor tables and umbrellas, Wi-Fi, an outdoor bar with a grill, an ice cream window, and a fire pit. You can have all that space to expand your business for free if you want to team up. Put our names together and create a local hotspot for the summer evenings."

Hattie's Café closed at two o'clock every day, and I wasn't sure if she wanted to commit to evenings. But the evenings on the lake were magical, and I'd been searching for ways to make it accessible for people.

Hattie cocked her head to study me.

"I was thinking to launch it Fourth of July," I continued, getting more excited. "Like the grand reopening of the marina. We could have outdoor games for the kids, like a jumpy house on the water. A weekend-long launch festival. What if we did it together? Brand the café with the marina. A joint venture."

She didn't say anything. She just continued to study me. I couldn't tell what she was thinking.

"I cook," she said finally. "My genius is in the food, not some evening bar scene."

"Your genius is being you," I shot back. "The food is simply what you choose to put your genius into."

"Huh." She stared at me. "That's the kind of thing I'd say to you. Well played."

I grinned. "We could be great together." I meant it, too. Hattie was a special force, and she galvanized me to believe in myself in a way I never had before. "You know we could."

She finally shrugged. "I'll think about it. Go check on Vinnie while I enter the contest. We'll deal with the dead body situation later." She gave me a wave and hurried off, her fuchsia hair standing out like a beacon in the crowds.

That wasn't a no.

Yes. I'd been planning to broach the idea of a joint Fourth of July celebration to Jake, with the idea that his Yacht Club and my marina could work together to turn the entire lake into a celebration, but working with Hattie sounded like so much more fun.

I spun around, then stopped when I found myself face to face with Beau Hammersley, an obscenely wealthy local mystery writer who prided himself on hating people. Tonight, he was wearing old jeans, flipflops and his T-shirt that had a bloody knife on it, in honor of his newest book, aptly titled *The Bloody Knife*. He looked like a homeless drug addict, but I knew that behind the grisly appearance was a smart, sassy, extremely wealthy creative genius. "Beau. What are you doing here? Isn't this too social for you?"

He didn't smile. "Did you just mention a dead body?"

"I did, yeah."

"You found another one."

"We did. Yeah." I started walking toward Hattie's booth, grinning when Beau hurried after me.

"Where?"

"Rogue's house."

He stopped. "Rogue? Is *she* dead?"

"Oh, God. No. Dee Dutch is. Rogue is missing, but not dead."

"How do you know she's not dead if she's not there?"

"Because she left a note that said she didn't do it."

He stared at me. "And you know her handwriting?"

I blinked. "I don't. Hattie said she wrote it—"

"So, there's a dead woman at Rogue's house, and Rogue's missing, and that's it? Everything's fine then? Did you even look around the place?"

I shook my head. "Hattie's certain that Rogue's hiding out at my house or hers."

"And that's enough? Have you learned nothing in the last two weeks? Nothing is ever as it seems when it comes to murder. And next time you find a body, call me. I'll pay you a thousand bucks for every corpse you show me."

"I'm not planning to find more bodies—"

"That's fine. They find you. I'm going to Esther's house. You want a ride?"

I was torn. Hattie had just managed to convince me that everything was all right with Rogue, and now Beau had reawakened all the concerns I'd had. "I told Hattie I'd check on her booth—"

At that moment, my phone rang. I pulled it out and saw it was Devlin. Frowning, I answered it. "What's up?"

"Mia," he said, his voice on edge. "I need you to come to Esther's house."

Fear congealed in my belly. "What did you find?"

"Just get over here. Fast."

CHAPTER 5

TURBOJET and I arrived at Rogue's house a few minutes later, with Beau behind me in his black Hummer with tinted glass. Chief Stone's car was there, along with a civilian pickup truck that I was guessing was Devlin's off-duty ride.

Chief Stone and Devlin were standing on the front step, waiting.

Why wasn't the coroner there? Had they already taken the body? I had no idea they were that speedy.

I hopped out of Turbojet. "What's up?"

Devlin didn't waste time with a friendly greeting. "I need you to show me the body."

I blinked. "I don't really want to see it again."

"Show us the body," Chief Stone snapped.

"I'd like to see the body, too," Beau chimed in.

Something about the way Devlin was looking at me made alarm shoot down my spine. "What's wrong?"

"Just show us the body."

Uh oh. I hurried by him into the house, past the tossed furniture, and into the kitchen. Rogue's note was no longer on the counter, and the pantry door was open. I hurried around the island and then stopped when I could see into the pantry.

Strawberries were still all over the floor, with a space where the body had been, but there was definitely no dead ex-beauty queen on the floor. "Where did you put it?"

Devlin sighed. "Can you point to where you saw the body?"

"Right here." I pointed at the floor. "It was right here." I turned around, scanning the kitchen. "Where is she?"

"She wasn't there. No body," Chief Stone snapped. "You reported a crime that didn't happen. I can arrest you for that."

Devlin said nothing, but he was watching me intently, clearly trying to decide if I was lying.

"Seriously? You actually have to decide if I'm lying?" The three men staring at me with varying expressions, none of which were all that supportive. "Dee was there!"

"How do you know it was Dee?" Beau asked. "Do you know what Dee looks like?"

I looked over at him. "Hattie said it was her. She would know."

"She would," he agreed. "But that doesn't mean she was telling the truth."

I blinked. "What? Why would she lie?"

"What happened when you found the body?" Chief Stone asked. "Walk us through it."

I quickly explained, leaving out the part how I unlocked the front door with my lockpicks.

"Hang on," Devlin said. "So, the minute you got close to the body, Hattie and Lucy pulled you away before you could get a good look, and then Hattie shooed you out the door without calling the cops?"

Chief Stone swore and threw up his hands. "There's no body. For hell's sake. It was a prank. You got pranked. My cousin is a pain in the ass. I'm going to arrest her."

"A prank?" I echoed. "What?"

"Whose idea was it to come here?" Devlin asked.

"Hattie's but—"

"There's no body in this house," he interrupted. "We checked the entire building and property. No body. I suspect there never was one."

"She was *dead*. I've seen dead people, and I know what I saw—"

Chief Stone barked out a laugh. "Put the pieces together, Mia. You were pranked. It was a good one." He pulled out his cuffs. "I'm arresting you for the false claim to the police."

I backed up. "Did you take the note that was on the counter? The one from Rogue?"

I ignored Beau's raised eyebrows, casting doubt into whether the note had been from Rogue.

"What note?" Devlin asked.

I pointed to the counter. "She left a note there that said she didn't do it."

"Didn't do what?"

"I don't know. We assumed kill Dee."

He looked at Chief Stone. "Did you see a note?"

"There was no note. Turn around. You're under arrest."

"No. You can't arrest me. I saw a body. It was moved."

"We looked carefully," Chief Stone said. "There's no evidence a body was ever there. Not even a stray hair." He looked thrilled by his statement. "You're under arrest, Mia Murphy for—"

"No." I held up my hands in protest. "A woman is *dead*, which means a murderer is walking around here somewhere."

"You were pranked, Mia. Welcome to Bass Derby." The Chief of Police slapped cuffs on me, and Devlin did nothing to stop him.

Twenty minutes later, I was in jail for the first time in my life.

————

EVEN QUAINT TOWN jails were still a total loss of freedom, and I didn't like it at all.

I leaned my head back at the mural of Diamond Lake that was along one side of my cell and closed my eyes, trying to think. Had

I been pranked? How sure was I that the woman I'd seen on the floor was dead?

I revisited every detail of the body...and eventually decided it was faintly possible it had been staged. I hadn't actually felt for a heartbeat, and—

No. The moment I thought that it could have been staged, my instincts resisted.

I wasn't a coroner, but I was sure that woman had been dead. She hadn't just looked dead, she had *felt* dead. Like the life that had once inhabited that body was no longer there in that little pantry.

I'd been there when Griselda, my FBI handler, had killed an assassin inches from me. I'd felt the life leave her body. I'd stumbled across too many bodies lately. Heck, I'd been attached to one. The bodies had a void to them, a life that wasn't there.

This woman had felt like that. I was so sure.

But if I were right, where was the body now? And who had killed her?

And if I were right, it meant there was an active murderer wandering around Bass Derby who the cops weren't trying to catch. Oh...boy.

I'd been allowed one call from the police station, and I'd called Griselda. His phone had been off, and it had gone into voicemail, so I'd left a message, and now I waited.

In my jail cell.

Thinking about the fact that Devlin hadn't believed I knew what I'd seen. That he thought I was stupid enough to be pranked.

I'd started to like Devlin. I'd started to trust him. But for him not to believe me? It pissed me off. I deserved to be believed.

Griselda had believed me when I'd told him that I'd found white powder in my China cabinet, and that it wasn't mine...but even as I thought it, doubt crept in. What if Griselda hadn't cared if it was mine? What if he'd decided that my ex was the big fish he wanted to catch, and I was just a tool?

I stood up, suddenly restless. Devlin's lack of faith in me had derailed me more than I wanted to admit, because it preyed upon the past I was trying to leave behind: the persona of being a criminal that no one should trust or believe in, which was who I'd been for seventeen years until I'd walked away from my mom.

What if Devlin was right? What if I had been pranked? What if the women I'd started to trust had turned their backs on me? What if Hattie and Lucy had messed with me?

No. *No.* I refused to believe that I was unworthy of real friends. I refused to let that old voice have any space in my brain.

I fisted the bars and closed my eyes, fighting off the years of indoctrination that had made me question myself and the people around me, made me doubt that I deserved the life I wanted, and that I could have it.

Hattie and Lucy were my friends, and I trusted them.

I should have called them, not Griselda. It had been over three hours, and he hadn't used his FBI magic to set me free. He'd left me there.

I slammed my palm on the iron bars. "Angelina!" I whispered the name of the Seam Ripper who worked at the police station, whose loyalty was on the side of sassy senior women with margaritas and sewing machines, not the cops.

Angelina Stefanopoulos peered around the corner, as if she'd been hovering there, waiting for my summons. "What's up?"

"Can you call Hattie for me? And Lucy? Tell them I'm here."

She grinned. "Already did," she whispered. "Hattie's working on a few things for you. This is going to be fun."

Relief rushed through me. *Thank you Hattie.* "Fun how?"

Before she could answer, I heard raised voices from the front of the police station.

Angelina winked at me. "I'll leave the door open so you can enjoy it. Put your sneakers on. You'll be out of here within moments."

She ducked out, and I draped my hands through the bars, resting my forearms on the horizontal rails. I could hear Chief

Stone shouting, a woman arguing with him, but I couldn't hear what they were saying.

The woman's voice sounded very chipper, very confident, and very familiar.

I was pretty sure it belonged to Ruby Lee Hanrahan, the slightly amoral real estate agent who had sold me my marina. What was she doing here?

Several minutes later, Chief Stone came striding through the door, looking completely annoyed. Trotting behind him in her six-inch heels and several pounds of glittery purple eyeshadow and hairspray was Ruby Lee Hanrahan, real estate agent extraordinaire. She gave me a cheerful wave as Chief Stone grumped over to the cell.

He unlocked it and glared at me. "You're free."

I grabbed my shoes and practically sprinted past him, eager to get out of that little box before he changed his mind. "Fantastic." I didn't ask how or why. I just wanted out.

Angelina held out some documents on a clipboard, clearly ready to participate in getting me sprung. "Here you go, Mia. Sign these."

I grabbed the pen and signed with a flourish while Chief Stone pulled out his phone and called the mayor, also his mom. "Mom! Ruby Lee just told me that I had to let Mia Murphy go—" He paused, no doubt listening to her questions.

He was an idiot, but his mom was smart, and we needed to get out before she told him how to keep me there.

"Let's go, Mia!" Ruby Lee took off in a ridiculously fast walk toward the front doors, and I jogged after her, after a quick thanks to Angelina.

Ruby Lee's huge Mercedes was idling in front of the steps, fully covering the No Parking sign painted on the asphalt. Right behind her was Rogue's Lamborghini, with Hattie at the wheel. She waved at me, and I waved back. "You're amazing, Ruby Lee."

"Oh, sweetheart, tell me something I don't know. My law degree comes in so handy. I just love it." Ruby Lee beamed at me.

"I need to thank you! One of my greatest joys in life is messing with Mayor Stone, and her son is a wonderful way to do that. How is your lovely marina?"

"It's getting better." Her comment about Mayor Stone caught my attention. I knew Lucy's aunt had grown up in Bass Derby. "Did you grow up here?"

"I did! Family headstone in the cemetery and everything." She blew me a kiss. "I'd love to stay and chat, but I have things to do. Call if you have more chances for me to thwart the Stone family. As I said, one of my greatest joys! Smooches!" And with that, she sprung her tiny little body into the massive car, tooted the horn, and shifted into drive.

"Wait!" I jumped in front of the car, and she shrieked and hit the brakes a split second after the car lurched forward and hit me just above the knee.

She flung the door open and leapt out. "What the bloody blazes was that? I almost pancaked you!"

"I'm resilient. Did you know Dee back then? Do you know why she left town?" She looked about the same age as Dee was, so I decided to ask.

Ruby Lee stared at me. "Dee who?"

She was lying. I could hear it in the pitch of her voice, which was the same tone she'd had when she'd told me the marina was in good shape, convincing me to buy it sight unseen. "Liar," I said softly. "What do you know?"

"Nothing." Her smile was gone. "Get out of my way, Mia."

"I need to know, Ruby Lee."

"Bye!" She jumped into her car, and I looked back at Hattie, who immediately hit the gas and moved her ride forward so it was pressing against Ruby Lee's bumper, blocking her in. Ruby Lee couldn't back up to get around me, and if she drove straight, she would kill me.

I was about seventy percent sure that Ruby Lee would choose not to kill me, mostly because we were in front of the police station and there were probably cameras recording everything we were doing.

I'd grown up around criminals and con artists, and Ruby Lee was definitely playing in that sandbox. To what extent, I didn't know yet, but that bonded us.

Plus, I liked her, and I usually didn't like people who were going to kill me. I had a good sense about people.

She stared at me through the windshield.

I smiled at her.

Finally, she rolled down her window. "Get in. Let's go for a ride."

Did I want to go for a ride with her? Probably not. But there was a murderer running around Bass Derby that raised my risk tolerance.

I also was cut from the same cloth as Ruby Lee, so I didn't trust her for a moment. "I'd love to." I waved to Hattie, beckoning her to join me.

Ruby Lee shook her head. "No. Now. We gotta go."

There was nowhere she could go until I moved.

Hattie trotted up beside me. "What's up?"

"Can you stand here until I'm in Ruby Lee's car?"

"You bet." Hattie leaned her knees against Ruby Lee's front bumper and braced both hands on the hood and stared at Ruby Lee's mutinous, glittery face. "If you run me over, I will hunt you down and destroy your life forever."

Ruby Lee blinked.

I patted Hattie's shoulder. "Perfect. Will you follow us?"

"You bet. Go get 'em."

I loved how Hattie didn't ask what I was doing. She simply trusted me, the way my mom and I had trusted each other when we'd been doing scams. Not that I was scamming anyone, but Hattie's faith in me felt great, especially after Devlin and Griselda had left me in jail. "Thanks."

I abandoned the front of Ruby Lee's car and hurried around to the passenger door. I tried to open it, but it was still locked. I knocked on the window, but Ruby Lee continued to stare down Hattie for a long minute, until she finally sighed and unlocked the door.

I immediately got in, and pulled the door shut. Hattie patted the hood, gave Ruby Lee a nod, then stepped to the side.

Ruby Lee hit the gas so quickly that I thought for a second that we'd run over Hattie's foot, but when I looked behind, Hattie was sprinting to the Lamborghini.

"I respect that old lady," Ruby Lee said as we tore down main street, which was thankfully quiet since it was after midnight. "I do her a favor and then she threatens to destroy my life. How do you not respect that? She's going back on my Christmas card list."

"Thanks for getting me out."

"My pleasure, like I said." Ruby Lee glanced at me. "You are unexpected," she said. "I thought you were a pushover when you didn't argue about the marina. I didn't see that 'jump in front of my car' move coming."

I grinned. "I wanted the marina, and I respected what a good job you did conning me into it."

Ruby Lee beamed at me. "I did do a good job, didn't I? I love being great at everything I do. That marina was junk, and you totally overpaid for it." She peeled around a corner, and I stole a quick glance behind me to see if Hattie was there, but she wasn't in sight yet.

I knew I had only moments before Ruby Lee dumped me on the side of the road. "Tell me why Dee left?"

"Dee left because she witnessed a murder."

I blinked. "What?"

"She was my best friend," Ruby Lee said. "One night, back then, she came over and said she got the code to the safe at Tony's Maine Gems, and she wanted to break in. I don't do things like that, so I said no."

"Of course you said no."

Ruby Lee slanted a look at me. "I would never break into

someone's house or business and steal something. That would be an embarrassment to my intelligence and charm."

Criminal pride. I got that. "So, what happened?"

"She said she was going anyway. So, she did. Around two in the morning, she comes racing over to my house, freaking out. She said she got the diamonds, but Tony, the owner, showed up, probably because she set off an alarm. She hid, but then someone else came. There was an altercation, and then Tony was shot."

I blinked. "Really?"

"Yep. She freaked out, stashed the diamonds, and then ran to my house."

Holy crap. "Who killed Tony?"

Ruby Lee shrugged. "Didn't ask. That's not the kind of info you want to have, right? That's a loaded gun right there. I told her to lay low, since no one knew she'd been there. She did, but then a couple days later, she came by. Said that the killer paid her a visit and told her she had twenty-four hours to hand over the diamonds or he was coming after her."

"Holy crap." I leaned back in my seat. Whoa. "He saw her there, then."

"He did. Of course, we all know that he'd kill her the minute he got the diamonds, right? If he killed once, he'd sure as heck kill to shut her up."

I had personal experience with that one. "The diamonds were the only thing keeping her alive."

"Damn straight. She didn't want to get murdered, so I helped her steal a car, and then she took off in the middle of the night and stayed away ever since."

"And the diamonds?"

Ruby Lee didn't answer.

"And the diamonds?"

She finally sighed. "I don't know where they are. They were never recovered. She said she'd hidden them well, and she was going to get them when it was safe. But she never came back."

"Until now."

Ruby Lee looked over at me. "Until now."

That could explain why Rogue's house had been tossed. Someone looking for diamonds. "What happened to make her come back?"

Ruby Lee shook her head. "I lost contact with her, and she didn't tell me she was in town. I didn't know she had returned until I heard she'd entered the baking contest. Didn't know she was dead until Hattie told me."

Ruby Lee was lying. Holy cow. Which part was she lying about? Had *she* killed Dee? I hoped not. Mostly because I was alone in a car with her with Hattie nowhere in sight. There were only trees around us, no houses, no buildings, no people. An easy kill and dump situation.

But I also hoped she hadn't killed Dee because Ruby Lee reminded me of my mom, and I liked her.

I decided to call her bluff, the one I wanted her to be bluffing. "You knew Dee was back," I said. "Why did she come back?"

Ruby Lee pulled over to the side of the road, but didn't put the car in park. She turned to face me. "Look, Mia. Dee was once my best friend. Someone killed her. That's wrong, and it needs to be avenged. If I find out who did it, I'll kill him. But then I'll be in jail, and that sucks. So, if you find them first, then maybe I don't get the chance to kill him."

I stared at her. "Have you ever killed anyone before?" Suddenly, the glittery eyeshadow and abundance of hairspray seemed more nefarious than it had moments ago.

"Hattie told me that the cops don't believe Dee was killed. So, no one is looking for her killer, except me. And you, right?"

She hadn't answered my question, which answered my question. *Holy cow.* Who had she killed? Had she been in the military? Or was she a vigilante? Or just a sociopath?

"Find out who killed Dee," she said. "If I find them first, and then have to kill them and I go to jail, I will be pissed at you."

Based on the recent information I'd just acquired about Ruby

Lee, I was pretty sure I didn't want this tiny little firecracker pissed at me. "I'll find him."

"Or her. Women can be murderers, too. Or it could be a them. It's important to be inclusive, even when it comes to murderers."

"I know." Yes, yes, I did know that men weren't the only killers around, as evidenced by my whole ex-mother-in-law's attempt to assassinate me. "What about the diamonds?"

"At the core of this all, I would imagine. Now get out. I have a real estate showing on the north end of the lake."

I didn't move. "Do you know where the diamonds are?"

She raised her brows. "I do not."

But she wanted them. She'd looked for them and hadn't found them. I could hear it in her tone. "If you find out anything, let me know."

She shook her head. "I *want* to find them. Which means I probably won't help you. So, you're on your own."

I stared at her. "Are you a sociopath?"

She blinked, and then started laughing. "I just grew up with different rules than most people, Mia. Different laws. My best friend was threatened, driven out of the town she called home, and then murdered when she came back. Doesn't that require action?"

"Yes, but not revenge killing."

"Which I understand, but when a woman has skills, it can be very tempting to use them to make things right."

I blinked. That was literally what I'd done with my pickpocketing and con artist skills over the last few weeks. "What skills?"

"Nifty ones. And that's why I told you what I know," Ruby Lee said. "Now get out and beat me to the punch before I decide I don't actually want your help."

Well, when she put it that way.... I opened the door and climbed out. "We'll find them, Ruby Lee. I promise. Dee will be avenged."

"Or her." She peered at me from a sea of purple glitter. "I didn't have a lot of friends, Mia. She mattered to me."

I heard the emotion in her voice, and suddenly understood that beneath all the bravado, Ruby Lee was the same as everyone else. Vulnerable. Staggered by the loss of her best friend.

I got that. "Ruby Lee—"

"If you see Rogue, tell her I say hi." She leaned across the car, yanked the door shut, hit the gas, and took off, the tires spraying me with dirt as she sped out of sight.

I clasped my hands on my head and took a breath while I waited for Hattie to find me.

Diamonds and murder made so much more sense than killing over a strawberry shortcake victory.

But Dee had entered the contest when she'd snuck back into town. Because she wanted to win, or because the two were somehow connected?

I didn't know, but if didn't figure it out, Ruby Lee would be going to prison, because I had no doubt she was going to figure it out, and fast.

Or, more likely, she was going to *think* she figured it out, and then an innocent person might die.

If you see Rogue, tell her I say hi.

Holy cow. That had been a message to me. She thought Rogue had killed Dee, and she was going to kill her.

We had to find Rogue first.

And fast.

CHAPTER 6

WE SEARCHED for her as soon as the festival was over.

Rogue wasn't at Hattie's house.

Rogue wasn't at Lucy's house.

Rogue wasn't at my house.

She wasn't at her own house, which we checked again now that the cops were gone.

She wasn't in the kitchen of Hattie's Café whipping up her batch of biscuits for Saturday's shortcake competition.

Not a single Seam Ripper knew where she was.

Beau hadn't seen her, alive or dead, which annoyed him.

We tried every single contact we could think of, and no one had seen her.

Rogue was gone.

Which meant our mood wasn't quite as chipper as Hattie, Lucy, and I gathered in my newly furnished and fumigated apartment at three in the morning.

Hattie sank down on my new couch, looking worried. "Son of a biscuit," she said. "I don't like this."

"Rogue is tough and smart," I said. "I'm sure she's fine, wherever she is."

"She's definitely fine. For now. But a murderer was in her kitchen, and Ruby Lee is hunting her."

"Ruby Lee is four feet eleven and weighs as much as a fork," Lucy said. "Rogue can take her."

"Maybe. But who killed Dee? How good is he at killing people? Maybe he's really good at it. Maybe he really enjoys it. Maybe Rogue's name is next on his list. Maybe he already got to her—"

"No." I interrupted her. "That was Rogue's writing on that note, right?"

Hattie looked at me. "Yeah, I guess. I mean, I think so. I didn't look that closely. I assumed."

"It was her writing," I said firmly. Doubt and fear weren't going to get us anywhere. My mom had drilled that into me growing up. It was important to be aware and strategic, but fear was debilitating. "Your job is to keep Rogue in the contest. She'll be back for the finals."

Hattie stood up and paced to the window, looking out. "I'll have to make her biscuits. She gave me her recipe. It's not perfect, but it's not ethical to make changes to it. I'm not entering the contest. I can't give it my all for her if I'm running against her. I'll have to beat that vegan woman with Rogue's recipe. Won't be easy."

Hattie was restless and on edge, and it was getting to me. She was usually unflappable. "Hattie."

She didn't look at me. "What?"

"We'll find Rogue. We'll find who she's hiding from so she can come out in time for the final. Your job is to make everything ready for the finals. Only you can do that." Giving her a job would help. It always helped.

She considered that. "That's true. The two of you can't make those biscuits."

"Not the way you can," Lucy said. "You're gifted."

"Again, true," Hattie said. "I am gifted." Her voice was stronger now, and she turned back to face us. "Let's get this figured out.

Rogue needs to win, not some butter hater or anyone else. She needs to be there on Sunday."

"Right." Relief rushed through me. Hattie was back. "So, where do we start?"

"Diamonds," Lucy said as she pulled my blender out from under the counter. "People will kill for diamonds. Hattie, do you recall anything about that jewelry store murder back then?"

Hattie paced away from the window. "They never solved it. Never found the diamonds."

I handed Lucy the bottle of margarita mix. "So, I'm guessing the murderer's been around all this time, waiting for Dee to show up. Maybe she hid them at Rogue's, and he caught her retrieving them, killed her, and then took the diamonds and hid the body."

"If no one has actually seen Dee in town," Lucy said, "then maybe he thought the cops wouldn't look for her. No one would know she was missing if he took the body. No one would try to solve a murder that they don't know happened. Rogue just got lucky, or unlucky, that she saw Dee."

Thinking of Devlin and Chief Stone, I looked at Hattie and Lucy. "Do you think it's possible that Dee wasn't really dead? That she was faking it, or that it was a prank?"

Hattie frowned. "No. I don't. I'm sure. She had that dead person vibe."

"I agree," Lucy said. "But Mia, you were closest. What do you think?"

"I think she was dead." I looked around. "That's all three of us. We're not coroners, but we can't all be wrong. So, we're in agreement that we have a murder."

They both nodded.

"So, we have a murderer on the loose."

"Wow." Hattie grinned. "It's been so long since we've been able to say that. It's good to be back."

"It's literally been less than two weeks," Lucy said. "And murderers aren't fun."

"Au contraire, my darling," Hattie said cheerfully. "It's all in your attitude. Life's an adventure. Embrace it or live like you're already dead." She rubbed her hands. "This is fun. We need drinks. Fireworks, maybe? The girls are back in business."

Lucy and I looked at each other, then we both grinned. "Hattie has officially lost her mind," I said.

"That happened years ago," Lucy said cheerfully as I handed her a bottle of tequila from Birch's Best, a local brewery and distillery.

She poured it with liberal abandon.

"Amen, sistah. Crazy sets you free. Your cat is on the roof, by the way." Hattie paced back into the room. "Okay, so what's the plan, kids?"

"Is he?" I hurried over to the window and peered out, relief rushing through me when I saw my big, black Maine Coon cat basking in the moonlight. When King Tut hadn't greeted us upon arrival, I'd been a little nervous, given all the murder chat that had been happening. "Hey, sweetie."

He flicked his tail once, which I knew was his way of acknowledging his deep and forever love for me.

"I'd prefer not to die tonight, so keep him outside, please," Lucy said as she dumped ice into my blender. "Well, we know for sure that the owner of Tony's Maine Gems was murdered twenty years ago. We know diamonds went missing at the time. Neither crime has been solved."

"Diamonds are in play," I said. My mom would love to be a part of this one. She loved diamonds. "Does anyone know how many?"

Hattie nodded. "I think it was a few million dollars worth."

"That's worth a murder or two," Lucy said.

"Is it, though? Who murders over diamonds?" Hattie scoffed. "I still think it's about the bake off. Food matters. Food is life or death. Diamonds are bling."

I decided not to open up a debate on that topic, and instead, tried to keep the discussion moving forward. "Well, we know that

Dee was present at the murder," I said. "So, that links her to the diamonds."

"Do we really know that? Ruby Lee isn't exactly a beacon of truth," Hattie said. "She might have made up that whole story just to distract us while she goes off and murders all the other four-time winners."

"Why would she do that?" I asked. "She isn't even in the contest."

"Yes she is. She's one of the four-time winners."

"Seriously?" Lucy threw up her hands. "You didn't tell us that! Of course she might have made up that whole story!"

Hattie shrugged. "She won hers during the boycott years. I didn't take her seriously as a competitor. No one would. She's not that good. Which would explain why she felt she had to murder everyone else in the contest in order to win. I hope she starts with that vegan woman. I think we should avoid intervening until Ruby Lee has taken her out."

"Hattie!" Lucy chastised. "Vegan baking is totally valid. And it can be delicious."

"Oh, I know it can be delicious, but morally, it's an affront to desserts everywhere."

"Boycott years?" I interrupted. "What are those?"

"Don't ask," Lucy said. "It's not worth it. So, we have Zoltan, Dee, Hattie, Ruby Lee, and Diesel as the four-time winners. Anyone else?"

"Not Diesel. His uncle, Stevie Coolidge," Hattie said. "He helps out at the Ugly Man tavern sometimes."

Stevie. I didn't know anything about him. "Anyone else?"

Hattie shook her head. "That's it. We should call them. Ruby Lee might be after one of them as we speak."

There were too many possibilities. Too many unknowns. "If we warn them all, we might be warning the murderer. Then the murderer will know we're onto him, and he'd need to shut us up."

"Ouch," Lucy said. "Good point. But if they're innocent and we don't warn them, and then they get murdered, the guilt will haunt us forever."

"Speak for yourself," Hattie said. "Everyone is responsible for their own well-being. Our job is to find the murderer and keep other folks from being murdered."

I raised my brows. "You literally just said that other people being murdered isn't our problem."

Hattie sighed. "We have to let people fend for themselves so we can save them. Obviously."

"Obviously. That's the soundest logic I've ever heard."

Hattie rolled her eyes at me as Lucy hit the crush button on the blender.

I grabbed a notepad and jotted down the names of the four-time finalists. "We should assign a watcher to each of them to see if they have Dee's body around or someone tries to kill them," I shouted over the roar of the blender.

"I'm out," Hattie said. "I need to bake and run my booth."

Lucy shook her head. "I have to deliver mail for part of the day tomorrow," she said. "Plus, I want to take action, not sit around."

I agreed with Lucy.

Thinking, I chewed the end of my pencil. The Seam Rippers would probably do it, but I didn't want to endanger them. "What about Vinnie's friends? Would they do it for money?"

"No, they only like to steal things," Hattie shouted over the roar. "Vinnie is the only one who is on board with legal acquisition of money. We can try the Seam Rippers."

"I don't want them killed!"

"I'll tell them to stay low profile. They'll love it!" She pulled out her phone and started texting.

I bounced my knee as I waited for the blender to finish. When Lucy finally turned it off, I spoke up. "I'm not convinced it's about the festival," I said. "I want to follow up on the diamond theft and murder."

Lucy nodded. "I agree. I think we need to check Ruby Lee's house and see if she has the diamonds or Dee's body."

I grimaced. "I think she was telling the truth. I don't think she's the murderer."

"Well, we need to prove that, then," Lucy said.

"Ruby Lee will be at the festival during the Biscuit Bake-Off," Hattie said. "You could search her house then."

"I'll get my route done early so I'm ready by then," Lucy agreed.

"We also need to search all the homes of the other four-time champions," Hattie said, pacing the room with increased vigor. "And the Ugly Man. The bar will be empty right now. It's a good time to go."

Going to the county's seediest bastion of unrefined testosterone in the middle of the night sounded like exactly how I wanted to spend my evening. "Awesome. I'm in." I paused. "I do think we need to keep the diamond possibility open, though."

Hattie sighed. "God, Fine. You're so anti-food, but whatever."

Lucy nodded. "We need to find out who was involved back then, and if Dee was a part of it. Confirm Ruby Lee's story."

"Hattie, do you recall who the sheriff was at the time? Anyone who was around then who we could talk to?" It would probably be efficient to break into the police station and search their files, but the wound of incarceration was still too raw.

She frowned, and I saw her sifting through her memories, then she hit her thigh. "Son of a biscuit. I do know. The sheriff at the time was a very attractive man that all the women in town had a crush on. I keep track of handsome men."

"As you should," Lucy said. "Who was it?"

Hattie grinned at us. "Justin Dutch."

"A Dutch?" Lucy and I looked at each other. "The Dutch family again?"

"Yep. He's probably Dee's uncle or something. He was sheriff at the time, but retired a few years later. He lives in a cabin on the north side of the lake, along the marshes. I hear he's a pure crazy loon nowadays. One of his nephews passed away a few weeks ago, and that can't have helped the situation. Ronald Dutch's twin, actually."

I raised my brows. "Really?"

"Yep."

"And he's still running the contest? He's not mourning? I thought twins were really close."

Hattie shrugged. "It was one of those awkward social moments. Richie wasn't a great guy. Not one of the Dutch family's proudest products. But Justin is a bit of a family patriarch, so it might have made him more crazy than usual."

Sounded like fun. I looked at Lucy. "Want to go visit a crazy recluse whose relative might just have been murdered?"

She grinned. "I can't think of anything I'd rather do." She handed Hattie a margarita. "Tonight, we brave insanity for the truth at the Ugly Man. Tomorrow, we risk our lives for justice with a crazed, in-mourning patriarch."

Hattie raised her glass. "No better way to live."

"No better way," we both agreed.

As long as we didn't die, of course.

CHAPTER 7

THE THREE OF us approached the Ugly Man by the dark of the lake, using Hattie's insanely over-amped ski boat. Her small boat was pink and glossy, but her ski boat? It was a whole other level. I was pretty sure there wasn't a boat on the lake that could outrun her sleek, gold beauty.

The boat breezed through the winding channel that connected Diamond Lake to Little Diamond Lake, which was where the Ugly Man was located. The water was very still, and the moonlight was bright, making it look like we were cutting through a mirror of polished glass.

Last time we'd been out on a lake at night, it had been a storm-filled adventure.

This time, the total silence of the night made our engine sound very loud, the lights on our boat very bright.

"If anyone's there, we're not going to be able to sneak in," I said. I'd brought King Tut with us, just in case the murderer decided it would be a good plan to kidnap my baby for ransom.

King Tut was wearing his orange life vest and a new heavy-duty leash for aggressive chewers. He was perched on the bow, his face lifted to the wind, his tail flicking with joy.

Okay, so I'd also brought him because his pure joy whenever

he got to be around the lake was infectious. I felt he might help the vibe of the evening.

"I'll cut the engine early and we'll pull it in," Hattie said. "Shoes off, ladies."

Lucy and I looked at each other, then we pulled off our shoes and rolled up our pants. Hattie pulled in close to shore, and then cut the engine.

Lucy and I vaulted over the edge of the boat. Lucy landed easily in waist-deep water, but my foot hit a rock, and I lost my balance and sprawled into the lake.

Lucy snickered as she grabbed my arm and pulled me up. "At least you're not attached to a body this time," she whispered.

"*Yet,*" Hattie corrected. "Never lose hope. It could still happen. The night is young."

"Ssh!" I waved at them to be quiet, then grabbed one of the bow ropes and began to pull Hattie's boat through the water. I was completely soaked, but the water was starting to warm up for the season, so it wasn't too bad.

Lucy grabbed the other rope and leaned into it. The ski boat began to glide across the water, moving silently while Hattie directed us.

My feet squished in the slimy lake bottom, sinking all the way to my ankles. The grasses felt like they were wrapping around my calves, sliding their fingers across my skin.

Lucy grinned at me and gave me a thumbs up. "So fun, right?" she whispered. "I love the water!"

Her excitement was contagious, and I gave her a thumbs up back.

Hattie leaned over the bow of the boat, squeezing beside King Tut. "Almost there," she whispered. "We're going to swing the boat around and tie it up facing outward so we can make a run for it if we need to."

"You know we will," Lucy said. "We always do."

"Maybe we'll get lucky this time," I said as the dock came into view. It was a large dock with about twenty slips. There were no boats tied up, which gave me hope we would be alone.

We quickly tied the boat up to the last slip, which was just out of sight of the tavern.

Moments later, Lucy and I were easing through the bushes, climbing the bank. Hattie and King Tut were waiting in the boat, ready to start the engine and untie if we were in a rush to leave.

"The lights in the tavern are off," Lucy whispered.

I let out a breath. "Awesome."

Emboldened, we ran up the steps from the lake and headed toward the kitchen door. I knocked lightly, just to be sure. When no one answered, I whipped out my lock picks and went to work.

Less than fifteen seconds later, I had the door open.

Lucy and I turned on our nifty microbeam flashlights that I'd ordered after our escapades a couple weeks ago. I'd actually ordered a number of items and stashed them everywhere we might need them: my car, their cars, Hattie's boat, the marina, each of their houses etc. Just in case.

The kitchen of the Ugly Man was clean and tidy, up to even Hattie's standards.

No biscuits were being baked, but Hattie had said most of the competitors would bake their biscuits right before the contest, so they would be at their freshest for judging.

I pulled open the walk-in fridge, half expecting to see Dee tucked away in the corner, but she wasn't in there, thankfully. There were a bunch of strawberries, vats of chocolate, and containers of organic whipping cream from a local dairy. Ready for the festival.

"What are we looking for?" Lucy asked. "Stolen recipes?"

"Diamonds in the chocolate? I don't know—"

The light suddenly came on in the kitchen, and we both dove behind crates as the low murmur of men's voices echoed, laughing about something.

"The walk-in fridge is open," one of them said.

I heard someone swear, and footsteps headed our way.

I met Lucy's gaze, and her eyes widened. There wasn't enough space for either of us to get completely out of sight. If he came in there—

King Tut suddenly sprinted into the fridge, spun around in front of me, then crouched down and let out a low, terrifying growl. His life jacket was off, and his leash wasn't attached, which meant that Hattie had probably unclipped it and set him free.

"Watch out," a man shouted. "A bobcat got in!"

King Tut then let out a scream that made the hair on my arms stand up, and he launched himself at the men.

The men shrieked, and I heard footsteps running as King Tut streaked through the kitchen. My heart thundering, I leaned out far enough to make sure my baby was okay, then almost started laughing. Two men were literally running for the door, shrieking as King Tut bounded after them, still screaming.

One of the men, who I could now see was the owner, Diesel, flung the door open and then tripped as he tried to get out. He landed on his face, and King Tut ran right over him, launched off Diesel's head, then disappeared into the darkness, unharmed.

"He's out!" Diesel yelled as he scrambled to his feet. "Shut the door!"

The other man in the kitchen turned toward us, and I dove back out of sight as he raced toward the fridge and slammed the door closed. I heard the outside door shut, and then the frantic voices of the men as they raced around looking for windows that the bobcat had gotten in through.

My cat was the best.

I grinned at Lucy, then almost started laughing when I saw that she was pressed back against the wall of the freezer, her eyes closed, her hands clutched to her chest. "Is he gone?" she whispered. "Tell me he's gone."

"The men?" I could hear them still outside, but they were too loud to be able to hear our whispers.

"No. Your demon beast."

"He just saved your life. How can you be scared of him?"

She opened her eyes. "I honestly believe your cat is the devil incarnate, and it's just a matter of time until he sucks my soul out through my clawed-out eyes."

I bit back a snicker. "He's on our side, Lucy."

"Is he? That's what he'd like us to believe—"

The door opened suddenly, and we both ducked.

But all Diesel did was shut off the light and close the door again, plunging us into darkness. I let out my breath, listening as the men's voices faded. The moment I couldn't hear them, I ran to the door and pressed my ear against it.

"What are you doing?" whispered Lucy.

"I didn't see who was with Diesel. We need to find out." I pushed the door open a crack, and I heard the voices drifting from down the hall. "Come on."

"Oh for heaven's sake." But Lucy followed me as I eased out of the kitchen and into a back hallway. We reached a partially closed door, behind which I could hear men talking in low voices. The door was slightly ajar, so I poked it with my finger and eased it open an inch. It creaked, and the voices stopped.

Lucy and I froze, and I held my breath.

"You sure you closed that window?" Diesel said.

"Yeah. The bobcat can't get back in."

I had to bite my lip to keep from grinning. It was so easy to fool people when their emotions were involved. They'd gotten so scared, that they hadn't noticed that King Tut was the wrong color and had a tail the size of a feather pillow instead of the tiny bobcat tail.

Granted, King Tut was probably as dangerous as a bobcat, so there was that—

I suddenly heard the man I didn't know mention Dee, and Lucy jammed her finger into my lower back, as if I hadn't noticed.

I leaned forward so I could see through the crack. A man with gray hair was sitting at the table, sideways, so I could see his profile. He was the man who'd been at the contest table with

Diesel. Diesel's uncle Stevie? I was going to go with that assumption.

Diesel leaned back in his seat. "You think Dee came back for the diamonds?"

Stevie moved in my view, a beer in his hand. "Why else would she come back?"

"The title."

Stevie laughed. "No chance. She'd never win."

"Of course she'd win. She was the best there was back then, and she's probably gotten better. She'd come back just to win."

"She'd do a lot. That woman is trouble." Stevie pulled out a chair and straddled it. "I want those diamonds. They're mine."

Diesel scoffed. "They're not yours—"

"They were supposed to be."

Diesel leaned forward. "Let the diamonds go, Stevie. They have blood on them, wherever they are. Let them be."

Stevie stood up. "Dee knows where they are."

"You don't know that. It's just rumors that she was there. It's a small town. Things get made up."

Lucy leaned in to listen, bumping me. I lost my balance and fell into the door. The door swung open, and I fell forward, landing on my hands and knees, caught in a stare-down with Stevie.

CHAPTER 8

Stevie shot to his feet, and before I had time to move, he aimed a shotgun at me. Where had he been hiding that thing? "Who the heck are you?" he barked.

Oh...crud.

Stevie might be about sixty, with salt and pepper hair, but he had huge shoulders, and a vibe that said he ran from nothing. Except my cat, so I tried to keep that in mind. "Hi." I waved at him, wondering if Lucy had scrambled out of sight in time.

He raised the gun higher. "You trying to steal my recipe?" He was pure backwoods male. Unapologetic. Unstoppable. "Who paid you?"

Seriously with the baking question? Maybe I needed to rethink my cavalier attitude about the high stakes of baking! Diesel was looking at me curiously, not nearly as alarmed by my presence. Because what could I do against these two? Besides sic my cat on them, which should not be underestimated.

I held up my hands. "I'm not here to steal your recipe." Why was I there? I needed to come up with an idea and fast.

He didn't lower the gun, and Diesel leaned back in his seat and took a sip of beer, apparently enjoying the show.

I cleared my throat, and realized I was still wearing my volunteer badge from the festival. I held it up. "I was sent by Ronald Dutch, the head judge. There are rumors circulating that some folks are cheating, so he sent a volunteer to each Open Division contestant to make sure they were baking their own biscuits with their own recipe." Oh...I liked that.

"At three in the morning?"

"Everyone knows bakers bake in the early morning," I said. I folded my arms and leaned against the door, trying to appear bored, sullen, and immoveable. "I'm to wait here and watch you bake. Maybe you can get started so I can go home?"

Diesel still hadn't said anything, but Stevie looked very annoyed. "I'm not baking until noon. The contest isn't until three."

"Noon?" I threw up my hands. "I'm not waiting around here for nine hours. I'm going home. If he asks, tell him I watched you the whole time. Cool?"

"Yeah, fine." He was still frowning.

I turned to leave, then paused, and glanced at Diesel. "So, not to be nosy, but when I was inspecting your kitchen, I heard you talking about Dee Dutch. Have you seen her? She missed her table today. No one knows where she is, or where she is staying."

The two men looked at each other, and a look passed between them. But then they both shrugged. "Not our problem," Stevie said.

"What about the diamonds? I heard you talking about diamonds. Are you guys talking about the ones stolen from Tony's jewelry store twenty years ago? I want in. How can I get in?"

Diesel sat up quickly then and turned to look at me closely, then he swore. "I knew I recognized you. You're that woman who was here making trouble a few weeks ago. Mia Murphy, right? Owner of the Eagle's Nest?" His gaze narrowed. "Ex-wife of a drug dealer."

"Yes, that is true," I said. "All of it. But seriously. What about the diamonds?" I was taking a chance if they were murderers, but Lucy, Hattie, and King Tut were around here somewhere, and I had a feeling they were ready to jump in to save my life if things got nutty all of a sudden.

"Don't know anything about diamonds," Stevie said.

Diesel agreed. "We didn't say anything about diamonds. You must have misheard."

"Did I? I don't think so." I paused. "Just so you know, I'm very good at picking locks and getting into places that you can't get into. So, if you need help and want to share the wealth, I'm your girl." It was amazing how easy it was to slip back into the old Mia, the one who lived by crime and sticky fingers. I didn't want to do that. But we were talking murder here. If there was a way to find out info without putting myself in danger, I had to do it.

They both stared at me and said nothing.

"By the way, it was me who let the bobcat in. Didn't mean to, but I did leave the door open after I picked your lock and let myself in. Because locked doors don't stop me. You know where to reach me. So, tata!" I waggled my fingers at them, then spun around and strode down the hall.

Lucy grabbed my arm as I walked into the kitchen. "You have to see this." She tugged me to the back of the kitchen, through the door and into a storage room. There was a big freezer humming, big enough to fit several moose.

"Look." She pointed at the edge of the cooler. Poking out from under it was a sparkly red high-heeled sandal, exactly like the ones that had been on Dee's feet.

"You've got to be kidding!" I dropped to the ground and shined my light under the cooler. My light reflected off a second matching shoe. "It's down here!" I slid the light under the cooler, trying to hook it on the strap. "What if Dee's not dead, and she came back here and ditched the shoes?"

"Or what if she's in the freezer right now?"

I went still, then looked up. Lucy's light was shining on a metal padlock glistening on the freezer. Slowly, I pulled back and stood up. "You think she's in there?" It was definitely big enough for Dee. And Rogue, too, for that matter. Oh…Rogue.

"I don't know. In the movies, she would be."

Suddenly, the gun that had been aimed at me a few minutes ago seemed much more sinister. "They were talking about Dee and diamonds," I said.

"They were," Lucy agreed.

We looked at each other, and Lucy gave me a little nudge. "Open it. Fast. Before Stevie and Diesel decide to come out here."

Oh, man. I so didn't want to find Dee tucked away in that freezer. I pulled out my phone. "I'll text Devlin—"

"And if he gets here and there's no body? You want my cousin to arrest both of us this time?"

"No." I shoved my phone in my pocket. "Keep the light on it." I pulled out my lock picks and went down on one knee. My hands were shaking a little, because that was one lock I really didn't want open.

Unfortunately, the padlock clicked open easy-peasy, and I slid it off the freezer. It slipped out of my fingers and clattered to the floor. She smacked my head, and I dropped down to grab it. I fished it quickly out from under the freezer, and as I did, something caught my eye. I reached deeper under it, and I found a large diamond and ruby hoop earring. My gut sank, and I held it up. "Doesn't Rogue have earrings like this?"

Lucy took it from me and inspected it. "I think so. There aren't too many people in town who could afford this besides Rogue."

We met gazes, and genuine fear tightened my chest. "Rogue's fine," I said. "She's probably trying to track down the murderer as well. Right?"

"Yeah. Right. Or Dee stole them, and had them with her—"

"When they put her in the freezer?" I finished.

"No one is in the freezer." Lucy put the earring in her pocket. "It's fine. It's just going to be meat. Open it, and we'll confirm it."

"Right. Okay." I flipped the latch out of the way. "All we need to do is see what's in there. If it's Dee, we just lock it back up and call Devlin. We don't confront them."

"Absolutely we don't," she agreed.

I grabbed the edge. "Ready?"

She nodded and held up her phone. "I'll take the picture."

"Okay." *Please don't let Rogue be in here.* I pulled on the lid, and it started to come open. It was dark inside, so I couldn't see in. I hauled it open the rest of the way, and we both peered in.

It was something large wrapped in a black tarp. And by "large," I meant something that could definitely be a person.

"Oh, Lordy," Lucy said. "That doesn't look good. No one puts away deer meat like that."

I poked it, but it was hard. Obviously. Because it was frozen. "Do you have a knife? We need to cut it open and see what it is?"

"Do we?"

"We can't call Devlin until we know." I looked around, but I didn't see anything sharp enough to cut the tarp. "I'll grab scissors from the kitchen." I raced to the door, flung it open—

And met the startled gaze of Stevie, who was holding a bag of flour. For a split second, we stared at each other in surprise, and all I could think about was that he might be sociopathic enough to be baking while a body sat in his freezer. *Holy moly.*

Then his gaze shot past me to the storage room, and I quickly realized he could see the freezer from where he stood.

"Mia's in the backroom!" he finally shouted. "She's still here! She has the freezer open!"

Uh oh.

"Get her!" Diesel shouted, and the door to the kitchen flew open.

"Run!" I wheeled around, and Lucy and I bolted for the back door. We burst out the door and raced down the steps, our feet flying as we sprinted for the dock. "Go, Hattie, go!" I shouted.

The engine immediately burst into life, and as Lucy and I thundered onto the dock, Hattie was already flipping off the dock lines while King Tut stood on the bow. We jumped into the boat and Hattie hit the gas as Stevie lunged for us.

I was pretty sure I felt someone's fingers brush over the back of my shirt before we were in the boat. Within a split second, we were away from the dock and speeding down the lake toward the canal.

I sank down in the seat as Hattie raced away.

Hattie looked over her shoulder. "Is that a gun in Stevie's hands?"

I twisted around and grimaced. "Yeah."

"He's not good with those. You're lucky you didn't get shot. What did you gals find?"

I looked over at Lucy. "Did you see what was in the freezer?"

She shook her head, "I couldn't get the plastic off."

I shook my head and groaned. "The freezer is open. They'll think we know what's in there."

"They'll move her, if it's Dee," Lucy said. "We can't call Devlin. There won't be anything for him to find."

"Wait. What? Dee was in the freezer?" Hattie looked startled.

"I don't know. Something large was in there wrapped in plastic. Her shoes were underneath it, though. And we found an earring that we think is Rogue's."

"What? Let me see."

Lucy handed her the earring, and Hattie shifted down. The boat eased down to a slow, quiet chug as she peered at it. I shined my flashlight on it, and leaned over her shoulder. It sparkled in the light of the beam, bright and beautiful and very expensive. "You think it's Rogue's?" I asked.

"I don't pay much attention to earrings, but it's pricey enough to be something she'd wear."

"I notice jewelry, and I'm pretty sure it's hers." I leaned my head back as King Tut hopped onto my lap and began to knead my thighs. *Good kitty.* "I'm guessing Dee stole the earrings from Rogue, or that Rogue was there at some point trying to find the murderer, just like we were."

Hattie rubbed her jaw. "If Rogue was there, she definitely left us the earring as a message. She's trying to tell us something." She tossed the earring carelessly in her hand, and I snatched it from her.

"Rogue will want that back," I said. Assuming she wasn't dead. Which I was going to assume. "I can't believe we didn't see what was in that freezer."

"You told them who you are," Lucy said. "They know where to find you."

Hattie looked over at me. "If Dee is in that freezer, and they think you saw her, they're going to come after you."

I swallowed. "I know." None of us acknowledged the possibility that Rogue was in that freezer, as well. "Would they recognize your boat?"

Hattie shook her head. "This is a new boat. I got it over the winter. They won't know it's me, so you can stay at my place for now."

"I have a marina to run. I can't hide."

"If Dee's in there, they're murderers," Lucy said. "You need to hide."

"I don't like hiding." I scratched King Tut's head to let him know how much I appreciated him and Hattie teaming up to save us, trying to think of next steps. "We need to know what was in there."

They both nodded. "We can't go back," Lucy said. "And if it's Dee, they'll move her quickly."

"There's one way to get it checked." I ground my jaw. "Did you get a picture of the tarp with the body?"

"We don't know it's a body, but yes."

"Text it to me." I leaned forward. "Diesel and Stevie talked about Dee and the diamonds, but Diesel said it was never confirmed that Dee was a part of it. Stevie said they were supposed to be his diamonds. We need to find out what happened back then."

My phone dinged and I looked down to see that Lucy had texted me the picture. I opened it and saw the sinister-looking bundle in the freezer. "That's so creepy."

Hattie slowed the boat and leaned over my shoulder. She swore. "That's definitely big enough to be a person. And those are the same shoes that Dee was wearing at Rogue's." She cursed. "I didn't want her to be dead," she said. "I wanted us to be wrong."

"I know," I agreed. "Me, too. Any objections to me sending it to Devlin? I want him to go check it out before they move the body."

"Do it," Hattie said as she put the boat into gear again. "We need to know."

"Agreed," Lucy said.

I nodded, and then clicked to forward him the photo.

Before I could type an explanation, my phone rang. Devlin. Did the man never sleep? It was three in the morning. Grimacing, I answered it. "Hi—"

"That looks like a body wrapped in tarp in a freezer. Tell me that's not what it is."

"I don't know what's in there," I said. "But we were just at the Ugly Man tavern, and found Dee's shoes on the ground by the freezer, along with an earring that might be Rogue's. We got the freezer open, but didn't have time to unroll the tarp because…we had to leave."

Devlin unleashed a string of profanities. "What were you doing in the Ugly Man at three in the morning?"

"I was assigned by Ronald Dutch to watch Stevie bake to ensure there was no cheating."

There was silence.

"Devlin?"

"Sorry. I was just marveling at how low your estimation of my intelligence is."

"Will you go check it out? Diesel and Stevie saw me there, and if it's a body, they'll move it quickly."

"Mia—"

"Dee's shoes were there," I interrupted. "You can see them in the picture."

He swore. "Fine. I'll go but—"

"Thank you," I interrupted.

"I'll be in touch." He hung up without a good-bye, and I shoved my phone in my pocket. "He's on his way."

"It'll be too late," Hattie said. "If that's Dee, she's already been moved. The freezer will be empty."

"It'll be empty even if it's not Dee," Lucy said. "Stevie shouted at Diesel that we'd seen what's in the freezer. Whatever it is, they didn't want anyone to see it, so Devlin won't find it."

"He's a good cop. Maybe he'll find something else. Like the shoes or something more." I knew he was grumpy about the call, but seeing Dee's shoes in the picture elevated the situation.

"Or maybe it'll all be cleaned out, he'll find nothing, and the possible murderers now know to look for us," Lucy said.

Hattie glanced at us, then shook her head. "We can do better than this, ladies."

I leaned back, rubbing my cat's head as Hattie slowed the boat to cruise the channel. "We're going to have to do better than this," I said. "Or we're going to wind up dead."

CHAPTER 9

An hour later, I had just flung myself into my bed to try to catch a few minutes of desperately needed sleep before we headed out to Justin's when I heard a knock on my door.

Holy crap.

I bolted up, grabbed my hairdryer from my nightstand, and vaulted next to the door. Would a murderer knock? Maybe? Suddenly, I remembered that I didn't have a bodyguard anymore.

King Tut didn't move from his nest in the middle of my bed.

"I'll get the door, Big Mike," I shouted. "You keep practicing your karate!" I wrapped the cord around my wrist and swung the hairdryer, perfecting the balance. Ready to defend.

"For hell's sake, Mia. I know there's no one named Big Mike there."

Devlin. Ah...no wonder King Tut hadn't gotten up. He had a crush on Devlin.

I unlocked the door and opened it. Devlin was on the landing, looking tired, cranky, and ridiculously handsome in jeans, sneakers, and a black sweatshirt. His gaze went to my hairdryer, which he knew from personal experience, that I was very handy with. "No. Do not use that on me."

I almost laughed at his crankiness. "At least it's not a nail gun."

That's what I'd actually hit him with a few weeks ago, not realizing who he was before swinging. I'd knocked him clean off my porch and into the parking lot.

As I said, I was a whiz with corded implements. I wish I'd had one at the Ugly Man—

Oh...that was why Devlin was here. Bad news he didn't want to deliver by text? My heart started pounding. "Did you find Dee? Oh, God. You found her, didn't you? That's why you didn't call me."

"I didn't find Dee."

My stomach dropped. "Rogue, then? Not, Rogue. Tell me Rogue wasn't in that freezer."

"Not Rogue." He didn't ask permission. He simply walked in. "Mia. The freezer was empty, except for a few packages of ground beef in store-bought packaging. Buns. Steaks. Exactly what should have been in there."

I blinked. "No tarp?" They'd sure removed that that quickly.

"No tarp. No red shoes. No earring. I searched the whole building and found absolutely nothing. Stevie wasn't there, but Diesel was. He was happy to let me look anywhere I wanted. He clearly had nothing to hide."

I sighed with resignation. "We thought they'd be fast, but I'd been hoping you would get there in time."

He sank down on my couch and leaned forward, bracing his forearms on his thighs. "Mia—"

"No lecture. I'm not staying out of it."

He looked over at me. "No lecture," he said quietly. "I can't doubt you on this one. I saw the photo with the tarp and the shoes. Clearly, whatever was in that tarp wasn't something they wanted anyone to find. It might have been bear meat from hunting without a permit. The shoes make me think it might have been something else. Tell me why you went there."

I stared at him in surprise. "You want my input?"

"Yeah. Griselda told me that you have a good mind, and I'm tired of fighting it. So talk to me."

Wow. This was amazing. "You literally left me in jail today."

"How could I deprive Chief Stone of so much joy? That would be cruel. I'm not cruel."

I raised my brows. "I feel like your priorities might be a bit misaligned. You know, choosing his joy over my freedom."

He shrugged. "You were safe in there, and not poking at any murderers, so I thought it was fine for the moment."

"Murderers?" My heart leapt. "So you believe there was a body?"

"I don't know, but I saw the photo, so I'm curious. Why did you go there?"

I told him about Hattie's theory about the quest for bake-off victory, and by the time I got done, Devlin was leaning back on the couch, his palms on his forehead in the classic pose of exasperation. "No one murders over strawberry shortcake, Mia."

"Well, that's what I thought, but then I saw the freezer—"

"No." He stood up. "For hell's sake, Mia. I can't believe I went over there tonight because Hattie told you Stevie and Diesel might have murdered Dee and Rogue to win the Strawberry Shortcake Bake-Off."

"What about the freezer? And the shoes?"

"Illegal bear meat, and the shoes could have been left there from a customer. Red heels aren't exactly unique. Could have been anything. People use tarps and big freezers all the time around here."

"What about the diamonds?"

"I'll look into the records we have from that case, but as far as I know, Dee was never even interviewed for it. There's no connection with her. And what's Rogue's connection to the diamonds?"

I shook my head. "I don't know. But you could find out."

Devlin walked over to the open door. "I'm a cop. I have to follow the evidence. There is literally no evidence right now. We don't even have a body. I can't even justify spending time on it."

"I saw her—"

"I believe you saw someone on the floor, but it might not have been what you thought. She could have been faking it, hoping you'd leave and then she could bail. Right? Did you check for a pulse?"

"No, but—"

"Was there blood? Any sign of injury?"

"No, she was just lying there, but—"

"Mia." He ground his jaw. "I believe you saw something, but I can't find a single shred of anything happening—"

"What about Rogue going missing? And her house being trashed? Can't you search for her?"

"It's been less than twenty-four hours, and she's an adult with all her mental faculties. Nothing I can do right now." He bumped his fist on the doorframe. "Mia, if there's a murderer out there, I want to catch him as much as you do, but I have nothing to take action on. Without any kind of evidence, I'm extremely limited in what I can do."

I stared at him, digesting what he'd just said. "I'm not limited," I said slowly, testing his response.

"No. Don't do anything. Stay out of it." But as he said it, his gaze met mine.

I stood taller. Holy cow. He was telling me to find out what I could so that he could get involved. I could see it from the look in his eyes. "All right," I said slowly. "I'll stay home and learn to knit."

He nodded. "Perfect. Just don't stab yourself with the needles, or jump in front of anyone else's needles."

"I would never."

"All right then."

As he stood there in my doorway, my heart started pounding. Not from fear. From something else. Excitement. Anticipation. Why did it feel so freaking good to have Devlin ask me for help? To have him believe me that something was going on?

He said nothing, but his eyes were full of things he wanted to say. Finally, he cleared his throat. "You still want to get dinner sometime?"

My heart rate increased. "Before thirty seconds ago, the answer would have been no. Leaving me in jail lowered your odds significantly."

"And now?"

"Sometimes I get hungry."

"Will you be hungry Sunday night after the festival is over?"

I swallowed. "Maybe."

He let out a breath. "How about the Bass Derby Inn? Seven o'clock?"

I hadn't heard of the Bass Derby Inn. "Okay. I'll meet you there."

A grin flashed across his face. "I'll be there this time. Promise."

I shrugged. "We'll see."

"I will." He paused. "Mia. About the knitting—"

"No." I didn't give him a chance to change his mind. I didn't want a lecture from him to stop being me. "Go away. I need to sleep. You have overstayed your welcome, Officer Hunt."

He let out his breath. "I can't stop you, can I?"

"No."

"All right then." He rapped his knuckles on the doorframe. "I'll let myself out, but lock the store door behind me. You can't be leaving it unlocked like it was tonight so people can come right up the stairs to your apartment door." He gave me a nod, then jogged down the stairs.

It took me a full minute to realize what he'd said.

I'd locked the front door of the store tonight. I always locked the door. Always. Having assassins after me had upped my "remember to lock the door" game significantly.

Which meant someone else had unlocked it.

Panic gripped me. "Devlin!" I sprinted down the stairs, taking advantage of the fact that a trained gun wielder was standing on my landing, and he was willing to save my life if it came to that.

The arms expert in question was already outside, and I heard the roar of his engine starting up.

"Devlin!" I ran out the front door and onto the deck, waving my arms, but he clearly didn't look back at the building, because he pulled around and drove out of the parking lot, leaving me alone on my porch in the dark of not-quite-dawn.

I turned around and looked at my store.

My phone was upstairs, but I had my hairdryer, still.

A part of me wanted to run for my car and bail, but I was done being afraid. This was my home, and I wasn't about to turn it over to fear.

I readied my hairdryer, then walked to the front door. "King Tut," I called out. "I need your help! You might get to kill someone!"

I heard the thump of his little paws hitting the floor, the scamper of him racing down the steps, and then he strode out into my store, his tail up and regal as he regarded me with his unblinking yellow eyes.

"Is there anyone here?"

He sat down and looked at me.

I waited for a moment, giving him time to sift through the scents.

When he continued to sit there quietly instead of transforming into demon assault cat, I decided there was no one in the store except us.

I flipped on the light by the door and scanned the store. When I'd first moved in, it had been an abandoned doomsday scene of dusty, outdated, yellowing product stacked in haphazard piles. Now, it was stocked with the new lakey items, merchandised with relative brilliance. Homey. Charming. Upscale. Professional.

Nothing looked out of place.

I bit my lip, trying to think of what someone would want in my store. Theft was always a possibility, but I kept the safe upstairs in my apartment, and nothing noticeable was stolen.

I walked over to the door and checked the lock. It had been jimmied open by someone who wasn't good at it, leaving scratches. I tried to lock it again, but it was broken. "Well, it wasn't my mom, because she wouldn't have broken the door."

Not that I'd heard from my mom in a decade, but I was certain that someday I'd walk into my kitchen and she'd be at my table with spreadsheets, planning our next con as if not a day had passed since I'd walked out.

I both dreaded and looked forward to that moment.

But at the moment, it wasn't her. Someone else had paid me an uninvited visit.

I closed the door and leaned against it, my heart starting to pound.

Nothing felt off, but someone had clearly broken in.

Keeping an eye on King Tut's state of mind, I began a slow walk of the store, looking for anything out of place. It was on the second walk around that I realized that the barrel of paddles in the corner had been moved to the left.

Tension gripped me, and I walked over. I grabbed a mini flashlight to look behind it, but I didn't see anything. I grabbed it and lifted the corner, but nothing was beneath it.

I dumped the barrel over and sent the paddles cascading across the floor.

And spilling out on top of the paddles was a white scrap of paper that looked very familiar. I grabbed it and looked at it.

I didn't do it.

It was the note we'd found at Rogue's.

Why was it here? Who put it here? And why? Rogue, telling me she was alive and well? But if so, why would she hide it in a place I wasn't likely to find it? Or had it been stashed by someone trying to set me up for a murder I didn't commit? Or the murderer telling me that they could get to me, so I needed to back off?

Hopefully the last one, because that meant we'd poked at the right sleeping dragon.

But who had we poked?

CHAPTER 10

By the time Lucy arrived in the morning to head over to the cabin of Justin Dutch, the former sheriff, I'd decided that the murder had nothing to do with baking and everything to do with the diamonds.

Diesel and Stevie had been talking about Dee and the diamonds.

Ruby Lee knew about Dee and the diamonds.

Hattie knew about Dee and the diamonds.

She might not have been officially a person of interest, but rumors always had an element of truth, and enough people knew about Dee and the diamonds to make it a viable pathway.

Plus, Devlin had agreed that people didn't kill over shortcake contests. We were both outsiders to the town, and therefore able to have some perspective.

It wasn't about the baking.

It was about the diamonds.

"You know," Lucy said, as we climbed into Turbojet and headed out of my parking lot. "If you get killed, Devlin's going to be wrought with guilt over telling you to get involved."

"I'm not going to get killed," I said as I pulled out onto the main road.

Hattie had already left with her wares for the day to meet Vinnie at her booth, taking Rogue's Lamborghini. We had all agreed that Hattie driving around publicly in Rogue's car might get helpful attention, and she'd been thrilled by the idea. She was going to come to the marina around lunch to bake Rogue's biscuits, and hopefully we'd be back by then with an update.

King Tut had stayed out the rest of the night, and I'd been getting increasingly worried for his safety and well-being, so when he'd launched himself off the roof with a yowl, scaring the daylights out of Lucy before landing with bared claws on my back, I'd almost cried with relief.

And I'd promptly put on his harness and dumped him in the front seat of Turbojet.

It took me several minutes to persuade Lucy to get in the truck with him, but she'd finally agreed only when I promised to hold onto his leash the whole time.

The little beast growled at Lucy for the first ten minutes of the drive, which I honestly believed he was doing just to amuse himself. I had a feeling he'd protect Lucy as much as he'd protect me, but it was fun to mess with her.

Cats, right?

The moment we pulled off the main road and began to wind our way through an overgrown dirt path barely wide enough for my truck, he forgot to terrorize Lucy and instead perched on the dashboard, his tail flicking as he inspected the woods.

The cabin that emerged at the end of the road made me glad that a scary, oversized demon cat was with us.

"Holy cow," Lucy whispered. "Someone lives in that?"

Perched on the bank of the lake was a tilted, metal shanty with a stove pipe coming out of the roof. The windows were boarded up, and underbrush had grown up high around it, almost obscuring it.

Only the front door was free from vegetation, and a very old, rusted pickup truck sat off to the right.

The scene looked long abandoned, except that the fire pit in front of the shack was roaring. An old Adirondack chair was pulled up beside the fire, and there was a plate with a half-eaten English muffin sandwich on the arm. Steam was still rising from the coffee cup that was sitting on the other arm.

It was eerily similar to the plucked-from-life experience when we'd first gotten to Rogue's house.

"You think he's got a gun trained on us?" Lucy whispered.

"Maybe." I executed a three-point turn so the truck was facing down the driveway, just in case we needed a quick getaway. I put it in park, but I didn't turn off the engine. Instead, I rolled down the window. "Hello? Justin? We brought some food from Hattie's Café for you."

Hattie's reputation was well-known, and her food was like crack. No one would turn down a delivery of Hattie's food. If his family had been taking care of him, it wouldn't be unheard of for them to arrange for a Hattie's Café delivery.

There was no response except the breeze rustling the trees. Even the water was moving so slowly that there was no sound. Justin did not come bounding out of his cabin, dancing with glee.

I looked at Lucy, and she shrugged. We couldn't leave the food, because we needed to talk to him, not just feed him. "Let's do this." I tied King Tut's leash to the steering wheel, then reached in back and grabbed the two big bags of food. I left the hairdryer there because how would I explain carrying a hairdryer around with me?

I needed to find another corded implement that would make sense to carry. Maybe I could disguise one in a purse? I wasn't really a purse person, but I could make exceptions for my own safety and well-being.

Lucy and I go out of the truck, and my boots squished in the mud by the riverbank as I stepped down. "Hello!" I called again. "Justin!"

Again, just silence.

"I really hope he hasn't disappeared as well," Lucy muttered. "Or I'm going to think we're living in a Stephen King novel."

"Stephen King does live on a lake in Maine," I said. "Maybe he gets his ideas from Diamond Lake. Maybe he comes over here to witness the ravages of real-life horror, and then writes about it in his books that everyone thinks are fiction, but they're actually about life on Diamond Lake."

She stared at me. "Really with that? Now? You're going to start talking about horror while we're literally walking into what looks like a man was plucked out of his life?"

I grimaced. "Right. Sorry. You're the one who usually does that. My bad."

"It does show me why you don't like it when I do that," she said. "It's very creepy."

King Tut suddenly growled, making us both jump. I turned around to see what my cat was doing. He had his front feet on the window frame, and he was staring past us, into the bushes to the right of the shack. His tail was flicking, and his fur was puffed up.

"Holy cow," Lucy whispered. "Your cat is terrifying. He's fifty pounds of clawed death."

"He's not fifty pounds." But he did look alarmingly fierce. I hoped he remembered we were friends. "What's he looking at?" I turned and looked toward the bushes. "Justin?" I held up the bags. "We have food."

Again, no response.

"Go knock on the door," Lucy said.

"Right. Okay." That made sense. I took a breath and then walked across the clearing, past the half-eaten sandwich and the still-steaming coffee. I knocked lightly on the door, really hoping he wasn't a shoot-first-look-later kind of recluse. "My name's Mia Murphy," I called out. "I—"

The door opened so fast that I shrieked and jumped back. I lost my footing and started to go down. I would have fallen, but a tall, strapping woodsman leapt out, snatched my wrist, and yanked me back to my feet.

He held me there for a moment, holding me close enough that I could feel the heat of his coffee breath on my face. He stared at me, clearly assessing every feature on my face. So I stared back, because I was also excellent at assessing people, and what else is there to do when being held at wrist-point by a tall, wiry recluse in the middle of the woods?

Justin Dutch was well over six feet tall. His skin was somewhat lined, he was lean, and his clothes were dirty and aromatic, but he still stood tall and strong. His blue eyes were like glaciers, glittering as he inspected me. There was an old scar under his right eye, and he wore what looked like a diamond stud in his left ear.

He was a man who still knew how to wield power, but there was a definite sense of no-nonsense with him. He was a man who would never waste time with words that didn't matter to him. Or people, for that matter, which was probably why he was in the woods living alone. He could definitely take us, and probably King Tut, bury us in the marshes, and no one would ever know.

That was a helpful thought.

"So, you're the one," he said. His voice was rough and scratchy, as if he hadn't used it in a long time.

"The one who what?"

"Who bought Rusty's place."

I blinked. "I did buy the Eagle's Nest," I agreed. "Were you friends with Rusty?" I hoped not. I'd never met Rusty, but he'd apparently been a crook with many talents and enemies.

Justin's fingers were digging into my wrist. "You busted your husband to the feds."

Apparently, fun news like that made it all the way out to the marsh. "I did," I agreed. Justin had been a cop. Maybe he kept track of things like that.

His fingers tightened around my wrist, and I fought not to wince. "Took guts."

I met his gaze. "I was terrified every single minute, and I still get panic attacks." I didn't know why I'd blurted it out. Instinct had made me say it, and I usually had good instincts about people. About what people needed to believe about me to trust me.

His icy blue eyes met mine, then he suddenly released my wrist.

I forced myself not to stumble backwards, holding my ground, still in his space where he'd dragged me.

He raised his busy gray eyebrows. "I like you."

I let out my breath. "Thanks. I'm pretty likable."

"I bet you are." He looked past me, and I assume he was looking at Lucy and King Tut, but I didn't take my gaze off him to check. He had an edge to him that made me not quite trust him. As for the crazy thing? He seemed completely sane to me. Sane and dangerous. He looked back at me. "What do you want?"

I held up the bags. "I brought food."

"That's not what I asked."

See? Not insane. Very, very aware. "I want to know about the murder at Tony's Gems twenty years ago."

I watched him stiffen as soon as I spoke. It was slight, but I was watching for it. His gaze snapped to mine, and he said nothing.

"I know it was unsolved, but as sheriff, you must have had leads. Suspects."

He didn't answer. He just stared at me.

"I think someone is back looking for those diamonds," I said. "And I'm afraid people are going to get hurt." I couldn't bring myself to tell him that his relative was dead. That wasn't my news to share. "I need to know what you found out."

He narrowed his eyes. "I heard about you sticking your nose into those murders around here."

"I do that," I agreed. News sure made it out to this little shack, didn't it? He was three for three. At the rate he was going, he'd probably dated my mom, too.

"Maybe you should stop."

"I probably should," I agreed. "Maybe next time."

He grabbed the bags of food from me, turned around, walked

back into the shack, and closed the door, a slight hitch in his gait from a right leg that didn't quite work as well as it could. I heard a lock click.

I looked back at Lucy, and she gave me a thumbs up. *Crud.*

I didn't want to do this, but I really didn't want anyone (else?) to get killed. I lightly tapped on the door. "I think Dee was involved," I said. "I think she's in danger." To say the least. Well, to be fair, she could be dead. She could also have been fake dead.

I heard him swear, and he yanked the door open again. "Is that your cat?"

I blinked. "In the truck? Yes."

"Let me talk to him."

"Talk to him?"

"Yeah. Bring him over."

Ah...now I got the crazy recluse thing. "If you try to hurt him, he will probably kill you."

Justin looked affronted. "I would never hurt an animal. What kind of monster do you think I am?"

"I don't know, but I love my cat."

"I know." His voice softened slightly. "Let me talk to him."

What the heck? If that got him talking, right? His claim that he'd never hurt an animal had felt genuine, and I could usually read people well. Plus, well, King Tut was King Tut. Anyone near him would be the one in danger, not him.

"Hang on." I walked back over to the truck, shooting Lucy a look. As soon as I reached the truck, King Tut leapt out the window and into my arms, the remains of his chewed leash dangling.

Silly me to think there was a way to contain the beast.

I carried the purring kitty back across the clearing, but the moment we got close to Justin, the purring stopped. The former sheriff leaned in to look at King Tut, and my cat stared back.

"I want to hold him," he said.

"No." My response was automatic. Chatting with King Tut was

one thing. Holding him? No. I had a duty to protect his mushy little feline heart.

Justin glared at me, and I glared back.

"No information is worth risking my cat," I snapped. "Look, I walked into Esther's house, and I found her missing and Dee on the floor of the pantry. Dee was either dead or faking it, but when the cops went to check, she was gone. I don't know what happened to her, but my friend is missing. Something is going on, and I think it relates back to that jewelry store theft and murder. I'll find out what happened to Dee, but I'd like your help."

His eyes widened, then he swore. "No wonder she hasn't returned my texts." He swore again, then sat down heavily on the Adirondack chair.

Okay, so now I felt like a jerk for letting that spill out. "I'm sorry, I didn't mean to—"

"No." He held up his hand to silence me. "She was always trouble." He leaned back in his seat and picked up his coffee. "She came to see me a week ago when she came back to town. Asked if she could stay here."

Holy cow. He'd spoken to her? "What did she say?" I tried to keep the eagerness out of my voice.

Lucy hurried over and stood next to me.

"Didn't say much. Said it was best if I didn't know." He swore again. "I let her put up a tent, but I didn't ask. Didn't care."

"When did she arrive?" I didn't see a tent anywhere.

"A week ago." He wrapped his hands around the mug and stared into the fire. "It was a Saturday night," he said, his voice getting rougher. "Got the call at two-thirty-three in the morning that shots were fired at the jewelers."

He'd dropped back into the past without warning. "What happened?"

"Got there. Saw Tony sprawled in the showroom, shot in the chest. Back door open. Safe open. Diamonds gone. No sign of who did it."

I looked at Lucy. "Did you get any leads?"

He continued to stare at the fire. "Got the security footage. It had been tampered with, but I saw my great niece on there."

Holy cow. "Dee? Dee was there?"

He didn't seem to hear me. "Couldn't be her. She wasn't a murderer. I buried the tapes, went to go see her. But she was scared. Wouldn't talk. Couldn't get anything out of her. But I know she was there. What did she see? I looked, but came up with nothing. And then she ran."

"That's not true," I said softly. "You did find something. No criminal is so good that he doesn't leave a trace. Who killed Tony?"

"Came up with nothing," he repeated again.

He was descending into the past, and we were going to lose him. I could feel it. Quickly, I started asking about the other finalists to see if any names triggered him. "What about Zoltan? Was he there?"

"Zoltan. He came to see me. Brought me desserts."

Holy crap. "When?"

"Nice young man. Nice young man. Nice young man. His dad would be proud. Proud dad. Happy dad. Nice family Christmas."

I leaned in. "What about Diesel? Or Stevie? Were they there that night with Dee?"

"Diesel. The Ugly Man." He leaned forward, staring more deeply into the flames. "I went there that night. I saw it. I saw him."

"Who? Who did you see?"

Justin started swaying back and forth, clasping his mug, humming softly.

Crap. "Esther? Was she friends with Dee?"

No answer. Just humming.

I tried again. "Ruby Lee?"

He looked up sharply. "Ruby Lee. Where is she? She said she would be back. Is she here?" He stood up and looked around. "Ruby Lee! When is Dee coming back? I need to talk to her! What does she know? What does she know?"

I saw Lucy over by the shed, digging through piles of trash, which I was super impressed with. Go Lucy! "What does Ruby Lee know?"

"Ruby Lee!" He was shouting now, getting almost frantic, pacing, and shouting.

Crap. I didn't know what to do. Should I call an ambulance or—

King Tut suddenly shot out of my arms. "Hey—" I lunged for him, but it was too late. He vaulted over a log, around the fire, and then literally launched himself at Justin. Dear God. He was going to kill the man! "Watch out—"

Justin spun around, and his eyes widened when he saw King Tut airborne. His arms went out to catch him, and King Tut slammed into his chest so hard the older man stumbled backwards. Lucy and I leapt to catch him, but he regained his balance, struggling to hold onto a growling cat.

He froze, staring at King Tut. "This cat is the size of a mountain lion."

"Don't hurt him," I warned my cat.

"I would never." Justin's arms softened, and he began to scratch King Tut behind the ear. "What's his name?"

"King Tut."

The cat in question flicked his tail, but remained still and didn't growl. Not in attack mode.

"Gorgeous cat." Justin crooned to the cat, all signs of distress gone. "He likes you," he said to me. "He says you're good to him."

I raised my brows. "You can talk to cats?"

"Sometimes. If they want to, I'll listen." He paused to study King Tut, then nodded. "Okay." He let King Tut hop down, and the massive cat wandered back over to me. I held out my arms, and he leapt up and settled down against my chest.

Justin studied me. "You save people, don't you? Cats, too?"

I shrugged. "I guess so. Sort of."

He nodded. "That's good. Good person." He sat back down in his chair and picked his coffee back up and started humming again. He was calm again, and I didn't want to mess that up by asking the wrong questions again.

But I had one more. "Justin?"

He looked up at me with a smile. "Yes?"

"Where are the diamonds?"

His smile faded into confusion. "Where are the diamonds?" he repeated. "Where are the diamonds? Where are the diamonds?"

I sighed. We'd lost him again. "We left you food from Hattie's café in your cabin," I said. "Make sure you eat it."

He looked up at me. "Hattie's the best chef," he said. "She's going to win the Strawberry Shortcake bake-off. She'll get to keep the trophy. Who will make the new one? We'll need a new one."

Lucy and I left him talking happily about trophies, strawberries, and cats.

We got in my truck, and I pulled out. "Well, we have confirmation of Ruby Lee's claim that Dee was at the murder, and diamonds were involved."

"And that something happened at the Ugly Man, but I don't know if it was back then or recently."

"And he knows Zoltan." I looked in my rearview mirror as I drove away. Justin was standing up now, watching us. His gaze was shrewd and sharp, with not even a trace of confusion on it, exactly as it had been when we showed up.

Was he really crazy? Or had he been playing us? I wasn't sure. Maybe a little of both. "Something happened that night with the murder," I said. "Either he was trying to cover it up, or it was so upsetting that it derailed him. Something to do with Dee and the diamonds."

"And Zoltan. And the Ugly Man. And Ruby Lee." They were all there. All a part of it. Whatever had happened twenty years ago had come back to life when Dee had reappeared. But what had happened? And how did it involve Rogue? He hadn't responded to her name, but that didn't mean anything.

Lucy held up a shiny piece of pink foil. "I was looking to see if

I could find anything indicating Zoltan had visited recently, and I found this. Think Zoltan brought it?"

I glanced over as I drove. "Is it a cupcake wrapper?"

"It is." She turned it over so I could see the bottom. "Recognize this? Is this Zoltan's logo?"

I looked closely. It was what looked like a pot leaf. Recognition shot through me. "I've seen that before. It's not Zoltan's."

"Whose is it?"

"Topsy's Vegan Cupcakes."

And just like that, we had another player, one who was also in prime position to win the contest.

Did that mean that the diamonds and the contest were actually connected? And if so, how?

CHAPTER 11

MY PHONE RANG at that moment, and we both jumped. I let out my breath and pulled my phone of out my pocket. "Can you answer it? This old truck doesn't have Bluetooth."

"Sure." Lucy answered the phone and put it on speaker. "Hello?"

"Where's Mia?" Devlin spoke without preamble, and his voice sounded both irritating and tempting at the same time.

I definitely needed to get over him. "I'm here."

"You're okay?"

I glanced at Lucy. "Fine. What do you want?" So sue me for not feeling all that friendly about his lack of faith in me.

"Griselda, I mean Hawk, can't get a response from Ivan, which is very concerning. Until we find out what's going on, you're to stay under my protection. If I can't be there, then he wants you at the police station. It's the safest place."

Lucy started laughing, which I appreciated. "There's literally no chance of me going to the police station, Devlin—"

"Mia. The highly trained bodyguard assigned to protect you from assassins has *gone missing*. Get your butt to the jail. Griselda, I mean Hawk, is going to send someone to pick you up, and he's going to relocate you until we can figure out what's going on."

My amusement vanished.

Lucy frowned. "He has a point, Mia. Getting murdered would kind of suck."

I thought about that. "If someone wanted me dead, I'd be dead by now. I'm not exactly a difficult target. If I'm still alive, then it's because no one wants me dead."

"They may want you for something else," Devlin said.

"Like what?" Lucy asked.

"Location of missing drugs and money."

Her eyes widened. "Is there missing drugs and money?"

"There is missing drugs and money," Devlin said. "According to Griselda. Hawk, I mean."

That news startled me. "Really?"

"Yeah. And the word on the street is that you took it."

Oh, *man.* "I didn't take it."

"Doesn't matter if certain people think you did. And with Ivan missing, we have to assume that they're closing in on you. Bass Derby isn't safe for you right now, Mia. You need to leave."

Lucy's mouth opened in silent protest.

My gut sank. "I'm not leaving."

"Don't be a stubborn fool," Devlin said. "These people kill."

"I know that. They've already tried to kill me. I know what they do." I hit the steering wheel in frustration. I didn't want to leave town, but I also didn't want to get assassinated, if I could help it.

"I can't watch you all the time. I have to deal with this murder and the festival. Hawk is on a case right now and can't shadow you. He's not sending another bodyguard until we find Ivan. He's going to send someone to pick you up and—"

I had a sudden idea. "I'll take care of my safety."

Devlin swore. "A hairdryer isn't going to save you against an assassin."

"It did once, but I have a better idea." I swung a U-Turn and headed toward the festival, instead of my marina, where Lucy's car was. "Tell Chief Stone not to arrest me again. I'm safe to be free."

To his credit, Devlin didn't call me a fool again. "What's your plan?"

"I'll tell you after I'm sure it's a go." I glanced in my rearview mirror, suddenly nervous. A black pickup truck was behind us. Had it been following us for long? I didn't remember seeing it. We passed two men on the street corner who both paused to watch me drive by.

Ugh. I was seeing threats everywhere. It was like when I was undercover and living on high alert all the time. I didn't want to go back there, to live like that again.

I put a little more weight on the gas pedal, and I saw Lucy slide her hand around the door handle to brace herself.

Devlin swore. "Mia, this isn't the time to be a hero. Ivan is special forces. He doesn't 'go missing.' Something serious is happening in Bass Derby."

"I know. This is my home and I want to find out what it is. I'm not leaving, and I'm not abandoning my new home to criminals. I'm going to the festival. You can find me there if you want."

"Mia—"

I nodded at Lucy, and she hung up on him.

"You're sure it's a good idea not to leave town?" she asked, without preamble. "I like having you alive."

I turned into the crowded parking lot, filled with hundreds, thousands, of people who could be hiding a murderer or two. "Here's the thing, Lucy." I pulled into a spot close to Hattie's booth, as close as I could get. "What's the point in being alive if you're not living?"

She didn't look convinced. "Well, there are some reasons, like getting a chance at another day, and then one after that—"

"Hiding in fear? No." I looked over at her. "I lived in constant terror for two years when I was spying on Stanley, but I never asked Griselda to let me quit. Why? Because even living in fear is better than giving up on what matters to you. Like this town, doing the right thing, and making sure the sassy rich Seam Ripper who helped save my life ten days ago is okay."

Devlin had fired me up, and I was in full fight mode. I wasn't stepping aside so bad guys could take over my town and my life. I hadn't before, and I wasn't now. "If someone killed Dee, then they don't deserve to get away with it. And Rogue deserves to be standing at her table on Sunday to fight for her victory."

Little things that mattered.

Lucy grinned. "All right then. I'm with you all the way. I'll watch your back, literally, and tell you to duck if a knife comes shooting toward it."

"Perfect. We're good then." I put the truck in park, knotted the leash that King Tut had eaten, and then grinned at Lucy. "Let's go find Hattie."

"Is she your plan? Because honestly, I'm not sure she'd sacrifice herself to keep you alive."

"She would. She just doesn't like to admit it. But no, it's not Hattie."

"Then...?"

"Follow me."

CHAPTER 12

I carried King Tut as we wove through the crowds, trusting him to warn us if someone was coming for me. He stayed relaxed, his tail flicking with delight as he watched people gape at the beast in my arms.

We reached Hattie's table, where she and Vinnie were setting things up. The festival didn't officially open until ten, but most of the food booths were already open. The boat parade was launching from Jake's marina and going past the town beach, so folks were already setting up their chairs and blankets to watch it. Boats were lining the lake all the way to the bend in the shoreline, lined up for front row seats.

I couldn't see the Yacht Club from here, but I'd seen the hustle and bustle at Jake's docks from my marina earlier, and I'd felt a little tinge of jealousy that he had all the action.

Soon. Soon I'd break through. Fourth of July launch for the Eagle's Nest, which I was beginning to think needed a new, clean-slate name. Honest Mia's Marina, maybe. Or King Tut's Royal Marina?

Hattie waved as we approached. "How did it go?"

Vinnie's T-shirt fit him a little better today, and he was deeply focused on arranging the muffins in Hattie's plexiglass display. He looked very happy working with muffins, and my plan suddenly seemed like it wasn't maybe the best idea. "Justin confirmed the robbery, murder, and that Dee had been there that night."

"What robbery? What murder?" Vinnie looked up eagerly.

We quickly filled them in on what we'd learned from Justin, and by the end, Vinnie was nodding. "Bet that lady got taken down by her partner. Happens all the time."

I blinked. "How do you know she had a partner?"

He shrugged. "I don't *know* that, but everyone has a partner. Breaking into a jewelry store and stealing diamonds? That takes planning. You need to case the joint, figure out how to get there without anyone seeing you. You need a lookout. An alibi. Tech skills for the safe. It's pretty complex. Dee was a high-school troublemaker?" He shook his head. "Not enough experience or background to pull it off herself. She had a partner who has been wanting those diamonds. Dee came back to town, the partner cornered her, and now Dee's dead. Makes sense. Easy enough."

"Well." Hattie said. "There we go. Who was her partner?"

Vinnie didn't have that answer, which was a little disappointing. It would have been so handy. "Ruby Lee would know," I said.

"Based on what you said," Hattie pointed out, "Ruby Lee *was* her partner."

"No. Ruby Lee definitely didn't kill her. She is out for revenge." I paused. "If we ask Ruby Lee who might have been Dee's partner, then Ruby Lee will go after them first."

"Wait a sec," Lucy said. "Wasn't Dee a beauty queen?"

Hattie nodded. "Miss Teen Maine and Miss Maine."

"Then that was her world, just like twirling was mine," Lucy said. "Everyone she was close to would have been in that world. Hang on." She pulled out her phone. "Let me look something up. I know what to look for." She stepped away and began typing on her phone.

Lucy was right. Everyone has a world they inhabit, a small circle of people who are on repeat in their lives. Mine had been the world of cons and celebrity. Lucy's had been baton twirling.

Hattie's was food. Today, I was building a new world, but it was still small.

While Lucy researched, I focused on Hattie. "So, Devlin called me. Since Ivan has gone missing, Devlin and Griselda think it's too dangerous for me here, and Griselda is arranging for me to be yanked out of town and relocated."

Hattie looked over sharply. "For how long?"

"They won't say. They don't care, honestly."

"You can't go. They'll toss you in some cesspool and forget about you until Stanley's appeal, which could be years. You'll waste away in a swampland of boredom and loneliness. Better to die living life than live in a swamp."

I grinned. "You'll miss me."

"I won't miss you at all," she snapped. "I just don't want someone else to take over the marina. I like your idea of becoming partners. You don't get to offer me that and then snatch it away. It's rude."

I loved Hattie. She was such a softie. "They won't give me another bodyguard until they find out what happened to Ivan. Honestly, I don't really want to get assassinated, but I don't want to leave. If someone killed Ivan, I might be next." Grisly, but true.

Hattie's eyes widened, and I saw the moment she understood there might be actual danger if I stayed.

I went in for the kill. "If I can convince them I'm safe, they won't make me leave."

"Safe? How? We'll find Ivan. He's probably shacked up with some woman somewhere having a little nookie time."

"What if he's dead?"

Hattie swore. "You need a bodyguard. We'll provide one."

"Oh…good idea. Do you know anyone?" I waited. It had to be Hattie's idea.

"Me?" She braced her hands on the table. "I don't. Vinnie! Do you know anyone who can keep Mia alive? You have friends who like guns."

He looked over, his hands full of croissants. "Her current body-guard is missing, and possibly dead? Is that what you said?"

"Maybe."

"So, it's a dangerous job."

Hattie looked over at me. "I'm sure it's fine."

"It is dangerous," I interrupted. After risking my life to put Stanley away, I would never ask anyone to do the same without full disclosure "My ex is a drug kingpin I put in prison. It's highly likely that someone will pay a professional assassin to kill me."

Vinnie's face lit up. "A professional? Really? That's so cool. I've never met a pro."

I grinned. "I disarmed one already and sent him to the hospital. It was fun."

Vinnie set down the croissants. "I want to do it. That'd be freaking awesome to take on a pro. Test my skills."

I grinned. "That would be fantastic." Yay for my plan!

But Hattie made a choking noise. "Absolutely not, Vinnie. You're my new second in command. You can't go around investing in a life of violence. I refuse to release you from your contract."

Vinnie raised his brows. "We didn't sign a contract. You're paying me with food to work your booth for the festival."

"But I see greatness in you. I have plans for you!" She turned to me. "Mia, I forbid you to hire him. He's mine. I found him."

The six-foot-four gun-wielding possible gang leader looked at Hattie. "No one owns me." His voice was soft, not angry, though.

Hattie looked at him. "I see greatness in you, Vinnie. You can be more than violence."

"Handing out muffins is my future?" He turned to face her. "No one gives a rip what I do. It blew my mind when you walked up to me and started talking cars like I was your best friend, when I was about to steal your ride. Then, you trusted me with your booth. No one does that for me. No one."

Hattie's bright blue eyes got a little misty. "I know. I could tell."

"That's why I'm hanging out at this festival handing out food this weekend. But I'm not going to work for you. This isn't my life. It's a favor paid back because you treated me like a human being. I honor my debts."

"You don't owe me for that."

"In my world, I do." He looked over at me. "But I want to work for Mia. I want to take on a pro. I want to see how good I am."

I heard the undercurrent in his words, because I'd also once been a criminal who had tried and was still trying to change the trajectory of my life. "Save a life instead of taking one?"

He glanced at me. "Something like that."

Hattie nodded. "I get that." She sighed. "Who am I to stand in the way of your dreams?" She threw up her hands. "Go keep Mia alive, and have fun doing it."

Vinnie grinned. "Awesome. When do I start?"

"Right now. 24/7."

"I have gear. I'm good. You want me to be obvious so I scare 'em off? Or should I be undercover, so they make an attempt, and then we take them down?"

It was actually a good question. It would be nice to find out who was after me and end that threat. But… "You're twice the size of every man in this place, with ten times the muscle," I said. "No one would overlook you."

"I can fix that. Hang on." He took a breath, then slumped his shoulders. He hung his head, and all the fight seemed to go out of his body. He instantly transformed into a gentle giant, who I was pretty sure would refuse to even step on an ant, let alone take down a professional killer.

"Holy cow," I said. "How did you do that?"

He gave me a sheepish smile. "I just changed my vibe. Easy."

I'd thought I was good at the con and becoming who I wasn't, but he was a master. "You're hired." I threw out a price that I thought was fair, and that I could afford, and he immediately stuck out his hand.

I shifted King Tut to my left arm and shook his hand. "Deal."

"Make sure she pays up at the end of every day," Hattie said. "If she dies, then you won't get your money."

"She won't die." Vinnie said it with such confidence that I believed him. "I'm wired for violence. I can feel it before I can see it. I'll know." He ripped off his shirt, showing insanely sculpted muscles that made me and Hattie look at each other.

He tossed it aside, then grabbed his gray T-shirt and pulled it over. It fit him much better, not showcasing every single line of corded masculinity that the pink one had revealed. He then grabbed a small duffel bag that he'd tucked behind the cooler of sandwiches. He slung it over his shoulder, and I was pretty sure I heard the clink of metal on metal. "Ready, boss. Let's do it."

He was still slouched over like a softie, but the edge to his voice was pure steel.

"Damn," Hattie said.

"I agree." The fear that had been trying to grip me since Devlin's call eased away, letting me breathe better. Vinnie might not be a pro, but the man had street smarts woven into his cells. "Just don't get yourself killed for me," I said. As I spoke, I realized the disadvantage of liking the man who was supposed to keep me alive.

"I won't." The confidence in his voice was absolute. "I got this."

I believed him. "All right, then."

Lucy came back over, her face glowing. "I found it." She waved her phone. "Dee almost got kicked out of the Teen Maine competition because she got caught smoking pot backstage during the finals. But one of the other competitors stepped up and said it was her stash, and Dee had just been walking by at the time. The other girl got kicked out and banned from other competitions."

"Oh...that's friendship right there," Hattie said. "Taking the rap for your friend like that. Commitment."

"It sure is," I agreed. "Who was it? Anyone we know?"

Lucy held out her phone. Staring back at us with the smiling visage of Hattie's favorite vegan baker, at the opening day of her cupcake store. "Topsy is from Peculiar, which is just down the road. She and Dee were arrested twice in Peculiar for breaking into the high school and vandalizing it."

Hattie nodded. "See? I told you Topsy was giving Bass Derby a bad name. No one who bakes without butter can be trusted."

"And eggs," I reminded her.

"It's literal blasphemy," Hattie said. "So, what's our little butter hater been up to for the last twenty years?"

Lucy shrugged. "She wasn't very noteworthy after she dropped out of the beauty scene. Her store website doesn't give much background, other than to say she has loved baking her whole life, and believes all creatures should be loved, not eaten. She's not on social media at all, which is honestly weird. She just opened the store last week."

"Well, we need to go see that store," I said. "She's probably baking right now."

"So, maybe we go see her house, then," Lucy said. "I mean, if she's not there."

"Her garage," Vinnie said. "That's where she'd stash a body. Not in her house. It would be in the freezer. Keep it cool until she can get rid of it."

We all turned to look at him.

He shrugged. "Just sayin'. Personally, I've never hidden a body in a freezer before, but it's a good plan."

"I can't go now. I need to deliver the mail. I'm already late starting," Lucy said.

"I need to run the booth and find someone to help me," Hattie said. "I'll be free later."

I felt very empowered to go visit a potential murderer with Vinnie in tow. "I'll go. Vinnie?"

"On it." He adjusted his little duffel bag. "I got your back, boss. Let's go."

CHAPTER 13

VINNIE HAD me drive Turbojet to the vegan bakery so he could sit in the passenger seat with his gun out and watch everyone around us.

He was very vigilant and dangerous-looking, and King Tut fell in love with him instantly. When Vinnie wouldn't let him sit on his lap, King Tut parked himself on the center console and simply stared at Vinnie with unabashed adoration.

I was going to call Devlin to tell him I had a new bodyguard, but he did me the favor of seeing me, turning on his blue lights, and pulling up behind us.

Vinnie turned around. "Don't pull over. Could be a fake cop. Keep driving. I'll shoot out a tire and—"

"Good heavens, no. Don't shoot out the tire! I know the cop. He's real." I put on my blinker to pull over.

Vinnie narrowed his eyes. "Fine, but I'll keep the gun on him."

Devlin would definitely appreciate having a gun pointed at him by the scary man in my passenger seat. "How about we don't get in a gunfight with him? Then you won't end up in jail with your gun confiscated, unable to protect me when the assassin comes?"

Vinnie narrowed his eyes at me. "You're positive this guy's for real?"

"Absolutely. His name is Devlin Hunt" I stopped the car and Devlin got out. His hand was on his gun, and he was moving carefully. I realized instantly what was going on. "Vinnie, Devlin thinks you're the assassin and you're kidnapping me. Put on your harmless vibe, and put that bag on the floor. It looks like it has guns in it." I quickly rolled down my window and waved cheerfully at Devlin.

He kept his hand on his gun as he approached, which was actually very endearing. His first thought was that I was in danger.

Vinnie immediately dumped the bag and slumped down in the seat, retreating into full harmless vibe just as Devlin reached the window. "Mia. Get out of the car. We need to talk." His gaze wasn't on me. It was on Vinnie, and every muscle in Devlin's body was taut.

Wow. He was a total badass right now, which was ridiculously attractive.

Beside me, Vinnie tensed, and I knew he didn't want me to get out of the truck with a cop he didn't trust. Which worked out great, because the cop didn't want me sitting in a truck with a dude he didn't trust. A win for all coming my way, unless I aced my hostess skills.

"Devlin. This is my new bodyguard Vinnie. Vinnie, this is Devlin, who has the hots for me and is trying to date me. King Tut likes both of you, so trust the cat."

The two men stared at each other, and Vinnie's harmless vibe was gone. He looked pretty terrifying, but honestly, so did Devlin. I'd suspected that he and Griselda had been on some black ops team together, and at this moment, I felt like I'd been right on with that.

"Get out of the car, Mia," Devlin said again.

"Don't get out, Mia," Vinnie said. "We don't know if he can be trusted. He could be on a payroll."

I looked back and forth between them, and then suddenly, I started laughing. The giggles bubbled up, and I couldn't stop. I just felt so safe wedged between these two gun-wielding, alpha muscle-heads. I hadn't felt this safe in a long time, and it unleashed a major attack of the giggles. "This is the best," I said. "No one would ever get to me with the two of you around. Vinnie, Devlin is definitely not going to kill me—"

"I might," Devlin said. "You're a little bit of a pain in my butt, not calling me to tell me you'd hired this guy."

Beside me, Vinnie tensed, and I rolled my eyes. "Read the room, Devlin. Not the time to joke that you might kill me. I'm literally paying Vinnie to make sure no one kills me."

Devlin narrowed his eyes at Vinnie. "You armed?"

"Got a bunch of stuff," Vinnie said, pointing to the bag at his feet. "No one's getting to her."

Devlin glanced at me, and he kind of looked like his head was going to explode. "Do you have permits for all your hardware?"

Vinnie's jaw clenched. "Yeah. I do."

Wow. I wouldn't have thought Vinnie would have gone legal for his gun. I'd hired well.

"Let me have it. Identification, too. And Mia, get out of the blasted truck until I'm sure you're safe."

I could tell Devlin was about to descend into over-protective protector freakout mode, so I nodded. "Vinnie, I'm going to get out now. I'm safe. Devlin gets a little overprotective of my well-being. Okay?"

Vinnie gave Devlin a long look. "If you try to hurt her, I will be on you before you have time to blink. It's legal to use deadly force in defense of others to protect against deadly force."

Devlin raised his brows, and then he gave a nod of acknowledgment. "I'm aware of the law." He grabbed my door handle and opened the door. "Mia. Out."

I raised my brows at Vinnie. "I'm impressed."

He grinned at me. "I feel like I've been practicing my whole life for this job. This is awesome."

I was still smiling as I stepped out of the car. King Tut took over my seat, his snowshoe-sized paws up on the window frame as Devlin took Vinnie's documents. "Bag, too," he said.

Vinnie looked like he was going to resist, but I nodded at him.

He sighed and handed over the bag, careful to handle it in a way that didn't alarm my edgy cop friend.

Devlin grabbed my arm and escorted me back to his SUV, his fingers tight around my elbow. I bumped into him on purpose, helped myself to his phone, then pulled away as we reached the sidewalk. "You don't get to drag me anywhere," I pointed out helpfully.

"Mia." He swore. "That guy looks like he just got out of prison."

"Well, then, he should be pretty good at handling violence, don't you think?" I clasped my hands behind my back, holding his phone loosely in my fingers. For an ex black ops dude, Devlin was surprisingly unobservant when it came to his digital devices and me.

"How do you know he's not going to kill you?" Devlin asked, still all worked up over the scary dude I'd been driving around. "Kidnap you? Or—"

I held up my non-phone-holding hand to silence him. "Vinnie befriended Hattie and saved my life a few weeks ago." I decided not to mention that his initial plan had been to steal Rogue's Lamborghini. "Hattie hired him to handle her money for her tent. She trusts him."

He stared at me. "And that's it?"

"We both have great people instincts, and we both trust him. So yes, good enough for both of us."

He scowled at me. "When I saw you driving with him in the passenger seat, I thought you were in trouble. Scared the crap out of me."

I blinked, surprised by his words. "Really?"

"Yeah." He ran his hand through his hair. "Look, Mia, the

threats against you are real, and I don't get the sense that you respect the level of danger that's hunting you."

"'Hunting' is a little dramatic—"

"I felt like drama was the best way to get your attention. Did it work?"

"Yes," I agreed. "Can I crawl into the back of your SUV and hide there for the next sixty years?"

He raised his brows, and a grin quirked the corner of his mouth. "You're mocking me."

"Yes. Definitely. It's my job to mock overly rigid law enforcement types who simply refuse to understand that I cannot be contained. I'm going to order a T-shirt that says 'I survived drug lord undercover work. I dare you to test me.'"

The quirk turned into a full grin. "Am I overbearing?"

"Yes."

"Any bonus points for the fact I don't want you dead, and it's not just a professional interest?"

My stomach did a little flip. "No. I can't date a guy who has caveman traits."

He narrowed his eyes thoughtfully. "So, if I bought you body armor for our anniversary, that would be preferred?"

"Throw in a bulletproof hairdryer, and it would be a win."

He studied me. "No flowers? No sweet nothings? No homemade dinner with candlelight and music."

I blinked. "No one has ever done that for me before."

His brows went up. "Not even flowers?"

"Not like that." I couldn't lie. It sounded incredibly nice. "Stanley gave me presents, but it was bling to win me over. It worked, because I was..." I almost called my younger self stupid, but suddenly, I didn't want to do that. I had to love her, because she had done her best. "It worked because it was all I knew," I said more gently. "But a homemade dinner with candles sounds..." I paused.

"Nice?"

"Maybe."

He cocked his head. "You're complicated."

"Isn't everyone?"

"Yeah." He studied me, and suddenly, there was that same tension in the air that there had been that night we'd sat out under the full moon after I'd almost killed him with a nail gun. That tension that was all about so much more. The tension that had made me say yes to dinner with him, even though I was committed to being single for the rest of my life.

I swallowed. How could I be thinking about him as yummy dessert when we were standing on the side of the road, with assassins, murderers, and bodyguards abounding?

At that moment, Vinnie leaned out his window. "Boss, we gotta keep moving. Murders don't solve themselves."

Devlin's gaze shot to Vinnie and back to me. "Boss? Murders?"

I folded my arms across my chest. "Yes." Waiting.

To my delight, Devlin nodded and didn't try to hold me back. "Why not go all in then, right?"

I smiled with relief. "Right." Were we finally past the battle of him trying to keep me small?

"Let me just run his documents and check his hardware. Give me that? You are riding around in a car with him, and Hawk did confirm that you've been the topic of some conversations in your old world recently."

Oh, goody. "Sure. Check away."

I stayed on the sidewalk while Devlin got into his SUV and ran all the little things he wanted to run. While I waited, Vinnie got out of Turbojet and walked over to me. He stood beside me, scanning our surroundings carefully.

He didn't interrupt my thoughts. He simply was present and doing his job.

King Tut put his paws up on the back window of Turbojet, watching me, his tail flicking. I had a feeling that I didn't need a human bodyguard. King Tut would take care of anything that needed handling.

I saw Devlin look up and watch Vinnie for a moment, then he

glanced at me. I gave him a thumbs up, and he nodded. A moment later, he got out of his car and handed everything back to Vinnie. "Keep her safe."

Vinnie fist bumped Devlin. "I got it covered, my friend. Twenty-four seven. Any tips on what I'm looking for?"

Devlin glanced at me again. "Drugs and money went missing during the raid on Mia's ex, who was the head of a very successful drug operation. The word on the street is that Mia has both the missing drugs and cash. So someone might search her stuff, or decide that getting her to talk is the fastest route. Or just make her an example."

I blinked at his bluntness. I already knew that, but having it stated like that made me almost want to take Griselda up on his offer to disappear.

Vinnie nodded. "Got it."

"And if Dee Dutch was really murdered, then Mia could be unleashing another target on her back if she gets too close to figuring it out."

"That would just be a 'shut her up fast' move," Vinnie said.

"Right. Most likely."

"I'll be prepared for it all, then." The two alpha males gave each other looks of respect, while I tried not to reveal that I was a little freaked out by their casual discussion of all the possible threats coming for me.

Vinnie nudged my arm. "Let's go."

"Right." I raised my brows at Devlin.

He took a breath, looked like he wanted to say something, but then he nodded. "You'll be at the Biscuit Contest?"

I nodded. "Wouldn't miss it."

"See you then." He looked at Vinnie. "I'm off duty from ten tonight until six in the morning. If you need a break, I can cover during that time."

My stomach dropped. He wanted to guard me at night? Um...

"I'll let you know." Devlin gave Vinnie his number and a list of instructions, which was actually quite detailed and more interesting than I would have expected.

"Were you ever a bodyguard?" I asked Devlin.

He looked at me and something flashed in his eyes. Tension. Pain. Regret. "Yeah, kinda."

Holy cow. Had he failed? Had his client died? There was definitely something there with that past, but I couldn't ask with Vinnie there.

"Gotta go." Devlin nodded at us both, then got back into his SUV and pulled out around us, lights on, bolting so fast that I knew I'd touched on a nerve.

I stared after him, thinking. When I'd first met him, I'd known he was more than a small-town cop, and I'd wondered how he'd ended up in Bass Derby. Now I was even more curious. I wanted to know his secrets.

Vinnie nudged me. "Ready?"

I blinked, pulled back to the present, and the task at hand, namely to break into a vegan cupcakery and see if I could find a body. "Right. Yeah. Let's go."

I headed toward my truck, but it wasn't until I went to open the door and found a phone in my right hand that I remembered that I'd taken Devlin's phone and forgotten to give it back.

I grinned as I set it in my center console. He was going to be so delighted when he realized that I'd bested him again.

Devlin was so lucky to have me in his life.

Or at least he better think so if he had any chance at more than a first date with me.

Did I even want a first date with him?

I turned on the ignition as King Tut settled between us, perched on the center console, his front paws on Devlin's phone.

Yes, I realized. I did want a first date with Devlin.

And just as quickly, I remembered that Griselda had banned us from dating. That he'd claimed that Devlin was not a guy I should date.

It was time to find out why, because I clearly was going to have some decisions to make when it came to Devlin.

And that moment, Devlin's SUV came flying back down the street toward us, sirens on.

Vinnie tensed. "Trouble."

"Nope." I grabbed Devlin's phone and held it out the window.

He pulled up next to me, rolled down his window, and took the phone. "You're a pain in the butt." But he didn't sound mad. Mad respect, maybe.

I grinned. "Don't you just love me? I make your day so much brighter."

He cocked his brow at me. "That's one way to put it." But he was grinning as he rolled up his window and hit the gas.

And so was I.

CHAPTER 14

Topsy's Vegan Cupcakes was not nearly as cute as her cupcakes were.

Her store was in a part of town that I hadn't been to yet, mostly because there was nothing cute about it. It was all local, not touristy, but not in a good way. It felt like the part of town that everyone had abandoned once Main Street had started thriving over by the Yacht Club and the town beach.

I pulled up in front of her store, which was identified by a vinyl banner stretched across the front glass window. Granted, maybe her nice sign hadn't arrived, but why would anyone pay money for a nice sign in this area?

It reminded me of how my marina looked when I'd first arrived.

Except no one had taken care to fix this little street of tired storefronts.

I pulled up right in front and parked the truck. "The woman who owns this was the best friend of Dee Dutch when they were teenagers," I explained.

"Her partner," Vinnie supplied.

"Maybe." I patted King Tut. "Stay in here for now. If it sounds like I'm going to die, come save me."

He flicked his tail and sat down on the center console.

"All right." I hopped out of the truck feeling quite chipper. Visiting the sketchy home turf of a possible murderer really wasn't that stressful when I had Vinnie with me. A real life-changer, honestly. I might have to keep him around forever. "Let's do this."

"I hope she tries to kill you," Vinnie said, unable to keep the eagerness out of his voice. "That would be so fun." He helped himself to a few weapons and strapped them in assorted places on his body.

"Right? Can't think of a better way to spend my day." Again, I was feeling light-hearted and chipper, even while making jokes about being killed. Vinnie was so empowering. Everyone needed a Vinnie. I could start a new business hiring out Vinnie and his friends. I'd get rich so fast—

"Front door's open," Vinnie said, "but the sign on the door says it doesn't open for two hours."

Right. I had to focus. "She's probably here baking biscuits."

"Then the door would still be closed. And locked." He eased up close beside me. "I should go first."

"What if someone comes up behind me?"

He glanced over his shoulder and swore, making me grin. "I got it covered. Me, first."

"All right." I stood on the porch as Vinnie eased the front door open and peered inside. He gestured me to stay put as he stepped inside, but as soon he went into the shop, I trotted right in after him.

The store had no cupcakes on display. The tables and chairs were old and not even arranged. I frowned. "This doesn't look like a store." But I knew she was a real baker. Her cupcakes had been amazing.

While Vinnie ducked around counters and furniture, playing spy, I headed toward the swinging door to the kitchen. The moment I stepped inside the kitchen, it was a totally different feel. The kitchen was well-stocked, immaculate, and shiny. The shelves were full of everything that one might need for baking cupcakes and decorating them, and there were boxes of cupcakes on the counter, already prepped for transport. Maybe she was a caterer?

Vinnie flung the door open, startling me. "Front is clear," he announced.

"Good job. No one's back here either—" At that moment, I heard a car door slam and an engine roar to life behind the building.

Vinnie and I both sprinted to the back door. I raced out in the alley just as a huge, black pickup truck shifted into gear. The driver looked over at me, and recognition flooded through me. "Rogue!" She was wearing sunglasses, but there was no mistaking her face and hair. I waved my arms and raced toward the truck, but she hit the gas.

Vinnie yanked me back as the truck flashed past us, not exactly close to running me over, but a little reckless, which made me even more certain it was Rogue. I ran into the middle of the alley, waving my arms at the fleeing truck. "Rogue!"

She put her blinker on, then hit the gas, the tires screeching as she peeled out of the alley. I put my hands on my hips as Vinnie spun around beside me, checking every direction for assassins.

"She's alive," I announced giddily. "She's alive!" I wanted to run back out to Turbojet and go after her, but there was no way my antique truck would catch Rogue and her deluxe piece of machinery.

"Who?" Vinnie asked. "You know who that was?"

"Our friend who went missing. We thought she was dead." I couldn't believe she'd been there. I pulled out my phone and texted Hattie and Lucy. *I saw Rogue! She's alive!*

Hattie texted back. *Really?! That's fantastic! I told you she wasn't dead.*

Yay! Lucy replied. *That's the best news!*

What did she say? Hattie texted. *Did you tell her she was an insufferable beast for taking off and not keeping us in the loop?*

I didn't talk to her. I just saw her driving away from the cupcake place. Driving a really nice truck, too. I was on foot and couldn't catch her.

Truck? Hattie typed. *She would never drive a truck.*

It was a really nice one. Deluxe.

She'd never drive a truck, Hattie insisted.

Well, she was driving one. You can ask her about it when you see her.

Did she leave another note? Lucy texted. *Or another earring?*

I don't know. I'll go inside and check. Humming with delight, I shoved my phone in my pocket. "Come on, Vinnie."

He followed me back up the steps I'd sprinted down, and I walked through the back hallway, scanning more carefully now. "Topsy," I called out. "Are you around?"

I was so excited. Rogue's presence meant that Topsy definitely did have something to do with Dee. We were on the right track!

There was no answer, but I didn't see a freezer in the backroom big enough for a body, so yay for that!

I went back into the kitchen, looking more carefully around, but I didn't see a note. Rogue hadn't left us another earring. What had she been doing there? I put my hands on my hips and surveyed the kitchen.

Biscuit prep was underway. Topsy had the trays out. Flour on the counter. The bowl of flour was half-sifted. The sifter was in the bowl, still partially full. The oven clicked, and I realized it was on.

Alarm began to prickle down my spine. For the third time, I was walking into a situation that felt like someone had been plucked out of their life mid-stride.

I looked around and saw a walk-in fridge at the end of the kitchen. The door was closed, but there was a towel peeking out from underneath the door. Based on the state of the kitchen, Topsy wasn't someone who would leave a towel on the floor like that. "Vinnie," I said softly, "be ready."

"Ready, boss." He edged up behind me as I walked to the fridge.

I reached for the door handle, and he blocked me. "Let me open it."

"No. You just be ready to shoot." I took a breath and then yanked the door open and jumped to the side. He leapt into the doorway, his gun up.

Nothing happened, but then Vinnie unleashed a string of curses that would have done a nun proud.

I immediately leaned around the door, and then my gut sank.

Dee was on the floor, again, sans pretty shoes, but wearing the same outfit as the last time I'd seen her on the floor.

And sprawled on top of her, not barefoot, was Topsy, wearing jeans, a white chef hat, and glittery sneakers.

Neither of them was moving, talking, or even baking their biscuits for the bake-off in three hours.

"Topsy?" I nudged her with my toe, but she didn't move. "Dee?"

They looked dead, but I wasn't going to make the same mistake as last time. "Keep your gun on them," I ordered Vinnie as I pulled out my phone and called Devlin.

He answered on the first ring. "This is why you don't take my phone. If you still had my phone, you couldn't call me."

I ignored his excellent point. "We're at Topsy's Vegan Bakery. Dee and Topsy are in a pile on the floor of the walk-in fridge, and neither of them is moving." Did I tell him I saw Rogue leaving the area? I didn't want to get her in trouble if she was innocent, but this didn't look good. Not with her earring and Dee's shoes at the Ugly Man, and now this...

Devlin swore. "Dead?"

"I'm no longer going to try to make that call," I said. "Maybe they've been baking really hard and they're napping. In a pile. In a fridge."

He swore again. "Stay there. I'm on my way. Don't take your eyes off them, and watch your back in case someone wants to move them, or if they suddenly come back to life and try to bolt."

Wow. So many high-stress options available.

"Okay." I hung up and glanced at Vinnie, who was looking a little shocked by the sight of the pile. "Last time I found Dee on the floor like that, her body vanished. So, someone might try to move her. Or they might not actually be dead. Keep ready."

Vinnie immediately swung his gun outward toward the kitchen, while I stood awkwardly in the doorway, watching Dee and Topsy for movement. Any sign of life. Any indication that the two of them were about to leap to their feet, laughing hysterically that they got me.

There was none.

CHAPTER 15

"They better not cancel the contest," Hattie said as she hurried up to Turbojet, before I'd even put the truck in park as I arrived at the festival. "Ronald Dutch called a meeting with Mayor Stone and the other judges to decide whether it needs to be cancelled." She pointed to the judges' tent, which had closed flaps and several volunteers guarding the entrance.

"Hattie. Dee and Topsy are *dead*," I pointed out. "I think that's a good reason to cancel the festival!" Upon arrival to Topsy's store, Devlin had quickly confirmed that both were dead, but there was no information yet on whether Dee had achieved that state yesterday or more recently. Mostly because Devlin had kicked me out once he got the info he needed from me, which was before the coroner had arrived.

"Is it *really* a good reason to cancel this party of joy and delight?" Hattie asked. "Dee was a toxic poison, and Topsy clearly was a drug addict and troublemaker. Neither of them had set foot in this town in years. This festival is all about good will and income for the town. Why should evil win? That makes no sense. Now is the time to feed love and goodness, not suppress it."

I stared at her. "How did that just make sense?"

"Because I'm right. Always right. But honestly, what am I

worried about? Ronald didn't even cancel his family's reunion lobster bake in April after his own twin brother died, so why would he cancel the festival for Dee and Topsy?"

I blinked. "Really?"

"Yes, but his twin was not a good man, so it was fine. Same situation as this one, so it's all good." She looked much more chipper now. "The show will go on, so let's go. We need to set up Rogue's table. Biscuits are all done, and Lucy just got here with all the displays for the table."

Vinnie was already out of Turbojet, scanning the crowd.

I lowered my voice. "Hattie. Someone *murdered* Dee and Topsy. Someone who is in this town. Maybe at this festival."

"I know," she whispered back. "We should probably thank him if we see him. It's a fitting end for a butter hater, right?"

She started to turn away, and I grabbed her wrist. "Hattie."

"Seriously, Mia, you're being so dramatic. Just because you got to have the adventure and I was stuck baking doesn't mean you need to rub my face in it—"

"What if Rogue did it?" I kept my voice low, but I saw Vinnie look over. "She was there," I whispered. "I saw her."

Hattie snorted. "She didn't do it."

"How can you be so sure?"

"Because she'd be so good at it that you'd never have seen her there."

"Every criminal makes mistakes."

"She wouldn't." Hattie patted my arm. "If you think it's Rogue, it's going to distract you from the truth. You have to let that go and focus on what you know."

What I knew was that Rogue had been there. And one of her earrings and both of Dee's shoes had been at the Ugly Man.

Hattie suddenly turned back toward me. "Did you tell Devlin she was there?"

"I told him that I saw a truck pulling away. I told him I hadn't seen who was driving it." I used to lie to the cops all the time growing up, but lying to Devlin about seeing Rogue there had felt uncomfortable. If Rogue had killed them, I couldn't protect her. I loved her, but I'd also loved my husband. Evil was evil, and I couldn't protect that just because I loved someone.

Hattie raised her brows. "You didn't lie to the cops about Stanley."

"No."

"If you saw Rogue murder someone, you would tell the cops."

"Yeah."

"So, the fact you didn't tell Devlin means that your gut believes she is innocent. If your instincts told you that she'd done it, nothing would have been able to convince you to protect her." She tapped my chest with two fingers. "You have a pure heart of gold, Mia. No bad person gets a free pass from you, and every good person gets your protection. It's how you are. So trust your instincts."

I shifted restlessly. "What if I'm wrong?"

"If you don't believe in yourself, who will?"

"You will," Vinnie interrupted. "You'll believe in anyone, Hattie."

She looked over at him. "No, I won't. I only believe in people who deserve it. So, yes, I believe in Mia. And Rogue. And you." She opened my truck door. "Now, get your lazy, self-doubting butt out of the truck and help us get Rogue's table set up. She has to be cleared in twenty-three and a half hours or she won't be able to be at the finals, and she can't win. We have work to do."

She walked away, leaving my door open. King Tut shot out of my truck and ran after Hattie, trotting happily beside her as they merged into the crowd.

With a sigh, I released my seatbelt and got out. "Vinnie? What's your instinct?"

He regarded me. "People lie and cheat and murder all the time."

I blinked. "Do they?" That sounded like a fun crowd he hung out with.

"Yeah. The people you expect to be your friends will stab you in the back the minute something is in it for them."

I stared at him. "Wow."

"Except you guys. I've never met people like you, Hattie, and Lucy." He grinned. "It's cool, how loyal you guys are. If this Rogue chick is anything like you three, she's good and she needs you at her back." He shrugged. "But maybe she's a really good liar, in which case, cut the ties and save yourself."

"That was helpful."

He nodded. "You're welcome."

With a sigh, I began to weave my way through the crowd back toward the competitor tent. I hadn't even made it halfway when an old, cranky mystery writer fell in beside me.

I looked over at him. Beau was wearing the bloody knife T-shirt again, jeans, and rainbow sandals. His gray hair was wind-blown, making me pretty sure he'd arrived at the festival via his very fast boat. "Hi Beau—"

He slapped a handcuff on my left wrist.

"What—"

He held up his right arm, which dragged my left arm up with it.

I stared at him. "You handcuffed us together?" What the heck? I looked around for Vinnie, and he was just standing there laughing. I guess a cranky old mystery writer didn't raise alarms for him.

"Two bodies," Beau said. "You found *two bodies.* A double homicide. Did I get a text? A call? Was I informed you were going to the lair of a woman who might be a murderer? No. I had to hear about it from my spy at the police station, and by then, the scene was cleaned up. You do realize I write about murder for a living right? That this is the passion that fuels my very soul? And there are so few chances in this world to experience a murder in real life. You know this. And you know how I feel. And yet you continue to encounter bodies and leave me out of it."

I started laughing. I couldn't help it. "So you handcuffed us together?"

"Yes. You attract bodies. I'm going to be around the next time you find one."

"It could be days. Months. Years," I pointed out.

"It'll be hours. I have a good feeling about this day."

"Hours?" Well, that was something to look forward to. "I'm not staying handcuffed to you for hours." I reached for my lock picks, and found my back pocket empty. Crud. Where were they? I suddenly remembered leaving them on the console of the truck. Shoot. "Uncuff me, Beau."

"No."

"I promise to keep you in the loop."

"I don't trust you. Your mother trained you to lie to people like me to get what you want."

"This is true." I knew he had a crush on my mom, so I took that as a compliment. "But that doesn't mean you can handcuff me—"

"Obviously it does."

I started laughing again. "You're such a weird man."

He grinned at me. "Thank you. I appreciate the compliment. Now, where are we off to?"

"Setting up Rogue's table for the Biscuit Bake-off."

He cocked his head. "Interesting. I wouldn't have expected a body there, but let's do it." He gestured with his free hand. "After you."

"*With* me, obviously, since we're attached." I started off toward the booth, mostly because I didn't have time to argue with him. "If you don't uncuff me, I'll never introduce you to my mother."

"You already promised you would," he said breezily. "We have a deal."

I looked over at Vinnie. "You let this happen?"

"Want me to shoot if off? I can do that." Vinnie started reaching under his jacket.

"No! God, no! Don't shoot in the middle of crowds!"

"Later?"

"Sure." I felt like that would be good payback for Beau handcuffing me, although I had to admit that I respected it greatly. It was a nice move.

"So, what have you found out?" Beau asked as he strode along beside me. "Who killed them?"

"I don't know. I thought it was Topsy, but clearly, that's not the case." I filled him in about the bake-off theory and the diamonds.

When I finished, he was looking thoughtful. "Fascinating."

"Any suggestions?"

"Many, but I won't share them. I'm observer status only." He smiled past me. "Good afternoon, Hattie. The biscuits look fantastic."

Her eyes widened when she saw the handcuffs. "Honestly, Mia. He's about eighty years old, and you couldn't keep your wrist out of his reach?"

"I'm not eighty, you mangy beast," Beau said easily.

King Tut was sitting on a pile of blankets, surveying the crowd while his tail flicked slowly. He was like a predator searching for his next meal. Human? Rodent? Fish? Who knew what he would choose.

"Beast, yes. Mangy? Never." Hattie tossed me a tablecloth, and my quick reaction to catch it nearly broke my wrist from the handcuffs. "Geez, Beau. You gotta be faster than that if you're going to be attached to me."

To my great joy, he was also rubbing his wrist. "This seemed like a good idea at the time."

I glanced at Hattie, and she nodded. "Mia, get to work."

I wrapped a towel around my wrist to protect my fragile skin from the handcuff, then I got to work. I moved fast, dragging Beau all over the booth while Vinnie stood guard, looking dangerous, which was fine with me. There were too many people around to track, so deterring an attack was better than dealing with one. Lucy was already there, and she helped me spread the tablecloth while Hattie directed us.

While we got the table beautified, I listened to and watched the crowds. No one was talking about Dee and Topsy, so I was guessing the news hadn't gotten out yet. Across the aisle, the same woman from yesterday was setting up Dee's table, which I thought was interesting. Clearly, she didn't know Dee was dead, right? Since Dee couldn't win the contest if she wasn't at the finals, there was no point in setting it up if she knew Dee was dead."

I nudged Lucy. "Who's the woman at Dee's table? She was doing the strawberries yesterday with some guy."

She looked over and frowned. "I don't know. Hattie?"

Hattie set a tray of champagne glasses on the red velvet table covering. "What?"

I lowered my voice as Beau leaned in. "Who is the woman setting up Dee's table?"

Hattie peered across the aisle, frowning. "She's a Dutch. I can't remember her name or which family she belongs to. But I've definitely seen her around."

I considered that. "She must have known Dee was coming to town, since she's doing her table. So, maybe she was close to Dee."

"Festival is on!" Bootsy came running up. "I was listening at the tent flaps, and the festival is on! Judges are on their way!"

"I knew it!" Hattie clapped her hands. "Let's get ready, ladies."

Bootsy grabbed a silver platter and began arranging delicious-looking brownies on it. "They decided not to make any announcements about Dee and Topsy. Just business as usual, since most folks don't know yet. Ronald said their job was to run the festival for the benefit of the town, and it was up to the mayor to deal with the situation with Dee and Topsy. She decided to keep it under wraps for as long as possible and put a gag order on Devlin and Chief Stone."

"See? Ronald's a food professional." Hattie sounded pleased. "Let's get this going."

I frowned as I helped put the table together, thinking about the fact that Dee had been related to Ronald, and yet he'd still wanted to go on with the contest. "How close were Dee and Ronald?"

"Oh, he had nothing to do with her," Hattie said. "She was

trouble, and Ronald was focused on trying to turn things around for his brother. He spent his life trying to help his brother get on the right track. I think it was a relief for him when his brother died. It freed him up to start living."

"Ronald was the good twin," Lucy agreed. "Everyone knew it."

I thought about that. "When did Ronald's twin die? You said April?"

They both nodded.

"And Dee came back a couple months later?"

They both stopped to look at me. "You think Ronald's twin is the one who killed Tony," Hattie asked. "That *he* was the one Dee was hiding from all this time?"

"The timing's right. What was the twin's name?"

"Richard. Ronnie and Richie Dutch. I could see it. Richie was trouble. They were identical, but you always knew who was who because Richie was always mean, and Ronnie was always kind. You can't hide that kind of mean. You could see it on Richie's face the minute he walked into a room. Plus, Richie had a tattoo of the devil on his left wrist. If you saw that, you knew you were in trouble. It was small, so you had to be close to see it, which was never good."

Huh. "So, Richie was the kind of guy who might shoot a jeweler?"

Hattie rubbed her jaw. "Absolutely."

"Well, interesting." I set the champagne down. "I'm going to go talk to the woman at Dee's table. I'll be back. Come on, Beau." The cranky mystery writer hated to be social, but he didn't have much choice, did he?

He grumped but followed me along as I hurried across the aisle to Dee's table. "Excuse me," I said. "Hello?"

The woman looked up, and habit made me do a quick assessment. Mid to late twenties. Fit. Clever. Clothes were simple, but expensive. Athleisure brands at their best. Her eyes were dark brown, her hair in a ponytail. She looked like she fit Bass Derby...

and also didn't. "We're a little busy," she said. "The judges will be here soon."

She was close to my age, and she looked a little flustered with the table prep. I knew exactly how to win her over.

I nodded to Beau. "Do you know Beau Hammersley? Famous mystery writer?"

Her gaze flicked to Beau, and her eyes widened. "Yeah. I've never met him. He never leaves his house."

"That's a patent lie," Beau said. "I go to breakfast every day."

"Where?"

Beau didn't answer, and I grinned as I held up our wrists. "He's my grandma's friend, and he thought it would be a great idea to handcuff us together for research for his new book. But he doesn't have a key." I made a little circle in the air by my temple to indicate that he was crazy. "Do you guys have a paperclip or something I can use to open these?"

She looked at the handcuffs, and then started laughing. "That's priceless. He handcuffed you and lost the key?"

"Yeah. Old, rich men, right?"

"Totally."

Beau looked even more cranky. "You two are why I don't like people."

"I'd love to help," she said, "but I don't have anything, and I'm swamped here, trying to get this together."

I beamed at her. "Can I help? It would be fun to drag Beau around your booth while I assisted you."

She glanced at Beau, and then grinned. "Yeah, sure, that would be great. My name's Leslie Dutch. If you can get the tablecloth out of that box over there and spread it out."

"You bet. My name's Jessie. Great to meet you!" I'd seen the display yesterday, so I knew the look she was going for. I immediately grabbed the red and white checked tablecloth and spread it out. "I'm just visiting Gram," I said cheerfully, careful not to mention names or give her the chance to ask who I was related to.

"I've never been to the festival before. Seems cool. Are you a baker?"

She laughed. "Heck, no. My aunt is, and I'm helping her, but she didn't show up yesterday." She glanced down the aisle again, apparently looking for Dee. "Honestly, I'm thinking she left town again," she whispered. "I don't think she had any intention of running this table, but I owe her."

Oh…juicy! "Why would she call in a debt for you to run her table if she didn't plan to show?"

Leslie shrugged. "I don't know. She's a little crazy. One of my uncles actually asked me to help her out. I hadn't met her before."

I put out fake lanterns and turned on the switches so they started flickering. "You have multiple uncles in town? How big is your family?"

She rolled her eyes. "Huge. We own like half the town. Honestly, you can't go anywhere without running into someone who will report back to your mom or dad or whoever. I'm saving money to move to Boston. I need to get away."

I got that. "I did the same thing," I said. "I ditched my mom when I was seventeen."

Leslie glanced over at me. "Did you miss her when you left?"

Ah…now I knew why she was still there. Because family was family, no matter how much it drove you crazy. "Every minute of every day, but I'm glad I did it."

She nodded. "Okay." She flashed a smile. "Thanks."

"You got it." I glanced down the aisle. "Judges are coming."

Leslie let out a yelp. "We're not ready!"

"Where are the biscuits? Get them out and I'll set up the rest." As I dragged grumbling Beau around the booth, setting stuff up, I watched Ronald and his team work his way along the aisle, and recalled that he was probably the one who had advocated to allow Dee into the contest. "Do you know the judges?" I asked.

She nodded. "The head judge is my uncle."

"The one who asked you to help out your aunt?"

"Yeah."

Oh, goody! Info was coming in fast and furious now. "Did you ask him where your aunt is?"

"Of course. He said it didn't matter if she showed up. We didn't need her. She'd already baked her biscuits, so I just defrosted them and warmed them before I came here."

Didn't matter? "Doesn't she have to be present to win?"

"Apparently not." Leslie set the biscuits out, quickly arranging them on an old wooden platter that looked like it was the cross section of a tree. "You can have family members rep you if you can't attend, as long as it's their prep. She has prepped everything, and it was verified that she did it, so I can just put it together."

Who verified? I needed to find that out. I set the plates on the table and arranged the napkins in a little spiral. "You can even represent her in the finals?"

"Oh, God. I hope she shows up by then. I don't want that pressure. But yes, apparently." She stepped back. "Okay, wow. We got it done." She hugged me. "Thank you! You're amazing!"

"You bet."

At that moment, Ronald and his little crew walked up to the table.

CHAPTER 16

I WANTED to stay and listen to the uncle/niece subtext, but Hattie gestured me frantically over to her table, so I gave Leslie a high five and dashed across the aisle, dragging Beau with me. "What's up?" I asked, as I gave my kitty a little head scratch.

He was being such a good boy. He hadn't wandered around, and he hadn't attacked anyone. Good kitty.

"Fill the champagne glasses," she ordered. "Fast!"

I grabbed the champagne and start pouring, but Beau's hand knocked a glass and champagne poured across the table.

"The biscuits!" Lucy lunged for the biscuits and yanked them off the table as the champagne oozed toward them.

"Beau!" Hattie whipped a strawberry at him. "Are you kidding? Did you kill Dee? Are you behind it all? Trying to sabotage Rogue?"

He looked slightly alarmed by Hattie's outburst. "Sorry! I didn't mean to—"

"We don't have time for an apology!" I grabbed for a towel, and yanked Beau with me. He lost his balance, and his head hit the corner of the table, and everything rattled.

"For hell's sake," he muttered. "Being handcuffed to you is like being strapped to a deranged five-year-old!" He dug into his pocket and pulled out a little key.

"You had the key all this time?" What a devious little monster! I was so impressed. I'd totally believed him that he didn't have it.

"Of course I had the key!" He stuck it in the lock, but then Lucy bumped him. The key went flying, landed in the grass, and bounced under the tablecloth.

"Crud!" I dove for it and yanked the tablecloth up to look underneath, and then froze. Staring at me from the shadowy underbelly of the table was none other than my missing body-guard. His eyes were open, and he was staring blankly.

"Hurry up, Mia," Hattie said. "We're next!"

I yanked on the handcuff and Beau fell to his knees beside me. "Look."

He gasped. "What the fruitcake! That is fantastic!"

"What?" Hattie bent down, then cursed. She dropped the table-cloth over Ivan and grabbed my arm. "The judges are almost here. We'll deal with it after!"

"Even better!" Beau looked thrilled. "What a brilliant response! Prioritizing biscuits over bodies. I love that! I need to write this down!" He grabbed the key and uncuffed us like a man who knew his way around cuffs, and then whipped out a little notebook.

"Hattie—" I started.

She held up a hand. "Talk to the hand. Don't you dare screw this up for Rogue. You only have to wait three minutes for the judging to finish!" At that moment, the judges walked up to the table.

"Good afternoon, Hattie," Ronald said. "Esther still not with us today?"

Hattie effused charm as she welcomed the judges, and I stood there stunned, my mind whirling. My missing, badass bodyguard was *under the table*. Clearly dead. Or stoned out of his mind, but I was pretty sure it was dead.

My bodyguard. Murdered. *Holy crap.*

Lucy elbowed me. "What's going on?" she whispered.

I toed the edge of the tablecloth up so she could see.

She smacked my arm. "Shut the front door! He's been under the table this whole time?"

Hattie did a reverse kick into Lucy's shin, and she yelped.

"Who was that?" Vinnie leaned over my shoulder. "Is he dead? He looks dead. Another baker? This is incredible. You're like a magnet for death."

"I'm not a magnet for death," I whispered. "It's my missing bodyguard."

He stared at me. "No kidding."

"Yeah."

"Was he good?"

"Not that good, obviously."

Vinnie looked very alarmed, and retreated to the corner of the booth, looking around the crowd with a much less confident swagger.

I also felt somewhat less confident. I'd been sort of pretending that Ivan had run off with some sexy lumberjack and was making happy times in a log cabin on the shores of Diamond Lake.

Seeing him dead made it very difficult to continue with that illusion.

"What are you going to do?" Lucy whispered. "Devlin and Griselda will lock you up if they know Ivan's been murdered—"

Hattie kicked Lucy again, and she yelped. "We need to get out of range of that monster," she said, backing up.

Beau dropped to his knees, crawled across the grass, and stuck his entire upper body under the table with Ivan. A beam of light showed under the edge of the tablecloth, and I heard him muttering to himself. So did Hattie, apparently, because she kicked at him through the tablecloth, while continuing to charm the judges and hand out biscuits.

Beau didn't yelp in pain, but Ivan's pasty hand flopped out from under the tablecloth onto the grass.

Lucy gripped my wrist and I saw Vinnie look over.

Beau reached out, grabbed Ivan's appendage, and pulled the lifeless hand back under the table and out of sight.

It slid back out almost immediately, thudding onto the grass.

I almost started laughing, and Lucy covered her mouth.

Beau's hand shot out again, and he yanked Ivan's hand back out of sight again more aggressively.

Lucy put her hand on my shoulder. "I can't believe Beau crawled under the table with a corpse," she whispered. "He's crazy, isn't he?"

"It must be a mystery writer thing," I whispered back. "I don't think he's actually crazy."

Hattie's cheerful voice grew louder, and she flipped us the bird behind her back.

"I think we're being too loud," Lucy said, covering her mouth. "What the heck, Mia. I mean it. What is happening right now? Ivan's under the table—"

She stopped as we watched Ivan's leg slide out from under the table. "His shoes are very polished," I commented. "He looks like a fed."

"No one would ever mistake him for a local." Ivan's leg was pulled back under the tablecloth, and a light flashed under the table. "Beau's taking flash photos," I whispered. "Someone's going to see that!"

"Hattie will kill him!" Lucy grabbed a tray and set a few glasses on it. "I have more glasses, Hattie!" She trotted over to the table, then fake-tripped extremely awkwardly, and fake-crashed down to the ground. She immediately stuck her head under the tablecloth, and I heard her low voice talking to Beau.

It took about a second before she scrambled back, moving almost in a panic. "Dear God, that was terrible." She looked pale. "I forgot there was a corpse under there—"

"Corpse? Did you just say *corpse?*"

We both jumped and turned around to find Devlin standing behind us. He looked unhelpfully attractive in his jeans, which I took umbrage with. "Why aren't you at Topsy's?" I demanded. "Don't you have bodies to inspect?"

"Chief Stone decided he wanted to take over." Devlin didn't look happy about it. "Did I just hear you say corpse?"

I glanced at the table and saw Hattie was still wooing the judges. "Did you find out how long Dee had been dead?" I asked, instead of giving Devlin a reason to hurl himself under the table and mess up Rogue's judging...

Hmm...putting a body under Rogue's table would definitely have a high likelihood of messing up her judging. My first instinct had been that Ivan's apparent demise had been a direct result of my inauspicious marriage choices, but what if even that had to do with the diamonds or the bake off?

"Did I just hear you say corpse?" Devlin asked again.

The man was much too persistent. "I say corpse a lot. They tend to follow me around. What did you learn about Dee?"

His gaze went past me, and I noticed the light flashing under the table again. "What's under the table?"

"Beau," I said.

"What's he doing?"

"Research for a book."

He looked at me as Lucy edged away. "What kind of research?"

I put my hands on my hips. "When did Dee die?"

"What kind of research?"

"Why won't you answer me?"

"Because it's an active murder investigation. Why won't you answer me about what Beau is doing?"

I saw the judges shake Hattie's hand and move toward the Yacht Club table. I smiled at Devlin. "It's actually really convenient that you're here. I was just going to text you."

He stared at me, and I watched his jaw tighten. "Why?"

"Maybe to tell you that I adore you and have been fantasizing about our upcoming date." The judges were shaking Zoltan's hand now. Was it safe to unleash The Devlin onto our table?

His brows shot up. "Even if that was true, there isn't a chance you'd text that to me. Why were you going to text me?"

Hattie gave me the thumbs up, and I relaxed. I had the green light. "We have a situation."

He regarded me. Waiting.

"Beau handcuffed us together, and then dropped the key."

To his credit, he didn't even blink at the idea of an old mystery writer handcuffing himself to me. "You didn't pick the lock?"

"Not the point, Devlin. Try to keep up."

A smile quirked the corner of his mouth. "All right. Keep going."

"The key bounced under the tablecloth." This was fun. I could see the tension mounting on Devlin's face. "So I pulled the table-cloth aside to look for the key."

His gaze went back to the table, where Beau's flipflop was sticking out. "What did you find?"

"Ivan."

Devlin's gaze snapped back to me. He unleashed a string of profanities, and practically launched himself across the grass. He bent over and yanked the tablecloth up. Beau was kneeling astride Ivan, taking a photo of his face, definitely messing up the crime scene.

I'd never seen Devlin move so fast. He grabbed Beau by the arm, hauled him out from under the table, and hurled him aside. He then leaned in and pressed his fingers to Ivan's neck, looking for a pulse, even as he pulled out his phone. He dialed with one hand and spoke in low urgent tones into the phone.

Hattie retreated back to stand beside me. She gave me a fist bump. "We got through the judging," she whispered. "They loved the biscuits. Nice work."

"Holy cow!" Beau bounced to his feet, apparently unaffected by his assisted flight across the grass. "That was insanity. I can't believe what just happened. His skin felt so interesting. Never felt that before. And looking into his eyes? No life. No life at all. It's the weirdest thing how you just know that the spirit is gone. I can

134

describe it now in a way I never could before. This is brilliant. Brilliant!" He threw his arms around me, his eyes glowing. "I'm so glad you moved to town, Mia! This is freaking incredible." He whirled around and crouched down in the grass, taking pictures as Devlin leaned over the body.

Devlin looked over. "Mia," he said quietly, his voice like steel. "Get Beau out of here. Now. All of you, keep everyone away from the booth until I get reinforcements. Now!"

Oh…he was pissed.

I grabbed Beau and dragged him back. "Enough," I said. "You gotta back off."

Beau seemed to realize that he'd crossed lines, so he quickly stood up and backed to the corner of the booth. But he was still watching intently. Around us, the festival was still going on as usual. No one had noticed the activity in our little space.

"And Vinnie," Devlin shouted. "Vinnie!"

Vinnie had been hovering at the edge of the scene, but he snapped to attention when Devlin shouted his name. "Yes, sir?"

"Do *not* let Mia out of your sight. No matter what. Got it?"

Vinnie glanced at me, and I saw the moment he made the choice to step up instead of being scared. "Yeah," he said, his voice lower. "Yeah, I got it."

Devlin then looked at me. "Mia. Do not screw around right now. Understand?"

At that moment, my phone rang. I looked down and saw it was Griselda. So that was who Devlin had called. I answered it. "Hi."

"Get Vinnie to take you to the police station. I'm sending someone to get you. You don't have the choice of whether to leave town. It's out of your hands. I'm on a plane. I'll be there in a few hours, but do not test me on this. Go to the police station and stay there. Say you understand. That's it. That's all I want to hear. *I understand.*"

Oh…he knew I didn't do well with orders. He must really be freaked out to try to boss me around like that. Did he have the ability to cart me away against my will? He might not have the right, but he definitely had the ability. *Crap.* "Look, Griselda—"

Hattie snapped her fingers to get my attention, and she shook her head at me. Then she pointed at my phone and nodded emphatically. "Say okay," she whispered. "Just do it."

Hattie was right. If I said no, Griselda would probably make Devlin take me himself. Or Chief Stone. "Okay," I said sweetly. "Whatever you think is best, Agent Straus."

"Don't sass me, Mia. I'm not in the mood. Just say you got it."

"I did just say that."

He paused, clearly trying to decide whether to believe me. "You're going to the police station?"

"Yes."

"Good. Watch your back." He hung up the phone without sending his love, and I looked at Hattie and Lucy. They both nodded.

I nodded back, then turned to Devlin. "Griselda said that Vinnie has to take me straight to the police station to hide out until he can rip me from my life and throw me in a hellhole in the name of justice."

Devlin swore under his breath. "Ivan is highly trained, and he has a knife in his back. You're not safe. I agree with Griselda. I mean Hawk."

"Okay, then," I said brightly. "Well, I'll just be off then. I guess our date is cancelled, then, right? Since I'll be on my way to some undisclosed location where they can suck the life from my very soul, and everything fun like that."

He narrowed his eyes. "Go to the police station. Death isn't a joke."

"Of course it's not." I looked at Vinnie. "To the police station we go?"

He nodded. "Yeah."

"Okay." I looked at Beau. "Find out as much as you can," I whispered. "Keep in touch."

He raised his brows. "Try not to die."

"I'll do my best."

"Mia!" Devlin snapped.

"Got it." I looked at Vinnie. "Let's go." I scooped up my sweet kitty cat, who had been sniffing around Ivan with a little bit too much interest, and off we went.

Vinnie stayed less than an inch behind me, off my left shoulder, while Hattie and Lucy flanked me. We moved fast, all of us aware that Ivan had indeed been murdered, and the crowds were dense and fluid. I got bumped a few times, and panic shot through me, but we kept moving fast and no one plunged a knife between my shoulder blades.

We reached the parking lot. "The Lamborghini," Hattie said. "We can outrun anyone in that. And your truck is too obvious."

A Lamborghini was more of an attention-getter than an old pickup truck, but I got her drift. "Good call." As a little pack, we hurried across the dirt parking lot, all of us tense, looking around, and hoping not to see an assassin hurtling through the crowd with a knife and a steely visage. Vinnie had his hand under his jacket the whole time, ready to pull out his gun. I stopped by my truck to grab my lock picks, then we hustled to the Lamborghini. Hattie got in the driver's seat, Lucy took shotgun, and Vinnie shoved me in the backseat and got in beside me.

None of us said anything as Hattie hit the gas and raced to the exit. She paused. "Which way?"

I knew what she was asking.

Left would take us to the police station.

I took a breath. Did I want to die? No. Did I want to submit to the feds? No chance. I didn't have a choice. I was who I was. I had to follow my path. "Go right."

Hattie didn't pull out. Instead, she looked at me in the rearview mirror. "You sure about this? Ivan's attack feels personal. A message to you. Someone got to him, Mia. They got to him when his job was to protect you."

"I know." I looked at Vinnie. "You up for this?" I couldn't risk him if he didn't consent. I wouldn't do it.

But he didn't hesitate. "Heck, yeah. Turn right."

I grinned. "Lucy?"

"I'm up for a right turn. I don't want you abducted by the feds."

"Hattie?"

She grinned at me. "Right it is." She let out a whoop, hit the blinker for a right turn, and then pulled out.

We were committed.

CHAPTER 17

"WHERE TO?" Hattie asked. "We need to regroup and come up with a plan, and I find it difficult to think when I'm looking over my shoulder for an assassin or a federal agent."

"Agreed," Lucy said. "We could go to my house."

"Too obvious." I bounced my feet restlessly while I thought. King Tut was on my lap, gazing out the window, kneading my thighs with delight.

"We can go to my place," Vinnie said. "No one would look for you there."

"Oh…that's a great idea," Hattie said.

"That would give us time," Lucy agreed.

"No." I checked behind us, but no cars were in sight. "The pressure is on right now. Ivan has been found. The cops and the feds are on his case, and Chief Stone is on the Dee and Topsy situation. The finals are tomorrow. If we go to Vinnie's, we give the murderers breathing room. They need to move now. Today. Tonight. Their time is almost out."

"Breathing room is bad," Hattie said slowly. "I agree. What do you suggest? Your marina? Put us right in the middle where they can find us?"

"Oh, Lordy," Lucy muttered.

"Yes, but not yet." I was already thinking of plans, of a net to cast, of illusions to cast, but it was too early to put the marina into play.

Lucy twisted around in her seat to look at me. "Oh...you have a plan. That makes me nervous."

Hattie grinned. "Where to, Mia?"

I took a breath. "Rogue's house."

"Where it all began. I love it," Hattie said approvingly.

Lucy frowned. "The cops will probably go back there now that Dee was found dead at Topsy's. And we don't know that the bad guys found what they were looking for when they tossed her place."

"It started at Rogue's house," I said. "We still don't know how Rogue fits into all this. It's time to find out. That's where tonight starts."

"But not where it ends?" Lucy said.

I leaned back in my seat. "Nope."

Vinnie grinned. "Will we need back up?"

I raised my brows. "We might. You have friends."

"I have friends."

"Call them."

He nodded and picked up his phone while Hattie turned onto the road that would circle us back toward Rogue's.

King Tut sat on my lap while I texted the Keep Mia Alive chat, which consisted of me, Griselda, and Devlin. *Hey, puppy dogs. Change of plans. Not going to the police station. Just wanted you not to freak out when I don't show up there. Have a sunshiny day. Smooches.*

I sent it, then started counting. I made it only to two and a half before Griselda called me.

I put it into voicemail and turned off my phone. I wasn't sure if the FBI could track me by my phone, but I wasn't taking the chance. But cutting off their ability to find me also meant they couldn't swoop in and save me.

A choice between bad and worse.

I took the worse. Or the bad. Or whatever it was I was choosing.

———

To keep the element of surprise on our side, we didn't take the driveway to Rogue's.

Hattie circled around behind the property, then drove straight off the road into the woods. She wove her way through the trees, literally snapping down small trees and bushes. Lucy braced her hand on the dashboard, Vinnie kept looking behind us, and Hattie hooted with delight each time another sapling gave way to the power of the Lamborghini SUV.

She pulled up behind the house, beside a thick cluster of blackberry bushes. "They can't see the car from the house," she said. "And I can pull forward and swing out toward the driveway or back through the woods. However we need to get out."

"I love you, Hattie," I said.

"Thanks. I love me, too. What's the plan?"

"Sneak through the back door," I said. "If anyone's in there, we surprise them."

I decided to leave King Tut in the car, because I wanted to be able to make a run for it without having to look for him. I clipped him to the seatbelt with a thin metal cable coated in rubber that was supposed to be chew proof and then got out.

We huddled at the edge of the blackberry bushes, watching the house for movement. We could see the driveway from where we were, and there were no cars in it.

"I think it's safe," Hattie whispered.

"Me, too." I paused. "I'll go first. If someone comes after me, there's no need for all of us to go down. You guys go for help. Or drive over them. Whichever seems to be the better option."

"Love that plan for us," Hattie said.

"Give us the sign when it's clear," Lucy said. "I wish we had weapons."

"I'm sure Rogue has a hairdryer," I said. "We'll load up when we get inside."

"I'm sure she has guns," Hattie said. "This is Maine. Everyone has guns."

"I have extra guns," Vinnie said. "You guys want one?"

Hattie and Lucy's faces lit up. "Oh. Yes, that would be great—"

"No!" Good heavens. "You guys don't get to make choices that could land you in prison for murder. No shooting!"

"I can make that choice, though?" Vinnie said.

"Yes, because you're hired to keep me alive. Defense of others, right?"

"Right. But just so you know, I'm not going to actually kill someone to save you," he said. "Juries are unpredictable."

I put my hands on my hips. "How are you going to protect me?"

"I'll scare them. I'll shoot at the area around them, making sure not to hit them. It'll be enough." He grinned. "I can look very deadly when I want to."

Hattie stared at him. "Wow. I have no words."

"Right?" He grinned. "It's a great plan."

"Yeah. Great." I felt so safe now. Vinnie was going to keep me safe from the people who murdered a trained FBI bodyguard by looking scary. "Let's go then." I shot Hattie a look, and she gave me a thumbs up.

Lucy looked worried. "The only reason I'm letting you go is because no one would think you'd be stupid enough to come back here, so I don't think your assassin is going to be coming after you."

"And if it's a local murderer, that's well within your skillset," Hattie added. "Go, team, go!"

"Right." I took another moment to inspect the grounds and the house, but I didn't see any sign of activity. So, I stepped out of the bushes and took off across the gorgeous, manicured lawn. I ran hard and made it to the back door without bullets kicking up dirt around my ankles.

Vinnie had kept up easily, though I was proud to note I wasn't breathing that hard. The workouts I'd been doing since I'd moved to town were starting to help.

I peeked in a few windows, but the house was still. The stuff was still on the floor like the last time we'd been there. No one had been in to pick it up, which probably meant Rogue hadn't been back. She would have cleaned up her house. "Okay. Going in."

I hurried over to the back door and crouched down while Vinnie stood guard. I picked the lock quickly and the door opened. I leaned in, listening, but the house was quiet. I gestured to Hattie and Lucy, then stepped inside.

While they crossed the lawn, I took a walk through the first floor, looking carefully around. Pictures were on the floor. Gorgeous crystals bowls had been tossed on the couch. Pillows were strewn about. Tables on their sides, their tabletop contents spread across the floor.

Hattie appeared in the doorway. "Watch for broken glass," she said. "In case the pictures broke."

I looked down, and suddenly realized that not a single one was broken. The crystal bowls were on the couch. Everything breakable had somehow made it to the floor intact. "Holy crap, guys. This search was done by someone who didn't want to break anything."

"Rogue?" Lucy appeared beside Hattie. "You think Rogue trashed the place?"

"Maybe." I crouched down. "Or else whoever did this wanted it to look like Rogue did it." I pointed to an end table on its side. "If the table was tipped with the books still on it, the books wouldn't still be in a stack. They would have slid. Everything was set up carefully." I rested my forearm on my knee and looked around, trying to put the pieces together.

"You know," Hattie said. "Rogue has plenty of money. She would be fine with breaking her crystal to advance her agenda. I bet you're right that this is someone who wanted to set up Rogue, but didn't know Rogue well enough to do it right."

I stood up, clasped my hands behind my back, and began to wade through the carnage, looking for whatever it was I needed to see. "Rogue was at Topsy's," I began, trying out facts to figure out how they came together.

"Was she really?" Hattie toed a picture aside. "You said she was driving a pickup truck."

"She was."

"I told you, Rogue would never drive a pickup truck."

"If she was trying to hide—"

"I know cars, and I know women who like cars. We have standards. Rogue would have borrowed a Hummer or an Escalade at the minimum. Maybe a Maserati. But there's no chance she would drive a pickup. She just wouldn't. It wasn't her."

I stared at Hattie. "I saw her."

"You saw someone who looked like her. But I assure you, it wasn't Rogue."

I thought about that. Hattie was correct in that all people had consistencies that you could count on. It was a matter of figuring out what those consistencies were so you could take advantage. I didn't know Rogue well enough to know about the pickup truck thing, but Hattie knew her. "You're sure?"

"Absolutely. I'd say that I'd stake my life on it, but I'd never offer my life to save anyone else, but that's how sure I am."

I rubbed my jaw while I replayed that brief sighting in my head. I had assumed it was Rogue. Was that because I'd been looking for her, or because someone had intentionally tried to make me think it was Rogue? What had made me think it was Rogue? "She had Rogue's hair. Her face looked like Rogue. But she had sunglasses on so I couldn't see her clearly. She was small, like Rogue."

Upon revisiting my memories, I still thought it was Rogue. She'd looked like Rogue. I wasn't a fool. I knew what I'd seen. But if Hattie was right…was Hattie right? I didn't know.

"I'm going to go check upstairs," Hattie said.

"Get me a hairdryer while you're up there."

While Hattie wandered off, I rubbed my jaw. "Lucy, do you think Hattie's right that Rogue wouldn't drive a truck?"

"Hattie knows cars for sure," Lucy said, "but she's also very stubborn. Just because she wouldn't drive certain cars to save her own life doesn't mean Rogue is the same."

I had to decide whether to believe Hattie's theory or my own eyes. I had absolute faith in Hattie. She was smart, worldly, and streetwise. But I also had absolute faith in myself. *Crap.* "We just seem to keep coming up with more questions than answers," I said.

"More bodies, too," Lucy said.

"Diamonds," Vinnie said from the couch, where he'd decided to park it. To my surprise, King Tut was sitting on his lap purring, clearly having defeated the chew-proof cable. "If diamonds are involved, it's about the diamonds. It's always about whatever has the highest stakes. Always. If there are two cars to steal, I'll take the better one."

"What if the cheaper one has the keys in it, and the nicer one doesn't?"

He looked at me. "It depends. Easy is better than impossible," he acknowledged. "But sometimes the thing that's easy is a waste of time, and the thing that's difficult is worth the effort. Like if diamonds are at play, this whole thing is about the diamonds."

"The whole thing? What about Ivan?"

"Cash and drugs are good too," Vinnie said. "I'd kill for that." He paused. "If I were a killer. Which I'm not."

Diamonds.

I walked across the living room. "Let's assume it's about diamonds. Let's assume even Ivan's death is about diamonds."

"We need a murder board," Lucy said. "Those always help. Let's use the extra shop at your marina for our murder board next time."

"Next time?"

She raised her brows. "No? You want to do it this time?"

"No, I meant, why would there be a next time?"

"Because you attract murder. It's your thing. I'm adjusting to it, though, so it's okay." She sat down on the couch opposite Vinnie. "Does Rogue have an office? Maybe she has a whiteboard in there."

"I don't know." I paced across the room. "Assuming for the moment that Ivan is involved with the diamonds, then the easiest possibility is that he stumbled across something having to do with this diamond thing, so they took him out."

"Oh...I like that so much more than the idea that an assassin targeted your bodyguard," Lucy said.

"Me, too," Vinnie agreed. "Let's go with that."

"All right." Because honestly, if Ivan had been murdered by an assassin, then that was really Griselda's situation to solve.

Lucy raised her hand. "I really don't think you can discount the theory that it's about the festival. Ivan was literally found under Rogue's table, and three contestants are dead or missing."

"No one would murder over shortcake," Vinnie said. "It's the diamonds."

"Who cares about diamonds?" Lucy retorted. "They're just sparkly rocks. This town cares about the festival. The trophy will get named after the first five-time winner, and they get to keep the trophy. That matters to the people in this town."

I watched Vinnie and Lucy argue about diamonds versus shortcake. We had to pick a path and start down it, but time was running out. "I have an idea," I said.

They both looked at me.

I paced across the room. "What if we start two rumors going," I said. "This is a small town. We can do that, right?"

"Absolutely," Lucy said. "What rumors?"

"First rumor is that Rogue and Hattie will be baking Rogue's biscuits at the café tonight for the finals tomorrow, and they'll be using Hattie's recipe."

Lucy's eyes widened. "Everyone will know that Rogue will win the contest if she's baking with Hattie."

"Yep. So if someone doesn't want her to win, they'll have to come stop them tonight."

"What's the second rumor?" Vinnie asked. "I hope it's about the diamonds."

"Yep. We'll start the rumor that we found the diamonds and they're in the safe at the marina."

Vinnie rubbed his jaw. "That'll attract anyone who wants diamonds. Not only the murderer."

It was always good to have a criminal's point of view. "Well, what if we say that we found what Dee was looking for that night twenty years ago. For people who know, they'll know."

"Oh… I like that." Vinnie nodded approvingly. "That works."

"Then we just wait there?" Lucy asked. "We invite all the possible people who might want to murder us or those we care about, then we wait at the marina for them to come try to kill us?"

"Yep. We see who shows up."

Lucy sat back. "That sounds like a stupid plan."

"Do you have a better one?"

"Maybe if we set up a row of guns and knives in the parking lot, free for the taking, and then tie ourselves to your railing. That might work better."

I grinned. "You have such little faith in my creativity."

"I've seen a lot of corpses lately. It makes me realize how easy it is to get killed in real life."

"Not that easy, actually," I said. "We're all still here, right?"

"What about your friend Rogue?" Vinnie asked. "How does that help you figure out what's up with her?"

"All we need is to get to the tipping point," I said. "To get that clue that starts to put everything into place. It won't be much. We just need that one thing. So, for the sake of efficiency, we'll bring all of it together."

"Are you going to add the rumor that you do indeed have the

cash and drugs from your ex?" Lucy asked with an admirable eye roll.

Fear slithered through me. "No," I said softly. "I'm actually scared of that person."

Her face softened. "Me, too," she said. "Griselda and Devlin are wrong that you don't respect the danger. You do, but you're not willing to give up living just because you're scared."

I nodded. "This is true." I heard a thump from upstairs and cocked my head to listen. "Hattie?"

There was no answer.

"Hattie!" I shouted.

No answer.

I looked at Vinnie and Lucy, and then we all took off for the stairs, King Tut on our heels.

CHAPTER 18

HATTIE WAS SPRAWLED on the floor of Rogue's bedroom, face down, not moving…the exact same position that Dee had been in when we'd found her in the pantry.

"Hattie!" I dropped to my knees beside her and felt for her pulse. "She's still alive!" I shouted.

"For heaven's sake," Hattie muttered. "You're so dramatic. Can you keep it down?"

Relief rushed through me. "You scared the daylights out of me!"

"Hattie!" Lucy knelt next to me, leaning over Hattie. "What happened?"

"I don't know." She sat up, rubbing the back of her head. "I was up here inspecting Rogue's jewels and then suddenly, I'm on the carpet, and you're yelling in my ear."

"That happened," Vinnie said, pointing.

Lucy and I both turned, and I saw that the closet door was open. "The closet hit her?"

"No. Look again."

I scrambled to my feet and walked over to the closet. I peeked inside and saw that there was a second door in the back of the closet. A door that was open, revealing what looked like an unfinished hallway. "Is that a secret passageway?" Holy cow. Leave it to Rogue to build a secret passageway into her house.

"Looks like it," Vinnie said. "I'm guessing Hattie walked in on someone who didn't want to get caught."

"And they ran through the passageway?"

"Yeah."

I looked at Hattie on the floor, rubbing her head. "They could have killed you, but they didn't," I observed. "That means they're not a murderer. Vinnie, let's catch up to them!" I turned my phone onto flashlight mode, then bolted into the hallway.

"Yeah!" Vinnie's heavier footsteps thudded behind me as we sprinted down the hall. We reached a set of steep stairs and I raced down them. Ahead of me, I could hear footsteps of someone running.

We were close!

I ran harder, and Vinnie stayed right behind me. "Vinnie! You're faster! Go get them!"

"Can't. My job's to keep you alive. Not leaving you."

I really appreciated that sentiment, but this was important. "We're the only ones in this hallway! Go!"

"It'll weigh on me for the rest of my life if I leave you here and you die. I love myself too much to torture myself that way. So, run faster if you want to catch them."

I shot him a glare over my shoulder. "You're sucking up to Devlin, aren't you?"

"He scares me."

"He's a puppy dog," I panted as I reached the bottom of the steps and sprinted down a long, narrow corridor.

"He's a freaking werewolf. You just don't see it because you have the hots for him." Vinnie wasn't panting like I was, but he was breathing harder than normal. "Werewolves eat people for sport. I'm not leaving you."

I thought about that as I leapt down three steps to a lower level. Devlin a werewolf? And why did I find that so interesting?

Vinnie suddenly grabbed my shoulder and hauled me to a stop. He held his index finger in front of his mouth to signal being quiet, then pointed ahead.

There was a heavy exterior door ahead, and it was closed.

He pulled out his gun, readied it, and then nodded. "Stay back after you open it," he said. "I'll go first,"

My heart suddenly started to pound, and I grabbed the door handle. It opened easily and I pushed it open. I raced out at the same moment as Vinnie. Ahead of us, a slim, fit gray-haired woman was running toward the same black pickup truck I'd seen before.

This time, I was sure who it was. "Rogue!" I shouted. "Rogue!"

She didn't look back. She leapt into the truck and hit the gas. The tires spun in the pine needles, and then the truck shot down the dirt road, around the corner, and out of sight.

I braced my hands on my thighs, trying to catch my breath. "That was Rogue," I said. "I'm sure of it."

"Why's she running from you?"

"I don't know. She freaking hit Hattie in the head. You don't hit old people in the head! Especially your friends! They could die!"

"Old? I'm not old. You're such a little thing of nastiness to call me old when I'm not around." Hattie hurried out of the passage-way. "I recant every nice thing I've said about you."

"It was Rogue," I said. "She was driving the truck again. I know it was her. She was fifteen feet away from me. I recognize her run."

Hattie's eyes widened. "She was driving a truck?"

"And she hit you," I said. "Hard enough to knock you out."

Lucy and King Tut came out of the corridor behind Hattie. Lucy was keeping a good distance behind him, and he was trotting happily, as if he'd really enjoyed scaring Lucy in a dark tunnel.

Hattie looked a little winded, and I caught her arm as she sat down on the ground. "There's only one reason I can think of for Rogue to attack me and drive a truck."

"What's that?"

Hattie looked up at us. "She's the murderer."

CHAPTER 19

I SANK down in the grass beside her, stunned. "You said you believed she wasn't the murderer. That she wouldn't do it."

"No," Hattie said. "I said that Rogue was fully capable of killing someone, and it wouldn't surprise me if she'd been an assassin in her prime. I said these murders weren't by her because she'd be better at it. But maybe I overestimated her. Maybe she's lost her edge and gone soft." She brightened. "I know! She's gone insane! That would explain her subpar performance and driving the truck. Clearly, she doesn't deserve prison, so we'll frame someone else for the crime and set her free. I think Chief Stone would be the best target, don't you?"

I raised my brows. "Really?"

Lucy put her hands on her hips. "That entire statement doesn't even deserve a response."

Hattie sighed and threw up her hands. "Okay, fine. You're right. It's rude to pin a murder on an innocent person, regardless of how unpleasant they are. But I don't believe Rogue deserves prison. If she did it, and it does look like she might have, then she had a great reason."

"Self-defense is the only acceptable reason to kill someone," Vinnie pointed out helpfully.

Hattie wrinkled her nose at him. "That's a very limited mindset," she said. "Growth mindset, Vinnie. Have a growth mindset. See archways instead of closed doors."

"We're lacking something critical for it to be Rogue." I leaned back on my hands and stretched my legs out.

"Competence?" Hattie asked.

"A video proving she did it?" Lucy suggested.

"Motive," I said. "What's her motive? Money? She doesn't need it. Success? She believes she's good enough to win the contest. Revenge? She could do it with money. I don't believe she has motive to kill anyone. But she apparently has motive to run, hide, and hit one of her best friends in the head, so there is that."

"She wants to keep Hattie safe," Lucy said as she sat down next to Hattie. "That's why she hit her. To keep her safe."

Hattie inclined her head. "I'd buy that. I'd hit either one of you in the head if it would keep you safe. Or for any other reason that might benefit you. Or me. However it shakes out."

"Rogue wants to keep Hattie safe from what?" Vinnie asked. He was still on his feet, his gun out, which I appreciated.

"Someone else attacking me?" Hattie suggested.

"Knowing something that will get you hurt," I guessed. "What if Rogue knows something that will get her killed, and she's trying to protect you and us from getting involved?"

"But we are involved," Hattie said.

"Apparently, there's more to know." I rubbed my jaw. "What does she know?" I mused. "What's she hiding that she can't share with us? That she would hurt you to keep you from knowing?'

Vinnie cleared his throat, and I looked over at him. "What?"

"Maybe she knows who did it, and she's trying to protect that person. She's helping someone else right now, someone she isn't supposed to help." He gestured to us. "What I see with the three of you is loyalty. You'd stand by each other no matter what. It's how I am with my boys. If Rogue's like you, she'd do the same."

I looked at Hattie, who was nodding. "Yes," Hattie said. "She would do that. That makes sense."

"Who would she protect?" I mused. "Friends. Family. Or maybe she's being forced because someone she loves is in danger. Maybe someone who has blackmailed her—" I bolted to my feet. "Holy cow. That's it. She's been coerced into this. It's like when I worked for the feds. That's why she's driving a truck. Because she's being forced to do it." Excitement rushed through me as Hattie scrambled to her feet.

"Yes!" she exclaimed. "That makes sense! She's not crazy! Thank God. I was getting worried. Because she's younger than I am, and if your friends start to lose it, then you start thinking you're next and—" She held up her hand. "Nope. Not going there."

"What would be enough influence to force Rogue to drive a truck?" I asked. "Someone she loves in danger?"

"A secret that she doesn't want to get out," Lucy mused. "Like a dark secret in her past."

"It would have to be really dark," Hattie said. "Rogue's pretty powerful with all her money. It would take a lot to make her scared."

"Someone she loves in danger, like kidnapped or something," I said. "Who would she protect? Does she have kids? A husband? A cat?"

Hattie frowned. "Her husband died a while ago. She has a daughter, Tessa, but she lives in Alaska."

"A best friend?"

Hattie shook her head. "Rogue's very independent. She's gotten close with the Seam Rippers, and I'm good friends with her, but she doesn't have a bestie like that. Maybe Bootsy Jones, I think. She's close with Bootsy."

"Bootsy." I frowned. "She's the grandma of Tyrone, right?" Tyrone worked at the Ugly Man and at Jake's Yacht club, and he'd been helpful to me on more than one occasion recently. He was a good kid, and I'd even offered him a job at the marina, but he hadn't taken me up on it. Yet.

Hattie nodded.

"Call her." I didn't want to turn my phone on. I had a feeling Devlin and Griselda would unleash the wrath of a man slighted on me when I did, and who needed that?

Hattie pulled out her phone and dialed Bootsy. She answered on the first ring. "Hey, Hattie. What's up? I heard about the dead guy at Rogue's booth. Where are you guys? Have you seen Rogue?"

I gestured for the phone, and Hattie gave it to me. "Bootsy. Hi. It's Mia. Are you okay?"

"Yes, fine. Why?"

"Have you seen Tyrone lately?"

"Tyrone? He's helping out at the Yacht Club booth today. Why? You want me to grab him?"

So it wasn't Tyrone who had been kidnapped. "We think that Rogue is being coerced. Blackmailed. Who would she be willing to sacrifice herself to protect? Or does she have a secret she'd need to protect?"

Bootsy was quiet. "You mean, that's why she's missing? She's protecting someone?"

"Yeah, maybe. Who would she protect?"

"I love her, but she's pretty much a believer in everyone fending for themselves," she said. "She thinks helping others disempowers them."

That sounded like Rogue. "So, there's no one she'd risk her life to help? Not even her daughter?"

"Tessa?" Bootsy snorted. "Rogue hasn't seen Tessa in years. Hattie? Don't you remember their huge falling out after Tessa got arrested with Dee that time? Rogue banned Tessa from hanging out with Dee, which of course didn't go over well. Their relationship never recovered from that."

I stared at my team. "Rogue's daughter was friends with Dee?"

Hattie threw up her hands, and Lucy gave a fist pump.

"Well, 'friends' was a little strong," Bootsy said. "It was more like Tessa followed Dee around and idolized her. Drove Rogue nuts that Tessa was following someone like Dee, when all Rogue wanted was for her to be empowered. Once Dee left town, Tessa moved away soon after. I don't think she's been back."

Wow. *Wow.* "Okay, well, if you think of anything else, let us know."

"Right on. Keep me posted!"

"Will do." I hung up the phone. "Tessa's back," I said. "And Rogue's helping her."

Lucy raised her brows. "Bootsy just said—"

"I know what Bootsy said, but she's wrong that Rogue wouldn't help her." My mind was whirling with the information. "I left my mom when I was seventeen," I said. "I haven't spoken to her since. But if she showed up here in trouble, I'd do whatever it took to help her. And she'd do the same for me. That mother-daughter bond is forever, and being apart doesn't change it."

Hattie nodded. "I agree. That connection is unbreakable."

I cocked my head, wondering if Hattie had kids. She'd never mentioned them, but the way she said it, made me wonder.

"My mom worked three jobs to pay for me to go private school," Vinnie said. "She sacrificed everything for me. She's the greatest human being to walk the earth."

I grinned at the emotion in his voice. Big, tough Vinnie was a secret softie. "She's lucky to have a son who appreciates her."

He shook his head. "I'm the lucky one." Then he suddenly looked at me. "Wait a sec. Did you just say you ditched your mother and never went back?"

His voice was a little judgy, which I didn't appreciate. "I ditched the life we had together," I clarified. "She refused to leave that life, and I couldn't stay."

"What life was that?" he shot back.

"Crime."

He blinked. "Crime?"

"One hundred percent."

"Oh."

While Vinnie chewed on that little bit of trivia about my past, I turned to my team. "Well, we now know why Rogue is involved. That's a starting point. What do we know about Tessa?"

Hattie shook her head. "I don't know anything. I wasn't friends with Rogue back then, and she never talks about Tessa."

Lucy was already on her phone. "Tessa doesn't have social media that I can find," she said. "No articles about her. She keeps a low profile."

"No social media?" I thought about that. "That's unusual. Maybe she doesn't want to be found." I paced as I thought. "She's a follower. She follows Dee around," I mused. "Maybe she followed Dee to the jewelry store that night. Maybe—" I stopped and spun around to look at my team. "Maybe she saw what happened. Maybe she knows who the killer was, and she knows where the diamonds are. She knows it all, and she's been hiding ever since."

"Until Dee came back to town and called her," Hattie said excitedly. "Told her to come back, for whatever reason."

"And she did, and then Dee wound up dead, and now Rogue's protecting her daughter," Lucy finished.

"But what is Rogue *doing*? If she knows who the killer is, then she would just tell the cops," I said. "Why is she running around in secret, getting seen near corpses? Leaving her earrings around? Running from her friends? Hitting Hattie in the head instead of telling her what was up?"

No one had an answer for that.

I put my hands on my hips. "It's time to find out. You guys up for a little action?"

Hattie clapped her hands. "Yay! Yes! Let's do it."

Lucy sighed with resignation. "Let's hear it."

Vinnie regarded me. "Is this going to put you in danger?"

"Absolutely. My whole life is danger right now. But don't worry. You won't be at risk."

He narrowed his eyes. "Why is that?"

"Because I have to do this alone."

"Oh, God," Lucy groaned. "I don't need to hear the rest to

know this is a bad idea. What's this con called, *Murder Mia?* Or *Death Day?* Or—"

"Relax," I said. "It'll be fine."

She folded her arms. "Okay, spill it."

I did. When I finished, all three of them were staring at me.

"I don't know if you're a genius or completely insane," Vinnie said finally.

"Genius," Hattie said. "Definitely."

Lucy shook her head. "A little of both."

"Well, we'll see. Everyone ready?"

No one hesitated.

The game was on.

CHAPTER 20

WHILE LUCY and I invaded Rogue's closet, Hattie and Vinnie stole a car.

It had to be done, and they were both delighted to get the chance to do it. And, to make it even more fun, they'd decided to steal an old, ratty pickup truck from the husband of one of the Seam Rippers.

Why?

Because Hattie was certain that the Seam Ripper in question would be able to force her husband not to press charges. Because who wants to go to jail? None of us.

While they were off retrieving the vehicle, Lucy and I got to work.

With her history of baton twirling competitions, she was a master at makeup.

With my history of being a con artist, I was a master at seeing opportunity and using it to my advantage.

Between the two of us, we managed to put together an outfit for me that made me several inches taller, fifty pounds heavier, fifteen years older, a mousy salt-and-pepper brunette with glasses, freckles, extremely thick eyebrows, and alarmingly dull fashion sense.

I was insignificant, unthreatening, and unremarkable, exactly the kind of person that could walk into a room that held other people, but not even register on their minds as present. As for a crowded festival? One hundred percent invisible.

We met Hattie and Vinnie at the Lamborghini as they were getting out of the truck that was to be my incognito transportation.

When I walked up, Hattie took one look, and started laughing. "You have got to be kidding," she said. "How on earth did you manage that? There's no way I would ever recognize you, and I know it's you."

Vinnie whistled. "That's awesome."

I pushed the glasses up on my nose, gave them both an uninterested look, and shuffled right past them, as if I didn't even see them.

The laughter stopped, and silence fell behind me as I kept going.

After a few yards, I stopped and turned around. "Excuse me," I said with my best Texas accent. "Where's the bathroom?" I didn't always get the Texas lingo or syntax correct, but the accent? I could nail it.

The three of them stared at me.

Finally, Vinnie said. "I'm so freaked out right now. Even your voice is different."

"This causes me all sorts of alarm and excitement," Hattie said. "I had no idea you could disappear from yourself so completely. It could be extremely handy and terrifying at the same time."

Even Lucy, who had helped create me, looked stunned. "You and your mom must have been really, really good criminals."

"We were," I said. "We stole a lot of things, and never got arrested." Disappearing from myself was an interesting way to put it. "It's been a long time since I've done this," I admitted. It felt unfamiliar, but also, it felt like coming home.

I'd forgotten what it felt like to completely disappear, as Hattie had put it. Right now, I could go out into the world and do anything I wanted. No one would know it was me. It was like a free pass to be whoever I felt like being. I'd spent most of my childhood in that state of lack of accountability, and it was weird to be back there.

Addicting? A little bit.

And lonely.

But mostly addicting. Shoot. I hated it when I was reminded of how much fun it was to be the woman I'd worked so hard to leave behind. "I appreciate the kudos. Glad it worked."

"Oh, yes, thank you," Vinnie said. "That's your voice."

I handed King Tut's leash to Hattie. "Keep him safe," I said.

"You bet."

I crouched down in front of King Tut and eyed him. "I need to you to protect the marina in case anyone shows up there early. So, when Hattie drops you off, stay there, be fierce, and you have license to kill."

He flicked his tail once and studied me with his yellow eyes. I suspected he hadn't even noticed the disguise. He saw me right through it, which actually felt good. I realized I didn't want to be invisible to the world anymore, sliding through life as a shadow that no one saw. Good kitty. "I'd take you with me, but people will know it's me if you're with me."

He flicked his tail once more, then turned, wiggled his butt, and shot up into Hattie's arms. To her credit, she didn't flinch when he dug his claws into her shoulders. She simply tucked him under her arm.

"Vinnie?" I asked. "You all set for the marina?"

He nodded. "I have friends meeting us there. I know what to do."

"All right." I took a breath. "Everyone ready? Meet back at the marina in two hours." It was almost five o'clock. We needed to be in place before dark.

Lucy threw her arms around me and hugged me. "Do not get yourself assassinated. Do you hear me?"

I grinned. "You bet."

"All right." She gave me a look of both worry and awe, then headed toward the Lamborghini.

Vinnie looked at me. "I agree with her."

"I'm fine. Go." It was making me uncomfortable how reluctant they were to leave me. It made my brain think that I was actually going to die, and that wasn't helpful. I caught Hattie watching me with a worried brow, and that was it. I knew I had to walk away before I lost my nerve.

"All right. Bye." I jogged over to my new ride, swung into the driver's seat, and started the engine. I put the car in gear, waved at my friends, and then drove out.

I didn't look back, because if I did, I'd see the worry on their faces.

Worry that I was going to die.

I didn't need that.

But before I got out of range, I couldn't resist the urge to glance in the rearview mirror. They were all standing there watching me drive away, including King Tut. My heart tightened. I had friends. People who cared if I died. I'd wanted that my whole life, and now I had it.

I wasn't going to mess that up by dying.

I PARKED at the far end of the parking lot on the town green. The festival was in full swing, with a local swing band, balloon animals, relay races, and lots of tailgating on the beach. They were going to shoot off fireworks from the beach later tonight, at nine-fifteen, which I was counting on.

The competitor tent was roped off, and I could see several FBI-ish vehicles parked outside of it.

Because when an FBI bodyguard gets murdered, the FBI gets interested. No wonder Griselda was mad. He probably had his boss riding him about me. It maybe didn't look good for him that he didn't know where the FBI's most valuable witness had gone.

I stared at the FBI SUVs for a long moment, the hair on the back of my neck prickling the longer I watched them. That was real danger right there. Real danger for me. I knew what the people in Stanley's world were like. I knew what they were willing to do.

And I knew it was time to make it stop. At least this particular chapter.

I pulled out my phone and turned it on.

The moment it turned on, my text messages and voicemails started popping up, fast and quick, on top of each other, all of them from Griselda and Devlin.

I waited until they finished so I didn't accidentally call the boys back when I touched my phone, then I went into my contacts and found the name I'd stored there. The one that Griselda didn't even know I had in there.

It was listed under Bunny Pumpkin, but that wasn't his real name (thankfully for him, right?). I'd never use his real name, or it would get him killed. And probably me. Because Bunny had killed a lot of people for Stanley. And then, he'd helped me take Stanley down. Secretly. For reasons he'd never given. Bunny was not a good person. But he was part of the reason I was alive and Stanley was in prison, so for those two things, I trusted him.

Or at least, I trusted him more than I trusted the person who had killed Ivan. Which wasn't a lot, but I needed help right now, and he was the one I needed.

I took a breath, then called.

Bunny answered on the first ring. "Peter's Pizza. Can I take your order?"

He had my number in his phone. He knew it was me. He also didn't work at a pizza place. But I appreciated the code. I was on it. "I have a question."

"What's that?"

"Is it true you had pepperoni and pizza dough go missing?" Pepperoni and dough were my code for drugs and drug money, and I was sure he'd know what I was talking about.

I didn't know if Bunny had taken over the business after Stanley had gone to prison, if that was why he'd wanted to help me. I hadn't asked, and I hadn't heard anything from Griselda about the state of the business since I'd left town.

Silence. Then… "Yes, so I've heard."

Ah…wonderful. So glad Griselda had been correct about that. "Is it true that some people think I took them?"

"Yes."

My pulse quickened. "I didn't."

"I know."

I believed him, that he believed me. Okay, so that was good that he wasn't going to come after me. "Can you please tell whoever might be interested that I have it in a safe in my marina garage?"

Silence.

"Hello?"

"No. I won't do that."

Aw…that made me all warm and fuzzy. I appreciated that he didn't want to set me up to be murdered. "My bodyguard was stabbed in the back and killed. I need to take control. I have a plan."

He swore.

I waited.

He was silent.

"I'll give you a free boat rental if you're ever in town."

He laughed then, a rough and rusty laugh. "I like you."

"Thanks. I appreciate that."

"I like you alive," he clarified.

"Me, too. That's why I need this favor." I'd never called him before this, but we'd traded phone numbers once. Just in case. Now was that case.

"Who do you have to protect you?"

Such a thoughtful guy. "My attack cat. Some gang members who like to steal cars. And a handful of old ladies who drink a lot and quilt. Oh, and a former champion baton twirler. And a hairdryer. Plus me. I'm my secret weapon."

Silence. Then, "You're serious? That's your plan?"

"Yeah."

He swore. "No—"

"I know what I'm doing. I know how the pizza biz works. You know I do. I need to do this. Just pass the word to the right person. I have it in my safe at the marina, and I'm moving it tonight at midnight. It'll be gone forever then. This is their last chance to get it."

He swore again.

"Do you know who to tell?" I asked.

"Yeah."

"Will it get you in trouble?" I asked. I didn't want him murdered for helping me.

"I can handle that."

"Then…? It's a nice lake. You'll be glad to have a free boat rental." I was literally negotiating with a drug lord's enforcer. Griselda would *kill* me if he knew. "I think it's a fair deal." It was probably a bad idea to owe a man like Bunny, but if I was dead, then there was no point in being debt-free.

He laughed again. "You're a crazy broad, but you've got guts like no one else."

I heard the respect in his voice, and I knew I'd won. "Thanks. Any tips?"

"Yeah. Be smarter than you've ever been."

I nodded. "I can do that."

He hung up without another word, and I did the same. Then I leaned back in my seat and rested my head against the headrest and waited.

The panic attack came hard and fast, as I knew it would. Suddenly, I couldn't breathe. Everything started spinning. My hands started shaking. I felt like I was going to throw up.

Oh…God…

I closed my eyes and took a breath, and then another,

breathing through the panic I'd known would try to take me down. I'd never had panic attacks before spending two years undercover against a drug king, and I knew it would hit hard. After all, I'd just invited my worst hell back into my life. The life that had given me panic attacks and nightmares.

Only this time, I didn't have the FBI to back me up. If Griselda knew what I'd done, he'd kidnap me himself.

It was all on me, and if I lost, I was dead.

So, yeah, a panic attack made sense.

Except I didn't have time for one. Not today. Tomorrow night? Fine.

Right now? No.

I took another deep breath and forced my hands to unclench. *I can do this. This is easy. This is going to be fun. I love challenges. I am undefeated against assassins. It's my zone of genius.*

I almost started laughing. My zone of genius was defeating assassins? Exactly what I'd been hoping for when I'd walked out on my mom.

I took another breath, and I realized that the tightness in my chest had eased slightly. My hands weren't shaking as much, and the dizziness had stopped. Look at me! Handling the panic attack like a pro—

My phone rang, and I screamed and hurled it across the cab of the truck in a split second of raw terror.

Okay. So, maybe not totally calm yet. "You're doing great, Mia," I said aloud as I retrieved my still-ringing phone. "Yeah, it's all good." I saw Devlin's name on the display, so I steeled myself.

I totally had this.

I answered it as cheerfully as I could. "S'up, pretty boy?"

"You're not dead."

"No. I'm fine."

"She's not dead," he said to someone. "Where are you?"

About fifty yards away? "It's a secret."

"Mia!" Griselda came on the phone. "What the hell are you playing at? Ivan went down without a fight. He got blindsided.

167

Whoever got Ivan is better than he was, which means they're better than you. Where are you?"

"I'm in Hawaii. If you could see me in this flowered bikini, you and Devlin would definitely get in a fist fight over me." A few weeks ago, it had come to my surprising attention that Devlin and Griselda both had the hots for me. Griselda had warned Devlin off me, and Devlin had ignored him. It was a law-enforcement, testosterone love triangle that I was both fascinated by and terrified by, especially since I had convinced myself that I was never dating again.

Leave it to hot law enforcement buddies to make a girl doubt her vow of celibacy and singlehood, right? Not that I'd caved yet, but—

Griselda swore. "I don't have time for you in a bikini—"

"Mia's in a bikini?" Devlin's voice drifted over the phone. "Where?"

Men. So predictable. "My cabana boy is bringing over a piña colada. Gotta go. Just didn't want you boys to worry. Gotta shut off my phone. It's an electronics-free resort." I hung up over his protests, then put my phone on airplane mode.

If I needed help, I wanted to be able to get my phone back fast.

And now…it was time for step two.

I took a deep a breath, then got out of the truck. I leaned against the door for a moment, then shook out my shoulders and headed into the crowd where my personal assassin and some local murderers could all be lurking, hungry for more.

Was that dramatic enough?

I was pretty sure it didn't do justice to the stakes, but it was the best I had right now.

Because I was about to find out how good my disguise was.

CHAPTER 21

My first stop was the competitor's tent.

Where the FBI and Griselda were.

I'd been hoping they would have been gone by now, but apparently, dead bodyguards required extra TLC.

I eased down the aisle, and made it to the Ugly Man table first, where Stevie and Diesel were still sitting back, feet up, handing out beer, chips, and biscuits to anyone who came by. Tyrone, Bootsy's grandson, was also there, and he was doing all the work while Stevie and Diesel enjoyed the love.

Tyrone knew me. Not as well as Griselda and Devlin, but he definitely knew me.

I slouched up to the table, summoned my Texas accent, and then pointed at a biscuit. "Can I have one?"

"You bet." Tyrone smiled at me as he put one on a plate, not realizing he knew me, which was awesome. "The Ugly Man tavern has its own baker," he said, clearly trying to summon his marketing chops. "Come by for more delicious pastries."

"Okay." I took a nibble, watching Stevie and Diesel kicking back. "Can I ask you a secret?" I whispered loudly.

Tyrone raised his brows. "What's up?"

"Is it true that a body was found at the Ugly Man?"

Just as I suspected, Diesel and Stevie both looked over. Belatedly, I remembered my little incident with them. I hoped my disguise was as effective as I'd planned.

Tyrone's eyes widened. "What? When?"

"I don't know, but I heard about it from my neighbor whose grandma's best friend's mom's husband's sister works at the police station." I leaned in. "I heard that it was about those diamonds that went missing in that jewelry store murder!"

Poor Tyrone looked horrified. "A jewelry store murder? When?"

"Oh, a long time ago," I said, "but they found the diamonds. Well, I mean not officially, but I heard that the lady who bought that marina and her friends found them. They have them in their safe in the marina garage. You think it's true? I heard that they killed someone to get them."

Tyrone blinked. "Mia Murphy? Mia killed someone to get diamonds?"

I snapped my fingers. "Yes! That's her name. Mia Murphy. She was married to a drug dealer, so she's definitely the murdering type."

"I'm pretty sure she didn't kill anyone," Tyrone said. "I'm sure you heard wrong."

Aw...I'd already loved him, but it was so sweet he was defending me. "I hope I didn't. It makes for fun gossip, doesn't it?" I gave a cheerful cackle. "All those diamonds in the safe at the marina. Can you imagine after all that time?"

Diesel stood up, so I quickly waved the biscuit at Tyrone. "These are good, but you aren't going to win. I heard that Hattie Lawless is making the biscuits for that Esther lady, using her own recipe. Ain't no one better at biscuits than Hattie Lawless."

Stevie stood up and leaned over Tyrone's shoulder. "Esther is missing. She can't win if she's missing."

"Oh, she's back," I cackled again. "She and Hattie are baking tonight at Hattie's café." I grabbed two more biscuits. "Good stuff. Keep it up." Then I wandered off, stumbling slightly. I decided to add a limp, so I started dragging my right foot just a little bit.

I was pleased with that little interaction. I'd dropped enough nuggets to get any potential murderers at that booth to head my way tonight.

I'd made it only to the Yacht Club table when Stevie caught up to me. He tapped my shoulder and I turned. "What?"

Zoltan and Jake were still handing out lots of desserts that looked delicious. Frankly, I didn't think that Zoltan and Jake were involved in any nefarious way, but they had to be brought in.

Stevie cleared his throat. "Did you mention diamonds?"

"Why?"

His eyes widened. "What?"

"Why do you care if I mentioned diamonds?"

"Because my grandfather owned the jewelry store. Those were his diamonds that went missing."

I cocked my head, trying not to look startled by that bit of news. "Were they?"

"Yes. Did you say you knew who had them?"

I shrugged. "Mia Murphy has them in a safe at the Eagle's Nest Marina. But that's just the rumor. Who knows?" I turned back to the Yacht Club table and wiggled my hands for a biscuit. Zoltan gave me one, and I took a bite. "Bah," I said. "Hattie and Esther will beat you tomorrow."

Zoltan raised his brows. "Hattie's not in the contest."

"She's helping Esther bake tonight at her café. Her recipe. Best damn biscuits on the planet."

"She does make the best biscuits," Zoltan agreed. "She's a genius. An artist, even, when it comes to food."

Ah...there was definitely a little bit of fawning admiration there. "That she is," I agreed.

He shrugged. "How can you be upset at losing to the greatest?"

Clearly Zoltan didn't care about winning the contest, and Jake wasn't even bothering with the conversation. He was flashing his pearly whites at a couple wearing expensive labels on their clothing. I decided right then that the Yacht Club wasn't a contender for the Murder of the Year award. They had a mission, and it wasn't diamonds or winning. It was simply exposure for the Yacht Club.

Jake and Zoltan were impressing the many visitors to town with a booth that spoke of luxury, competence, belonging, and success. If I had a nice boat, I'd definitely go there.

My marina was nowhere to be seen. Why was that? Because I'd totally dropped the ball on this little marketing opportunity. Le sigh. That was fine. July Fourth was going to be the official launch of my new biz.

"Excuse me." Ronald Dutch, the head judge, strode up. "We have a bit of a situation tonight, and we're going to be moving all the tables out of the tent for the rest of the evening. Our volunteer staff will help you set up by the beach. If you can start to pack up, that would be great."

That danged FBI. Taking all the joy out of everything.

Stevie put his hands on his hips. "Ronald. This lady here says that Hattie and Esther are going to be baking at Hattie's Café tonight. That's not fair, is it? Esther can't have help."

Ronald didn't look like he wanted to deal with the question, but he managed a charming smile. "All competitors have to do their own baking, but there's no rules that say that others can't be with them or advising them."

"What if Esther's not there tomorrow?" Stevie continued. "No one has seen her."

"She must be present," Ronald said congenially. "Do you need crates or boxes to move your supplies outside?"

Stevie would not be derailed. "So, if she doesn't show up tomorrow, then she can't win?"

I looked sharply at Stevie. Was he plotting to overthrow Rogue? Maybe he would be visiting me tonight. Wouldn't that be fun and nifty?

"That is correct," Ronald said. "Now, if we can move this all outside, that would be great. Volunteers will be stopping by in a few moments to show you to your new location." He started to walk past us, but as he did, I recalled that Dee was related to him.

I also recalled that he'd let Dee into the contest, against the desires of pretty much everyone in town, and that Dee would have been a runaway winner if she'd stayed in the contest.

"Excuse me," I said, limping after him as he started to walk back toward the section that was cordoned off and swarming with FBI. "May I have a word with you?"

He glanced at me, impatience in his eyes, but charm in his voice. "Of course."

"You're the head judge, right? Ronald Dutch." At his nod, I smiled. "My name is Jenny Doody. I'm writing an article for the *Boston Globe* about this festival, and how the Dutch family has been the core of it for decades."

He glanced toward the FBI section, then nodded. "I must run an errand, but you may walk with me."

"Great." I limped faster, but he didn't slow down. "Your niece, Dee Dutch, was a front runner to be the first five-time champion, then she disappeared right before she could win. And now she's the favorite to win again. You must be super proud of her."

He looked over at me sharply, clearly trying to decide if I knew she was dead.

I smiled innocently, but watched him with razor-sharp acuity, looking for his reaction.

It wasn't agonized grief. Instead, he looked...suspicious. "Dee is an excellent baker, and she deserved to be in the contest this year. It's unfortunate it took her this long to come back to town and claim her spot as the first five-time champion."

"Why did it take her so long to come back?"

"I don't know. I didn't keep track." He was nearing the glob of FBI agents.

"Is it true she was involved with the jewelry store murder a few years ago? Is that why she left?"

He stopped and spun toward me suddenly. He grabbed me by

the forearm with surprising strength, and dragged me to the side of the aisle. "What the blazes do you want?"

I blinked, startled by the venom in the "nice twin's" voice. "I want to find out what happened with the diamonds," I said. "And if that has anything to do with the festival. What do you think?"

His jaw flexed, and I saw the vein in his forehead get all worked up. Not sadness, though. Not grief. More like aggression and anger. Wow. That had been a quick emotional shift. "My niece was innocent of all wrongdoing," he said. "All she wanted to do was bake, and I gave her the chance she should have had a long time ago. The Dutch family supports this town and this festival. We always have, and we always will."

I smiled brightly. "Wonderful! I wanted to write a feel-good story. My editor wants some drama piece, but I want to bring sunshine into the world. Tell me something great about the festival! Is it true that Hattie Lawless is the best there is? And that she might beat your niece?"

"Hattie isn't in the contest, and cheating won't be tolerated. And my niece—" He paused.

I waited.

"If anyone tries to stand in the way of my niece's success, the Dutch family will take care of it. Put that in your article." And with that, he spun around and strode past the FBI scrum and toward the judges' tent.

Had that been a threat? A threat he'd wanted me to publicly announce to the world? That was so juicy. And—

Two men I knew quite well burst out of the FBI huddle and charged toward me. I had no time to move before Devlin plowed my shoulder and sent me flying. I crashed into an abandoned table and rebounded onto a flat of strawberries. *Mother trucker!*

Devlin cursed and spun around. "Sorry. Sorry. We're in a hurry."

I waved him off, keeping my face away from him. He wasn't an idiot. There was only so much that makeup would hide from a man trained in details. "I'm all set," I said, loading on my Texas accent.

"Let me help you up—" He reached for me.

I let out a shriek and scrambled backward! "No! I don't touch people!" Was my wig still in place? God, I hoped it was. If Devlin and Griselda realized I was standing in front of them, I'd be locked up within seconds. I locked my hands behind my back and backed up, dragging my gimpy leg behind me.

Devlin held up his hands in an innocent gesture. "Sorry. I didn't mean to scare you."

Griselda hit his arm. "I'm going to the parking lot! She has to still be around!" He turned and sprinted down the aisle, the flaps on his little suit jacket flapping.

The parking lot? He'd tracked my phone? Suddenly, I remembered that during my spy years, he'd had a high-tech GPS locator installed on my phone, just in case I got thrown in the back of a van and driven out to a graveyard for dismembering. Son of a biscuit. He'd used that on me! Did it work when my phone was in airplane mode? Obviously not, because he hadn't realized I was right here.

But holy cow. I couldn't ever take it off airplane until I figured out how to get him off my phone.

Devlin was frowning at me suspiciously, and I realized I'd gotten distracted from my role playing. I flashed him a cranky, somewhat passive aggressive glare with squinty eyes. "Apology accepted." Then I turned and limped down the aisle. I hunched my shoulders and listed to the side, forcing myself to move slowly, even though I could feel him watching me.

His cop brain was definitely telling him that something was off about me, but he wasn't quite figuring it out. I needed to get out of there before things clicked in. *Crap.*

That had totally been my bad, walking so close to the FBI party. My gut had told me I needed to talk to Ronald, and I'd taken the risk. But who would think that Griselda and Devlin would have come charging out?

I mean, yeah, if I'd remembered that Griselda could track me, then I would have thought they'd come charging out, but other than that—

"Hey!" Devlin's voice rang out.

That was so authoritarian. He didn't deserve a response.

I didn't turn around, but I heard him jogging up behind me. My mind raced, trying to think of a way to throw him off.

He eased to a walk beside me, shortening his long strides to stay even with my agonizingly slow limp. "May I escort you somewhere?"

"Nope." I kept my head down, trying to read his tone and body language. "Just going to set up on the beach for the fireworks." If he knew it was me, he would have called me out. If he merely suspected it was me, he would have probably also called me out to see if I caved. So maybe he didn't know it was me, but he definitely suspected something was off about me.

"What were you doing by the FBI agents?" he asked.

Seriously? He was interrogating me? "Interviewing Ronald Dutch," I said, trying to focus hard on my accent and keeping my voice low and gravelly.

"Why?"

"For the Boston Globe." I took a breath. "My name's Jenny Doody, and I'm a freelance writer. I'm trying to sell a feel-good story about the festival."

"Jenny Doody?" he echoed, skepticism dripping from his voice.

That was it. I had to take the offensive. I spun around him. "Are you mocking my name? Because that's rude."

To his credit, he didn't back down. He actually looked pleased that he'd gotten me to face him. "You keep switching what side you're limping on."

Well, great. That was good to know. "I'm ambidextrous."

"You're also trying to hide your muscle tone," he said. "And you keep slipping out of your accent. Who are you?" His hand went to his gun, and suddenly I realized that he thought I was the assassin who'd killed Ivan.

Wow. That was such a compliment to be mistaken for an assassin! I was so proud of myself! It did, however, mean that Devlin was on high alert and he was going to take me down in about thirty seconds if I didn't provide proof that I was a nerdy, harmless, freelance reporter with Texas roots.

Since he wasn't going to buy that anymore, my only other chance was to decide I owned him and his attitude. It was time to claim control of the situation.

So, I glared at him, dropped the accent, and used my real voice. "If you tell Griselda I'm here, he'll lock me up and you'll never see me again. So back off and let me do my thing."

Devlin's mouth dropped open in absolute shock, which felt really good. He had totally not realized it was me. How awesome was I? "What the fu—"

"Don't curse around me," I interrupted. "That's rude."

"What are you doing? Running around here without a bodyguard? Oh, hell. Is Vinnie missing too?"

"No. He's fine. I have a plan. He's in on it."

He was still looking stunned. "A plan? There is an assassin looking for you, two women were shot and then dumped at a cupcake store and you're poking at the murderer, Ivan was stabbed, and you're wandering around out here with a *plan* as your only defense?"

"You didn't realize it was me. And neither did Griselda. How is a stranger going to recognize me?" And wow! Topsy and Dee were shot and then moved. I was pretty sure Devlin didn't realize he'd just let that info slip out, and I didn't point it out.

His mouth opened again, and then closed without him saying anything. Because I'd scored an excellent point.

"I'm completely safe out here," I continued, trying to sound like I absolutely believed it. "But if Griselda knows I'm here, he's going to kidnap me. You know it. I'm not going to die, but you have to let me handle this."

"What's the great plan you have?" His tone said he didn't believe there was any chance it could be a great plan.

I looked over his shoulder and I saw Griselda heading toward us. "I gotta go. Don't tell him."

Devlin swore again. "What if I need to reach you?"

"Call Hattie."

He ground his jaw. "Hattie? Of course she's in on it—"

I turned and began limping away. Griselda was closing fast, and I needed to get out. As I walked away, every one of my senses strained to hear what Devlin was doing. Would he come after me? Would he tell Griselda it was me? There was every reason for him to blow my cover, and not many to let me go. But something told me that he might be willing to stand on his own on this one, and not be Griselda's minion. *Come on, Devlin!*

CHAPTER 22

"I COULDN'T FIND her or her vehicle," Griselda said as he walked up. "What the hell? I can't believe Mia's here. I'm going to kill her when I find her."

I kept limping away. Devlin didn't answer.

Griselda spoke again. "Why are you watching that woman? What's going on with her? Is she a problem?"

Really, Devlin? He couldn't fake it better than that?

"No," Devlin finally said. "I just wanted to make sure she was all right. I knocked her pretty hard when I hit her."

Relief rushed through me. He wasn't going to turn me over to my favorite federal autocrat.

"I'm sure Mia's around here somewhere," Devlin said. "I'll look for her while you deal with your FBI bureaucracy."

"Great. Keep in touch. I'll keep an eye on my phone, and I'll let you know if she turns hers on again."

What a stalker! How often had he been spying on me in the last few months? I felt so exposed and nekkid. I glanced back as Griselda clapped Devlin on the shoulder and headed back toward the top-secret area. Devlin glanced at me, raised his brows, then started following me.

Because that wouldn't be obvious! I waved him off, and he

shook his head, but angled his walk in a different direction. I realized he was going to keep an eye on me, but not make it obvious.

Except it would be obvious. How long would it take for Griselda to notice Devlin's special interest in the weird, limpy, Texas woman with ginormous eyebrows? Or my personal assassin might notice his interest? Those were trained people. As good as it felt to have Devlin at my back, I needed to ditch him.

I just had one more stop to make.

I eased into the crowd by the beach, scanning for the sparkly gold pop-up tent that Hattie said would be set up near the south end of the town beach. I found it almost immediately, and started laughing. The Seam Rippers had glittering gold streamers wrapped around the four posts, along with white Christmas lights. They had portable lounge chairs set up, along with a table with three blenders, multiple bottles of margarita mix, and cartons of assorted juices, which I was pretty sure contained tequila. Numerous Seam Rippers were present, laughing, shrieking, and having more fun than pretty much anyone on the beach.

Beside them was a black pop-up tent that said "Society Sisters" on it. They had a table full of artifacts about the town, and a sign inviting folks to see if they qualified for membership by being related to one of the headstones in the original town cemetery. A few women were handing out flyers to people who passed by, and they were offering free apple juice to anyone who wanted it.

Standing at the main table was the head of the Founders Society, Agnes Higgleston, who I'd thought was supposed to be in jail. But she clearly wasn't. Were we friends? I was pretty sure we weren't.

I limped up to the Seam Ripper's tent. Although they were seam rippers for hire and well-sought after, they didn't have a single sample quilt on display, and no photo boards of their accomplishments. They were simply there to enjoy the evening for themselves, to bask in the freedom that their seventies, eighties, and nineties gave them.

At the first blender was Bootsy, who I needed to speak with.

I limped up and walked into the group. I bumped Bootsy and lifted her wallet out of her purse. She had no clue, chattering merrily with the others.

I circled back out of the tent, then came back in, waving her wallet. "Is there a Bootsy Jones here? I found her wallet."

Bootsy whirled around to face me, her hand going into her purse. "What? I lost it?" She looked horrified, and hurried over. "Thank you so much—"

"It's Mia," I whispered, as she took the wallet.

She paused, stared at me, then burst out laughing. "Holy drunken cupcakes. That's outstanding!"

I grinned. "Thanks."

"Wow. I'm stunned. Honestly." She raised her voice. "Hey, you guys, look it's—"

I slapped my hand over her mouth. "Really?"

"It's just so good. Everyone would appreciate it."

"I literally have an assassin after me, and an FBI agent."

"Right. I know. But if the Seam Rippers know this is you, they'll be guarding your back. We're all over the place at the festival. You'd have little spies watching you all the time."

How sweet was that? "I appreciate it, but I'm not going to endanger any of them by getting them involved."

She put her hands on her hips. "Well, that's rude. You're going to make us all live boring, old lady lives when there's adventure to be had? What kind of friend are you?"

"The kind that keeps her friends alive. I feel like that's a good friend." But yay, friends! That felt so good.

"Well, we don't want those kinds of friends, the ones that keep us safe. The minute you start running away from danger, you get old, you lose your spark, and you die. You want that for us?"

I blinked. "No—"

"Then shut up." She grabbed the arm of a nearby Seam Ripper and yanked her over to us. She pulled her in and whispered in her ear. The Seam Ripper, whose name I didn't even know, stared at me with wide eyes, then grinned. "No kidding?"

I sighed. "Honestly, Bootsy—"

"See?" Bootsy exclaimed. "That's her voice. Go spread the word. We'll keep an eye on her."

"Got it!" The Seam Ripper grinned at me, then hurried over to a group of quilters.

Four silver-haired heads leaned in, they all glanced my way, and then moved on to tell others. As I stood there, I could literally see gossip happening in front of me. It went through the tent, then out into the grounds, jumping from person to person, skipping around from here and there, moving with lightning speed.

"Holy cow," I said. "That's stunning how fast information moves."

"When you want the best, hire the best." Bootsy put her hands on her hips. "Now what's up?"

I had a feeling I had to get out of the festival quickly now. It wouldn't take much for the wrong person to hear information moving that quickly. "I need you to spread another rumor."

She grinned. "We're fantastic at that."

"I can see that." I leaned in and whispered the rumor to her.

Her eyes widened. "You're kidding. You don't want us to spread that."

"I do."

"Mia. That's going to get you killed."

"I'll be fine. I have a plan."

"A good plan?"

"It better be, right?"

She chewed her lower lip. "I don't like it."

"Well, you don't have a choice now. What if the assassin is wandering around here looking for me and they overhear a Seam Ripper tell someone who the chick with the eyebrows is? I'll be dead before I make it to my car."

She waved her hand. "We're very good at what we do."

I could feel people watching me, and heads were turning. Were they all Seam Rippers, or were other people finding out now? I'd underestimated the small-town effect. "I need to go. Will you do it?"

She sighed. "All right, but don't get killed."

"I won't." I blew her a kiss, then turned and hurried away, heading back toward my truck.

I could feel the presence of people behind me, but when I looked over my shoulder, I could see no one watching me. A few sassy seniors were nearby, but I never caught them looking. I didn't even see Devlin. Had I lost him? Had he decided to trust my plan?

I felt like someone was watching me, though. Intently. And not with great love. Was my imagination working me over, or were my instincts on point?

My mom had always, *always* told me to trust my instincts. Better to overestimate the danger and risk than to underestimate it.

Which meant I had to assume that right now, I was being followed by someone who didn't want the best for me in life.

I stopped where I was, and focused on calming the sudden pounding of my heart. I was in the middle of a crowd, so the odds of someone taking me out right now were low. Most people didn't want to commit crimes in the middle of a public area. Of course, some people didn't care, or were so good that it didn't matter, but right now, it was my best chance.

I was fifty yards from an FBI party. Surely that would help, right?

But as I stood there, the hair on the back of my neck began to prickle, and goosebumps popped up on my arms.

I spun around and faced the crowd that was behind me, scanning for anyone who was out of place, but I didn't see anyone that triggered my alarms. It was simply families and friends, milling about, enjoying the festival, and making their way to the beach for the tailgate.

Everyone looked relaxed, normal, and oblivious to my presence.

Someone bumped me, and my hand instinctively went to my back pocket, covering my phone, but no one tried to grab it. Crap. Was I becoming paranoid?

I let out my breath and turned and began weaving my way through the crowd. I gave up the limp and simply moved fast, circling back toward the parking lot. I'd done what I needed to do, and now I wanted to get out of there.

The parking lot was full, with people setting up barbeque grills on their tailgates, and arranging chairs in the parking lot. It looked like fun, and I wanted to stay, run around, introduce myself and talk about the marina.

But I didn't dare.

I hurried down the aisle next to my purloined truck, checking behind me using all the windows and mirrors of the adjacent cars, but I didn't see anyone closing in on me. My heart pounding, I dropped low, so my head was below the level of the cars, then I crawled around to my borrowed truck. I hopped inside, yanked the door shut, locked it, and then shoved the key in the ignition.

I backed up so quickly I almost ran over a barbeque grill, but then hit the gas and charged out of the parking lot. I hung a quick left, away from my marina, just in case, and then pulled out.

Behind me, two pickup trucks pulled out of the parking lot and headed in the same direction I was going.

That could be a fluke. There were only two directions to turn when leaving the parking lot. And the way I was going, led into the town center, where more action and fun was.

It was fine.

No one was following me.

But neither truck turned off as I drove through the downtown.

I approached the police station and decided to pull in. I circled around the lot and pulled up alongside the front door and paused, the truck still in gear and my foot on the brake.

Neither truck pulled in, but they both slowed as they passed. Or did they? Maybe I was imagining things.

I let out my breath as they moved past, watching as they went by. One black pickup. One navy one. Both shiny and clean. Nice trucks. Tinted windows, which made it impossible for me to see who was driving. My gaze went back to the black truck, and I felt a flash of recognition. I'd seen it before, but where? Had it been following me at other times?

They both went around the corner and out of sight. Okay, right. See? Fine.

But I didn't pull away from the police station, and I couldn't quite loosen my grip on the steering wheel.

It had been a long time since I'd been that scared, and I didn't like it.

Maybe Griselda was right. Maybe I should walk into that police station and let him hide me. I didn't have hand-to-hand combat skills, gun skills, or evasive driving expertise. All I had was a keen sense about people, my wits, and sass, none of which were handy when faced with people ready to Grim Reaper me.

Without the ability to call or text anyone, I felt isolated. Alone.

I could turn on my phone and sit here. Griselda would come find me, throw me in his backpack, and lock me up for my own safety. And right now, that didn't feel like such a bad idea.

I wanted to go into that police station. I wanted someone else to protect me. I wanted—

I realized suddenly that the first truck, the black one, had looked like the one Rogue had been driving. Holy crap! Had it been Rogue? Or was it being driven by the person who was forcing Rogue to go on the run?

My heart started to pound again, this time with excitement.

I could go after that truck. Follow it to see if I could find Rogue. Or follow it until it realized I was following it, and then have it turn on me, run me off the road, and kill me.

My knee began to jiggle as I bounced it restlessly.

Go into the police station and be safe?

Go after a truck that might lead me to an innocent old lady who was in trouble?

Dammit. When I put it that way, what choice did I have?

I took my foot off the brake and hit the gas. The old truck shot out of the parking lot, and the wheels squealed as I took the corner a little fast. As soon as it straightened out, I hit the gas again, urging my little stolen sweetheart onward in pursuit of justice.

We hurtled down the road, and I scanned the road ahead for the truck, but I didn't see it.

I didn't slow down.

This was my chance. My speed inched up as I raced after the truck, checking side roads and driveways as I drove, but it hadn't pulled off that I could see. I didn't see the blue one either.

I kept my foot on the gas and kept driving, heading out of town. I had to be only moments behind it, so I kept thinking I'd see it around the next curve. But I didn't.

After another ten minutes of reckless endangerment to the well-being of my ride and myself, I finally had to acknowledge that I'd lost it. With a sigh, I pulled off to the side of the road and put the truck in park, trying to think.

There was no way I hadn't caught up to it. It had to have pulled off somewhere.

But where?

What had I missed?

I hit my palms on the steering wheel in frustration. My fault for being a wimp and hiding at the police station like a pansy. If I'd kept driving, I would have recognized that truck while I still had it in my sight. I could have done something to help Rogue.

Instead, I had to get back to the marina. I'd set it up for a lot of malcontents to show up there tonight, and I had to be ready for them.

With a sigh, I put the truck into gear and pulled out onto the road. I swung a U-turn and headed back toward the marina.

But as soon as I pulled out onto the main road, I saw the black truck heading toward me.

Fast.

In my lane.

Heading right at me.

I yelped and swerved to the right. My truck shot off the road and skidded down the gravelly shoulder right toward the trees. I yelped and hit the brakes as the trees came at me with alarming speed. The truck slowed, the trees came, and I closed my eyes and threw my arms up over my face.

And slammed right into a tree.

CHAPTER 23

THE FIRST THING I did was realize I was still alive.

The second thing I did was open my eyes.

The side of the truck was resting against a tree, but the window wasn't broken, the airbag hadn't deployed, and I was still alive. I'd hit the tree, but not hard enough to kill me or the truck. Hurrah for brakes!

Holy cow. That had been close.

I leaned my head back against the seat, then heard footsteps racing toward the truck...and remembered that someone had just run me off the road.

I quickly tried to shift into drive, but before I could move, a shadow appeared by my window, pointing a gun right at my head. I couldn't see it clearly, but it was definitely not Rogue. It was a man, and he was tall, and he had a *gun.*

I didn't freeze. I didn't put my hands up and be a good little girl. Instead, I ripped the steering wheel to the left and hit the gas. My truck shot forward, careening to the left, while the man dove out of my way, shouting at me.

My tires skidded as the truck scrambled back up the embankment. I reached the top, and saw that the black truck was right there, the driver's door open, headlights on.

I glanced over my shoulder and saw the man was scrambling after me, but his feet were sliding on the debris I'd left behind.

I had maybe two seconds. Two was plenty!

I threw my truck in park, grabbed my car keys, shot out of my vehicle, launched myself into his, hit the gas as I was pulling the door shut and took off down the street. I watched as he ran into the road, waving his arms and shouting.

I had no idea who he was. I'd never seen him before.

He ran for my truck, but unless he could hotwire a car, he wasn't going to get far in it.

I glanced down at the console as I drove, and I saw that his phone was on the seat. I quickly picked it up and turned it off as I drove. I then leaned over to peer in the back of the cab to make sure no one was hiding out, but it was empty. The truck bed was covered, so I couldn't see in there, so I'd done all I could.

I hit the gas, and drove fast, speeding through town as I headed back toward the marina. The longer I drove, the more the enormity of what I'd done settled on me. *I'd stolen a truck.* Well, two, actually, but the second one felt much more aggressive.

I hoped he wasn't FBI. That would be so awkward.

I turned into my marina parking lot. Hattie came out on the porch, aiming a shotgun at me. "Hey!" she shouted. "Stop!"

I rolled down the window. "It's me," I yelled. "Open the garage! I need to hide this!"

Her eyes widened, but she quickly hoisted the gun over her shoulder and jogged toward the mechanics building where Cargo, my sole employee, who I had yet to meet, worked on the few boats that came to me for service.

I pulled up to the huge doors, and Hattie hurried over and opened it.

I quickly drove in, and she pulled it shut behind me. "What the heck's that?"

"It ran me off the road," I said as I opened the door. "The driver came at me with a gun, so I almost ran him down, and then I stole his truck."

"Wow!" Lucy leaned over the railing of the loft, where she'd apparently been working. "That's so great. Good job!"

Hattie was surveying the truck. "It's an upgrade from the one you had. Excellent work."

"I think it's the one Rogue was driving." I waved as Vinnie came in. "We need to search it. There might be something in the back."

"We don't have much time," Hattie said. "The rumors are spreading. People could come at any moment."

"I'll keep an eye out." Vinnie handed me a phone. "It's a burner. All our numbers are in there. I have my boys stashed out in the woods along the road. I knew you were coming."

"Awesome. Thanks." I shoved the phone in my back pocket. "Before you go, let's see what's in the truck bed. Just in case it's a serial killer or something."

Hattie raised her shotgun and aimed it at the truck. "I got you covered."

"Hang on!" Lucy ran to the back of the loft, then came back with a hunting rifle, which she also aimed down at the truck. "Okay. Ready."

I put my hands on my hips. "Both of you, put those away. I'm not having you go to jail for shooting someone."

"Better jail than the morgue," Hattie said. "Who knows what's under there. Open it up, Mia."

"I'll help." Vinnie went to the back corner of the truck.

With a sigh, I went to the other. We both unlocked our corners and rolled it back...revealing an empty truck bed.

Hattie sighed and put her gun over her shoulder again. "I'm so disappointed. I really wanted a gun fight."

"I'll go back outside," Vinnie said. "Keep your phones on."

Lucy leaned on the railing. "Check the glove box," she said. "There has to be something in there."

I climbed in the truck and opened it. "Empty." I checked the visor and the console, but there was nothing. "Just his phone." I held it up.

"Who the heck was he?" Hattie said. "Tell me what happened."

As I retold the story, Lucy came down the ladder from the loft. "And you didn't recognize the driver?"

"No. But he had a gun."

"What kind? Handgun or rifle?"

"Handgun."

"Okay, that's much more aggressive," Hattie said.

"Look, we don't have time for this," Lucy said. "The sun is setting, and anyone could come at any time. We need to be ready." She raised her brows. "Are you sure you don't want to tell Griselda and Devlin about the trap we set?"

"No. They'll just mess it up." I shook out my shoulders, trying to focus, but I was so distracted by the truck I'd stolen. He'd followed me out of the festival, which meant he'd known who I was. He'd recognized me. He had to have been the one I'd felt following me.

I wished I hadn't run from the scene now. I'd gotten scared and bailed, which left me not knowing who he was or why he'd come for me. But he knew who I was, which meant he might be heading to the marina shortly to find me.

Would my plan hold?

All our phones buzzed, and we all pulled them out to check what was going on. *That mystery writer is approaching by boat.*

"Beau." I didn't want him getting hurt. "I'll send him away."

"I'm going to the kitchen," Hattie said. "In case someone comes to stop me from baking."

"I'm going back to the roof of the garage," Lucy said. "I have a great viewing from up there."

We split up, and I hurried down to the dock as Beau pulled up. "Beau, you have to leave."

He raised his brows. "What by all that's bloody and bestselling are you wearing?"

"It's a disguise."

"God, that's a relief. I thought that was your actual fashion sense. You'd definitely die in one of my books. No one like you lives past the first chapter. You'd probably walk right into a murderer's knife, thinking that they just wanted a cheese plate or something."

I grinned. "Perfect. That's the image I wanted to give."

"No." He leaned on his windshield. "See, it's still obvious it's you, but you look like you need to be killed. I thought you didn't want to be killed."

I frowned. "How is it obvious it's me?"

He shrugged. "Just is. You give off a vibe. Are those slugs on your forehead?"

"They're eyebrows."

He leaned in to peer more closely at my forehead. "They look like slugs. I take it back. I don't think I'd kill you. No one would care if you die, and you gotta get the reader to care."

I blinked. "That's incredibly rude."

"I'm too rich to care about being polite. Why do I have to leave?"

"Because I put out a bunch of rumors to try to get assassins and murderers to descend upon the marina tonight so we can set a trap for them."

He stared at me. "That's the stupidest freaking idea I've ever heard. You'll all get killed."

"Thank you for your support— Hey! Why are you tying up your boat?"

"Are you kidding? This is fantastic. I can't wait to see how this plays out. You're practically writing my next book." He hopped out onto the dock with the spryness of a man half his age. He grabbed his notebook and his phone. "Is that Lucy on top of the garage? That's a good vantage point, but too far away if things get interesting. Plus, she's very obvious. She's one good sniper away from plummeting to her doom with a bullet in her heart." He scanned my marina. "I'll go to your apartment and watch out the windows. It has good 360-degree visibility, but only one entrance, so easy to protect. And if someone comes, I can go out the window onto the roof with King Tut. Best seat in the house. That's perfect. Is the store unlocked? I'll let myself in."

He didn't even wait for an answer. He just started jogging away.

"Beau! You might get hurt!"

He waved his hand. "No chance. I'm not going to get involved. Just a bystander out of harm's way. Best of luck."

I put my hands on my hips as he jogged up the boat ramp, through the parking lot, and into the front door of the marina store.

I didn't like this. Too many people were in danger. I pulled out my phone and called Lucy. "Get off the roof. If Beau were a sniper, you'd be dead already."

"What?"

I signed. "You're too obvious. You need to get down."

"I have a great view. No one will see me when it gets dark."

"Then you can go back up after dark. Please come down. I don't want you killed."

"Oh, fine." She hung up, and I shoved my phone in my pocket.

I glanced around to make sure no one was racing toward me with murder in their eyes, then I jogged back up to the marina, and I headed into the café. The door was unlocked, and the bell jingled loudly as I walked in.

Hattie leapt from the kitchen with her shotgun aimed at me. "Freeze!"

I jumped, startled. "Hattie. You're going to kill someone with that."

"Only if they deserve it." She holstered the gun over her shoulder. "Your weapon is on that table. Come on back."

I saw a nail gun and a hairdryer on the table by my hip. I grabbed both, slinging the hairdryer across my shoulder like a beauty queen's sash. I wrapped the cord of the nail gun around my hand, so that the gun itself swung freely, ready to become a projectile. "Hattie?"

"Back to the kitchen." She beckoned to me. "I'm getting things ready."

I started to follow her back, then the bell rang. We both spun around as Lucy walked in.

She waved. "I'm back."

I felt better having her there. "Great."

The three of us filed into the kitchen. I leaned up against the wall by the back door, peering through the window. "Do you guys think I should call in Devlin and Griselda?"

Hattie raised her brows. "Why?"

"I don't want people getting killed. I set a trap to try to attract possible assassins and murderers. We've made ourselves sitting ducks against people who are really good at killing. I'm not sure that's such a great plan." Now that the sun was setting and the night was getting dark, it was feeling like an incredibly bad idea. "At least, I think you guys should leave."

"Us? No." Hattie folded her arms over her chest. "I love you, Mia, but you're not exactly a badass. Leaving you alone would be detrimental for your long-term wellbeing, and I prefer to safeguard that."

Lucy opened the walk-in freezer, checked inside, then gave the all-clear and shut it. "Someone's going to come," she said. "If Devlin and Griselda are here, they'll get scared off. We'll never know who it is."

"We don't even know if we'll get the murderer," I said. "We don't know what the motive is."

"It's diamonds or the festival," Hattie said. "And we've set the lure for both. Someone will come."

I thought of the call I'd made to Bunny. At least I knew that an assassin would kill only me. They didn't like to give out freebies. I texted Vinnie. *You guys have all approaches covered, right?*

His reply came back via a group chat called *Gold Eagle #1. No one is getting to the marina undetected. We have the roads, lake, and woods being watched.*

I texted back. *How many people are on this chat?*

Eleven watchers, plus your team. Everyone check in.

A quick reply of the numbers one through eleven lit up my phone, and I relaxed. Everyone was still okay. *Okay, thanks.*

I put the phone in my pocket, watching as the sun dipped further. We hadn't turned on the outside lights, but the lights in the kitchen were blazing. Those were the only lights on anyone on the property.

I knew from past experience that the lake could get very dark at night.

I cracked the door a hair to listen, but I couldn't hear the hubbub from the town beach. It was around the bend from the marina, and out of hearing, apparently.

I let the door fall shut. "I don't like sitting around." This was feeling very wrong to me. Very, very wrong. I couldn't see what was coming, and I had a feeling that a trained assassin could probably slide by the watchers pretty easily.

I paced across the kitchen. "You guys, this isn't feeling right."

"Where are your nerves of steel?" Hattie asked.

"I have nerves of steel. I also have instincts." I looked out the window again, into the darkness. "You guys, we need to get to the roof of the garage."

"But—"

"No. Now. We need to get to safety." The urgency was almost debilitating, with the need to get out of here. "We'll take photographs."

"At night? We won't see anything."

"Then we'll turn the lights on. Let's go." I shoved them both out the backdoor. "Get to the roof. We'll each take a direction and watch."

"No." Hattie refused to move. "That's stupid. Being a wimp never served anyone."

"I'm not being a wimp. I'm being smart—"

"You're caving," she said. "Life is short, and you can either live it as a grand adventure, or huddle in fear."

"Easy for you to say," I said. "You're—"

"If you say I'm old and close to death, I will shoot you right here, right now, bury your body in some back woods where no one will ever find you, and laugh about your untimely demise every day for the next fifty years."

I was feeling desperate. I needed to get them out of there. "I don't want you hurt—"

"We made our own choices," Hattie said. "At the end of the day, what matters is that my friend Rogue is out there somewhere, and my friend Mia has an assassin hunting her. If that's not a reason to get involved, then what's the point of being alive? Friends make life worth living, Mia. Surely you understand that now?"

Lucy nodded. "She's right. Wouldn't you risk yourself to save Rogue?"

"Well, yeah…"

"So, let's do it." Lucy patted her gun. "We aren't defenseless idiots," she said. "They might think we're clueless women, but we're not. Let's do this."

I took a breath. "You guys are sure?"

They both nodded. "Go next door," Hattie said. "Lucy will stay here with me. And we'll wait."

I let out my breath. "Okay. Okay." I hugged them both, and they squeezed me tight.

Then, without a word, I slipped out the front door and walked the few yards to the front door of the marina. I walked inside, and without turning the light on, quickly ran a fishing line across the threshold, and along the side of the door and up the staircase to my apartment.

I attached it to a fishing pole I'd wedged by the railing.

If someone tripped the fishing line, the pole would move, alerting me that someone was there.

I checked on Beau, but he refused to come down, so I made him promise to shout a warning if someone came in through my apartment.

Then I settled back on the landing and waited.

CHAPTER 24

IF ANYONE TELLS you that it's fun to wait in the pitch black for an assassin or murderer to show up, they're lying.

It didn't take me long to realize that it was very stressful, very isolating, and the perfect environment for worst case scenarios to run through my brain with reckless abandon.

I leaned my head back against the wall and shifted my weight, listening for the sounds in the night. I knew King Tut was upstairs with Beau, so I didn't worry about him.

The night was incredibly silent.

And nothing was happening.

What if no one came?

The thought was almost as alarming as if someone did come.

If no one came, then what? What next?

I stared at the fishing pole, watching for any movement, while I thought, trying to put the pieces together. I felt like I had a million possible leads, and nothing fit together.

Nothing made sense.

What did I know?

Dee was dead, but I didn't know if she'd been dead when we'd found her at Rogue's, or if she'd died later. And did it matter?

Topsy was dead.

Dee, Topsy, Tess, and Ruby Lee had been pals back then, back when diamonds had gone missing and the jeweler had been murdered.

Justin Dutch had been the sheriff, and hadn't made any arrests, and now he was crazy, or pretending.

Diamonds.

Strawberry shortcake.

And assassins...

I kept circling back to dead Ivan. If someone had wanted me dead, why was I still alive? They'd gotten to Ivan easily enough, and yet no one had actually made a play for me. Other than the truck incident, but that hadn't been planned well enough for it to be an assassin.

I'd been around assassins enough to know that they were efficient, precise, and excellent.

I sat up as a sudden epiphany hit me. No one wanted me dead. If they did, I'd be dead. Relief rushed through me. I wasn't a target! At least not for death.

So, why was Ivan dead? Who would kill him? Someone who wanted him out of the way. Of what? Following me? I didn't believe that anymore. I was often away from the marina. If someone wanted the cash and drugs, they would have had plenty of time to search the entire premises and not find it.

I stood up, my heart racing as I tried to piece the things together.

What if Ivan had stumbled across something else? Something having to do with the murder? That would mean he'd seen something at the festival. He'd been standing at Hattie's tent with us, and then he hadn't followed us when we'd run.

I thought back, trying to think of when I'd last seen him. What had he been doing?

He'd been looking over his shoulder. I thought he'd just been scanning around, but what if he'd seen something? He'd been looking into the booth next to Hattie's.

I pulled out my phone. *Hattie. What booth is next to yours?*

Dutch's Nail Salon.

My heart started beating fast. Dutch's again. *Did you see anyone we know in there yesterday? Before we went to Rogue's?*

They were super busy. Lots of folks.

Did you see Ronald there? Or Justin?

Ronald stopped by. He was making the rounds, as head judge.

And as a Dutch. *Any chance that truck I stole is owned by a Dutch?*

Sure. There are a lot of them around.

I need to run those plates. I'm going to the garage. I slipped down the stairs, and hurried through the store, being careful not to step on my fishing line. I was less nervous about an assassin now, pretty certain that I'd be dead if they'd wanted me dead.

I slipped out the door and hurried across the parking lot.

A meow echoed across the night, and I paused to look up at the roof. Both Beau and King Tut were on the roof, leaning over the edge, looking down at me. I waved at them to stay there, and then hurried to the garage. I slipped in through the side door, and pulled out my burner phone and my regular phone.

On my regular phone, which I still had on airplane mode, I found the phone number of my favorite Seam Ripper spy who worked at the police station. I texted her from the burner phone. *Angelina. This is Mia. Can you run a license plate for me?* I hoped she was at work.

I can't get into that database. Why? What's up?

I chewed my lower lip, thinking. *Did anyone report a stolen truck today?*

You bet. A Seam Ripper's husband had his truck stolen.

I grimaced. *Anyone else?*

Jeremiah Dutch came in here an hour ago, shouting about how someone stole his truck.

Excitement pulsed through me. *Do you have his address?*

Now that I can do. There was a pause, then she texted me an address in town. *It's out in the woods, on the west side of Diamond Lake.*

Got it. Thanks. My heart was racing now, as I texted the news to Hattie and Lucy. Before they could reply, the Gold Eagle #1 text group lit up my phone.

Three people coming through the woods along the south side of the lake.

A black Escalade approaching from the north.

I swore under my breath. *Does the Escalade look like FBI?*

Don't know. Wait. There's another one. And a third. It's like a presidential escort.

Hattie chimed in. *Griselda must have found you, Mia. You have to bail.*

I can't. We need to know who the three on foot are.

They'll leave once the FBI shows up. You gotta go!

I hurried to the window and looked out, but the night was still, with the exception of the fireworks bursting over the trees, flashing their gorgeous sparkles across the night sky. The booms were loud, aggressive, thundering through the metal building.

If the Escalades were coming from the north, I could drive out to the left. *How far away are the vehicles?*

Quarter of a mile.

Shoot. They would see me if I pulled out in the truck.

I had to go south, on foot, but that was where the visitors on foot were coming from.

Mia! Get out!

I bolted for the side door of the building, then raced through the parking lot toward the trees. King Tut meowed, but I didn't look back before I disappeared into the trees.

It's Mia. I'm in the woods. Where are the visitors? The woods closed in around me like an inky cloak of darkness. I went down on one knee staying low behind some ferns.

About two hundred yards from you. Moving fast. Silent. They know how to travel in the woods. I can see the glow from your phone. You need to shut it off. They'll see it.

Shoot. I shoved my phone in my pocket, but instead of getting up, I closed my eyes and took a deep breath, focusing on the sounds of the woods in between booms. I'd learned how to focus in times of stress as my mom's protégé, and I took a minute to go back to that place.

My mind seemed to focus, and senses awakened into hyper awareness. My heart rate slowed to a steady, even pulse, and my breath evened out. It took only a moment, but when I opened my eyes, I was back in full teenage Mia mode.

I was ready.

The trees shielded some of the light from the fireworks, but the booms were loud, drowning out any sounds that might clue me in on my visitors' location. I eased through the woods, moving from shadow to shadow, keeping just close enough to the shoreline to be able to see it.

My guess was that they'd come by boat, and they would be keeping close to the shore.

I saw the first one quickly. He was walking along the shore-line, a few feet off the lake. I crouched low, watching him. He looked familiar. I knew I'd seen him before, but it was hard to tell. He was a murky silhouette in the darkness.

Then a firework flashed and lit him up. *Stevie.*

At that same moment, he looked right at me. I froze, knowing that he wouldn't recognize me with my slug eyebrows.

But to my surprise, he shouted. "That's her! The one who was talking about the diamonds! She knows where they are! Get her!"

And then he charged me.

At that same moment, I heard footsteps behind me, and I knew they'd spread out. Shoot! I bolted to my right, away from the marina, while I organized my nail gun. Stevie was so much faster than I was, but before he could reach me, someone grabbed the back of my shirt and threw me to the ground.

I gasped as I hit, but before I could get my gun, someone was on my back, and my hands were trapped behind me.

Stevie crouched in front of me. "Where are the diamonds?"

I couldn't see who was behind me, but he had my hair and

was pulling my head back. "Was it worth killing over the diamonds?" I asked.

"I didn't kill anyone."

"Their bodies were in your freezer! I saw them!" I knew the FBI was at my marina by now, and I had watchers in the trees who would come to my rescue, so I had only moments to get up close and personal with my new pal before rescuers would descend.

"You saw them?" He frowned. "That's impossible. There weren't any bodies in there—" He swore suddenly. "Holy crap. It's you." He looked past me. "It's the one who searched the freezer."

"You killed them for the diamonds," I said. "Why would they have the diamonds? Why them?"

"Dee took them," he said. "She had them that night, and she took them. She hid them, and then she left town. Where did you put them?"

I needed more from him. I needed something to prove he killed Dee. "Why would you kill Dee before she told you where they were?"

He narrowed his eyes, then pulled out a gun and pressed it against my forehead. "You have three seconds to tell me where they are."

My gut went cold with sudden terror. No one would be able to get to me in time if he pulled that trigger. "They're in my freezer," I whispered, my throat suddenly dry. "In my apartment. Upstairs at the marina."

"If you're lying, you're dead."

I blinked. "I'm not lying. Go check." Yes, yes, go run out of the woods with a gun while Griselda was in the parking lot looking for me.

Stevie looked at whoever was behind me. "Keep her here. I'm going to go check."

He stood up and ran past me.

I couldn't get to my nail gun or my hairdryer. Whoever was behind me had me pinned too well—

He suddenly went limp, and then his weight disappeared

from my back. I scrambled to my feet and spun around. Behind me stood a tall, muscled twenty-something guy with a gold chain, bling earring, and a visage I'd seen by Hattie's booth yesterday. Vinnie's pal grinned. "The FBI is raising hell up there. Get out of here."

Lying on the ground was a guy I didn't recognize, and I didn't waste time looking for his identification. "Thank you!" I spun around and ran toward the water, working my way along the shore. I didn't know who the third guy was, and I hoped he wasn't there.

As I ran along the bank, I heard the rumble of an engine coming up from behind me.

I whipped around, but at that moment, the sky lit up, and I saw my cat perched on the bow of Beau's boat. The running lights were off, and the boat was drifting, almost wakeless. The grumpy old man didn't wave at me, but Hattie and Lucy leaned over the edge of the boat. "Jump in."

"You're amazing! I love you guys!" I ran down to the edge of the water and plunged in. The boat didn't slow as it passed me, but I grabbed the edge and hauled myself up as far as I could. Lucy and Hattie dragged me in, and the moment I fell onto the floor of the boat, Beau opened up the gas and his nifty little number took off into the lake, shooting down the firework-covered mirror that the lake had become.

That had been close.

Too close. "There are too many people with guns in this town," I shouted over the roar of the motor.

At that moment, Beau shifted to neutral, and the boat slowed down so quickly that I fell backward. Lucy landed on her knees, but Hattie managed to sink gracefully down into one of the luxurious seats on Beau's boat.

"You okay?" he asked.

Aww...he was such a liar, pretending he didn't care. I nodded. "It was fine. I like having guns pressed against my forehead."

As their eyes widened, I waved off their concerns, downplaying the situation as we floated in the middle of the lake, just below the fireworks that were lighting up the sky. They all leaned in as I told them what had happened. "I don't think Stevie killed them," I said. "But he wants the diamonds, and he was certain Dee took them that night and hid them."

"So, what now?" Beau asked.

"We go to Jeremiah Dutch's place. He owns the truck." I read them his address, and Hattie nodded. "That's in Loon Cove. Beau?"

He didn't turn the boat back on. "You want to go to his place? What if he's there?"

"He won't be there," I said. "It's not even ten o'clock on a Saturday night. What guy is going to be home? He's out looking for me."

"Agreed," Hattie said. "He's not home."

"I'm in," Lucy said. "If Rogue was driving that truck, then we need to get to his place."

Beau looked at the three of us, then shook his head. "If things go south, I'm saving myself and leaving you guys there."

"Perfect." I sat down on one of his benches, and King Tut snuggled down on my lap. "I love a challenge."

"I really will leave you."

"Okay." Hattie and I exchanged knowing glances, then we all stretched out on the luxurious cushions as Beau hit the gas and the boat shot forward.

It was too loud to talk with the engine on, so I simply leaned back and watched the fireworks as we sped away.

It really was beautiful.

I was glad I hadn't died earlier and missed it.

CHAPTER 25

JEREMIAH'S HOUSE wasn't visible from the lake, but Hattie and Lucy figured out which dock was his.

It was in a remote part of the lake on a cove where all the houses were on a hill above the lake. It was impossible to see the houses through the trees. All that was visible was the occasional dock, with a pathway that went up the hill and into the woods.

There was a fishing boat tied up at Jeremiah's dock, but the left side was empty, so Beau pulled up there, cutting the engine as we drifted in. Like a pro, I helped catch the pilings, and we looped the dock lines around it.

Despite his "I'm not involved" disclaimer, Beau opted not to stay in the boat, but instead, followed us up the trail as we headed up to the house, recording every moment on his phone. King Tut stayed close to my heel, because I hadn't any industrial strength chains to attach to him to make sure he stayed in the boat.

But he was sticking close to me, so it was fine.

It was so dark, we were almost at the house before we noticed it. I caught Hattie's arm and pointed. No lights were on, and it was very still.

"I doubt he's in bed already, so I think we're good." Hattie led the way to the back door, which opened lakeside, and knocked loudly on the door.

I realized that we'd left Vinnie behind, which had been fine in the moment when I'd decided that no one was trying to kill me, but not so fine now that I was alone in the woods with only some corded implements. "Anyone want the nail gun?"

They both held up their rifles.

"Seriously?"

"Always," Hattie said.

"Knock again," Lucy said. "Louder. We want to be sure no one's there."

Hattie banged on the door again, and then I shouted. "Hello! Jeremiah! Are you home?"

Then we waited...and there were just the distant booms of the fireworks.

Hattie stepped back and gestured to the door. "Have at it, Mia."

I stepped up and tried the door. It was locked, but it was a doorknob lock, so I had it opened quickly. I eased the door open and stepped inside. "Hello? Anyone home?"

We all waited for a moment, then, when no one greeted us, we filed in. "I'll go upstairs," Hattie said.

"I'll take the first floor," Lucy said, her gun ready.

Beau looked at me. "Where are you going?"

"Basement. We're on a hill, and I saw glass below the deck. There's a bottom floor here."

"Oh, good. Let's go." He continued to video me as I walked through the first floor, looking for the stairs that led to the basement. He began to narrate. King Tut trotted along beside me, his fur brushing against my calf. "We're following Mia Murphy and her massive cat," he said. "She has a knack for finding bodies, so if there is one to find, she's the one who will do it."

I looked back over my shoulder as I opened a door and found stairs. "Really?"

"Mia is a former con artist and FBI covert operative, so she believes she's unstoppable," he continued. "That will be her downfall, but it will be most interesting to witness the moment of unraveling."

I started to jog down the stairs, with King Tut charging down ahead of me. "Beau. Enough with that."

"I'm going to start a new series, and I'm modeling my heroine after you. So, I'm feeling out the tone with my narration. It's how I work."

I couldn't decide whether to be pleased or horrified that he was modeling his new series heroine after me. "Is she a cool chick?"

"I'm still deciding. Impetuous. Takes ridiculous risks. Overmatched. Unfocused. An underdog."

I shined my mini light around the basement, which screamed "man cave central!" It was furnished with a full bar, a keg, a ping pong table, and a foosball table. A few leather recliners, and a TV that took up an entire wall. King Tut was strolling through the basement as if he owned it. "That's flattering. Thanks."

"Underdog stories sell the best," Beau said, "because you gotta write the protagonist as rootable."

"Rootable? Like a carrot?"

"No. Someone that the reader roots for. That's everything to make a story successful. She needs to be intensely loyal. Funny. Resilient. The average human being that rises above their limits to beat the odds. It's what everyone wishes they were."

Wow. I was rootable. I loved that. A warm feeling settled over me as I shined my light on an interior door that looked like it was a closet. It definitely didn't have windows, as it was on the backside of the basement. King Tut wandered over to it, sniffed along the bottom edge, then put his front paws up on the door and meowed.

Not an aggressive meow, like he was going to inflict death and serious bodily harm on whatever was on the other side. More of a communicative meow, like, "hey, this door is pretty adorable, don't you think?"

I walked over to the door and tried the handle. The doorknob turned but the door didn't open. I shined my light again, and I saw a deadbolt lock on it. "Why do you think they have a keyed deadbolt on an interior door?"

Beau didn't say anything, but he kept recording me.

"You'll record it if someone leaps out and kills me when I open it?"

"You bet. The police will have an easy time solving your murder, so no worries."

He could have said he'd save me, but since he'd already told me I was rootable, I decided to just hang onto that positivity for the moment. I pulled out my lockpicks and went to work on the lock. It was new and shiny, high-end, and it took me longer than I expected to open it.

While I worked on it, King Tut wound around my legs, purring, which was reassuring. If there was a threat behind that door, he would know it.

When the lock finally clicked, I grinned at Beau triumphantly. "Is she going to be able to pick locks?"

"I haven't decided. It's a little bit dull, honestly. How is that a life skill?"

"It's not dull. It's clever and the ultimate underdog weapon."

He grunted.

I decided to ignore him, and I pushed the door open. It was dark inside, but no one jumped out at me, and King Tut didn't charge into the darkness yowling, so I felt emboldened to shine the light around the room. I found a floor freezer like the one at the Ugly Man, shelves of assorted garage-type stuff like paint and extension cords, and then my light landed on a cot in the corner.

On the cot, facing the wall, was a woman lying on her side with her hands behind her back. "Holy crap!" I leapt forward, my heart racing. "Are you okay?"

At the sound of my voice, she rolled over to face me, blinking at the light. I quickly averted it as I ran over, but not before I saw she was gagged. Fury roared through me. Who tied up a woman and left her gagged in an empty house?

I quickly untied the gag first. "Are you okay?"

"My wrists. Quick. My wrists. He'll be back soon."

As King Tut hopped up on the cot and tapped her forehead gently, I looked at her wrists. "Zip ties? What the heck? Beau. We need scissors."

He was still recording. "Scissors? I don't have any—"

"Get them from the kitchen! Go! And get water!" She had to be thirsty from the gag.

He swore under his breath, but grudgingly turned and backed out of the room, still recording, and shouted for Hattie.

I crouched next to the cot. "My name's Mia Murphy. Who are you? Why does he have you here?" She looked to be in her mid-forties, maybe a little older or younger. She was wearing jeans and sneakers, and a blue tank top with lace around the edge. She looked casual, but capable. It was still dark in the closet, so I couldn't see her clearly, but she looked vaguely familiar.

She tried to sit up, and I helped her. "My mom," she said. "Have you seen my mom?"

"Who's your mom?"

"Esther Neeley. Have you seen her?"

Esther! I knew it! *I knew it!* No wonder she looked familiar. She looked a lot like Rogue. "You're Tessa?"

She nodded.

Footsteps raced down the stairs, and Tessa tried to stand up. "Hurry! It's him—"

"It's me," Hattie shouted. "I have scissors!" She ran into the room, with Lucy and Beau on her heels. She swore when she saw Tessa. "Are you kidding me? The bastard!"

I took the scissors and snipped the zip tie that was around her ankles, and then her wrists. "I've seen your mom twice, but I don't know where she is."

"We need to find her. He's got her doing something for him. I don't know what." She tried to stand up, and her legs gave out.

"How long have you been in there?"

"I don't know. I tried to attack them with stuff I found in the room earlier, which is why I got zip tied." She let me sling her arm over my shoulder, while Lucy helped on the other side.

Hattie was swearing up a storm, and I felt the same. "When did you last see your mom?"

"I haven't seen her for a couple days. They let me talk to her through the door a few times, but that's it." She took the water from Hattie and guzzled it. "Thanks."

"What do they want from her?"

"I don't know. Let's get out of here."

King Tut sat down in front of us, blocking the pathway. He didn't move, and he gave me an unyielding yellow stare when I told him to move.

He just sat there, and suddenly, I understood. He was telling me not to rush out of there. Why? Because she was trying to rush us out of there. Maybe it was because she was scared. And maybe not.

I let go of Tessa and moved forward to stand beside King Tut, also blocking the way. "I don't believe you, Tessa. You know exactly what's going on."

Lucy gave me a look. "Mia. She's been tied up for heaven knows how long. Now is not the time—"

"On the contrary, it is the time." I folded my arms over my chest, remembering what Bootsy had told us. "Tessa, is it about the diamonds? The murder at the jewelry store? Or the festival? We know it's one of them. You were friends with Dee and Topsy, and they're both dead—"

"What?" Her eyes widened, and I didn't *quite* believe her. "They're dead? When?"

What was up with her? Because she definitely hadn't tied herself up. "Yesterday. Day before. I'm not really sure. But they're dead. And you and Ruby Lee are still alive. It's either about the festival or the diamonds, and we need to know what's going on."

Tessa scowled at me. "Can we get out of here first?"

"Yeah," Lucy agreed. "I don't think it'd be great to run into him here."

I noticed Beau was still recording.

Hattie shot me a look, then walked over and sat down on the leather couch. She put her feet up on the coffee table. King Tut hopped up beside her, and they looked like they were there to spend the evening watching baseball and drinking.

I grinned. Hattie also thought something else was going on. "Tessa. People are *dead*. Your mom is missing, and probably going to be blamed for it. We need to know what you know."

Her eyes narrowed, and suddenly, she didn't look quite so sweet and innocent. "You're just like him."

"Like who? Jeremiah?"

"Look," she said. "My mom is in danger because they're using me as leverage. We need to find her now."

I felt Hattie shift. Rogue's safety was most important to all of us, but I tried not to show it to Tessa. "What is she doing right now? What's his plan?'"

"Can we just go get her?"

"No, we can't just go get her," I snapped. "What is going on, Tessa? Talk to us. What happened that night?" I was listening intently for the sound of a boat or a car, indicating that we were running out of time, but the fireworks were still booming, so I figured no one was coming home yet. But they'd be over soon.

Tessa stared at me, and her jaw went mutinous. "You wouldn't understand."

"No? I was married to a drug kingpin, and I didn't even know it. Sometimes you get yourself in bad situations and it's not your fault. But what you do afterwards? That's when you get to choose who you are and who you want to be."

She stared at me.

I stared back.

King Tut purred.

Beau recorded.

As I engaged in a staring contest with Tessa, I studied her carefully. The set of her shoulders and her chin spoke volumes about defensiveness and anger, but the way her eyebrows were knitted, and her shallow breathing told me that there was distrust under the surface.

She was guarding herself, and possibly Rogue, against us. All on her own, and that wasn't going to work this time.

"You can trust us," I said softly. "We love your mom, and she helped save my life a few weeks ago. I owe her, and I honor that. We've been running her booth at the festival so she can still win."

"I baked the biscuits today using her recipe," Hattie said. "I didn't even change it, even though I could have made it better. I'm Hattie Lawless, of Hattie's Café, and when I say I could have made them better, I mean it. But that would have made the biscuits ineligible, so that's friendship right there."

"And we all set up the table both days," Lucy said. "It looked really great."

"We hid a dead body so that it wouldn't interfere with her biscuits being judged," I added.

"And I even sacrificed my pride to drive her Lamborghini around to try to attract the murderer's attention," Hattie said.

Tessa looked around at us. "You hid a body for her?"

"Absolutely," I said, as we all nodded. "And you better delete that, Beau."

"I don't share my research," he said. "You're good."

Tessa's shoulders suddenly sagged. "It's my fault," she whispered. "I got her involved."

And…now…we were off. "What happened?"

She sank down on a recliner. "I followed Dee, Topsy, and Ruby Lee that night. When they got to the jewelers, there was a fight with the three of them. Ruby Lee took off with the car, leaving them stranded."

Ah… so that was what drove Ruby Lee. Guilt because she'd left them there.

"What happened?"

"They went inside. I knew they were going to steal the

diamonds. Dee had gotten the safe combo from a boy in her class who worked there. But they were going to give them back. It was just a lark, to see if they could do it," Tessa said. "They were going to take them from the store, and then sneak them into the jeweler's home. Dee loved to do stuff like that—steal stuff just to give it back."

Hattie, Lucy, and Beau all looked at me meaningfully. "Mia understands that," Beau said. "Don't you, Mia?"

I sighed, realizing that a confession might help my bond with Tessa. "I grew up as a criminal, and I do still enjoy pick pocketing phones and giving them back," I admitted. "It's fun."

Relief rushed across her face at the realization that I wouldn't judge her friends. "Right! That's what they did. Everyone thought Dee was such a bad person, but she wasn't. She just liked to challenge herself and have fun."

I cleared my throat. Yes, that sounded like me. "So, what happened?"

"Well, I had my car there, so I jumped out and told them I could drive them home. They always told me to leave because I was younger and they wanted to protect me, but they needed a ride, so they told me to wait outside."

I walked over to the window and peered out at the lake. The booms were still going on, and I could see the moonlight on the lake through the trees. Not much of the lake, but enough to see that nothing was moving out there. I could see the tip of Beau's boat. "Then what?"

"Well, I was waiting, right? And this truck pulls up right in front. I couldn't see who got out because the driver got out on that side. I freaked out because I knew they were in there. But before I could warn them, the jeweler pulls up and races in, shouting."

"He must have had a silent alarm," I said. Those silent alarms had nearly busted me more than once.

Tessa nodded. "I didn't know what to do, and then I heard shots. Gunshots!"

Hattie leaned forward, and I looked over at her, taking my gaze off the lake. "And?"

"At first nothing, then Topsy and Dee came running out the back door. They ran to the car, freaking out, saying that he'd shot him, but I didn't know who they were talking about. They said to leave, so I hit the gas. As we were driving out, the man came running out the front door. Not Tony. The other man."

The silence in the room was riveting. "Did you see him?" I asked.

She nodded. "We all did."

"Who was it?"

"Richie Dutch. He died a few months ago. That's why we came back."

Holy cow. Ronnie's twin brother. Justin's nephew. Dee's uncle. The fireworks started booming like crazy, like the grand finale was cheering on the revelation.

Hattie let out a low whistle. "He was always a nasty sort," she said. "It doesn't surprise me at all that he killed that poor man."

"Or that Justin didn't want to arrest him," I said. "No wonder Justin retired. It was that or arrest his own family."

"Why'd Dee come back?" Hattie asked softly. "For the diamonds?"

Tessa nodded. "She hid them that night. When she heard Richie's truck pull up, she hid them. She was going to go back, but then Richie came to her house and told her she had twenty-four hours to hand them over, or he was going to shoot her and the rest of us. So, she took off. We all took off."

"Where did Dee hide the diamonds?" I asked.

Tessa looked over at me. "In the trophy."

"The trophy? What trophy?"

"The bake-off festival trophy. It was at the jeweler's getting engraved. She hid the diamonds in the bottom."

We all stared at her, then Hattie started laughing. "Son of a biscuit! That's why everyone wants to win? So they can get the trophy and get the diamonds out of it?"

Tessa shrugged. "Well, they keep it under lock and key at the town hall. No one can get to it. The only time it comes out is at the festival, but the winner just gets a replica."

"Except a five-time champion," Hattie said. "They get to keep the actual trophy." She stood up. "I can't believe that the sanctity of a baking event has been tainted by diamonds! Does no one appreciate the fine art of dessert anymore? I'm so annoyed. I'm going to enter tonight. No one deserves to win for diamonds. I'm going to enter, and my biscuits will be so delicious tomorrow that they'll win even though I didn't enter the other two stages. What the flipping pancake!"

While Hattie grumped about dessert ninjas, I stayed focused on Tessa. "So, what is Jeremiah having your mom do?" If she said, "killing my friends," I wasn't sure what I'd do.

"He wants the diamonds," she said.

"I gathered that, but what is your mom doing?"

"Putting things together for tomorrow. For the finals."

"Who is he setting up to win?" Hattie asked. "Ruby Lee? Zoltan? Not Rogue, because he's not letting her do it."

"All of them," Tessa said. "It doesn't matter which one it is. He has a plan for any of them. My mom will be back for the finals. And if she wins, she trades the diamonds for my life."

I looked over at Hattie and Lucy. Everything she said made sense...until the part about Rogue. Hattie and Lucy both gave me a look that said they agreed. "Tessa," I said. "What's your mom really doing?"

"I told you! I don't know exactly what he's having her do."

At that moment, I saw movement down on the water. Belatedly, I realized that the night was quiet. The fireworks were over. Boats were cruising by with their lights on, heading back home after the night's festivities were over. "We gotta go. Let's go. Now. Everyone to the boat."

I yanked the door open. Tessa ran out first, sprinting down toward the water. "Beau? You didn't leave the key in there, did you?"

Hattie and Lucy hurried after her, but I waited for Beau and King Tut.

I closed the door behind us, then we filed down to the water. I went last, wanting to make sure that Hattie and Beau made it down the steep stairs okay. As we hurried down the steps, the roars of boat engines from the lake filled the night air.

As we reached the dock, I paused, looking back up at the house. "You think Jeremiah wrote down his plan? If we could find it—"

"Get in the boat," Hattie said. "Regardless of how much of Tessa's story is true, he left her tied up and gagged. You don't want a piece of that. Let's get out of here. We'll get more info from her when we get home—"

At that moment, the engine of Beau's boat roared to life.

He let out a curse as the driving lights came on, then Tessa put the boat in reverse and backed out of the dock. "Hey!" I took off first, reaching down to the water and waving my arms, but she hit the acceleration and Beau's boat shot down the lake.

Beau strode up next to me, unleashing a litany of curses.

I set my hands on my hips, watching as his boat disappeared into the night. "You didn't learn your lesson about leaving your key in the boat?"

"No one steals boats around here."

"Except Rogue and her daughter."

"I didn't know her daughter would be here. I was preparing for a fast getaway."

Hattie was laughing as she and Lucy walked onto the dock. "The man writes about the most nefarious minds in fiction, and he assumes that no one will steal a million-dollar boat if he leaves the keys in it?"

"It's Bass Derby. I've left the keys in my boat for years. No one steals boats in this town."

"Except the same people who steal diamonds," I said.

"I don't know about you guys," Lucy said, easing to the side as

King Tut strode out onto the dock. "But I think we need to get out of here. Any suggestions?"

"Let's steal a boat." Hattie hopped off the dock into the little fishing boat. "I can get any engine started. Get in. Just need a moment."

While Lucy and Beau climbed in, I walked to the end of the dock with King Tut, and looked down the lake. There were so many boats coming up the lake. Any one of them could be Jeremiah.

I watched each one, listening for the sound of the engine slowing.

I'd stolen his truck already. And now his hostage. And his boat.

I crouched down next to King Tut, sliding my hand through his harness to keep him from diving in after a fish. "If he catches me," I whispered. "He's not going to be happy."

King Tut leaned over the edge of the dock, watching the water.

"Can you chew through zip ties?"

His tail switched, and I tightened my grip. "Tessa was lying," I whispered. "About some of it. Not all of it. There was truth mixed in there. And lies." But what was what? I needed to replay Beau's video and watch for her tells.

King Tut launched himself off the dock so fast that I had no time to brace myself. My fingers stuck in his harness, and the massive cat dragged me right off the dock. I landed face first in the water, and got it up my nose, in my mouth, and down my throat.

Sputtering, I came up, still holding King Tut by the harness. He had a wriggling water snake in his teeth, which was just gross.

"I can't believe I got that on video," Beau said. "That was brilliant."

I didn't have time to get mad at Hattie and Beau laughing, because Lucy gestured me to hurry. "There's a boat slowing down. Get over here!"

I sloshed across the water and tossed King Tut into the boat, making him lose the snake, as Hattie began to pull away from the dock. "We don't have time to pull you in," she said. "Just hang on and stay low."

Holy cow. Hang onto a speeding boat? "You've got to be kidding." I grabbed the side of the boat, and Lucy locked her hands around my wrists.

"Zip ties," Hattie said. "That's your motivation. Now, quiet." She pulled away from the dock. Navigation lights were off, and she kept close to shore, close enough that my shins kept hitting rocks. I tried to scramble over them, but since I couldn't see them, I just kept hitting them, and tripping.

Lucy tried to hang on, pulling me up each time I fell. "Hattie," she whispered. "Get deeper."

King Tut sat on the seat nearest me, watching me with moderate disdain. He was dripping wet, and not impressed that I'd deprived him of a fishy snack.

"Can't go deeper," Hattie said. "We need to stay in the shadows of the trees."

"A boat is docking there," Beau reported.

"Turn your phone off," I whispered. "The flash from the video is bright."

"Oh, whoops." Beau turned off his phone just as we heard a curse from the dock we'd just vacated.

I met Lucy's worried gaze, dimly visible in the moonlight. "If he sees the boat, take off," I whispered. "Hattie can outrun him. I'll just go to shore."

She shook her head. "We can't leave you."

"You have to. If you stay, we'll all be caught. If you take off, then he won't look for me." I was on the far side of the boat, where he wouldn't be able to see me.

Hattie kept the boat moving, and we all stayed silent as she pulled me along, creeping along the shoreline. Jeremiah was shouting and storming around. I could hear his boots thudding on the dock, and then a light flashed across our little boat, lighting up Lucy's face.

"Hey! That's my boat!"

I met Lucy's gaze. "Go," I whispered. Then I let go, and sank beneath the water.

Hattie hit the gas immediately, and the propeller buzzed past me, churning up water.

Leaving me alone in the lake.

CHAPTER 26

I SWAM UNDERWATER along the shoreline as far as I could. The sound of Jeremiah's boat starting up echoed through the water. His spotlight was bright, flashing across the surface of the lake above me. Had he seen me submerge after all?

I was in so much trouble if he came after me. I didn't want to be zip-tied. Or gagged. Or murdered. Or any of it.

I sank lower beneath the surface, until my lungs were burning. The urge to inhale began to build, but still I stayed under. The light was still bright above me. Was he looking for me?

His propeller roared to life, and I heard the hum of the blades as he backed up and then hit the gas. The boat shot right toward me, and I realized I was in the way.

Horror shot through me, but I had no time to move.

His boat cut through the water, inches from my shoulder, and water from the propeller hit me with such force that I flew backwards.

And then, he was gone. Past. And I wasn't puréed into little pieces.

"Holy cow." My heart was pounding like crazy. The propeller would have chopped off any body part they hit instantly, including my head. And it had been so close.

I wanted to cry a little bit for how near I'd come to being dismembered, but I had no idea how quickly he'd return. I knew Hattie was a great driver, and if she had enough horsepower, she'd lose him in the night quickly. But if she didn't have enough speed to outrun him, he could catch up to her and—

No. They would be safe.

I only had to take care of myself.

I swam along the shore, staying close, in water that was only about three feet deep. Enough that I could touch the bottom if I needed to, submerge if necessary, but keep swimming and moving, putting as much distance between myself and Jeremiah as I could.

The water wasn't all that cold, and as long as I kept moving, I didn't feel cold.

But I did feel isolated, vulnerable, and lost, so that wasn't all that fun.

I'd never been in this part of the lake, and I didn't have enough lake knowledge to know where I was or to have a good exit plan.

Exit plans were everything, and I'd totally forgotten to have one. My mom would be so disappointed in me.

Or maybe not. I mean, it had been kind of an on-the-run escape while chaos had been going down at the marina.

Plus, I'd sacrificed myself to protect people I loved. I think she would appreciate that. But maybe not. It had been a long time since I'd been privy to the unpredictable recesses of her mind.

I had no choice but to keep moving, the silence and darkness of the night settling down around me. I settled into a steady rhythm, touching my feet to the bottom occasionally, as I worked my way along the shore. Progress was slow, and I wanted to be around the bend from Jeremiah's by the time he got back.

But then what?

———

AN HOUR LATER, I changed my mind about how cold the water felt.

I was shivering so much my teeth were chattering.

I had no idea where I was, or how far I'd gone.

Every dock I passed had boats tied up, so I knew people were there. I didn't dare go up to the houses and ask for help, in case they were friends of Jeremiah.

So, I kept going.

I was so cold.

My muscles were cramping.

And it was so freaking dark. And quiet. And isolated.

So many pine trees crowding out the moonlight along the shoreline.

But what choice did I have?

No new solutions would present themselves if I stayed where I was, so I had to keep moving.

Moving.

Moving.

Come on, Mia.

I gradually became aware of the sound of a boat engine behind me. I turned around, and saw a spotlight directed onto the shore.

Was it Jeremiah?

Oh, crap. I honestly felt like crying. After all this, he was going to find me?

Then I got annoyed. No man got to make me feel like crying! Stanley had forfeited that right on behalf of his entire gender.

So, I eased over to shore, looking for a rock to hide behind, but there were just tall grasses and lily pads. I sank deep, trying to swim as quietly as possible as I wove between the vines that seemed to reach out and wrap around my ankles. I got in the middle and sank low, so that only my mouth was out of the water.

And I waited.

The boat got closer, and the light flashed right over my face, blinding me.

Then the engine turned off, and there was silence. Was he fishing? Or listening for my breathing? I was going to need to breathe soon—

"Mia!" A man's voice whispered out across the water. "Mia! Are you in there?"

I eased my head up out of the water to look at the boat. I could see the outline of a man, but his silhouette didn't look familiar. He looked solid and strong, but definitely not Jeremiah. The boat was a little canoe with a tiny motor on the back. It looked familiar. Who had one of those?

"Mia!" he whispered again. "Hattie sent me to find you. It's Cargo."

"Cargo?" I blurted out the name in stunned surprise. My sole employee, who had managed to avoid me completely since I'd arrived. I'd find his coffee still steaming, a blueberry muffin half-eaten, his boat at my dock...but never Cargo. He always got the work done, and the boats were always ready on time, but I literally never saw him. He'd helped save me once, but he'd managed it without showing his face, or even a pinkie toe.

"Mia!" He sounded so relieved for a man who'd never met me. "Where are you?"

"In the grasses." I didn't dare come out. "Give me proof that you're Cargo."

"You owe me for a month of wages."

"Because you never signed your paperwork to become an employee!"

"That's right. Now let's go. This isn't as fun for me as you might think."

I grinned. "It's not that fun for me either." I began to work my way out of the grasses, watching the canoe as he moved his light across the shore, trying to find me.

The light suddenly blinded me, and he said, "I've got you. I'm coming over."

"Avert the light!" I put my hand over my eyes, unable to handle the brightness after being in the dark for so long.

"No," he shot back. "If I can't see you, I can't rescue you. So deal with it. Head back to shore. I heard you're not exactly Princess Grace around water."

I smiled again. I liked his attitude. There was no room in my life for namby-pambies, as my mom used to say. Since I didn't want to almost get run over for a second time that evening, I did as he said, keeping my eyes shielded from the light as I sloshed back toward shore.

About the time I reached ankle-deep water, the canoe bumped against my calf.

I turned around as he finally turned the light away. "Get in carefully. Canoes tip over easily, and I'm not in the mood to be wet."

"Are you always this cranky when you rescue people in the middle of the night?" I braced my hands on both sides of the canoe, and carefully stepped in.

"Yeah."

I settled down in the bow of the canoe, facing him. He'd turned off his light, so it was dark again. I couldn't see him at all, other than a silhouette. "Thanks."

He grunted as he used his paddle to get us out of the grasses. "There are towels and blankets on the bottom of the boat if you're cold."

"Great." Now that I was out of the water, I was already warming up, since the night was balmy. "Nice to meet you."

He didn't say anything else, but he started his engine and began a leisurely pace out into the middle of the lake.

"Where are we going?"

"Hattie's."

"So, they made it there safely?"

"Yeah."

I sat back, watching him. Now that we were away from shore, the moon was casting a silvery light on him, enough for me to start to make out his features. I realized he looked vaguely familiar. "Have we met before?"

"No."

I continued to watch him. I'd definitely seen him before, but I couldn't place him. He looked to be about sixty, but it was difficult to be sure.

"Stop staring at me," he said.

"You're so attractive, I can't help myself."

It was too dark to see if that made him grin, but I felt like he'd thought that was funny, since we both knew it was too dark to see him well. "Why have you been hiding from me?"

"I never hide."

"You do hide. You're like one of those subway rats in New York City. You know, the ones who can't handle sunlight, so they scurry into the dark recesses of the city's underbelly whenever sunshine tries to find them."

"I'm a rat?" There was definite amusement in his voice now.

Which was good. I had a feeling he was going to dump me at Hattie's, and continue to hide from me once the adventure was over. "Did you agree to rescue me tonight only because it was dark, so I wouldn't be able to see you well?"

"Shut up."

"So, that's a yes," I mused. Why didn't he want me to see his face? Because I knew him? Because I'd recognize him from somewhere? "Let's play twenty questions. It'll take forever to get to Hattie's at this rate. How long have you lived in Bass Derby?"

I thought he wasn't going to answer, but he surprised me. "I used to come here as a kid every summer. I retired about ten years ago and moved here. I like what you've done with the marina. Looks good. I like having new boats to work on."

Holy cow. That had been like an entire speech! He was such a chatty Cathy in the safety of darkness. "Did you know about the jewelry store murder?" I asked, changing the subject. If he'd been around his whole life, maybe he'd seen or heard a little tidbit that would make all the pieces fit together.

"Tony's Maine Gems? Yeah. Everyone knew about it."

His voice was beginning to sound familiar. I'd definitely met him before. "Did you know the girls involved? Ruby Lee, Dee, Topsy and Tessa?"

"Nah. They were locals. I was a summer kid. I was older than they were."

The way he'd said that triggered a memory. A song from a movie. About summer. I remembered his voice saying summer that way. Hmm... "Let's sing." The words popped out unexpectedly, but I trusted my instincts.

Silence.

I started to sing the summer song.

"You're a terrible singer."

"I sing with joy and delight. What more could you ask for?" I went back to singing.

It wasn't until the third verse that he started to sing with me.

His voice was rich and melodic, and exactly as I'd remembered. *Holy cow.* Cargo was actually Phillip Harding, an incredibly attractive, very well-known Hollywood A-list actor. He was my mom's generation, not mine, but he'd been huge! *What the heck?* What was he doing working my maintenance garage?

He was a celebrity, superstar, and world dominator of the level that my mom would have targeted in a split second. She would have tossed me in the deepest ocean to get a chance at Cargo's income.

We finished the song, and then the night fell quiet. Just the sound of the little engine chugging along, and the water lapping at the boat. "Interesting," I finally said. "Your voice is very similar to the actor who originally sang that song for the movie. Can't remember his name, but he was quite unattractive." I went with sass, because if I was serious, he'd shut down. Or that was my guess, since he'd been hiding out in my garage under an assumed name.

"What are you going to do about it?" he finally asked, an edge to his voice.

"About what? That you're impersonating Phillip Harding? Nothing. He can chase you down himself."

He was quiet for a moment, clearly trying to decide if I really thought he was a look-alike, or if I knew he was the real deal.

"You know Beau Hammersley?" I asked.

"Yeah."

"He's also very famous, and he hates people. But you know? He loves me. Because he's just Beau to me, and he needs more friends. Even cranky celebrities need friends. Did you know that? It's a fact."

He sighed. "You know it's me."

Ah…I'd been pretty sure it was him, but he'd confirmed it. No wonder all the Seam Rippers had giggled like teenage girls when they mentioned his name. "Is that why you hid from me? Because you don't want me to know you're alive and living in Bass Derby?"

"I hide from everyone. I don't want to be bothered. I just want to fix boats, go fishing, and be away from all that."

"I'm infamous," I said.

"I know. I know all about you."

I grinned. "So, I get what it's like to not want your past to define your future." I tried to think of the last movie I'd seen him in, but it had been a long time. "Why did you leave the business?"

"None of your business."

"Right."

We were quiet for another moment, then he spoke again. "If you use my name to try to get people to come to the Eagle's Nest, I'll quit."

"I would never do that." I trailed my hand in the water. "My mom is an excellent con artist. She used to take me to parties with celebrities when I was a kid. She'd con her way into vacations in the Hamptons, people's jewelry, lavish gifts and lifestyles. I spent a lot of time with celebrities as a kid, and it was always with one foot pointed toward the door, ready to run when they realized we were crooks."

He was quiet. Listening.

"I left her when I was seventeen, and I've never talked to her since, even though she was my whole world. But I can't live that life, and I need to move beyond my past and that identity." I decided not to mention how much fun I was having every time I had to do something illegal to help my friends. "So, I understand you wanting to stay off the radar, and I don't have celebrity awe. Honestly, if anything, I'd probably just start looking for ways to con you."

He started laughing then. "You'd never succeed. I'm incredibly brilliant."

"I am, too. It would be a level playing field, then. All the more fun."

I could feel his energy relaxing. "You're a strange one, Mia Murphy."

"You're a paranoid hermit with an attitude. I think we'll get along great."

"We just might," he mused.

"You going to fill out paperwork now that I know your real name? So I can pay you?"

"Nope."

"Why not?"

"Because I don't actually want any money from you. I do it for fun. If I fill out paperwork, then it gets tangled."

I thought about that. "You work for free?"

"Nope. I work for me. I do it my way. You can deal with it or not."

"Must be nice to be able to do whatever you want."

He snorted. "Everyone does whatever they want, but most people are on autopilot. They go to a job they hate. They think they *have* to, but they're actually making that choice to walk out that door and go to work. They could make a different choice. Sleep 'til noon. Move to Havana. Start a business. But they choose to go to the job they hate. So don't give me any of that crap that you don't get to do what you want. You do exactly what you want. People that choose to go out the door and live a crappy day every day? That's what they want to do. They'd rather make that choice than a harder one, which is to break the cycle."

I raised my brows. "You're so aggressive with that attitude."

He laughed softly. "You appreciated the advice."

"I did actually." I leaned back. "It's very empowering. And you're right. I do exactly what I want. We all do."

He nodded. "Most people don't understand that."

"I do." I sat back. "So, if you want to work long hours doing amazing work for me and not get any money for it, I won't stand in your way."

"Appreciate that."

"Are you still going to hide from me?"

He laughed. "Depends on my mood."

"Hiding sucks. I did that for most of my life. Try standing in the sunshine. It feels so much better than you think."

"Life advice right back at me?"

"Yep. I'm fun like that. You're lucky you finally met me. Your life will be brighter and more sunshiny every day because of it."

"You think?"

"For sure."

He grunted noncommittally. "You get off here."

I realized that he was pulling up to Hattie's dock. Jeremiah's boat was nowhere to be seen, and I wondered where they'd left it. "Awesome. Thanks." I grabbed the ladder and carefully eased myself out of the boat. "I appreciate the rescue. And the conversation. It was great to meet you, finally."

He looked up at me from his little boat. "I'll see you around, Mia Murphy."

I grinned. "You got it."

He gave me a little salute, then pulled away from the dock and chugged slowly down the lake. I put my hands on my hips, watching him go.

How did someone walk away from the life he had? He'd had it all. I was pretty sure he'd even won an Oscar.

I thought about Googling him, but just as quickly, I decided not to. His story was his, and whatever was in the papers was just outsiders trying to write the story they didn't know.

I'd give Cargo his space and his privacy.

But I wasn't going to let him live in the shadows anymore.

I might not be paying him for his work, but if he worked in my garage, that made him part of my tribe. He was mine, and I was going to keep him.

"Mia!" Hattie shouted at me from the house. "Come on up! We have a situation!"

And with that, back to reality.

CHAPTER 27

I HURRIED up the path to Hattie's sprawling and gorgeous house, where Hattie was on the deck. King Tut was beside her, but as I came up the stairs, he sprang off the top step right at me. I caught him, staggered under his weight, then hugged him to my chest. "I'm so glad you guys are okay."

Lucy came out onto the porch, carrying a margarita. "Hattie is a master at evasive maneuvers. I don't know how she managed to lose Jeremiah when his boat was faster, but she did."

Hattie winked at me. "The darkness helped."

"And the rocks you ran him into," Lucy added.

I raised my brows. "Really?"

"He might have a broken propeller now," Hattie acknowledged. "But honestly, it's on him. If you don't know where the reefs are in the lake, then you shouldn't be boating at night."

Lucy grinned. "Maybe he'll bring the boat to the Eagle's Nest for servicing."

"Either way, he's probably still trying to row back home. That propeller made quite a sound. It's definitely fried."

"Way to go," I said. "You impress me more every day."

"Girl power," Hattie said. "Go us." She held out her phone. "Now, you have to call Devlin. He's about to have an apoplectic fit. When I didn't put you on the phone and couldn't promise your safety, it didn't go over well with him."

I grabbed the phone and dialed as I followed Lucy and Hattie into the house. Beau was by her fireplace, on his phone, looking annoyed. I was pretty sure he was calling his minions to find his boat.

I didn't blame him for being annoyed. His gorgeous boat had been stolen.

"Hattie!" Devlin came onto the phone. "Is she back?"

"That's so sweet that you're so worried about me," I said, "but I'm also offended that you underestimate my scrappiness so significantly."

"Mia." The way he said my name with so much relief and irritation was incredibly adorable, which immediately made me cranky. "You're okay?"

"I'm fine. What do you want? Why did you all descend upon the marina like that? I had a trap set up, and you scared everyone away with all those official vehicles."

He swore under his breath. "Griselda got a call that there was a team on their way to the marina to find the drugs and cash you stole. Apparently, there was a tip that you had it at the marina, and you were moving it at midnight."

I tried to look alarmed. "Wow, really? That's a surprise."

He paused. "You're the one who tipped them off?" He swore again. "I should've known."

"What? I don't know what you're talking about. Why would I send bad people to my precious Eagle's Nest? Did you guys set up a sting or whatever you call it? Or just scare them away with all the official vehicles?"

"We got it covered. We're in process. You did have a couple visitors from your old life, but we're on it."

A little warm fuzzy settled in my heart. "I forgot Griselda is actually good at his job."

"He'll appreciate that. I'll let him know."

"Yes, do that." I sank down on the couch, King Tut on my lap.

Someone had set a huge fire in the fireplace, and it was romantic and warm for my wet little body. "What's up?"

"You're really okay?"

I smiled. "I'm fine. What's up?"

"I wanted to give you a heads up. This is off the record."

I sat up, surprised. He was giving me a tip. "What's up?"

"There's a warrant out for Esther's arrest for the murders of Dee and Topsy."

My gut sank. "Oh, *no.* What happened?"

Hattie looked over from the kitchen, where she was putting together sandwiches. Because what else did you do in the wee hours of the morning, except make and eat sandwiches, right?

"Chief Stone found the apparent murder weapon in Esther's dresser."

I thought of when Rogue had stumbled upon Hattie in her bedroom and hit her, before escaping out the wall tunnel. Had she been trying to get the murder weapon back? Or was she stashing it there? No wonder she'd come back to her house. A murder weapon was worth taking a risk for. "Oh, crap."

He paused. "You're not going to tell me she didn't do it?"

"She didn't do it." But I didn't know that. Would she kill for her daughter? She might, if pushed far enough. My mom would kill for me. Well, not if she would get caught, but if she could do it without getting busted, she'd definitely be willing to play the Grim Reaper on behalf of her favorite and only daughter.

"What do you know that I need to know?" Devlin asked.

I looked over at Hattie. "Can we tell him?"

"Tell me what?" Devlin interrupted, weirdly not appreciating our strategic moment. "What do you know?"

Hattie glanced at Lucy. "Tell him that Tessa told us that Rogue was out running around doing bad things to keep Tessa from being killed? You think we should tell him that?"

"No. Maybe not," I agreed.

"What did she say?" Devlin asked. "I couldn't hear her."

He was so adorable thinking that he could talk us into doing or telling anything we didn't want to do/tell.

But he did have connections, being a cop and the buddy of an FBI agent, so how could I take advantage of what he could offer?

I stood up and paced to the window, watching the lake. "We found a witness who was there the night of the jewelry store murder," I said slowly, thinking. "The witness said that Dee and Topsy hid the diamonds in the trophy for the festival. The witness also saw Richie Dutch leaving the building after hearing gunshots."

"Richie Dutch?" he echoed. "The guy who died a few months ago? Ronald's twin?"

"That's why Dee and Topsy came back to town. Since he was dead, they weren't afraid anymore. Apparently, he threatened them, so they left town."

"What does that have to do with Esther?"

Hattie and Lucy were leaning in, listening to the call now. We all looked at each other. If we brought in Tessa, Rogue had motive. I didn't want to give her motive unless it was real. "Nothing that I can find," I lied.

Devlin accepted that, but I suspected he didn't really believe me. "Who's your witness?" he tried.

"Can't tell you."

"Mia—"

"Rogue didn't kill them," I said. "Someone planted the gun there." Maybe Rogue, but if so, why? Why would she incriminate herself? I had a sudden idea that I didn't like at all. "Go check the trophy for diamonds. I gotta go." I hung up the phone and turned it off. "Rogue is setting herself up," I said. "She's going to take the fall for Tessa."

Hattie's eyes widened. "You think?"

"It all makes sense." I paced around the room. "Tessa was never accepted by Topsy and Dee, right? She was always an outsider. So, she's pissed, and even after all these years, it still eats away at her. Maybe she went back and took the diamonds. Maybe she stashed them in Rogue's house. And Dee came after her for them. A little fight in Rogue's kitchen, and then oopsie, Dee's dead. Rogue walks in and she's like, 'what did you do?'"

"So, she takes off with her daughter to formulate a plan," Lucy said.

"Tessa goes AWOL and then kills Topsy. Rogue's trying to do damage control, and you see her there," Hattie said.

"But why were Rogue's earrings at the Ugly Man? Why Dee's shoes?" Lucy asked.

I shook my head. "My guess is that Dee's body was there. Maybe Tessa was trying to set up Stevie? Or Stevie was helping her? And then they moved it to Topsy's?"

"A mother sacrificing herself for her daughter," Hattie said. "That's a classic storyline right there. Very valid."

I nodded. "I know Rogue's tough, but what mother could let her daughter go to jail?"

"Maybe Rogue tied up Tessa to keep her from killing Ruby Lee," Lucy said. "Maybe Jeremiah was helping Rogue. Maybe he was looking for you so you could help Rogue, not to kill you."

Hattie and I both looked over at Lucy in surprise. "Well, heck, girl," Hattie said. "That's an idea."

"Do Rogue and Jeremiah know each other? Does anyone know?" I asked.

"Doesn't matter," Hattie said. "She could be paying him for his help. She'd be able to pay enough to hire anyone for anything."

Beau cleared his throat. "Ladies."

We all looked over at him. "What?" I asked.

"You all just ran right past an important point. Ran over it, more accurately. Trampled it with your big feet."

"What point?" Lucy asked.

He cocked an eyebrow, then turned on his phone camera and began to record us.

I stared at him, replaying our conversation. I could see from the looks on Hattie and Lucy's faces that they were doing the same.

And we all realized it at the same moment. "Tessa's on her way to kill Ruby Lee," I said. "She's not going to find Rogue. She's going to go after Ruby Lee, the third one of the group who rejected her." I grabbed my phone (so grateful for the new water-proof iPhone) and turned it on, not even hesitating even though it would tell Griselda where I was.

I had Ruby Lee's phone number from when she'd brokered the deal for the marina, and I had to use it.

She didn't pick up. "Ruby Lee. It's Mia. I think Tessa may be on her way to harm you. Watch your back." I hung up. "We gotta go to her house."

Hattie was already running for her keys. "Try calling her again."

"I am." We all ran for the door, and Beau followed us, still recording. King Tut ignored me and stretched out in front of the fireplace, basking in the warmth. "I'll be back," I told him.

Then we bolted outside.

Somehow, Hattie had retrieved the Lamborghini, so we all climbed in, and Hattie hit the gas. The tires spun out, and I texted Ruby Lee and Hattie from my phone. *Ruby Lee. Watch out for Tessa. She might be coming for you.*

Still no response, so I quickly turned off my phone and switched to Hattie's. *Ruby Lee. I'm on Hattie's phone now. Text me here.*

No response.

"It's past midnight," Lucy said. "She's probably asleep."

"Or dead," Beau said. "Tessa did have quite the head start. My boat is very fast."

I shot him a look. "I like Ruby Lee. Don't say that."

"You gotta look at all possibilities all the time," he said as he reclined in the back seat. "This *is* a nice ride. I think I might need to get one."

"Right? It's freaking awesome," Hattie said. "If Rogue goes to prison, I'm going to claim this for my own. I think she'd want that for me."

"Hattie!" I interrupted. "We need to find Rogue, not allocate her belongings."

"As long as you all agree the Lamborghini is mine, we can move forward."

"Oh, for heaven's sake." I turned around to face Lucy, who was the only one besides me not obsessing about the vehicle we were in. "We need to figure out where Rogue is. She was clearly out doing something when Tessa was tied up. What would she be doing?"

Lucy shook her head. "I don't know."

I still couldn't fit all the pieces together. "Even if Rogue was trying to protect her daughter, it doesn't make sense that she'd zip tie her and gag her. There are more humane ways to keep her from murdering people."

"Rogue might be annoyed," Hattie said. "I'd be annoyed if my kid was running amok popping off women who ignored her as a teenager. It's just not a valid reason to kill people."

"I still don't see Rogue doing that." I bounced my knee restlessly. "I mean, maybe Jeremiah tied up Tessa and Rogue doesn't know, but still. She wouldn't condone it. She just wouldn't."

"Well, maybe." Hattie hit the steering wheel. "Okay, fine. Something's not adding up. What are we missing?"

Beau grinned. "Even I don't know, but I'm going to just say that the three of you are a treat to follow around."

Hattie's phone rang, and I saw it was Devlin.

I silenced it, my mind spinning. I just couldn't figure out how Rogue fit into all this. "Rogue," I whispered. "What are you up to?"

Hattie turned into Ruby Lee's driveway, and as we shot down it, my gut started to tighten. I didn't want Ruby Lee dead, and I didn't want Tessa to be a killer. How would Rogue continue on her reckless, uproarious, shameless life if her daughter was a murderer? I really liked her the way she was.

Hattie pulled up and put the car in park. "The front door's open."

And then we heard a scream.

CHAPTER 28

ALL FOUR OF us ran right for the house.

I charged inside first, my hairdryer ready. "Ruby Lee! We're here!"

There was another scream, and this time, I could hear it was from the back of the house.

"That way!" Lucy yelled, pointing down a hallway.

I raced down there, Lucy on my heels. Hattie and Beau fell behind, but we didn't wait.

I burst out into the kitchen and saw movement on the back lawn. I sprinted across the tile and out the back door.

A silhouetted person was racing across the lawn, but in the middle of the grass was a slumped figure. *Crap!* "Ruby Lee!" How many times could she survive a deadly assault? I ran to the figure on the lawn and dropped to my knees. I rolled her over and saw her face. "It's Tessa." Her eyes were closed, and she was limp. *Uh oh.* I shook her shoulder. "Tessa?"

"Tessa?" Lucy asked. "Someone took her down?"

"Someone was running for the woods. Stay alert!" I leaned in and put my ear to her mouth. "She's breathing." Relief rushed through me. "She's still breathing!"

Hattie and Beau caught up. "Another body?" Beau exclaimed. "This is fantastic!"

"No. She's not dead." I didn't see any blood on her. "What happened to her?"

"I'm calling 9-1-1," Lucy said.

"Yes." I stood up and looked toward the woods where I'd seen the figure run. Had it been Ruby Lee? Someone else? Who had attacked Tessa? I could see movement in the trees. "No one look. We're being watched," I said softly. "In the trees. To the right."

All three of them immediately turned and scanned the trees to the right.

"Honestly, guys. What is wrong with you?" The person watching us was actually on our left, but I'd decided to make sure the gang would follow directions before telling them.

Clearly, a good plan.

"I don't see anyone," Hattie said. "Does anyone have binoculars?"

"I have some in my boat," Beau said. "Wait! If Tessa's here, then my boat is here." He immediately took off at a jog, heading toward the lake, abandoning murder talk for boat rescue. So, now I knew his priorities: boat over murder.

"I still don't see anyone," Hattie said. "Are you sure you saw someone?"

"Yes. We're being watched." I crouched beside Tessa, watching her carefully. Her eyeballs were moving under her eyelids, and her breathing wasn't even. I was pretty sure she was faking it. "Everyone, come down here. We need to talk."

Hattie and Lucy crouched beside me. I gestured at Tessa, make a slicing sign across my throat, while I made a face and shook my head.

Hattie's eyes widened, and then she glared at Tessa. I saw her open her mouth to call her out, but I put my finger over my lips and shook my head. I leaned over her again, and this time, I shook my head. "She's not breathing anymore. I think she's dead."

"That's too bad, but honestly, not such a loss," Hattie said. "Now Rogue doesn't have to sacrifice herself to protect her."

"'You think we should call 9-1-1?" Lucy asked, watching me.

"No. I have a plan," I said aloud. "As long as Tessa's dead, we might as well take advantage of the situation to find the murderer. Since it's clearly not her, right?"

"Clearly," Lucy said.

"Agreed," Hattie said. "What's the plan?"

"Let's see what she has on her." I patted down her pockets and found a bulge in her jacket. I pulled it out, and then I swore as I held it up. "It's a wig."

"It looks like Rogue's hair," Lucy said.

Understanding dawned on Hattie's face. "You never saw Rogue, did you? It was Tessa, dressed up as Rogue."

"They do look alike," Lucy said. "But honestly, there's a big age difference, Mia. How did you not see that?"

Had I seen Rogue? Or had I seen Tessa dressed up as Rogue? Given the wig, I had a feeling that I'd been duped, which impressed me. "I don't know." What the heck was going on? "Devlin's going to arrest Rogue. We have to figure out what's going on." I kept searching Tessa's pockets, grinning when I saw her face twitch.

She was trying so hard not to give away the fact she wasn't dead. Or probably not even injured. A total fake, which I had taken the time to notice after facing the possibility that Dee hadn't been dead when we'd first found her.

I found a paper in one pocket, and I pulled it out. The moment I saw what it was, I sat back, crumbling it in my hand. "She's incredibly unhelpful for a dead person," I said aloud.

"Right?" Hattie sat back. "So, what do we do with her?"

"Let's use her as bait for the murderer."

Lucy grinned. "How?"

"You brought your gun, right?"

Her smile widened. "I did."

I shrugged. "So, let's shoot her, then."

Tessa's eyes snapped open in alarm. "Shoot me?"

I grinned. "Don't move," I whispered. "Who is watching us?"

"No one. Why? Who hit me? Who are you? Why am I in the grass?" Her gaze frantically went from face to face, clearly trying to figure out what to do, now that she'd blown it.

"You have two seconds to tell us what's going on," I said, "or we turn you over to the FBI."

"I didn't do anything, so that's fine."

"Your mom is going to be arrested for murder," I said, still watching the woods. The person hadn't moved, but I could see their silhouette. What were they waiting for? "Is that okay with you?" I asked Tessa.

Her eyes widened. "My mom didn't kill anyone!"

"Then who did?"

"I don't know!" She sat up. "I already told you what's going on!"

"Why are you at Ruby Lee's? Where is she?"

"I don't know." Her gaze darted to the side, and I knew she was lying.

Alarm settled in my gut. "*Where is Ruby Lee?*"

"Not here. She's not here."

That was the truth. But where was Ruby Lee? "Why did you scream? And who's watching us?" My skin was starting to prickle. I didn't like that I didn't know what was going on in the woods. "Do they have a gun?"

She stood up. "You have to let me go," she whispered. "Don't stop me, or my mom is in trouble."

"She's already in trouble." I glanced at Hattie and Lucy. "Let us help you."

"No. I can't." She began to back away. "Don't follow me. Pretend to believe what I shout. I'm lying, but you have to pretend to believe me. Ruby Lee isn't in the house."

I stood up, clutching the piece of trash in my fist. "Tessa—"

She shook her head. "I gotta go." Then she turned and ran toward the woods where the person was watching us.

"Do we go after her?" Lucy asked.

Hattie said nothing. Like me, she was watching the woods. Waiting.

"Guys?" Lucy prompted.

"We need to find Rogue," I said softly. "Tessa knows where she is. That's our priority." I had a feeling I knew where she was. The piece of trash had given me an idea, but I needed confirmation. A second piece of information. I needed to know who was in those trees waiting for her.

I watched carefully as Tessa slipped into the shadows. The other shadowed figure met her, and then they moved away swiftly through the trees. The moment I saw him move, I knew.

"It was a man," Hattie said. "I couldn't see his face, but she came up to his shoulder."

"So, he's about six-two—"

Tessa suddenly shouted at us. "Ruby Lee is in the basement! She needs help!" Then she turned and ran.

That was our cue. She'd given us a reason to race into the house, which we were going to do, and then keep running through it and to the cars. "Let's go, guys." I started to run toward the house. "He walked with a limp. His right leg. Very slight. Did you see it?"

"Yep," Hattie agreed, hurrying to catch up to me. "Do we know any man who walks with a limp like that?"

"Yep." I knew one. "Lucy?"

She looked over at me, her face furrowed. "We do?"

"Yeah." We reached the kitchen door, and I handed her the piece of trash I'd found in Tessa's pocket as we ran inside.

She looked down, and then her mouth dropped open. "This is from Topsy's cupcakes."

"So, she was at Topsy's?" Hattie said.

Lucy looked up. "Maybe, but we found a wrapper like this at Justin Dutch's."

"The ex-sheriff?" Hattie asked.

I nodded. "Wasn't Richie his nephew? What if he knew Richie

239

killed the jeweler, and that's why he buried the evidence and quit?"

Hattie's eyes widened. "And how he's trying to cover it up. Because Topsy, Tessa, Dee, and Ruby Lee all know the truth."

"And probably Rogue," I said. "I'd bet that Tessa told her, if not originally, then when she came back."

"We gotta go to his shack," I said. "He probably has Rogue there."

Down by the dock, a boat started up. "That's Beau's boat," Hattie said. "I know engines."

"We don't have time to wait. Let's go." We sprinted through the house and made it to the Lamborghini. Within seconds, we were all strapped in, and Hattie hit the gas. "To Justin's?" she asked.

I nodded, my brain whirling. "When we were at Justin's, I thought I saw movement in the bushes," I said.

"You think Rogue's in the bushes?" Hattie was driving fast, and I was grateful for it.

"Someone was there. Tessa? Rogue? I don't know." My foot bounced restlessly. "We need to beat Justin to his house."

Lucy leaned over the seat. "Where is Ruby Lee? And why did Tessa scream and fake her death?"

"I don't know." I hated that we were racing over to Justin's without facts and information, but my gut was telling me we needed to get there fast. I always liked to prep for a situation, but there was no time. "Hattie, give me your phone."

There were multiple messages from Devlin. I called him back. He answered on the first ring. "Mia." His voice was low. "Don't come back to the marina right now."

I gripped the phone. "Why not?"

"Griselda's on a rampage. He's not happy with you."

"What else is new? Can you check Ruby Lee's house? I'm worried she's next on the list."

"Why?"

"Because Dee, Topsy, and Ruby Lee were best friends back

then. They probably all know what happened the night of the jewelry store murder. Ruby Lee's the only one still alive."

"I'll send someone to her place. Where are you going now?"

"To get bagels."

"Why won't you let me help you?"

I bit my lip. "Because I don't know what we're going to find. If we find something that makes Rogue look guilty, then I don't want you there."

He swore. "Trust me to do my job."

"I can't. Bye." I hung up the phone and set it on the console.

Hattie side-eyed me. "How are you going to date him if you don't trust him?"

"I'm not going to date him. It's obviously too complicated." Why did that bum me out? It shouldn't bum me out.

"Life is complicated," Hattie said. "You still have to live it."

"You don't trust him because of your past," Lucy said. "That's not his fault."

"He even warned you not to come back to the marina, and he didn't rat you out to Griselda," Hattie pointed out. "Seems to me that you set your boundaries, and he's accepted them and he's working with them."

"I know, right?" Lucy clapped her hands. "Well done, Mia."

I looked back and forth between them. "Are you guys insane? I can't date him. I don't want to date him. I—"

"You don't?" Hattie shot me a look as she peeled around the corner. "Can you honestly say that? Really? He's attractive. Dangerous. Willing to disobey his FBI bestie on your behalf? But also willing to stand up to you when you're being stubborn. I think he's a winner."

"Me, too." Lucy leaned forward between the seats. "He was so freaked out when you were missing. He clearly cares about you."

"He barely knows me."

"That's how all relationships start," Hattie said. "They start at the beginning and move forward."

I looked back and forth between them. "We're driving to a

potential murderer's house right now and you guys are talking about me dating Devlin?"

"Yep. It's a tension reliever," Hattie said. "We don't know what we're going to find, so you gotta just kick back and chill out."

"Plus, if Hattie and I die, then who else is there to tell you to date Devlin? No one. You'll die alone and miserable. So you need our great advice while we're still alive to give it." Lucy was grinning now.

"We're not going to die," Hattie clarified. "But in theory. Because when you're approaching your possible demise, you have to tie up loose ends. Like the sex lives of your friends."

"To be fair," Lucy said. "If you trusted Devlin and let him help us, then he could be driving to Justin's instead of us. We could be home drinking margaritas."

Hattie looked at Lucy, then burst out laughing. "Who would want to miss this? We're not telling Devlin because we want to have all the fun!"

Lucy rolled her eyes, but she was laughing. "You know, I have to admit, driving around with you two hunting murderers is starting to grow on me."

I threw up my hands. "Okay, fine, I admit that it's fun, but only until we die."

"So, we won't die," Hattie said. "Everyone have their weapons?"

I held up my hairdryer, and Lucy held up her hunting rifle. I sighed. "Honestly, Lucy. Where's the nail gun?"

"If I shoot someone, then it will be self-defense and I'll be fine. But if they have a gun, the hairdryer won't be nearly as helpful as we'd all prefer."

"It worked before against a gun. More than once."

"Luck runs out eventually," Hattie said. "But wisdom is forever."

I laughed. "It was strategic with the hairdryer. It's my superpower."

"Well, we can't all have good superpowers. Keep looking. I'm sure you'll find something better," Hattie said. "This is his driveway."

We fell silent as Hattie turned off her headlights and drove in the darkness. The trees let in just enough light for us to see the road, but the woods felt dangerously dark. "He wouldn't be in the woods," I said softly. "We moved fast. He wouldn't have had time to get ahead and wait for us."

"If he went by water he might," Hattie said. "It's more direct if you go by lake."

I thought of Beau down at the water. "I hope Beau didn't run into them down there."

"He'll be fine. He got a head start on them."

Lucy leaned forward between the seats. "It's around the next corner," she whispered.

On a whim, I texted Beau from Hattie's phone. *We're at Justin Dutch's. We might need a fast exit by water.*

I'm not leaving my boat again.

Relief rushed through me. He was alive and texting. *Did they leave by boat?*

They might have tried, but weirdly, their dock lines got untied and their boat floated away.

"Beau sabotaged their boat. He bought us time." *Beau, you're a star.*

I know. Stay alive. I'll cruise by and see what's doing.

Thanks.

I put the phone down and Hattie pulled up in front of the shack. She whipped the vehicle around so it was pointing down the driveway for a fast exit, then put the SUV in park. "Plan?"

"Lucy, you check the shed," I said. "I want to go look in the bushes where I saw activity. Hattie, you keep an eye out and let us know if you see them approach."

"On it." She turned off the ignition and rolled down her window. "A car is a deadly weapon. I'll stay armed."

I raised my brows as I got out. "Sometimes you're a little terrifying."

She winked at me. "As long as one person says that to me every day, I'm doing something right. It's barely past midnight and I already got my quota for the day. That means it's going to be a great day. Go have fun, kids. I'll say a little prayer that I get to run someone over tonight."

Lucy and I looked at each other, both of us pretty sure that Hattie was at least partially serious.

We walked across the dirt side by side. Justin's abandoned Adirondack chair was where it had been before, with a cup of coffee on the arm. The campfire was out, and there were no lights on in his shack. "Maybe we should stay together," Lucy suggested.

I kind of thought that wasn't a bad idea. Who knew what we were going to run into? We weren't exactly trained. "Yeah. Let's be quick." We broke into a run, shining our mini flashlights all around, but no one jumped out at us.

We reached the shack and the door opened easily under my touch. No need for lock picking! I opened the door and we both leaned in, shining our lights.

CHAPTER 29

I<small>T DIDN'T TAKE MORE</small> than a few seconds to see that it was unoccupied. It was exactly what it looked like from the outside. Old wood floors. A cot against the wall, with faded blankets tossed on it. An ice box. A wall with several rifles and handguns that were bright, shiny, and well-cared for. "We need to make those disappear," I said.

"Absolutely."

We ran over to the wall and helped ourselves to all we could find, Lucy checking first to make sure they weren't loaded. I grabbed a bag of zip ties on the way out, because, hmm…what a coincidence he had zip ties, right? We hurried out to the Lamborghini, and Hattie's face lit up when she saw our load. "Christmas in June! That's fantastic!" She popped the back. "Load 'em up. I have presents for all the Seam Rippers now."

"Hattie!" I set the guns in the rear of the SUV, and Lucy put hers on top. "Seriously!"

"Just kidding, but joy to the world, right?" Hattie leaned out the window as she shut the back. "No Rogue in the cabin?"

"No."

"Any clues?"

"We'll go back and look again if we have time." I was itching to get into the woods. I had a feeling that's where we needed to be. "Keep an eye out."

"On it."

I headed toward the bushes where I'd seen something before, Lucy keeping close. I pushed the bushes aside, and then gasped. "It's a tent."

Lucy came up beside me. "Justin said that he let Dee set up a tent. This must be it."

"The question is, what's he keeping in it now that Dee's not using it." I crouched in front of the tent, then saw a small padlock on the zipper. "It's locked."

"Yay for you."

"Yep." I pulled out my picks and popped the lock. Then I grabbed the zipper and unzipped it. The first thing that hit me was a terrible smell, the smell of subway tunnels and...pot? I flashed my light inside, and saw two sleeping bags on the ground, thick and round, as if people were inside. "Hello?" I whispered. "Rogue?"

One of the sleeping bags kicked at me and I heard a squeal.

Lucy and I both gasped, and we crawled into the tent. I went first to the one that had kicked and shined my light. The familiar face of a sassy seventy-something rich-as-sin Seam Ripper blinked at me, a gag across her mouth. I nearly cried with relief. "Rogue!"

Her eyes widened, and she started talking rapidly, with great excitement, but the gag muffled her. "I can't understand you," I said. "We need to get the gag off."

"This one is Ruby Lee," Lucy said. "She's gagged too."

I unzipped the sleeping bag. "She's zip-tied. Go find scissors in the cabin!"

"I'm on it!" While Lucy scrambled out of the tent, I quickly unzipped both women and untangled their feet from the sleeping bags, making their escape a priority over their talking. Once they were free, I untied Rogue's gag. "Rogue! Are you okay?"

She grinned at me. "Mia. This was an adventure. You look so

pretty tonight. Did you know my daughter's back in town?" She tried to whistle and failed. "She's in trouuuubbbbblllleeee."

I stared at her. "Are you stoned?"

"Stoned." She thought about it. "Maybe. Maybe indeed."

No wonder he'd been able to keep her quiet. He'd drugged, gagged, and tied up my friend. That was not okay with me.

I untied Ruby Lee's gag. "Mia," she said, exhaling terrible breath in my face. "Murder. It's everywhere. And diamonds. Esther has diamonds. Lots of them. Did you know how rich she is? I need to sell her some houses."

Yep. Also stoned. "Why don't you lie back down until we cut you free?"

"Lies. Lies. Lies." She started singing the word. "I love lies. I'm so great at lies. You're great too. Let's lie together!"

Holy cow. "Let's not."

Lucy crawled back in the tent. She held up a terrifying looking hunting knife. "That man likes his weapons."

"Do Rogue first. And watch out. They're stoned."

She glanced at the women, who were both lying on their sides making faces at each other. "Well, it's good they're not stressed, right? Stress isn't good for old people."

In unison, they both lifted their heads to glare at Lucy. "Old?" Rogue said. "I'm taking you out of my will. Begone, irreverent youth!"

"Esther's the old one," Ruby Lee said. "I'm simply fabulous."

"No. I'm fabulous," Rogue retorted.

"Au contraire, 'tis I, thouest silver-haired swan."

Lucy and I looked at each other, and we both burst out laughing. "Let's get them out of here," I said.

"Right." She quickly snipped Ruby Lee free, and then handed me the knife.

Getting them free was easy.

Getting them to stand up and walk out of the tent toward freedom? Not so much.

Once they were both liberated from their plastic binds, all they wanted to do was sit cross-legged and make faces at each other.

I put my hands on my hips and watched them. "He must have given them an awful lot," I said. "I think we should run them by the hospital."

"Agreed. But how do we get them out to the car? Short of tying them back up and throwing them over our shoulders?"

Hattie bolted into the tent. "I see headlights coming—" Her face brightened. "Rogue! Ruby Lee!"

"They're stoned," I said. "We can't get them out of the tent."

"Stoned? That's easy." Hattie waved her hands in front of their faces to break up the weird-face contest. "I have chocolate chip cookies in Rogue's Lamborghini outside. First one into the back seat gets them all!"

"Food!" Rogue shot to her feet. "In my car? That's a sacrilege!" She stumbled out of the tent, while Ruby Lee lurched to her feet.

"Hattie brought cookies? She has the best cookies ever!" She wove out of the tent after Rouge.

"This is why drugs are bad," Hattie said as we followed them out. "It makes you totally unable to appreciate the fact you were kidnapped by a murderer. They'll be so sad tomorrow when they realize that they totally missed out on the experience."

I hurried after them. "I hope they're okay. You think Rogue's been in that tent all this time?" She was staggering now, and I wasn't sure if it was because of the drugs or the fact she'd been tied up for so long. I caught her arm as she stumbled, guiding her to the car.

She went for the driver's door, and Hattie jumped in front to block it. "The keys are in the back seat," she said. "You'll have to get them from back there."

"You get them." She tried to open the door.

I looked at Lucy, and together, we scooped Rogue up and literally carried her to the back seat, over her outraged protests. "I hope she doesn't remember this," Lucy said. "She might get me fired from my job."

"She'll appreciate being manhandled, I'm sure." Ruby Lee was already in the back seat, looking for the cookies, and we basically tossed Rogue inside.

Lucy climbed in with them, and I ran around to the other side. I climbed in the back to keep Ruby Lee from climbing out that door. Once Lucy and I had them sandwiched, Hattie started the engine. But instead of driving out, she hit reverse and backed us into the woods. "It's a one-way driveway," she said as she kept backing up. "We need to let Justin get past us, then leave. Everyone quiet."

The Lamborghini's engine went quiet, and we all waited in the shadows. The Lamborghini was red, but in the darkness of the night, it simply looked dark. We were off to the right, behind the bushes.

"What are we looking at?" Rogue whispered.

"Justin," I said as the headlights came into view. "He's coming back with Tessa—"

"Tessa! My baby!" She lunged for the door. She got it open, and Lucy locked her arms around her stomach, trying to hold her in the car.

"Get her back in the car," Hattie hissed. "They're coming!"

"Trying," Lucy said. "She's unbelievably strong!"

I leaned across Ruby Lee and grabbed Rogue around the waist. "Rogue! We have to be silent to save Tessa!"

"Tessa!" Rogue shrieked, and I slapped my hand over her mouth.

I bent my head so my mouth was right next to her ear. "Esther. Shut up and freeze right now or Tessa will die."

She froze, going completely stiff, like a coiled spring ready to explode.

I hated saying that to her, but I didn't want Justin coming after us. "Now, ease back into the vehicle," I whispered.

She shook her head, and gripped the door more firmly.

"Rogue!" Hattie hissed. "Get back in the car!"

Rogue turned her head. "That's my kid out there with him. I'm not leaving." The grogginess was gone, replaced with raw determination and terror.

I sighed. No amount of drugs could completely obscure a mom's fear for her daughter's safety.

And she was right. How could we drive off and leave Tessa there? Maybe Rogue was the only thing keeping Tessa alive? "All right," I said softly. "We'll stay. Lucy and I will go get Tessa, but you have to stay here."

"Seriously?" Lucy said. "He's a murderer."

"With Rogue's daughter."

Lucy sighed. "I hate that you're right."

Justin's pickup truck pulled up in front of the cabin. The way we were angled, his headlights didn't go in our direction. I realized that Hattie had done that on purpose. She was a genius with cars. "I agree," she whispered, her hands on the steering wheel. "We can't leave Tessa."

"They're going to realize Rogue and Ruby Lee are gone any second," I whispered. "Hattie, be ready. Rogue, if you and Ruby Lee get out of this vehicle, you're going to risk Tessa's safety. He drugged you, and you're in no condition to help. You need to stay put. Got it?"

Rogue looked at me, and I saw her fighting to understand. "Mia?"

I nodded. "Rogue, you have to leave it up to me. Hattie won't leave, but you have to stay in the vehicle, and you have to make Ruby Lee stay there too. No matter what. You guys are a mess right now. Got it?"

She nodded, and I saw her fighting for clarity in those blue eyes. "Got it."

"Ruby Lee?"

"Where are the cookies?"

"Ruby Lee!"

She dragged her gaze off her fingertips and looked at me. "Are you going to sue me for misrepresenting the marina? I did a great job with that. You were so stupid to buy it from me. You know that. I know you do. You're a smart gal."

"If you stay in the car and don't make any noises, Esther will give you a million dollars in cash tomorrow."

Rogue started to protest, but I held up my hand to silence her.

Ruby Lee's eyes widened, and then she zipped her lips shut and threw away the key.

"Money solves everything," Rogue whispered. "You need to be rich, Mia. It's so fun."

"I can see that." I looked at Lucy. "Let's go."

She gave me a look, then rolled out of the SUV and landed on her hands and knees. I did the same on my side. We both eased the doors shut, then met behind the Lamborghini. I was wearing my hairdryer, and she had her hunting rifle. "We need to get Tessa free," I said. "I'll distract him, and you grab Tessa and get her in the truck."

She narrowed her eyes. "If you tell us to leave without you, I'll shoot you myself."

I grinned. I loved having friends. "He has no reason to kill me, so that's really the best strategy."

"Not in this town, it's not. We're not leaving."

"All right, then." I thought it over. "We need to take him down, then."

She leaned in. "I don't actually want to shoot him," she whispered. "I think it would traumatize me."

"Good. Don't shoot him. But you can fake it, right?"

She nodded. "Yep."

"Okay, let's do this."

"But what's our plan?"

"Split them up. Get Tessa the info that Rogue is safe, then she can help us." A car door slammed, and we were out of time. Justin was out of the truck. "Let's go."

Staying to the shadows, I led the way around the back of his shed so that we were on the side with the tent. I gestured for Lucy to stay by the shed, while I wove through the underbrush and hid behind a thick tree that was on the path to the tent.

I unwrapped the hairdryer from across my body and wound the cord around my hand. I'd have one chance as he ran past, one chance to take down a six-foot-two deranged sociopath.

Fun. I loved a challenge.

CHAPTER 30

I CROUCHED behind a tree and watched as Justin stared at his shack. My gaze followed his, and I saw that we'd left the door open.

Tessa got out of the truck and headed toward the tent. She would be passing me momentarily, and I wondered if I could signal to her when she passed. "I'm checking on my mom."

"No." His voice stopped her hard. "What did you tell them?"

"Tell who?" She sounded tired and defeated.

"Mia and the others. At Esther's house. Did you mention me?" His voice low and hard. He didn't sound insane. He sounded strategic and angry.

"No. You have my mother. I'd never risk her."

"Your mother—" Swearing, he spun around and sprinted for the tent. He shoved Tessa aside and I stood up, swinging the hairdryer to get momentum, then, as he neared, I reared back and then swung as hard as I could.

I hit him right in the chest.

He gasped and stumbled, and I charged out and tackled him. "Lucy!"

She let out a Tarzan screech and launched herself onto him,

knocking us both to the ground. "Your mom's safe," I shouted. "Help us get him!"

"Baby!" Rogue flung herself out the car door. "Take him down! Make me proud!"

"Mom!" Tessa ignored us and ran for Rogue, which was super sweet, but Justin was already recovering.

"Stay down, you scumbag," Lucy yelled as she pressed the rifle to the back of his neck and shoved his face into the dirt.

I grabbed a zip tie, and tried to get it around his wrist, but he was moving too much. "We're going to lose him," Lucy shouted.

I thought that would go very badly for us if we lost him. "Hattie—"

"I have an idea!" She bolted for his truck as I threw myself on Justin's back, fighting to hold onto his wrists to keep him from pushing up. Lucy was using her full body weight on his head, trying to hold him down, but he was strong and mad.

I heard an engine start up, and I looked behind me. Hattie was driving Justin's jacked-up pickup truck right at us.

"Holy cow, Hattie," Lucy yelled. "Stop!"

"No!" I realized what she was doing. "Stay on him, Lucy. This will work!"

"You're freaking insane!" But she stayed where she was, pinning his face to the dirt.

The headlights bore down on us, and I glanced under my arm, checking the height of the undercarriage. It was high enough. I gestured to Hattie to keep coming.

She stuck her hand out the window and gave me a thumbs up.

"Come on!!"

She drove forward, keeping our little trio between the tires. The front bumper was almost to his struggling feet, and then she drove over it, trapping his feet under the car. She kept coming, and I hit Lucy's arm. "Lucy! Heads up!"

She turned around, and her eyes widened when she saw the grill of the truck inching forward over Justin's body. "Crazy. My friends are crazy!"

I scrambled up Justin's body, keeping just ahead of the bumper. Justin's hips went beneath the truck, but he hadn't noticed yet, mostly because his face was still in the dirt. Hattie reached his lower back and I scrambled forward, over his head. Lucy shoved his head to the ground, then we both dove off him as Hattie shot forward over him.

Justin let out a roar of victory, braced his hands in the dirt, and tried to shove himself to his feet. He slammed into the undercarriage of the truck and rebounded back into the dirt.

He let out a curse and looked up, swearing even more when he saw he was under the truck. He scrambled forward to get out, and I shouted. "Hattie! Forward!"

She hit the gas and the car lurched forward a few feet, keeping even with him.

He glared at me and tried to roll sideways between the tires.

"Hattie!" She rolled forward again, and Justin had to pull back to keep from getting run over.

He rolled onto his stomach and glared at me.

I was on my hands and knees in front of the truck, crouched low enough to see him, but far back enough not to get hit if Hattie had to hit the gas again. "I dare you to move again," I said. "Hattie would love to run over you."

He swore and scrambled forward again.

"Hattie!"

The car jerked forward a few feet, keeping pace with him.

"You're going to run out of space," he snarled as he scrambled forward again.

I looked behind me and saw the trees and realized he was right.

I also saw the unzipped tent. I waved to Lucy and pointed to the tent.

She nodded and gestured to Hattie.

Justin was scrambling fast now, trying to get ahead of the truck so he could get up, and Hattie kept moving forward.

The tent was getting closer. Hattie turned her wheels sharply, and he swore, pausing for a moment, then he started moving again, off to the left, trying to stay between the tires.

It was dark and Hattie's headlights were still off, which made it almost impossible for Justin to see the dark tent.

He lunged again, and this time, Hattie stopped the truck with the bumper pressed up against the tent. Justin scrambled out, right into the tent.

"Back!" I shouted.

The truck flew backward, and Lucy and I lunged for the tent flap. She held the sides together, and I zipped it and got the lock on before Justin had made it to his feet.

He stood up, ripping the stakes out of the ground. Shouting like a lunatic, he lunged for...whatever he was lunging for. The tent wrapped around him, and for a moment, it was as if this killer tent was trying to suck the life out of him.

"It's like a horror movie," Lucy said, watching the tent and Justin battle.

"Attack of the Killer Tent," I agreed. "No child will ever go camping again."

"Horrifying, really."

"But fun," I said, as the tent wound tighter and tighter around Justin. "I think this is going to work out really well for us."

"Agreed."

Hattie got out of the truck and walked around, watching Justin fight against the tent. "This is why you always bring scissors with you whenever you go. Or a knife. One well-placed stab and he could rip that sucker right open."

"Nylon is surprisingly hardy," I said as Justin fell and started a horizontal tango with the tent.

"That it is."

As we watched, Justin finally appeared to concede defeat. The tent stopped moving, and Justin lay there, panting heavily, completely tangled.

"At least he can breathe," I said cheerfully.

"It's unfortunate, really, that he can," Hattie said. "I feel like suffocation might be a valid ending for him."

Justin didn't move.

I pulled out my phone, turned it on, and called Devlin.

"Mia! Where are you? Ruby Lee wasn't at her house."

"We found her and Esther. They were tied up, gagged, and drugged in a tent on Justin Dutch's property."

He swore. "Where are you now?"

"We're on Justin Dutch's property. We have Rogue and Ruby Lee. And Justin is a little tied up as well, so to speak. We'd love a visit from our favorite cop."

"I'm on my way."

"Wonderful. Call an ambulance for Rogue and Ruby Lee, please."

"Will do."

I hung up and crouched beside Justin. "Justin."

He didn't answer.

"Did you really kill all those people to protect the reputation of a man who was already dead?"

He didn't answer.

"Or was it for the diamonds?"

He was still very unhelpful, so I stood up and scanned for Rogue, Ruby Lee, and Tessa. They were sitting on the ground in front of the shack. Rogue and Tessa had their arms around each other, and Tessa was resting her head on Rogue's shoulder. "Keep an eye on him, will you?" I said to Hattie and Lucy.

"I would love for him to try something," Hattie said.

"I'll try to keep Hattie from killing him," Lucy said, "but I can't make any promises."

"Good enough. We've kept Hattie out of prison before, so it will be fine." We traded grins when Justin groaned, and then I walked over and sat down with the zip tie gang. "How are you guys doing?"

Rogue smiled. "Got my baby back, so I'm good."

"Yes," Tessa said.

Ruby Lee stretched out on the ground. "I need to nap. Wake me when the cookies arrive."

"Will do." I had a few questions to ask before Devlin and his gang arrived. "What happened?"

Rogue looked at Tessa, who sighed. "It was about the diamonds," she said.

"Where are they? Are they in the trophy?"

Rogue and Tessa looked at each other, then they shook their heads. "I have them," Rogue said. She seemed to be regaining her clarity.

"How?"

"I went back and got them," Tessa said. "The next day. I heard Dee say where she hid them, and I knew that trophy was going to be in the festival. So I went back and got them, and hid them in my mom's safe."

Wow. What a simple, logical place to store them. "Your mom's safe?"

Rogue closed her eyes and looked like she was starting to fall asleep. So maybe not totally okay.

Tessa nodded. "I hid them in the back. I was going to give them to Dee, but then Richie came by her house and threatened to kill her if she didn't turn them over. She went back to get them, but they were gone, obviously."

I grimaced. "Did you tell her you had them?"

Tessa bit her lip and shook her head. "No. I was scared. She freaked out. Topsy did too. They left the next day. I didn't know they were going. They just left. So I had the diamonds, but I was afraid, too."

"Why did you leave?"

She swallowed. "Richie came to see me. He tracked down my license plate, so he knew me. He was terrifying. I truly believed he would kill me. So I left, too."

"You didn't tell your mom?"

"No." Tessa looked at Rogue, passed out on her shoulder. Asleep, Rogue looked old and weary, without any of the fire that coursed through her when she was awake and not drugged. "We didn't get along back then, and I think I used it as an excuse to leave town."

I nodded. "What happened the day Rogue disappeared?"

"I came home and surprised her. The minute I saw her, we both started to cry. It had been so long, and we'd been apart for no reason. I told her everything. She was horrified, and wanted me to go to the police, but what was the point, right? Richie was dead. We went upstairs to see if the diamonds were still there, and then when we came down, we found Dee in the pantry."

Close to what I'd guessed.

"Last week, I told Dee my mom had them, so when we saw Dee on the floor, we realized that she must have told someone else. So we took off. We needed to find out who was back in action, right? But we couldn't tell the cops because I'd stolen the diamonds."

I nodded. I got that. It was so inconvenient to be a criminal.

"So, we put the diamonds back in the safe, made it look like the house had been ransacked, and then ran outside…right into Justin. He took us both and then used my mom to make me do errands." She hugged her mom. "Errands that would make it look like my mom had killed people. When I got to Topsy's and saw her and Dee in the pile, I freaked out. I knew I was next. Once everything was set up, I would be last, and my mom would get the blame for all of us. When he got Ruby Lee, I knew he was setting up for the final showdown."

I thought about that. "Is that why you went to Ruby Lee's after we released you?"

She shook her head. "I didn't know he had her at that point, but I knew he was after her. I went there to warn her, but he'd already taken her. He'd just returned to the house to search it for the diamonds when I appeared, so yeah, not the best timing there."

I smiled. "It worked out perfectly, because then we were able to figure out Justin was involved."

Sudden tears filled her eyes. "Thank you for not giving up, Mia. My mom kept telling me that you guys wouldn't give up, and she was right. She told me if I left that note in your marina, that you'd know to keep going. She said to hide it so no one else found it, but she said you'd know it was there. Somehow, you'd figure it out. And you did."

My throat tightened with emotion as I recalled finding that note in my store. "It's great to have friends. Real friends."

She nodded. "It is. And a mom."

And a mom. Seeing them together, reunited after all this time, made my chest ache for my mom. "Did you see Justin kill Dee or Topsy?"

She shook her head. "No, thank heavens. That would have been the end of what I could cope with." She put her head on Rogue's. "I love you, Mom," she whispered. "I'm so sorry."

A tear trickled down my cheek and I stood up as I heard the sound of sirens in the distance. "The police will be here soon. You'll need to tell them everything."

She didn't open her eyes. "They don't need to know about the diamonds."

"Yes, they do." Suddenly, I needed her to not have to live with that shadow. "Look, Tessa, my mom is a criminal, and I was one for most of my life. It's time to set yourself free."

She opened her eyes. "Can you promise no one will send me to prison for stealing them?"

I stared at her, and my gut sank. "No," I said. "I can't. The police can't always be trusted."

She nodded. "Then Dee only thought I had them. I didn't have them. If the cops don't find them in the trophy, then I don't know where they ended up. No one ever will." She met my gaze, pleading. "Right?"

What could I say? It wasn't my story to tell. "Okay."

She nodded and closed her eyes again, hugging her mom while Ruby Lee napped on the ground.

I stood up and walked back to Hattie and Lucy, who were

explaining to a newly arrived Beau all that had occurred. He was busy taking pictures of Justin, the tent, and the car. "This was brilliant. I'm using it in my new series. It's perfect. It's a takedown of luck, opportunity, and—"

"Luck?" Hattie put her hands on her hips. "We rocked this, you nasty little billionaire. Don't undercut our brilliance."

"I can do whatever I want." But he winked at me as he took another picture.

I wedged myself between Hattie and Lucy and put my arms around their shoulders. "Nicely done, my friends."

Hattie patted my hand. "Well done," she agreed. "Now you see that I was right that life was getting boring? We were born for this."

Lucy laughed. "It was fun," she agreed. "I'll never look at tents the same way."

"I told you that you needed to lose your bodyguard," Hattie said...but as she said it, her smile faded. "I hope they solved that little situation."

"Agreed." I wasn't going to leave, though. No matter what Griselda wanted. Facing down Justin and dealing with the threats to me and my friends had made me realize that I was capable of living my life. I wasn't going to live in fear anymore, especially not fear from the FBI or cops.

Sirens began to echo, and I looked at Rogue, asleep on her daughter's shoulder. "You think she'll be ready by the bake-off later today?"

"She'll be at that table with the best strawberry shortcake in the festival, no matter what," Hattie said. "Because we'll make it happen."

I grinned. "Yes, we will.

CHAPTER 31

FOURTEEN HOURS LATER, we'd done it.

I stood back against the side of the tent with Lucy, watching as Rogue and Tessa chatted with Ronald Dutch and the judges. Her table looked amazing. The biscuits had come out of the oven less than twenty minutes ago, because we'd waited as long as possible for Rogue to recover.

Rogue was laughing, her eyes sparkling with joy as she and her daughter worked together. "She looks so happy," I said. "She was always sassy, but she looks like pure joy."

"That she does." Hattie stretched her arm. "The biscuits came out amazing. I really thought we needed to use my recipe, but she did great work. She'll win this on her own, and that's the way it should be."

I glanced at the table where Diesel was handing out beer and shortcake. "I can't believe that Stevie let Justin hide Dee's body in their freezer. That's so freaky."

"He thought Justin would give him part of the diamonds," Hattie said. "He gets off scot-free because he is willing to testify against Justin."

"Well, not scot-free," I said. "There is still the incident from last night when he attacked me and went after my marina. And it looks like Diesel fired him." I watched the owner of the Ugly Man. "Do you think Diesel really thought it was Stevie's stash of illegal meat from hunting off season, as he claimed?" I asked.

Hattie shrugged. "I'd have to say yes."

"I can't believe Justin confessed to murdering Dee and Topsy," Lucy said. "Who admits that? No one actually saw him do it, so he could still have maybe gotten off."

"Guilt," Hattie said. "He's been sitting on it for decades. That eats away at a soul."

"Mia."

We all turned to see Griselda walking up to us. He was wearing jeans, a navy T-shirt, an FBI hat, and sunglasses.

"Damn, he's hot," Hattie muttered under her breath. "Forget Devlin. Take him."

I elbowed Hattie as Griselda reached us. "What's up?" He hadn't come by Justin's last night because it hadn't been an FBI issue. He'd stayed at my marina dealing with the remnants of my past, and I'd stayed at Hattie's. I didn't know what had been solved regarding my federally interesting life.

He nodded at Hattie and Lucy before turning to me. "I need a word with you."

I didn't move. "Are you going to kidnap me? Or try, rather?"

He didn't quirk a smile. "No. Not today."

"All right then." I gestured to Hattie and Lucy stay behind, then I followed Griselda to the end of the tent. He guided me out the flap and herded me to the edge of the crowd, near the beach.

When we reached an empty picnic table, he gestured for me to sit down.

I did, curious. He wasn't usually a sit-down-and-chat kind of guy. "What's up?"

"I thought you should know that we have accessed all our channels, and we can find no evidence of Ivan being assassinated by a professional."

I sat back in my seat. "Really?"

"Yeah. The knife wound in his back was a match for a knife

found at Justin Dutch's property. The one you guys apparently used to cut Ruby Lee and Esther free."

I blinked. "Justin stabbed Ivan? Why?"

"My guess is that Ivan stumbled onto him doing something related to the other murders and Justin killed him, but that's pure conjecture. We're still interviewing Justin to find out what happened. But it was a local attack."

I sat back. "So, I'm not in danger."

"I didn't say that. You'll always be in danger, for the remainder of your life."

I let out a breath. "The price of marrying a drug kingpin."

"And betraying him, yeah." He was quiet for a moment.

I watched the families playing with their kids on the beach. That looked so normal. I'd never had that. Could I have it? Could I dare have kids if they would always be in danger? The thought surprised me. I'd stopped thinking about the fairytale of a family once I'd realized my fairytale life depended on a drug lord. "What happened at the marina last night?"

"A couple wannabe entrepreneurs from Stanley's old life showed up to try to liberate the cash and drugs. They were low-level, not the type to send an assassin. Just opportunists."

I let my breath out. "That's great news. Did you arrest them?"

"Yes." He paused. "Devlin indicated that you set that up. That you basically invited them to show up."

I cleared my throat. "How would I have done that?"

He leaned forward. "Are you still in contact with people from your old life?"

I met his gaze unflinchingly. "No."

He narrowed his eyes, and I didn't look away. I saw the moment he accepted my lie as truth, and pride flickered through me. I still had it. "Are you going to try to get me to leave again?" I asked.

"No."

I looked at him, surprised. "Why not?"

He leaned forward. "Mia. In the two and a half years we've

worked together, you've been..." He paused. "You've surprised me. Impressed me. And challenged me. Repeatedly."

I nodded. "Okay."

"But since you've been here, in this town, I've seen what you can do, who you are, when no one is calling the shots in your life."

I let out my breath. "I love being here."

"I know. I can tell." He ground his jaw. "Devlin got on my case last night. He was furious that my pressure on you had made you turn off your phone, which made it impossible for us to reach you or find you or help you."

Wow. Go Devlin.

"I don't listen to a lot of people, but Devlin and I go way back. I respect his opinion. And he had some valid points."

I sat back. What else had Devlin said to him?

"I won't force you to give up your life just so I can have a witness when Stanley's case goes up on appeal."

I could see the effort it took for him to say that. "Thank you." I felt such relief I could barely breathe. *I was free.*

"But I will be pissed as all hell if you get yourself killed." He let out a breath. "I had to say that."

I laughed, lightness in my chest. "Well, if it's any consolation, I'll be pissed too."

He shook his head. "I don't get how you don't take your safety seriously—"

"I do take it seriously." I leaned forward, wanting him to understand. "Life is short, Griselda. You can live it in the shadows, hiding, afraid. Or you can live it to the fullest you can, in every moment. I have to do the latter. It's how I'm wired. Try it. You might like it."

He stared at me. "You're so freaking vibrant."

I grinned. "I am."

He let out his breath, drumming his fingers on the table. "Devlin wants to date you. He's going to try to grab you for dinner tonight."

My heart turned over. "He mentioned that." Did I want that? I wasn't sure.

Griselda studied me. "You like him?"

"He has some palatable qualities, I guess."

Griselda grinned then. "You want to date him?"

"I don't know," I said honestly. "I don't know if I want to date anyone."

He let out his breath again. "So, you're not madly in love with him?"

I made a strangled sound. "No."

He leaned forward suddenly. "Then I'm throwing my hat in the ring, too."

I stared at him. "What hat? What ring?"

"You told me that you don't date men named Griselda. Which is fine, since that's not my name. What about men named Hawk? Because that's my actual name, in case you forgot. Would you date a guy named Hawk? 'Cause I'm officially asking you out."

My mouth formed a silent "O." I had no words.

"If it's a hard no, say it. Let's move on and put it behind us. If it's a maybe, say it. If it's a yes, then admit it and let's see what might happen. Regardless, I'm still going to be your handler. I'm still going to work to keep you safe. I'm still going to call you as a witness when Stanley's appeal comes up. This is off the rails to do this, but I'm doing it. You have three choices for an answer. Which one is it?"

A few weeks ago, I would have said hard no.

But ever since Devlin had hinted that Griselda was interested in me, I'd looked at him differently. I'd looked at him as a man, not just as a control freak who was trying to wrangle my life into submission. But it was also impossible to ignore Devlin's interest.

I didn't want to date anyone.

But at the same time, both men were incredibly tempting. Which made them both that much more annoying. "You're a pain in the butt," I said.

A grin flashed across his face. "That wasn't one of your

options."

I leaned forward so my face was in his space. "You're a control freak. You're bossy. You don't respect me."

"The first two, I admit to. The third one is a bald-faced lie. I respect the hell out of you. If I didn't, there's no chance I'd ever want to date you. I don't have time to date. But I'd make time for you."

I stared at him.

He stared back.

Finally, I sighed. "Go back to your life, Griselda."

A slow grin pulled at the corners of his mouth. "A maybe it is. I'll take that." He stood up. "I'll be in touch, Mia. " He rapped his knuckles on the table. "And good job. Again. The world is lucky to have you in it."

And with that ridiculously sweet announcement, my most and least favorite FBI agent wandered off into the raging Bass Derby festival crowd.

I sat back and watched him go. Date Griselda? And Devlin? Two guys were bad enough, but they were pals. That wouldn't go well for me, or for them. This would not work. I was telling them both no—

My phone dinged and I looked down. A text from Devlin. Confirming our dinner date for the Bass Derby Inn tonight? I didn't know if I wanted to go. I didn't want to commit.

My heart started to race as I opened the text.

Mia. It's been a long weekend. How about we meet at the hot pretzel truck in ten minutes instead of trying to make dinner?

I relaxed. A food truck at the festival sounded just about right for me. *Make it eleven and a half minutes and I'm in.*

Deal. See you then.

I sat back. Devlin was handling me the right way, and I appreciated it. Maybe it was time for me to get back in the game. Or not. But a pretzel was fine. A place to start. See if I liked pretzels or not.

"Mia!" Hattie and Lucy strode up. "What was that about?"

"Griselda officially gave up keeping me locked up. And he told me that Justin killed Ivan. It wasn't about Stanley." I knew that all the issues about my past had not been resolved. But for now, I was free to be me.

They both sat down across from me. "What else?" Hattie said. "He had that look in his eyes that men get."

"I told Hattie she was wrong," Lucy said. "But she's convinced that Griselda declared his undying love for his favorite amateur undercover spy."

I spread my hands out on the table. "It's a battle between cops for my sweet little heart," I admitted.

Hattie slammed her palm on the table. "I love that."

Lucy grinned. "Me, too. Who are you going to pick?"

"I'm going to get a pretzel with Devlin in a few minutes."

"Good start. The twisted pretzel is one of my favorites," Hattie said, wiggling her brows.

I laughed. "I'm not twisting my pretzel with anyone—"

"Are these seats open?" Rogue and Tessa walked up, arm in arm.

I grinned, my heart so happy to see them together. "You bet. Come join us."

Rogue sat down next to me, and Tessa sat next to her. She had that sparkle in her eye again, and her walk had a definite bounce to it. "We didn't get a chance to talk because we had to get baking when I got out of the hospital, but I just want to say thank you. To all of you."

My heart tightened at the genuine appreciation in her voice. "We'd never have let you down," I said, and Hattie and Lucy agreed.

"I knew that. It kept me going." Rogue grinned. "I want to buy you all dinner. My place tonight? I will have a catered meal, and we can drink and eat while we clean up the house."

Lucy and I burst out laughing and Hattie raised her brows. "After we saved your life, you're literally trying to trick us into helping you clean the house that you messed up?"

"Absolutely."

Hattie grinned. "Okay, I'm in."

"Me, too," Lucy said.

"And me," I agreed.

While the conversation continued, I sat back, watching everyone, my heart so full. These were good people, and they had become my tribe. I was so grateful—

I saw Devlin watching us from a distance, and my heart started racing. I pushed back from the table. "I'm going to go get that pretzel now," I said. "I'll meet you guys at the awards ceremony at four. Save me a seat."

Hattie looked behind her and gave me an approving nod. "Good girl. Have fun."

"I don't know about that." I stood up and stepped over the bench, but Rogue caught my arm as I started to move away.

"Mia." As she spoke, she slipped something into my hand and closed my fingers over it. "Find their true home. I trust you."

Then, before I could ask, she gave me a little push and then turned back to the table.

I saw Hattie and Lucy watching me, but I shrugged. As I walked toward Devlin, I looked down at what she'd given me. It was a little zippered pouch. Plain. The kind you might find at a pharmacy for nail clippers. I unzipped it. Inside was a plastic baggie.

The last plastic baggie I'd stumbled across had contained vast quantities of cocaine that had changed my life.

This one had a bunch of white, sparkling stones worth as much as the cocaine had been worth. Inside there was a little notecard with writing on it, explaining where the diamonds were from and apologizing for taking this long to give them back.

Holy cow. She'd given me the missing diamonds. *Find their true home.*

She wanted me to give them back to the family of the murdered jeweler.

CHAPTER 32

"Mɪᴀ."

When Devlin said my name, I quickly zipped the bag up and shoved it in my pocket. "Hi." I smiled up at him, but my thoughts were on the diamonds in my front pocket.

His smile faded. "There's always something with you," he said softly. "Does your brain ever slow down?"

"I don't know. Maybe."

"You don't have pretzels on your mind. What's up?"

I both loved and hated that Devlin could read me so easily. "The jeweler who was murdered. What was his name?"

"Tony D'Amario."

I couldn't believe that was the first time I'd heard his name. "Did he have any kids? Grandkids? Any of his family that is still around?"

Devlin raised his brows. "I don't know."

"Okay." I took a breath, the diamonds burning in my pocket. "Look, I'm going to have to take a raincheck on the pretzels. I have to take care of something."

"With Tony's descendants?"

"Yeah. Someone asked me to do a favor. I need to do it."

He held up his hand and pulled out his phone. "Hey. It's me.

Can you text me a list of all living descendants of Tony D'Amario. Thanks." He hung up and looked at me. "How about we talk and stroll toward the pretzel stand. It'll take a few minutes to get the list."

I was restless and edgy with the diamonds, but I decided I was less likely to get mugged if I was walking with Devlin. "Okay."

He walked beside me silently, and I could feel him watching me. "Bad idea to get a pretzel with me?"

I turned to face him. "Griselda officially declared his interest in dating me. He asked me out."

Devlin's face went stoic. "What did you say?"

"I told him to go back to his life."

His jaw flexed. "That's not a no. That's a maybe."

These men were much too versed in dating talk. "I said yes to your pretzels."

He thought about that. "Why?"

"Because it didn't scare me."

He nodded, and I saw the corner of his mouth curve up. "I'll take that as a place to start." At that moment, his phone dinged.

We both looked down as he tapped the text. "He has two grandkids. A granddaughter named Leslie Dutch, and a grandson named Stephen Coolidge." He frowned. "That's Stevie from the Ugly Man."

Ah...no wonder Stevie felt like the diamonds belonged to him.

I wasn't the hugest fan of giving it back to him...but I knew the name he'd mentioned of the granddaughter. She was the woman who Ronald had asked to run Dee's table. She'd still been at Dee's table earlier, running it in her name, even though Dee was officially not able to win since she wasn't present. "I need to go find her."

Devlin nodded. "Want me to walk you?"

"No. I got this." I paused. "Devlin," I said softly.

He cocked a brow. "Yeah."

"Thanks for accepting me as I am. For how I need to handle this. Us. Thing."

He smiled. "You're welcome. I'm in no rush."

I nodded. "Okay, thanks." On a sudden whim, I reached out and lightly brushed my hand over his forearm. It was the first time I'd touched a man voluntarily in a long time, in a way that had potential, and to my surprise, it felt good. "I'll talk to you later."

"You bet." His eyes were dark, searching mine, but he made no move toward me, which I appreciated.

I shot him a smile, then turned and jogged back toward the competitor tent. Devlin was becoming a definite maybe. A different maybe than Griselda. A real maybe. A maybe that I was getting more and more tempted by.

Who knew? Maybe my dating life wasn't actually forever dead. Maybe it was simply in hiatus and could be resurrected someday.

By the time I saw Leslie at her table, I was actually feeling excited to hand over the diamonds and maybe grab a pretzel before the award's ceremony. "Leslie!" I waved as I walked toward her.

She looked up at me, frowned, then her face brightened when she recognized me. "Hi, Jessie. It's good to see you."

Right. I'd forgotten that I'd introduced myself as Jessie. That was probably best. It would be more difficult to trace the diamonds back to Tessa. "Good to see you, too. How is it going?"

"Oh, great. Just cleaning up."

"Want help?"

"Sure!"

I started helping her, bumped her side, and slipped the bag into her back pocket. But the moment I did it, I realized that I couldn't just walk away. I had to tell her. I didn't want them to fall out of her pocket, or for her to toss it when she didn't recognize it. "Leslie."

"Yeah."

"Are you Tony D'Amario's granddaughter?" I probably should have asked that before sticking the diamonds in her pocket.

She froze and looked over at me. "Yes. Why?"

"Did anyone ever find those diamonds?"

She put the crate down, her eyes narrowing. "You want the diamonds? Everyone wants the diamonds. Even my freaking cousin wants the diamonds. I don't have them."

"You do, actually," I said quietly.

"I do not. God. Seriously? You're like everyone else. I'm so over this—"

"Your back pocket."

"My back pocket? Are you kidding? I'm—" Her hand went to her back pocket, and she froze when she felt the bag there. "What?"

"Don't open it here, but don't lose it."

Her fingers tightened on the bag, and she pulled it out. She looked down at it, and then looked at me. "What is this?"

"Someone rescued the diamonds from the murderer way back then, and then hid them. They just came to light, and someone gave them to me and asked me to make sure they got back home. So I'm giving them back to you."

Her fingers tightened on the bag. "You could have kept them."

I definitely could have. "It's not what I do. They're yours."

She stared at me. "Did you look in the bag?"

I nodded.

"Are there a lot?"

"It looks like a lot to me."

She closed her eyes and pressed the bag to her heart. "You don't understand how much I need this right now. I—" A tear slipped out of her eye, and she looked at me. "I'd given up," she whispered. "I thought that there was no way and then you gave me this—"

"They're yours," I said. "I'm sure your grandfather is happy right now, knowing that they came back to you at the right time." I didn't know what she was going through, and it didn't matter. What mattered was that she had hope again, that whatever she was facing was going to be better because we'd found the diamonds that were hers.

She threw her arms around me and hugged me. "Thank you," she whispered. "Thank you."

Happiness flooded me. All the times I'd stolen jewels in my life, I'd left behind a wake of enemies, of loss, of personal transgression. This was the first time I'd done the complete opposite: finding jewels and giving them back, making someone whole again.

It was freaking *awesome.*

She pulled back. "Can you do me a favor? Can you finish packing this stuff up? I need to go."

I grinned. "You bet. Go ahead."

"Thanks!" Clutching the bag in her hand, she sprinted off, ducking around people.

I grinned, watching as she ran. I couldn't believe how good it felt—

Someone came up to her, and she stopped running. I frowned, watching them chat. It was the young man who'd been running the booth with her the first day.

They talked briefly, and then he put his hand on her elbow and they headed toward the judges' tent.

I watched them carefully, with rising alarm. Her body was stiff. Tension was radiating off her.

Something wasn't right.

Quickly, I pulled out my phone and texted Lucy and Hattie. All I got typed was the letter *S* before I heard a man clear his throat.

I spun around. Ronald Dutch was leaning against a tent pole, his arms folded across his chest.

I tensed when I saw him. How long had he been standing there? "Um, hi."

"Mia Murphy, right?"

I nodded. "Yes."

"I heard you were instrumental in solving the case of my

niece's murder. On behalf of the Dutch family, I want to thank you."

I nodded again. "You're welcome." Ronald was giving off a very weird vibe. Something wasn't right.

"We were all very surprised to learn that my uncle Justin had killed Dee and her friend Topsy. And that my twin brother killed Tony. It's difficult when you discover that your family is made of murderers." His voice was even. Too even.

I became aware of how empty the tent was. We were the only ones I could see. The band had started playing outside, and everyone had gone out for the concert. The walls of the booth obscured my view of the rest of the tent. "I can see that."

"The Dutch family takes care of their own issues," he said.

I recalled Hattie basically telling me that, and her initial guess that Rogue was on the run from the Dutch family, not the police. "Family loyalty is good. I'm meeting Officer Hunt in a couple minutes, so I need to be going."

"No, you don't." His hand moved to his back pocket.

"Yes, I actually do." I moved to the right, so Leslie's crates of strawberries were between us. "He'll come looking for me."

"Good." He moved then, fast.

Moving on instinct, I instantly dropped to the ground behind the crates as I heard a thud above my head. I looked up and saw a hunting knife lodged in the wall of the booth, right where I'd been standing. *Holy crap!* Anyone want to guess who had killed Ivan with a knife at the festival? No wonder Justin hadn't admitted to it.

I vaulted to my feet and lunged for the knife, at the same moment Ronald launched himself across the crates to grab it.

I couldn't get it free, and I dove out of the way as he wrenched it out of the wall. He spun to face me before I made it to my feet. I was on my knees, and he was crouched a few yards away, the knife in his hand. "My brother didn't kill Tony," he said. "He was a good man."

"Okay, great. That's fine. I don't even care who killed Tony." I looked around frantically for a weapon or a shield, but nothing was in reach. Getting stabbed to death felt so much worse than a one-shot-kill. This was not the way I wanted to go.

"It was me. Not my twin. He was the good brother."

My skin went cold. The only reason he just told me he'd killed Tony was because he knew I was about to die. Of course, it made sense. They were twins. Dee and Tessa could easily have gotten them confused, especially if Ronnie had dressed like Richie—Oh! Alert! "Why did you make yourself look like him if you didn't want him to get the blame then?"

"Because that's what we did. We created Richie when we wanted to cause trouble, and Ronnie when we didn't. We both played both roles."

Oh, that was a great idea. My mom would have found it so useful if I'd been a twin. Too bad for her, right? "Are you really Ronnie? Or was Ronnie the one who died? And you're Richie?"

He smiled then, a terrifying creepy smile, then held up his arm, sliding his watch back just enough for me to see a tiny devil tattoo on his wrist. "Smart girl."

Oh, fantastic. Bad twin alert. Had he murdered the good twin? Maybe. That added a fun element of surprise.

The last time I'd been facing down a murderer, I'd been smart enough to pretend I didn't know he was a murderer. This time? I'd been stupid. He'd have to kill me now. But since he'd already been planning to kill me, maybe not such a significant mistake. "Why do you want to kill me?"

"Because my uncle needs to go free. You're going to kill yourself with a suicide note. Justin's going to say that he took the blame because he thought I did it, so he was protecting me. But at the end of the day, you did it all, including your stupid bodyguard who found Dee's body in my truck. Or your truck. Because there is now Dee's hair in that rundown truck of yours."

Oh, *Ivan*.

"My family will not be brought down. You're an outsider who deals drugs. Of course you'd kill people."

"Of course I would. That makes sense," I agreed, trying to stay focused. How was I going to get out of this? There were so many people only yards away, and yet I was completely alone with a murderer.

"I'm getting the diamonds from Leslie, and my family's name will be clear again." He looked past me and grinned. "Time to die."

Someone was behind me. What the hell? There were two people? Who had I overlooked?

They'd killed Ivan by stabbing him from behind, but they couldn't do that if I was going to kill myself. They'd have to do it from the front. A strange calm suddenly settled over me. I had this.

I stood up and put my hands on my hips, facing down Ronnie. On the table were the glasses that Leslie hadn't packed yet. In the reflection, I could see someone behind me.

It was the young man who'd escorted Leslie to the judges' tent. What had he done with her?

Keeping my attention on both of them, I eased to the left, trying to put myself directly between them. Ronnie (aka Richie) turned with me. His knife was in his hand, and he looked very focused and confident, which was always fun in a murderer.

Then, just as suddenly, I heard a bird "ca-caw" from behind the wall to my right, and relief burst through me.

That was the call of the Seam Rippers. Hattie and Lucy must have come to find me!

Sudden power coursed through me, and I moved to the right, toward my friends. I saw movement between the panels, and then I saw Hattie's blue eyes peering at me.

Ronnie's gaze went to the wall, and I saw him realize someone was behind there. "Run," I screamed, then I charged him.

He shouted and threw the knife...except I was already diving behind the table by the time he let go of the knife.

Behind me, I heard his pal grunt, and I spun around. Just as I'd hoped, he'd been standing in the path of the knife, and without my body to block it...oopsie.

He went down on his knees. "You stupid idiot!"

Ronnie swore. "Give me the knife! We need to finish it!"

"It's in my thigh! My freaking thigh!"

"I'll get it!" Ronnie charged past me, but just as he reached Thigh Guy, Hattie, Lucy, Rogue, and Tessa all burst out from behind the panel swinging blenders by the cords. They swung hard, and all four of them connected with the men.

Ronnie went down.

Thigh Guy went down.

And neither of them moved.

"Wow." Rogue grinned. "That's so freaking powerful! I love that so much!"

"Time for a zip-tie party!" Tessa tossed some zip ties at Lucy and me, and we quickly went to work returning the zip-tie favors they'd bestowed upon Tessa, Rogue, and Ruby Lee.

"Call Devlin," I instructed Hattie, who was busy congratulating Rogue on her great aim and delighting in the joy of corded implements. "Hattie!"

"Right on it." She quickly called my favorite cop while the three of us finished up.

By the time we were done, both men were awake, but entirely unable to move. Or talk. Because who likes gags? We liked them, at least in this particular instance.

Lucy sat back. "Do you think we were a little enthusiastic with the zip ties?"

Both men had been zip tied multiple times from shoulder to ankle. We'd basically tied them up everywhere we could, including tying them to each other and to the tent pole. "I don't think you can ever have too much fun with zip ties," I said.

"Agreed." Tessa hopped to her feet. "Ronnie did all this to defend his brother's name?"

"No. He's Richie. He's the one you saw that night."

Tessa stared at him, then nodded. "That explains so much."

"Mia!" Devlin's shout echoed through the tent.

Hattie grinned at me. "I'm the one who called him, but he shouts your name. That's true love right there, my friend."

"Right?" Rogue grinned. "He's a good man. I'd take him."

I ignored them. "Over here," I called out.

Devlin came running down the aisle, gun out, then slowed when he saw the men trussed up on the ground. Slowly, he lowered his gun. "I'm going to have a lot of questions about this."

"As you should," Hattie said.

I raised my hand. "That's Richie, not Ronnie. He admitted to killing the jeweler, and I'd look into him for the knife death of Ivan. I think he was the one who killed Dee and Topsy, as well, but I'm not sure. Justin might have taken the blame for it to protect his nephew. Not that he's innocent, of course."

Devlin saw the knife in Thigh Guy's leg, then swore. He looked around at us. "You guys are all okay?"

We all nodded, and then Chief Stone came running down the aisle. "What's going on? What happened? More bodies?"

Devlin sighed. "This is going to take a while."

"As long as we're done by the time they announce the winners," Hattie said, "it's all good."

He raised his brows. "I can't promise that."

She met his gaze. "Rogue has been tied up and drugged for two days. You're going to deprive her of her moment of glory?"

"If I have to, yeah—" He paused when we all looked at him. Then he sighed. "I'll see what I can do."

CHAPTER 33

IT WAS ALMOST two in the morning by the time I made it home.

Rogue had won, and we'd celebrated at her house with the rest of the Seam Rippers. Even Ruby Lee had come by. Leslie Dutch had been found safe and sound in the judges' tent, and her cousin had been happy to rat out Richie for the murders of Topsy, Dee, and Ivan. Justin, Jeremiah, and Stevie were still in trouble for their participation, but the murder card was hanging only on Richie's shoulders.

And so we'd spent the evening celebrating strawberry short cake, murder, and women. They'd even invited Beau as an honorary woman, but he'd refused to come. Next time, maybe.

The story that Tessa had told about almost getting caught by Hattie putting the murder weapon in Rogue's bedroom and then trying to run down the passageway like her mom instead of herself had been one of the funniest stories I'd ever heard. Tessa was hilarious, and I loved listening to the mother-daughter rendition of the last two days. They had the same great sense of humor and indomitable spirit, and I was so glad they'd found each other again.

It had been the best night I'd had in a long time, maybe ever.

So many women there together, supporting each other, working together for victory.

The trophy would now be called the Esther Neeley Challenge Trophy, which was amazing.

As I got out of my truck at home, King Tut meowed at me from the roof of the marina.

I grinned up at him and threw my arms over my head in a victory pose. "We did it! Another murderer shut down!"

He watched me with his yellow eyes, his tail flicking.

"I know, you're so proud of me." I spun around, dancing in the moonlight. "You know, kitty cat, this is the first time that I've been truly free of my past," I called up to him. "Griselda gave up trying to get me to leave."

It felt so good! So amazing! So—

A shadow moved on my deck steps, and I froze. "Who's that?"

He stepped into the light, and I saw it was Devlin.

"What's wrong?" I asked, slightly alarmed by his presence.

"Nothing," he said. "I just wanted to see you."

My heart started racing as he walked across the parking lot toward me. "Why?"

He held up a pretzel wrapped in paper. "It's not hot anymore, but they reheat well. They're the best around. Didn't want you to miss it."

My tension eased, and I accepted the pretzel. "Thanks."

"My pleasure." He paused for a moment. "You'll always throw yourself into the flames to protect others, won't you?"

I nodded slowly. "Seems to be that way, yeah."

"You're good at it."

I smiled. "Thanks."

He nodded. "Telling you to stay safe and not get involved won't work with you."

"Never."

He rubbed his jaw. "It's instinct to try to keep you safe. I can't promise I'll stop."

I cocked my head. "Try."

"I will." He moved closer. "I'm going home. Gotta get some sleep. But before I do…" He paused.

My fingers tightened on the pretzel. "What?"

He studied my face for a moment, then he reached down, took my hand, and raised it to his lips. He pressed a kiss to the back of my hand, his dark gaze fixed on my face.

Then, without another word, he released me, walked across the parking lot, and down to the dock, where his boat was tied up.

He never looked back, and I didn't try to get him to stay.

But when I turned to go inside, I was smiling.

——————

What to read next?

IF YOU LOVED *GONE ROGUE,* make sure you order the next book, *Margarita Mayhem* today! When one of the Seam Rippers gets arrested for a mixing up a deadly margarita, it's up to Mia and her pals to figure out the truth before it's too late!

Sign up for my newsletter here to be notified when the next Mia story is released! New to the series? Grab the first Mia Murphy mystery, *Double Twist* today!

——————

IF YOU ENJOYED the Mia vibe and also enjoy mixing it up with a little magic and romance, try my *Immortally Sexy* romantic comedy series (a little steamy!) or the *Guardian of Magic* paranormal mystery (contains some profanity!).

If you love cowboys, try my deeply heartwarming, family-oriented (but with a little spice!) *Wyoming Rebels* series or the spinoff *Hart Ranch Billionaires* series. Grab the series starter for the Hart family, *A Rogue Cowboy's Second Chance,* or start with the first first book in the *Wyoming Rebels* series, *A Real Cowboy Never Says No.*

If you want more small-town stories with heart-melting, emotional romances, you'd love my *Birch Crossing* series! Get started with *Unexpectedly Mine* today, in which a billionaire hero gets stranded in a small town and gets his world upturned by a sassy single mom and her daughter.

Is dark, steamy paranormal romance your jam? If so, definitely try my award-winning *Order of the Blade* series, starting with book one, *Darkness Awakened.* Jump into the world of soulmates, passion, danger, and immortal warriors who will do whatever it takes to save the woman who steals his heart, no matter what the cost. Don't we all want a guy like that?

SNEAK PEEK: TO DATE AN IMMORTAL

AN IMMORTALLY SEXY NOVEL

"I couldn't put it down! It was funny, heartwarming, sexy, and badass all rolled into one. Keep em coming!!!!" ~Christa S (Five-star Amazon Review)

————

DEREK LAVALLE HAD less than four minutes to save his cousin's life, break the Curse that would kill him and his twin in a week, and prove to his family that he wasn't insane for believing in curses, dragons, and immortality.

It was kind of a loaded four minutes.

Which was why the billionaire, no-carb-soft-pretzel mogul was in a bit of a rush as he vaulted up the crumbling steps of the hovel that his less-than-impressive cousin, Les LaValle, was currently living in.

As a general rule, it might seem pretty easy to make sure an unemployed pothead doesn't die in the next three and a half minutes. But when it came to thirty-one-year-old LaValle men, it was a little tricky. Like the kind of tricky that boasted a zero percent success rate for the last two hundred years. Dead. Dead.

Dead. Dead. Dead. And dead a few more times. For four generations. As odds go, those aren't exactly fantastic ones.

But Derek had an advantage, because he was the only one who'd realized it was a curse that had been knocking off each LaValle male at the precise moment he turned thirty-one years, forty-six weeks, four days, six hours, three minutes, and five seconds old.

Yeah. A freaking *curse*. What are the odds?

Maybe not that high, under normal circumstances. But if you have in your hot little hands a two-hundred-year-old journal by your ancestor that explains very clearly that the men in your family are cursed, then, yeah, the odds are pretty high that could be what's going on.

Derek had the journal.

His family? Not so much on the bandwagon. As in, spend-the-last-ten-years-trying-to-get-Derek-committed not on the bandwagon. Lucky for Derek, he had vast amounts of disposable income and had bought his way to freedom several times.

In truth, his entire extended family had disowned him because they thought he was a freaking whack job who besmirched the family name with his insanity. Understandable on some levels, but for Derek, breaking the Curse that had damned his entire lineage trumped trying to win his family's approval.

It was a no brainer. Screw playing by the rules when the rules wind up with you dead, right?

Derek wasn't super interested in dying in a week, and he sure as hell didn't want his math professor twin brother, Quincy LaValle, to die two minutes after him.

Which meant he had to break that damned Curse.

For those unclear on how curses work, it's hard as freaking hell to break a damned curse. Derek was a master of chasing down leads on how to break curses, but guess how many times the assorted mumbo jumbo tricks and other stuff had worked?

That's right. Zero. A big fat goose egg.

So, now, it had come down to this: break the Curse by beating it mano-a-mano in the battle for his cousin's life or death. Derek had come armed (thank you, baseball bat, for being a deadly weapon masquerading as sporting equipment) and ready to fight.

Yeah, granted, keeping Les alive wasn't exactly a public service, and might even be considered criminal in some societies with basic human morals, but death was death, and Derek was so not going there right now.

But Les was not making it easy.

The disbelieving bastard had been avoiding Derek for the last two weeks, from the minute Derek had showed up and told him he was keeping him alive.

And now, death was three minutes away, and Derek still couldn't find his cousin anywhere, which was, obviously, a major impediment to defeating the Curse.

He was down to his last chance.

If he didn't find Les here, he'd be out of time, and death would roll on through, thumbing its nose at Derek once again.

Derek had been by twice already today, but he was trying a third time, because there was literally nowhere else Les could be. He'd been by Les's favorite bars, the park bench, and a couple alleys he liked to pass out in, but Les had been nowhere. The dude had to be home. His life literally didn't include any more possibilities. "Les! It's Derek! Open up!" He gripped his baseball bat tighter as he hammered his fist on the peeling front door.

Still no answer.

He tried the doorknob.

Still locked.

Derek glanced at his watch. Less than two minutes. *Shit.*

Fuck it. He was breaking in.

Derek shifted the bat to his right hand and sprinted around the side of the house. The rusted gate was closed, wedged in place with a pile of old kegs, a couple bald tires, some strange looking lead pipes, and other thoughtful lawn décor.

No problem.

Derek scrambled over the gate, clearing it easily, courtesy of his slight obsession with assorted martial arts and fitness. Hey, if something was going to try to murder him next week, he was going to make damn sure he was fit enough to fight for his life, right? Amen, brother.

He raced up the rickety stairs to the back deck, and nearly tripped over his cousin, who was sprawled in a lawn chair. Elated disbelief rushed through Derek. He'd found him! "Les! Didn't you hear me?"

"Jesus. You just don't know when to drop it. Fuck off." Les was holding a reflective cardboard piece across his chest to catch some rays. A horrifyingly small bathing suit stretched to the limit across his hips, the yellowing fabric barely visible beneath his expansive gut. His hairy feet were partially covered by the green, murky water of a plastic wading pool.

Oh, damn.

That was just not a sight anyone needed to see.

Honest to God, the things a guy needed to do in order to break a family curse, right? Derek averted his eyes before the sight could be entrenched forever in his brain. "It's time, Les."

"I'm not interested in your shit." Les didn't even bother to open his eyes.

Derek scanned the backyard, searching for rabid chipmunks and homicidal yard implements that might develop a mind of their own. "You're supposed to die in less than two minutes. I'm here to save you."

"I already told you. I don't need saving. I'm a fantastic model of male perfection exactly as I am." He paused to belch. "Take your insanity off my property, dude."

"Damn it, Les. I'm not insane."

"Are too."

Are too? Really? Because every grown man should throw out retorts worthy of a six-year-old brat. "Listen to me, Les," Derek said urgently. "You're going to hit the expiration date for LaValle men in just over a minute." He raised the bat into the ready position, settling it on his shoulder. "You might want to get off your ass and grab a metal rake or something to help me defend you." *I know you're out there, you murderous son of a bitch. I'm ready for you.*

"Fuck that." Les took another drag of beer and waddled his ass deeper into the lawn chair. "Everything always works out for me."

"Everything? Really? You're so sure about that?" Derek eyed the rusted motorcycle sunken into the weeds. Could that come flying at Les? That would be deadly, for sure. Shit. There was so much junk in the yard that could be lethal.

"Hell, yeah." Les waved his hand around the broken-glass and weed-filled backyard. "Look at this glory. I sit out here, drink beer, and get high, then go play Internet poker. I haven't punched a time clock in six years, because I'm a freaking genius at working the disability game. I'm one of those lucky bastards, Cuz. Hell, they just made pot legal in this state. I have shitloads of cannabis in my house, and my health insurance *paid* for it. I live a gifted life, my friend. *Gifted.*" He stretched his arms up and then clasped his hands behind his head. "The other LaValle men were unlucky sons of bitches, but that's not me. I'm a fucking *god.*"

"*Unlucky*? Hell, Les, it's not a matter of bad luck." Derek's dad had made the same claim, but that hadn't stopped a wayward butter knife from taking him down, right in front of seven-year-old Derek, while they'd been sampling a no-calorie waffle together. Derek had managed to perfect a no-carb-soft-pretzel recipe by the time he was eighteen, but replacing his dad? Not so much.

And how could bad luck explain his Uncle Jack, who'd been lethally impaled by a cotton-ball? Or Grandad Howie, who'd choked to death on lemonade? And let's be honest, folks, newborn babies don't usually generate enough power with their kicks to give fatal brain damage to tenth degree black belts, like his cousin Tony. The fact that his fifth cousin, twice removed, had shot himself in the head while cleaning his gun could have been bad luck, except, of course, for that precise age he'd been when it had happened. And pet hamsters? Really? How many of them maul a three-hundred-pound iron worker to death?

Every LaValle man had died, and every single one of them had died at the same age, down to the *second*. There was no chance that could be anything but supernatural, as if fate was grabbing whatever was available at that precise moment. Who the hell could be stupid enough *not* to realize that there was something supernatural going on? "I'm staying, Les."

"Then I'm calling my mom and telling her you're over here talking about the Curse again," Les whined. "And then I'm going to call the cops and—"

"Shut up and let me concentrate." He glanced at his watch. Forty-five seconds to go. "Maybe you should go inside. You could drown in that pool." His bat wasn't going to be much good if the water suddenly swelled up in a massive tsunami and swept Les away. Mouth-to-mouth resuscitation with Les was just not something that he wanted to be thinking about right now.

"You go inside. Get me another beer." Les let his head drop back against the lounge chair straps. "Order a pizza while you're at it."

Derek looked up at the sky. No lightning bolt could come out of that blue sky, could it?

Ten seconds.

He kicked an old pizza box off the deck. He wasn't sure how cardboard could be deadly, but he wasn't taking any chances.

Les yawned. "I'm gonna take a nap."

Five seconds.

Les belched again and picked up his beer.

"Give me that bottle. I don't want glass near you." Before he could grab the bottle, Derek's phone alarm went off, and a huge rock came careening over the back fence, heading straight for Les's head.

Les screamed and dove out of his chair. Derek swung for the rock. It shattered his bat but ricocheted away from Les and smashed through the living room window.

Derek whirled around, ready for another incoming assault, but the yard was quiet.

Nothing else was happening.

Nothing else was coming in for attempt number two.

Slowly, a stunned disbelief settled over him. He'd done it. He'd intervened and stopped the Curse from getting his cousin. Son of a bitch. *It was over.* Letting out a deep, shuddering breath, he lowered the handle of the bat, barely able to let himself relax. "Believe me now, Les?"

There was no response, not even an obnoxious, ungrateful whine.

Derek spun around, then swore. His cousin was lying on the deck, motionless, his neck twisted at an angle that was unnatural and very, very wrong. His eyes were open and staring, without nearly enough alcohol-induced haze for him to still be alive.

Son of a bitch. Dead. Right on time. "Dammit, Les. Why didn't you listen?"

No one listened. And everyone died.

Well, Derek wasn't going to die, and his twin wasn't either.

So what if he had less than a week to solve a problem that he'd spent his life failing to fix? Deadlines were fantastic motivators, right? So, it was all good. He was going to figure this shit out, and he was going to do it in time.

He glared at the overgrown backyard. "You've just taken your last LaValle man, you hear me?"

There was a weird cackle, almost like maniacal, possessed *laughter.* It didn't sound human. It didn't even sound like it was of this world. It sounded like a freaking nightmare coming for him.

Chills crept down his spine.

A Curse with a warped sense of humor?

Or he was officially starting to crack.

Neither option felt really fantastic, so yeah, he was going to just pretend he hadn't heard that.

But as he pulled out his phone to call 9-1-1, he couldn't deny the truth.

He'd heard it.

Someone...or rather...some*thing* had laughed.

SNEAK PEEK: A ROGUE COWBOY'S SECOND CHANCE

★★★★★ "Absolutely swoon worthy, lovable and emotionally driven. Family is everything." ~Madison (Five-star Amazon Review on *A Real Cowboy for Christmas*)

———

BRODY WAS LATE.

And he still wasn't sure if he was staying.

He kept his head down, his shoulders hunched, and his cowboy hat tilted as he strode through the quiet tunnels leading into the stadium.

There were a few people in line for beer or pretzels, but it was mostly empty.

Everyone was in their seats, screaming for Tatum, who had been on stage for a half hour already.

Brody knew, because he'd sat in his truck and watched the social media feeds. He wasn't about to go in before she was on stage. But once she came on...he'd just sat there in his truck, watching as fans posted grainy clips of her performance.

Then, thirty minutes in, someone had posted a clip from up

close, close enough for Brody to see her face. She'd looked up, as if she were looking right at him, telling him to come in.

So he'd shoved his phone in his pocket and gotten out of his truck.

And now, he could hear the thud of the music as he neared the doorway that led to Floor Section 4, Rows 1-10.

He paused to show his ticket to the usher, and then was waved inside.

He shoved his hands in his front pockets and stepped inside the stadium. The music hit him like a wave of raw power. The lights flashed. Smoke rose from the stage. An assault on his senses that he ignored, his gaze going right to the stage to find her.

His breath seemed to catch in his chest when he saw her in person, for the first time in fifteen years. She was at the far end of the stage, one arm over her head, her stance wide and strong in red, sparkling heels. Her halter top matched the shoes, showing off her muscled torso, while her black leather pants showed off every curve. She radiated a passion and gloriousness that the photographs never did justice to.

She was moving to the fierce beat, working the fans up into a frenzy.

Her voice was glorious, radiating through the stadium like heaven itself had unleashed its greatest glory through her. It wasn't country. It wasn't soul. It wasn't pop. It was all of those together, mixed with a magic that no one else had ever been able to mimic.

Tatum Crosby was legend, and she was right there, fifty feet from him.

The front row was less than five feet from the stage. She would see him. And the moment she did, he would be close enough to read her expression and know if she'd sent the ticket and back-stage pass. He would know whether to stay.

But still he didn't move.

He stood there, silently, watching. Breathing in the woman who had been a part of his soul for fifteen years. With the lights from the stage, he knew she wouldn't be able to see him from where he was standing.

He could watch her entire concert, and then slide away into the night.

She would never know.

But then, neither would he.

Keegan was right. He had to know. This was his chance to begin to live again.

He waited until she was at the far end of the stage again, singing to the crowd on that side of the stadium. The moment she turned her back on him, he pulled his hat down to hide his face, and then he went on the move.

* * *

Brody wasn't coming.

The realization wound tight around Tatum's chest, making it difficult to get enough air to sing.

She fought for the energy her fans deserved. She shouted her love for them. She poured all she had into her music. But she couldn't keep looking at the empty seat in the front row.

She'd known it was a long shot he would come. It had been so long since she'd seen him. Since everything had fallen apart. Since she'd run.

Movement in the wings caught her eye, and she saw Donny shouting at her, gesturing with his palms up for her to step up the energy. He would be angry at her performance.

Her chest tightened even more, dreading the after-show recap with him.

Beside him stood Nora, her clipboard clutched to her chest. She shrugged at Tatum, indicating that she, too, had noticed the empty seat in the front row.

He wasn't coming.

She had to get over it. She'd come this far on her own. She didn't need him. Wasn't that the point she'd been trying to prove her whole life? That she didn't need anyone? Her mom had quit on her, choosing drugs over her own daughter. Her dad? She didn't even know who he was. Foster care? All hell, except for a gray-haired old man named Roger who had given her his old guitar and changed her life.

No. The guitar hadn't changed her life. *She'd* changed her life, and she didn't need anyone.

It was fine if Brody didn't show. Absolutely fine.

She could do this. She'd been on her own since she was ten, tossed between foster homes when her mom was in jail for drugs, sitting in their crappy apartment, watching her mom's chest to see if she was still breathing, or if she'd finally died of a life not worth living.

Her mom had finally died. And on that rainy day in June so long ago, Tatum had decided she was going to become the star she'd always dreamed of, the celebrity who was so incredible that everyone would love her. That everyone would see how special she was.

And she'd done it.

She had money. She had success. She was a star. She didn't need anyone or anything, especially not Brody. But even as Tatum told herself that, she stumbled, panic starting to close in around her.

Emotion caught in her throat, filling her eyes with the tears she worked so hard to keep at bay every moment of every day. The loneliness, the fear, the isolation—they were all lies and illusions. She *had* what she needed. She was *enough,* all on her own.

She spun away from the wings, away from Donny and Nora. She focused on her fans, on the people who filled her soul and kept her going.

Still singing, she moved to the edge of the stage and bent down, holding out her hand for a high-five. A woman in her forties with red hair screamed and high-fived her, making Tatum smile. She moved along, holding out her hand to her fans.

Two adorable young men, early twenties, stopped holding

hands long enough to high-five her. "We love you, Tatum!" One of them yelled.

"I love you, too!" she shouted back.

The next in line were three girls that looked like they were in college, screaming and shouting and jumping up and down, filming her as she high-fived them.

Next up, a man in a cowboy hat with his head down.

In Brody's seat.

At that moment, he raised his head and met her gaze, dark brown eyes that she'd never forget.

Brody.

Tatum was so shocked she forgot the words for a second, the music thundering on without her. She caught up almost immediately, and she knew that no one except Donny would notice, but she couldn't take her gaze off Brody.

He looked the same. And different. A beard. Muscles. Heavier. Fancier.

Still singing, she held out her hand to him for a high-five, her heart pounding.

He reached up and caught her hand. It was a split second of skin brushing over skin, but it was the touch of a man she'd never forgotten.

WHICH BOOK IS NEXT?

What's the easiest way to know when a new book is out?

My newsletter.

It's a quick read, it goes right to your inbox, and it has the info you're looking for. No ads or commercials flashing in your face! Just me and books you enjoy!

I also make sure you know when I have a free book, a cover reveal, or any other important book info. I post reader surveys, give away Advance Review Copies, and provide insider scoop on my books, my writing, and the author life (it's super glam, trust me…).

Give it a try. See if it works for you. If not, you can always unsubscribe at any time!

Go to www.stephanierowe.com and click on the newsletter link to sign up!

Stephanie

A QUICK FAVOR

Hey there, my friend!

It's Mia! Tell me, tell me! What did you think of *Gone Rogue?*

I hope you loved it, and my suffering wasn't for naught.

Just kidding. No suffering here! I love my life. And my hairdryer. And my cat. And my friends. And… well… the list goes on and on. And just wait until my next book comes out. More fun on the way!

I hope I gave you some feel-good entertainment in these pages! If I did, it would rock if you'd do me a favor and help get the word out, so that other folks can find their way here.

Tell a friend. Tell an enemy. Leave a note for your barista.

Reviews are also incredibly helpful to encourage new readers to make that leap and try a new book. It would be super fab if you'd consider taking a couple minutes and jotting one or two sentences on the *etailer* and/or Goodreads telling everyone how freaking amazing I am. Or King Tut. Because we all know that he's the best. Even the short reviews really make an impact!

Thank you again for reading my story! I can't wait for you to see what happens next!

Smooches,

Mia

BOOKS BY STEPHANIE ROWE

MYSTERY

MIA MURPHY SERIES
(COZY MYSTERY)
Double Twist
Top Notch
Gone Rogue
Margarita Mayhem

ROMANCE

PARANORMAL

ORDER OF THE BLADE SERIES
(PARANORMAL ROMANCE)
Darkness Awakened
Darkness Seduced
Darkness Surrendered
Forever in Darkness
Darkness Reborn
Darkness Arisen

BOOKS BY STEPHANIE ROWE

Darkness Unleashed
Inferno of Darkness
Darkness Possessed
Shadows of Darkness
Hunt the Darkness
Darkness Awakened: Reimagined

IMMORTALLY SEXY SERIES
(FUNNY PARANORMAL ROMANCE)
To Date an Immortal
To Date a Dragon
Devilishly Dating
To Kiss a Demon

HEART OF THE SHIFTER SERIES
(PARANORMAL ROMANCE)
Dark Wolf Rising
Dark Wolf Unbound

SHADOW GUARDIANS SERIES
(PARANORMAL ROMANCE)
Leopard's Kiss

NIGHTHUNTER SERIES
(PARANORMAL ROMANCE)
Not Quite Dead

NOBLE AS HELL SERIES
(FUNNY URBAN FANTASY)
Guardian of Magic

THE MAGICAL ELITE SERIES
(FUNNY PARANORMAL ROMANCE)
The Demon You Trust

BOOKS BY STEPHANIE ROWE

DEVILISHLY SEXY SERIES
(FUNNY PARANORMAL ROMANCE)
Not Quite a Devil

CONTEMPORARY ROMANCE

WYOMING REBELS SERIES
(CONTEMPORARY WESTERN ROMANCE)
A Real Cowboy Never Says No
A Real Cowboy Knows How to Kiss
A Real Cowboy Rides a Motorcycle
A Real Cowboy Never Walks Away
A Real Cowboy Loves Forever
A Real Cowboy for Christmas
A Real Cowboy Always Trusts His Heart
A Real Cowboy Always Protects
A Real Cowboy for the Holidays
A Real Cowboy Always Comes Home
SERIES COMPLETE

THE HART RANCH BILLIONAIRES SERIES
(CONTEMPORARY WESTERN ROMANCE)
A Rogue Cowboy's Second Chance
A Rogue Cowboy's Christmas Surprise
A Rogue Cowboy Finds Love (Coming in 2023)!

LINKED TO THE HART RANCH BILLIONAIRES SERIES
(CONTEMPORARY WESTERN ROMANCE)
Her Rebel Cowboy

BIRCH CROSSING SERIES
(SMALL-TOWN CONTEMPORARY ROMANCE)
Unexpectedly Mine
Accidentally Mine
Unintentionally Mine
Irresistibly Mine

MYSTIC ISLAND SERIES
(SMALL-TOWN CONTEMPORARY ROMANCE)
Wrapped Up in You (A Christmas novella)

CANINE CUPIDS SERIES
(ROMANTIC COMEDY)
Paws for a Kiss
Pawfectly in Love
Paws Up for Love

SINGLE TITLE
(CHICKLIT / ROMANTIC COMEDY)
One More Kiss

ROMANTIC SUSPENSE

ALASKA HEAT SERIES
(ROMANTIC SUSPENSE)
Ice
Chill
Ghost
Burn
Hunt (novella)

BOXED SETS

Order of the Blade (Books 1-3)
Protectors of the Heart (A Six-Book First-in-Series Collection)
Wyoming Rebels Boxed Set (Books 1-3)

For a complete list of Stephanie's books, go to
www.stephanierowe.com

ABOUT THE AUTHOR

New York Times and *USA Today* bestselling author Stephanie Rowe is the author of more than fifty published novels. Notably, she is a Vivian® Award nominee, and a RITA® Award winner and a five-time nominee. She loves her puppies, tennis, and being as as sassy and irreverent as her heroines. She's pretty sure dead bodies are better in fiction than real life, but hey, never say never, right? She has a pretty fantastic newsletter thing happening, so if you want in some good entertainment, go to www.stephanierowe.com and click the newsletter link!

ACKNOWLEDGMENTS

Special thanks to my beta readers. You guys are the best!

There are so many to thank by name, more than I could count, but here are those who I want to called out specially for all they did to help this book come to life: Alyssa Bird, Ashlee Murphy, Bridget Koan, Britannia Hill, Deb Julienne, Denise Fluhr, Dottie Jones, Heidi Hoffman, Helen Loyal, Jackie Moore Kranz, Jean Bowden, Jeanne Stone, Jeanie Jackson, Jodi Moore, Judi Pflughoeft, Kasey Richardson, Linda Watson, Regina Thomas, Summer Steelman, Suzanne Mayer, Shell Bryce, and Trish Douglas. Special thanks to my family, who I love with every fiber of my heart and soul. And to AER, who is my world. Love you so much, baby girl! You are brilliant, kind, funny, sassy, and a fantastic athlete. I am so proud to be your mom, and I look forward to watching you grow and thrive through life! And to Joe, who keeps me believing myself. I love you all!

Thank you to Elizabeth Turner Stokes for the most AMAZING cover. I am in awe of your vision and your talent.

Printed in Great Britain
by Amazon

23108282R00182